Stone

STONE

Joe Donnelly

ARROW BOOKS

Arrow Books Limited
20 Vauxhall Bridge Road, London SW1V 2SA

An imprint of the Random Century Group

London Melbourne Sydney Auckland
Johannesburg and agencies throughout
the world

First published in 1990 by
Barrie & Jenkins Limited,
the Random Century Group
20 Vauxhall Bridge Road, London SW1V 2SA

Arrow edition 1992

1 3 5 7 9 10 8 6 4 2

ISBN 0 09 983110 4

Photypeset by Intype, London
Printed and bound in Great Britain by
Bookmarque Ltd, Croydon, Surrey

In memory of
Charlotte Kerrigan Donnelly

PROLOGUE

Winter

The girl balanced on the dead pine trunk, arms spread
out on each side of her skinny frame. It was getting
dark, and darker here, in the trees where the shadows
were long, and beyond the trunks the shade crowded
in.

It was winter. The day after new year. Night was
falling early and soon the girl would have to go home.
She had been playing with the boys in the field across
the road beyond the trees, but she'd got bored when
they started their game of football, so she had left them.
She'd taken a short cut, over the crumbling dry-stane
dike and into the stand of trees.

Overhead the wind was soughing through the high
tops, shivering the canopy of pine needles and rattling
the thin twigs on the tall, bare beeches.

Chrissie Watt had skipped along the path until she'd
come to the jumble of deadfalls that had been brought
down by the gales a year ago. Here the scaly trunks lay
tangled, spreadeagled and jagged. She leapt nimbly up
on to the first and felt it see-saw under her weight. The
movement caused a creak further in as the log shifted
slightly.

Humming to herself, the girl bent her knees and
bounced gently up and down, letting the momentum
build up in the spring of the fallen log. Up above,
the wind shook the tops more strongly, moaning and
keening as it picked up strength over the firth. Chrissie
swung her narrow hips and bounced along the trunk,
every step in time to the jouncing vibration, keeping

1

her balance, every step avoiding the jutting, broken-off twigs that stood out sharply at right angles every foot or so. At the thick end, where the fallen trunk was pinned down by a more massive log, the bark flaked off with the motion. Wood sawed on wood with the sound of an old door opening on rusted hinges.

The shadows lengthened imperceptibly as the afternoon faded towards a midwinter early evening.

Across the log jam Chrissie, still humming a school-yard tune just loudly enough to hear it over the rising wind, clambered lightly. At the far end of the tangle where a number of pines had swatted each other into an assault course of slanted trunks, the big stone loomed up, dark against the gloomy sky. One of the pines angled upwards, balanced against the massive block. Chrissie never missed a step as she crossed from one fallen tree to this bigger one and continued up the slope of rough bark.

It was then, when she was slowly edging upwards, arms outstretched on either side for balance, that the change came. In the wink of an eye, the night seemed to fall harder, turning the shadows inky black. Above, the wind whipped fiercely, twisting the tall pines which creaked in response. Chrissie stopped suddenly, half-way up the long slant, and turned, suddenly aware of the dark and the shadows. There was a screeching crack as two pieces of dead wood rubbed jarringly against one another. The small girl turned to face the way she had come. Around her was wind and noise and shadow and Chrissie was alone in it.

She shivered, vulnerable to the sudden cold and to the strange *change* in the air. The pine logs creaked against each other with a shriek that was close and loud enough to startle her.

And then the ground shook, *hard*.

The girl felt the vibration jar through the trunk on which she balanced, almost jolting her off the perch. The blowdown rolled slightly against the top edge of the big stone and Chrissie's arms windmilled as she fought to keep from falling. Around her the trees and shadows looped crazily, then steadied, and as she regained her balance, the shock came again with such an intensity that Chrissie was bounced up into the air as the tree trunk buckled. A small cry of fright escaped her as she twisted in the air and fell with a smack that burned pain across her hip. The leg of her jeans ripped on a stubby branch and blood welled from a gash that scored the outside of her leg. She flopped across the trunk and cartwheeled off head first, spinning down on to another log several feet below to land so heavily the air was punched out of her lungs.

Dizziness made the world spin before her eyes.

And as she lay, labouring to draw breath, the earth next to the great dark stone shifted and heaved again. The old scaly pine tree thrummed again and was sprung off the top of the stone, turning as it went. The top end crashed with a mighty rending sound on to the log on which Chrissie lay spreadeagled and the girl was flipped up, heels over head, to thump so hard against the big stone that blood seemed to pop from her snub nose.

The darkness now flooded in, blotting out the last vestiges of grey.

In that dark the big pine rebounded, rolled, hitting off a still-standing conifer, and careened over the log jam with a splintering crash. Its broken-off branches whirled like knives as it fell.

The immense weight hit the sprawled and dazed girl with such force that it smashed her face from the nose down and caved in all of the ribs on the right side. As the far end rolled down, Chrissie Watt's still living, broken body was flipped upwards against the stone. The massive trunk came down again, squashing her against the hard surface.

A mass of blood flew out to the side as one of the sharpened branches plunged into her, ripping through the tough denim of her tomboy's jeans, and impaling her on the spike so violently that it ruptured her intestines in several places, punched through her tiny, undeveloped womb and smashed two of the bones in her lower back.

Chrissie Watt's heart continued to beat despite the catastrophic injuries and a small sound escaped past the blood that was backing up in her throat. As she sprawled, crumpled and broken, and mercifully unconscious, her heart pumped her life blood out through the horrendous wounds on to the cold grey stone. The blood ran in rivulets down the smooth sides and into the ground which seemed to drink thirstily in the dark.

And when the blood slowed at last, there was another change.

Between the great stone and its twin, yards away through the swaying trunks, the dark of newly fallen night went blacker still. And the stones themselves seemed to thrum in the wind, as if they had life of their own.

ONE

Summer

Tommy waited until his heart stopped hammering against his ribs and his laboured breathing started to slow down.

His hands were still shaking and, try as he might, he couldn't stop the sickening rolling in his stomach, the sudden switchback lurch that felt as if his insides were being squeezed by an invisible hand.

The blue-checked cotton shirt, fresh and neatly pressed that morning, was burr-stuck and torn in two jagged rips where the brambles and hawthorn had snagged and spiked it in his headlong rush through the trees. His whole left side, from ankle to cheek, was slick with mud from his sudden, skidding stop that had almost tumbled him into the stream.

Tommy was eight. He was fair-haired and blue-eyed, tall for his age and bright as a button.

He was also scared. Scared in the way no eight-year-old kid should ever be. More scared than he had ever been in his short life. So *gut-gripped* fearful he thought he was going to be sick.

His flight through the trees, whipping past the clutching thorns and runners, had spanned maybe a hundred yards or so, and perhaps sixty seconds at the most.

To Tommy it had felt like miles and his adrenalin burst, like an explosion in his belly, had concentrated his perception so finely it had seemed like hours.

It had seemed like *for ever*.

He had run blindly, crashing through the thickets and barging into the silver birches that barred his way, desperately, *frantically*. He had made it to the edge of the coppice and between the span of the great, grey standing stones and out into the moonlight.

There was only another fifty feet of short-cropped grass beyond the stones until the ground gave way in a smooth green slope down the sides of the gully in which the stream burbled its way to the sea loch. Tommy had scooted across the silvered patch like a startled fawn, then he'd skittered and slid over the lip and down towards the clear water.

It was there, lying on his side and waiting for his heart and lungs to idle down from their supercharged clamouring, that he realized it had gone.

It had *gone*.

As soon as he passed out of the trees and into the light, the *bad thing* had stopped. The shadow that had flowed after him, flitting between the tall trunks like a cloak of night, bringing its dark shades to blot the shadows into deeper black, had vanished. The blackness that had stretched the tendrils of anger and hate, that had made the very air taste thick and slimy, was no longer behind him.

No longer *chasing* him.

Tommy was a brave little boy, and he was determined not to cry. Maybe he had got beyond the stage of being *able* to cry. His heart still pounded like a fast and jittery drum, his stomach gripped in another switchback spasm, and he blinked back against the light thrown up from the sparkling stream.

Here he was safe. Out of the trees and past the stones and down by the stream, he was in the clear. He could feel it. Here was a refuge against all the bad things that had been happening, and the bad things that were coming. *Oh yes*. Tommy knew there was more to come, and worse. There was no escape from that.

The air may have been soft and warm, the moonlight at the edge of the cloud that seemed to swirl over the house a magical light that reflected from the water, and the murmuring of the stream a soothing balm on his panic. But Tommy was a bright boy.

This was just a break; a little capsule of calm before the terrible storm that he felt was building up all around him.

Instinct told him he was safe here, although he was too young to know why. He felt it inside where the real things are. But he knew he couldn't stay there beside the clear water. He knew he wouldn't be safe for long.

Tommy felt his heart quicken again, revving up from the faster-than-normal idling pace it had settled into, and there was a slither of walking fingers up the length of his spine as he stirred from his sprawl and hauled himself to his feet. He gathered himself up, stiff and sore, to his full big-for-his-age height (feeling awfully small) and his blond hair, almost white in that light, gleamed a contrast against his tan. His breath hitched a little, but he willed himself not to cry. One slow step at a time, he started to go back.

Back was where it waited. The thing that brought the shadows.

And that was the way Tommy Crombie had to go.

TWO

'Well, what do you think?'

They stood in a hushed little group beside the BMW.

'Hey. At last I've struck it lucky,' Alan Crombie said, his smile widening into a grin. 'I've got a family that's been shocked into silence.'

Helen Crombie, neat in a bright headscarf as she leaned against the cooling bonnet, shot him a quick look that flicked meaningfully towards the two small girls who gazed up at their father in awe. He caught the look, and the brightness in his eyes faded for an instant, then his exuberance batted away the momentary shadow.

'Aw, come on, you lot. Say something. We're here. I've driven five hundred miles and my dumb bum's numb.'

Tommy laughed out loud.

'At last, a reaction from somebody, even if it is tricky Tommy Tractor,' Alan said. He ruffled his son's shiny halo of fair hair.

'Right, team,' Alan started again, 'what do you think?' He gestured expansively, taking in the iron gate that swung from two massive smooth stone pillars, the gravel-bordered driveway that snaked through an undulating lawn, the stand of trees that stood tall beyond the clumps of rhododendron, and finally the house.

Tommy's giggle subsided and he stared at the mansion that sat, solid and imperious, at the end of the driveway.

'But where are we going to live?' he asked.

This time Alan Crombie laughed out loud. 'This is

the place, sunshine boy. This is the home of your dreams,' he said, again gesturing expansively.

'But it's a castle,' Tommy said. 'We can't stay in a castle. You have to be rich.'

'Rich! That's rich,' Alan barked in his stage barker's mode. 'You wanna be king of the castle, m'boy, then step *right* this way.'

Tommy was about to ask the obvious question when his mother broke up the act.

'It's too big,' she said, her voice just a shade chilly in the cooling afternoon air. 'We'll never be able to run a place like this.'

'Nonsense, Nell. Wait until you see the inside. It's got everything.'

Helen wasn't disarmed. 'Don't call me that. You know I don't like it. And it looks too big for me. And old-fashioned. And,' she said with a longsuffering sigh, as if explaining to a child, 'it's miles from nowhere.'

'Aw, come on. Take a look inside. You'll love the place. And anyway, it's not so far away as it looks. I can be in the office in thirty minutes, and you can be up to your armpits in hypermarkets and beauty salons in less.' Alan paused and watched Helen's face as her eyes took in the whole scene. He was willing her to show some hint, some suggestion that she was going to be positive about this. 'And you can get to the airport in next to no time whenever you feel homesick for the dearly beloved dragon lady . . .'

Helen's expression remained stony. There was a slight downturn at the edges of her lips.

'So come on, folks,' Alan said, as brightly as he could muster it, 'let's see how the rich folks live.' He smiled at his wife and chucked Tommy under the chin. He left the car where it sat and scooped up the twins, who watched adoringly as always, saying nothing as always, and sat each on the crook of his arms. His long strides carried him up towards the house.

'Is this really our house, Mum?' Tommy asked in wonderment.

'Unless there's been some ghastly mistake, or unless there's a miracle,' Helen said, with a weary sigh.

Tommy turned to watch his father walk up the slow curve of drive, and then scanned past him to take in the house. There were lots of windows on the stone front, dark and shiny. Behind them there was a darkness that was magnified by the reflections on the sheen of glass. As he watched, there seemed to be a shift, a change in the darkness beyond the panes, as if the squares of glass themselves had flexed and bulged, like muscles. Like eyes. Then a cloud moved and the sun scattered shards of light into the boy's eyes, watering them up, killing the fleeting image. When they cleared, seconds later, the house stood square at the end of the drive. Big and solid. But just a house.

Alan Crombie was determined to make a good life for his family. Sometimes it was tough going. Sometimes it was *very* tough going, but what the hell. You take the good with the bad, and while the last couple of years had been as bad as things probably could get, being back in Scotland, being back *home*, was good. It was wonderful.

Well, close to home, anyway. Levenford, home of childhood memories and summer sunshine, was out there, across the narrow expanse of the Finloch and further up the firth. The house commanded a magnificent view for miles, even as far as the Kilpatrick Hills, purpling in the distance. The old pull had dragged him back, as he knew it would, to this part of the west. Not too far from where he was born. Here the air *did* smell clean and sharp, with a trace of salt from the sea loch, and a hard tang of summer. And the land felt *right*.

And now Cromwath House.

Probably the most desirable residence on the whole

10

of the peninsula. Tommy was right, Alan thought, as he gazed down at *his* view. It *is* like a castle.

Alan Crombie. Thirty-three years old. Corrieside Primary Dux, Levenford Secondary with a string of A-levels and a bursary walk-in to Glasgow University to step out of his father's footsteps and into precision engineering. Only there weren't any ships to build on the Clyde any more. The yards were starting to hollow themselves out by the time Alan was set to leave school, gutted by the recession, and the flow of money out of industry and into speculation. By then Alan wasn't interested in ships. He wanted to build big. Maths, science and civil engineering. More studies in architecture, business administration and computers. Five years of hard graft and the beer bar, and then the big fish were fighting over his qualifications. Alan had settled for a small but well put-together company with guts and a bit of vision and no creaking old fogeys at the top. Then he started to *really* work. Two years in Hong Kong, another in Malawi, followed by a chance to lead the team on a vast contract on the Colorado River, and then an associateship – only two steps from the top – in London.

More success, more hard work, more travel. Alan was the coming man in civil engineering. The big consortia still tied themselves in knots and eventually settled for the use of his services as a consultant.

And now this.

A full partnership in MacKenzie-Kelso. Voting rights. Share options. The chance to pick his own team to make the world of design engineering stand on its ear.

Helen had gone upstairs half an hour before, tired and a bit grim-faced. Maybe he shouldn't have surprised her. Women like to choose their own nests.

But Cromwath House. What a place. What a bargain. It was something he just couldn't ignore.

He'd heard the property was on the market six

months before, just when the offer of the partnership had been made over smiles and large brandies in the oak-panelled head office in Park Circus.

Mike Toward, the big bluff American whom he'd recruited on the Colorado job, and who'd decided to come across for a holiday and then stayed for the offered job, had taken a couple of the boys from the surveying office down to the peninsula and given the house a thorough going over. He had sent Alan a thick report. A thick, *enraptured* report on the house.

It wasn't until Alan realized just how much his semi-detached in Surrey had appreciated in the internal combustion of the south-east property market that he was forced to conclude that he really could afford the house. And the speed at which Scots law eases property transactions was a helter-skelter that whizzed him around dizzily to land, breathless and excited, with a bunch of keys jingling in his hand.

Helen had taken the news with less than great enthusiasm. But what the hell. She'd come round.

Maybe she didn't share Alan's native pride, being only half-Scottish, and that was understandable. But the house wasn't as remote as she'd suggested, and without doubt it was magnificent. Ten good rooms and eight acres of land, including a forest walk and a stream that cut through near the boundary at the north end. And the house had been built – Alan knew from his own experience and from Mike's report – with no expense spared. Someone had put a lot of thought and a great deal of love into building this place.

And now it was theirs. To love and to cherish.

Tommy was pretending to be asleep when his father opened the bedroom door, but as soon as Alan's hand touched his shoulder, he couldn't contain his excitement.

'Hey, are we really going to stay here, Dad?' he

blurted, whirling round and getting tangled in the sheets in the process.

'For ever'n ever ay-men.'

'It's great, Dad. Just *great*.'

Tommy untangled himself and scrambled out of bed to scoot across to the window. He looked past his faint reflection and pointed out at the gathering darkness.

'Look, you can see the lights right down the water. I saw two boats, one after the other,' he said. 'And there was a rabbit in the grass too, but it ran away.'

'I think there's lots of rabbits around here, TC,' Alan said, easing himself down to sit on the edge of the bed. He still felt stiff from the long drive. 'You probably get squirrels up in the trees, and there's a stream over there where we might catch some tiddlers.' He patted the bed. 'Come on now, son, hop back in. It's been a long day, and it's getting late.'

'Can I leave the curtains open for a while?'

'Sure. There's no street lights here to keep you awake. And maybe you can see the stars shining when you lie down.'

Tommy came back from the window and burrowed under the duvet that he'd left in a rumpled heap. Alan straightened it around him and pulled it up to the boy's chin. He leaned down and kissed his son, and when Tommy snuggled in closer Alan felt that familiar burst of pride and pleasure in his boy.

'That's m'boy,' he said. Tommy giggled softly.

When the door closed gently behind his father, Tommy settled back against the soft pillow and stared at the deep blue rectangle that was the window set against the surrounding black.

Gradually his eyes accustomed themselves to the darkness and the shapes in his room; the chest of drawers, the unpacked boxes that held his toys and books slowly made themselves visible, as if they'd been waiting for quiet to come out and show themselves. His room was high up in the house and it was vast by

13

comparison to the little boxroom he'd had all to himself in Surrey. He hadn't quite got the geography of the place in his head, but that would sort itself out. Outside, the stars pricked a plush velvet sky. From far down the firth there was the faint moan of a ship's horn, or it could have been the echo of a train's whistle. Somewhere out in the trees at the far end of the garden, an owl hooted, low and comfortable, close but far away, and was answered by another on the opposite side, where Tommy hadn't been and which was still a mystery to be explored. Just before he fell asleep, Tommy heard, faintly, the cracking of a twig out there in the trees, and a muffled scuffling sound, followed by the plaintive cry of a small animal in pain and fear. He was aware of nothing else until the sunlight speared him through the bare window in the morning.

Alan Crombie had quietly slipped into the other bedroom to check on the girls before going to bed. No pretence there. Both of them were sound asleep on their divans, set close side by side. He stumbled over one of the boxes that had slipped from the pile and cursed very quietly to himself. In the semi-darkness he could just make out the lustre of the girls' hair, identical mists of white silk on each pillow, and in the quiet he could hear their soft rhythms of breath.

Again he felt that deep-down swell of love that was a physical surge just under his ribs. Kathryn and Elaine, his babies, touched by the gods, perfect in their symmetry. As he watched, Kathryn turned in her sleep, a half-smile on her angel's face. Instantly, Elaine followed suit, as if they were tied each to the other by invisible strings. She too had that little smile, as if she shared the same pleasant dream as her sister. Alan watched them for a moment, then quietly backed out of the door and closed it gently against the picture of innocence.

Helen was almost asleep. Her eyes opened blearily

when Alan tiptoed into the room, but she said nothing. Alan undressed quickly, trying to make as little noise as possible when he pulled down his cord slacks. He gingerly sat on the edge of the bed when he realized he'd forgotten to take off his Treks first, and bent, a little ungainly in his shirt and with his jeans at his ankles, fumbling with the laces. Helen turned and hunched the duvet over her. He couldn't tell what kind of mood she was in, but after the journey, and the excitement of showing the family their new home, he was too tired to give it much thought. He put his shoes in the corner, then slung the cords and shirt after them. It was too late to look about for somewhere to put his clothes. Tomorrow would be soon enough. He thumbed the push-button that killed the bedside light with a small click and the room was suddenly black and strange. He slipped out of his jockey shorts and flipped them across to where he thought his clothes were lying (but wasn't quite sure now, in the dark) and slid into bed. Helen grunted once, though faintly, and poached another half-yard of quilt. In a minute or two he could tell by her breathing that she was asleep.

Alan lay in the darkness, feeling the tension stream slowly out of his back and arms. Inside, his emotions were still shunting around like a busy railway junction, as pride and anxiety fought for pole position against a motley team of uncertainty, delight, annoyance (at Helen's first reaction) and the still-fierce thrill of love he'd been jolted with when he looked in on his boy and his babies. Very soon the darkness in the room damped down all of this and swallowed him in sleep.

He woke once in the night, and panicked because he didn't know where he was, confused by the unfamiliar shape of the room and its shadows. But in minutes he was sound asleep again and didn't wake until Helen nudged him in the ribs and asked him to stop snoring.

THREE

'Well, everybody,' Alan called from the corner of the
kitchen where he was unsuccessfully attempting to turn
over an egg to go with the rashers of salty bacon sizzling
under the grill, 'check your supplies and eat hearty.
We're going on the grand inspection.'

'Where?' Tommy asked past a mouthful of egg on
toast.

'Here, of course,' Alan said. 'We're going on a walka-
bout round our castle.' He turned to point the egg-
scoop across in the rough direction of where the family
were at breakfast. 'And I'll thank you, sir, not to spray
egg on the walls. We like 'em just the dirty green way
they are. At least until your mother decides what she
wants in its place.'

Tommy choked on a laugh, but managed to confine
the egg-spray to his plate. The twins, sitting side by
side and making a dual mess of their soft-boiled eggs,
followed suit. Alan glanced over and winked at the
three of them, then managed to encourage his own egg
on to his plate, negotiated with the bacon until he had
a plateful, and came to join the kids at the table.

He sat down at the end, opposite Helen, who was
sipping coffee absent-mindedly while leafing through a
woman's magazine. She was managing to ignore the
chaos, a fact for which Alan was surprised but grateful.

'Oh, Casey, that's a nice picture you're making there.
We'll hang it on the wall as soon as it dries. And Easy,'
he turned to Elaine, 'mix me some more egg cement,
there's a good girl. I may want to build a wall in the
garden today.'

Tommy spluttered again and the girls pealed with

tinkly laughter. Helen looked up over the top of her magazine. They all knew she disapproved of Alan's nicknames for his children, but again they all knew that it was hardly likely to stop him. In any case, instead of frowning, she smiled.

The previous day, they'd had what Alan described as the mini-tour. Alan had led them all round the inside, showing off the big bedroom with its oriel window, the ballroom of a living-room with its classy Adam-style fireplace, the impressive wood-panelled stairway with its smoothly polished banister. They'd inspected the little rooms at the top of the house with their sloped ceilings. Of course there was more that they still hadn't seen. There were outhouses and a greenhouse and a garage, and there was a vast basement that ran the full length of the house down in the depths, where Tommy hoped he might be able to explore.

Alan had taken them along a little corridor that jinked to the left and opened a narrow door into a neat little room that was built into the turret-shaped formation that stood on the north-east corner of the house.

'And this is *my* room,' he said with a proprietorial air. 'It's just perfect for working in. And quiet too. I'm going to put up a big notice on the door saying "Do not disturb" and I'm going to lock myself in there when I've had enough of you lot.'

He looked round with pretend menace. 'But don't worry. You've all got your own places. You guys can have one of the spare rooms upstairs for all your toys, so that means you can have tidy bedrooms for a change. And I don't see any problem in making that little dress-ing-room into a workroom for you,' he said, turning to Helen. 'There's plenty of light, and a great view too.'

Tommy loved the vastness of the place. The stair-way, old and shady, but with wonderful warm wood.

'Tomorrow, I'll show you the garage,' Alan had continued. 'It must have been an old stable block, but it's clean and there's space for six cars.'

'We only have the one,' Helen said.

'Yes, that's true. But I've already arranged to go down to Watkinsons in Levenford next week to see if I can't get some kind of a deal. We can afford it, and you mustn't be without wheels.'

'That's a relief,' Helen said. 'I thought I was going to be stuck out here with no chance of escape.'

Alan sighed, trying to keep it to himself, failed, and turned to his wife. 'I really hope you like it here,' he said. 'I really do. If I had to come to Scotland – and I did have to because of the promotion – there isn't a better place to live in, believe me. All right, it's not quite Guildford, but nobody I know could afford to live in a place like this down there. And I'm sure this is just what you need. Some space. And some peace and quiet.' Alan looked directly at his wife. She turned and smiled at him. Two in one day was almost a record.

Despite all that Alan had said about the house, there was another important reason for uprooting his family and bringing them to the west of Scotland.

The past four years, ever since the twins had been born, had been rough on him and Helen. This place, he hoped, would give them the opportunity to try to get back to where they'd been.

Helen hadn't come home from hospital with the babies. She'd merely been transferred from the maternity wing to a clinic half a mile away for treatment for the severe postnatal depression that had swamped her after her twins had arrived in the world.

At first the doctors had been sympathetic but firm. They'd told Alan that many mothers get depressed after a birth. They explained about tiredness and changes in hormone levels. It was this. It was that.

Whatever it was, the doctors only took it seriously three days later when Helen calmly slipped under the lukewarm water – the auxiliary nurse had taken her for a bath – and then started to breathe in.

They'd had to resuscitate her and keep her under constant observation. Helen didn't get better. She got worse. By the time Kathryn and Elaine were allowed home – in their father's arms – Helen was almost catatonic.

They'd been marvellous at the clinic. They put less stress on pills and potions than in spending time with patients, bullying and chivvying for a response. After two months Helen had started to come out of the dreadful torpor and could recognize people around her. After three months she was well enough to come home for short visits. By the end of the year, four months after the babies were born, the doctors thought she was well enough to stay home. But by then she was a shadow of the pretty, laughing girl who had waddled, stout with imminent delivery, into the maternity unit.

A year after that, it was becoming apparent that there might be a problem with the girls.

They were bonny babies who always found it easier to laugh than to cry, even when they started teething. Alan had had to cut out foreign trips altogether and kept jaunts to far-flung sites to a minimum so as to be with the children as much as possible. He took them for weekend walks, made bottles and changed nappies with the dexterity he'd acquired with Tommy four years before.

Kathryn and Elaine Crombie became KC and EC within weeks, and Casey and Easy by natural progression. They laughed and giggled, and seemed to understand a great deal of what was said to them.

But they never spoke a word. By the time they were two years old, it had become apparent that they were not making any attempt to talk.

Alan had taken them to speech therapists who held their hands in the air, puzzled expressions on their faces. He ran them through a gauntlet of child psychologists, psychiatrists and paediatricians, and eventually trailed them to a neurologist whose surgery looked better equipped than a space-station. He put them through an exhaustive – and exhausting – battery of tests, and they never complained once. He then pronounced them fit and well, except, he said, when he was explaining everything to Alan, for one thing.

'What's that?' Alan had asked, feeling a slow, worrying lurch of fear deep inside him. And to himself he said: *'This is it. They're brain-damaged. He's going to tell me they're retarded.'*

'The brain scan shows one small abnormality. If we can call it that, although I'm not so sure that we should,' the professor said. Before Alan could blurt out his demand to be told, the elderly man produced an oscilloscope reading that had been taken during the brain scan.

'It's their alpha rhythms from the electroencephalograph,' he said, holding up the graph-paper sheets where the gentle curves undulated on, perfectly smoothly. 'I shouldn't say it's an abnormality,' Professor Jamieson said. 'But they are remarkable.'

He cast a critical eye over the sheets again, then looked at Alan over the top of his half-moon glasses. 'They're identical,' he said.

'Yes. We know that,' Alan said, almost sharply. 'They've always been identical.'

'Oh, I don't mean the girls. Of course they're identical. Classic split-gamete twins. But actually I was referring to these,' he said, pointing at the long strips of hard copy. 'Look at this. I had the electrodes on each of them fed into the machine simultaneously. What I wanted was a measurement of their alpha waves. They're the impulses the brain makes when we're awake. These are perfectly normal, nine to the second, which tends to indicate that the twins are happy and healthy, and share what you might call a high degree of peace of mind, and I hope this helps yours too.'

Alan nodded. The consultant moved on. 'Now here,

we have a second series of wave-lines. What is unusual is that they're the kind of rhythms we tend to associate with REM sleep. That is, we get them when we're dreaming. It's unusual, but not unheard of, to record these in waking subjects.' He fiddled with yards of print-out. 'There. Now look at that. These beta rhythms are exactly the same,' he said, pointing to curves which mirrored each other perfectly. 'They are perfectly matched. There is no deviation whatsoever. It's as if this were one reading from a single brain.'

'What would cause that?' Alan asked anxiously.

'I'm not sure. I've never come across this before, but I rarely have identical twins to work on. I have a colleague in Edinburgh who is working on sets of twins. Would you mind if I showed him this?'

'No, go ahead,' Alan said absently. 'But does this mean anything? Can you say what's wrong with them?'

'I don't really think there is much wrong with them,' the doctor said with an encouragingly paternal smile.

'From what I can ascertain, they both appear to be very healthy, and from the looks of them they are very happy. The other scans we have done show that the speech centres seem to be operating as normal, in the correct places on the cortex, and there doesn't appear to be any sign of damage. In short, they appear to be well equipped to be chatting their heads off. The fact that they don't is perhaps a puzzle, but I expect that when the time comes, they will talk. And I would hazard a guess that their vocabularies will be quite extensive. They may not start talking in baby language.'

'What about these rhythms. The beta thing?' Alan asked.

'That's unusual, I must say. But apart from the precise matching, they're not exactly unique.' The doctor paused, searching for a way to explain. 'You see, a regular wave on the alpha level shows a strong pattern that I would tend to associate with very healthy brain

21

rhythms. By that I mean they seem to have the ability to precisely concentrate their thoughts. It also means, because of the smoothness of those rhythms that your daughters seem to operate on, shall we say, a fine degree of peace of mind. As for the beta factor, it's odd to have them showing during consciousness. It's as if they are, at times, in a state between dreaming and waking. It certainly shouldn't affect them at all. I would say that they are perfectly normal in every way – and beautiful too, I might add – and I would also suggest that you have very little to worry about. They haven't spoken, and while I cannot explain why, there is no evidence to suggest that they cannot. On the contrary. And there is none whatsoever to suggest that they will not.'

'But what about the rhythms matching? Does that mean anything?' Alan asked.

'What it might mean,' Professor Jamieson said, removing his glasses and looking directly at Alan, 'and remember, this is not my field, is that you see evidence of two human beings who are very highly attuned to each other. I understand that in twins, identical twins, this kind of attunement is manifest in various ways in other cases. But your daughters, Mr Crombie, I won't go so far as to say they can read each other's minds, but they are almost certain to have a very clearly defined empathy with each other. If the cell in your wife's womb hadn't split at the right time, your daughters would have been one daughter.

'But that's neither here nor there. Watch them as they get older, and see if I'm right. They should be very clearly bonded to each other, and I certainly can't see that as anything but an advantage.'

The doctor stopped and regarded Alan calmly. He put his spectacles back on, pressing the bridge further up on his nose. 'What I would suggest is that you don't worry about them. I rather think they'll be fine. Let time and nature take its course.'

Alan took some comfort from the doctor's explanation. The twins still didn't speak, but at least there was no sign of anything seriously wrong with them.

But Helen blamed herself for her daughters' silence. Her relapse was slow but steady, and finally cataclysmic.

At first she believed she might have passed on some recessive gene which had made her daughters dumb. But her self-doubt and guilt because of the fact that she had been away from the babies after their birth, *in the loonyward* was how she described it, made her think she was being punished in some way for past misdeeds. Those misdeeds were a vague collection of small things that built up in her mind until she was swept away on a black wave of panic and anxiety.

Just as Alan was beginning to think everything in their lives was fitting back together again, Helen started to crack.

Alan would come home to find her sitting in the small kitchen, her head in her hands and a blank look of deep gloom on her face. She had fits of blackest depression that alternated with bouts of savage anger. Once she found that Tommy had accidentally cut a table-cloth with the scissors he was using to snip a newspaper into patterns, and she had slapped him so hard that he was thrown violently off the seat, and gashed his head on the Welsh dresser. She had stopped taking care of herself, and her dark, lustrous hair became lank and lifeless. Alan was run ragged. He would come home in the evenings and find that his work was only beginning.

The final crash came when Helen went suddenly berserk one night as they were sitting at dinner. The twins watched wide-eyed, Tommy in fear, and Alan with a sinking feeling of horrified dismay, when Helen leapt up from the table with no warning and started smashing every item of crockery she could get her hands on. Alan had tried to stop her, and was shocked at Helen's amazing strength. She didn't even seem to know he was there. As shards of plates, cups and saucers flew, bouncing back off the walls, Alan had grabbed the children and hustled them into the living-room. He called the clinic, finding it hard to explain to the doctor he eventually was connected with, over the crashing noises that were coming from the kitchen.

It took another four months before Helen was allowed home again. Four months of relying on baby-sitters and mother-in-law while Alan made up for his time away from his job.

This time, however, her improvement was slow and agonizing, but there *was* improvement. Step by step, day by day, Alan's despair began to fade. He had stopped expecting that his wife would ever smile again, and steeled himself not to react badly when she became bitterly angry and confused. He began to hope that she would find her way back to what she had been before. He wanted the fun-loving, energetic and bright-eyed girl he had fallen in love with. He worked hard at bringing her back. By the time he announced the news of their move to Scotland, he reckoned she was more than half-way there.

Now they were here he forced himself to put his doubts to the back of his mind.

'Some peace and quiet, I guarantee it,' Alan said as he opened the window in the dressing-room that adjoined the master bedroom. There were two other doors leading off the big room, one to a bathroom complete with shower, and another to a side-room that felt more like a corridor, but was lined on either side with floor-to-ceiling wardrobes.

As he adjusted the catch, a slight breeze carried in the smell of fresh flowers and new-cut grass. Some-where out of sight a blackbird warbled a complex melody in liquid notes.

'This is yours, of course,' he said, and Helen gave a small smile. 'If you like, I'll get a phone up here, plus all your favourite books and comfortable chair. And when you feel you can't stand the sight of me any more, you can just beat a retreat and lock the door.'

'It *is* lovely,' Helen said. 'You can see the water from here.'

'From this house, you can see the water from almost anywhere.'

'But don't you think it's too big? There's so many rooms. And it's *old*.'

'Old, yes. Just over a hundred years, but it's got character. And it's not too big. You'll see. It's like money and lifestyle. Your needs expand to spend the available cash. More, usually. Here, we'll get used to the space. We'll just spread out to fit. I'll bet that in a couple of months you'll wonder how we ever managed in Surrey.'

Alan stepped across to the window and rapped his knuckles on the wood surround. 'Mike Toward has been through this from roof to basement. It's in great nick. Spectacular, in fact. There's not the slightest trace of anything amiss. No damp, no rot, and not a worm in sight.'

'It is a bit remote,' Helen said. 'And I don't know anybody here.' She sounded a little unsure, almost timid.

'It is a bit remote by comparison to what we've been used to. It's only remote because you've been huddled with the swarming masses all your life. Here space *is* a way of life. And there are some fine people round here. We'll get to know them pretty quickly, I'm sure of it. Honest.'

Helen tried to smile again, and Alan felt himself willing her on. She finally made it and he was glad.

Honest. It hung in the air like something tangible. More an expression of hope than certainty, Alan admitted to himself. He *hoped* that Helen would accept this as a new start and show a major improvement. It was a stab at getting over the black times. A chance to close the chapter on the past and write a fresh one that was sunnier and brighter.

'You can see most of the garden from here,' he said. 'And because there's hardly any traffic on the road, the kids can play almost anywhere without us having to worry.'

Helen nodded absent-mindedly. Outside, the blackbird's song crystallized in the sunlit garden.

'Tomorrow, we'll have a good look around the place. Our policies. You can be the lady of the manor,' Alan said. He looked across at her. She was still miles away. 'In a manner of speaking,' he punned lightly. There was no response to that. Helen sat with her head cocked to the side, as if listening to some small sound.

FOUR

'Daddy!' Tommy's cry echoed up the stairwell and startled them both out of their thoughts.

'*Daddee!*' This time louder, and with a rising edge of concern.

'Oh God,' Helen said on an intake of breath. 'What's happened?'

Alan was across the room and through the door before she had time to finish the sentence.

'Daddy. Come *quick*.'

Tommy's voice had risen an octave, making the hairs on Alan's neck tingle. He went down the stairs three at a time, his heels clattering on the polished wooden treads, sliding his hand on the banister and spinning his weight with centripetal force on the landing.

Tommy was standing at the foot of the stairs. His big blue eyes were wide with anxiety.

'I've looked and looked, Daddy, but I can't find them,' he said in a voice that was close to a wail.

Alan let out a sight of relief when he saw his son standing there. For a moment he'd thought it was something serious. 'Can't find what, TC?'

'Katie and Laney. They were right beside me, and then . . .' He paused, trying to get the words right. 'And then, they weren't. I've looked and looked, and they're not there.'

Alan swung his glance up and down the wide hallway at the bottom of the stair.

'Well, they won't be far,' he said, putting an arm around his son's neat shoulders. 'They can't reach the snib, so they can't be outside, so there's nothing to worry about, is there?'

27

Tommy shook his head slowly, but the expression on his face belied his agreement. He looked worried. In fact, he looked plain scared.

'They can't be far away. This is our house, and you can't get lost in your own house, even if it *is* new.' He took Tommy by the hand and called to Helen who was coming downstairs. 'Tommy can't find the girls. I think they're playing hide-and-seek.'

'But they were *with* me, Daddy,' Tommy protested. 'I just turned around and they weren't there.'

'Don't worry. We'll find them in a minute. They've got more places to hide in here. Just think of the games you can have.'

'Where were they?' Helen asked.

Tommy pointed at the big lounge with the picture window that viewed the firth in two directions. 'In there. We were watching a boat,' he said. 'And then they weren't *there*,' he blurted out, with a little catch in his voice. 'But I looked in all the rooms, and they weren't there either, and I don't know *where* they are.' He looked up, and his eyes flicked back and forth, between his mother and father. 'I *always* know where they are. And I don't know now.'

Alan shot him a puzzled look. 'Let's go and look for them. We'll find them in two minutes flat.'

The three of them went back into the big room, and Alan made a point of looking behind the settee that was sitting against the wall. There was no sign of the twins. They looked in the sitting-room and the empty library where there was an ornate stone fireplace set in a panelled wall. Alan opened all the cupboards in the kitchen and checked out the cloakroom and bathroom at the end of the hallway. The twins weren't downstairs.

'They must have followed us up,' he thought. He was just about to lead them upstairs when he passed the small door that led down to the basement. 'You haven't been down here, Tommy, have you?'

The boy shook his head.

'Good. I haven't had a good look in the basement. There's a lot of rubbish and all sorts of old things heaped about. It needs a good clean out. I don't want you down there until I've checked it out myself.'

Alan tried the door anyway, and found it locked. The big mortise key was dangling from a hook that was well out of the twins' reach, and probably too high for Tommy to get at on his own.

'Right. Let's try upstairs,' Alan said. 'And when we find them, it'll be our turn to hide.' He smiled down at Tommy in a gentle attempt to soothe the worry that was written on his son's face.

Within ten minutes, Alan and Helen had scoured all of the upstairs rooms and opened every closet. They inspected all of the little rooms up near the roof of the house, and when they found no sign of the twins, they both started to feel the first jittery pangs of anxiety.

'Where can they be?' Helen asked. Her face seemed two shades paler.

'They have to be somewhere,' Alan said with much more confidence than he felt. His mind was poring over its own plan of the house, trying to think of some room they'd missed. 'There must be somewhere we haven't looked. You didn't open any of the outside doors, did you, son?'

'No, Dad, honest. We were just looking out of the window.'

Alan stopped at the bottom of the stairs. 'Kathryn!' he called out. 'Elaine!' A little bit louder.

From somewhere, it seemed a distance away, there was a small noise. It could have come from anywhere. It sounded like a giggle.

'I told you they had to be inside,' Alan said, feeling the tight band ease on his chest. 'Did you hear them?'

Helen and Tommy both nodded, listening out for the noise which faded as quickly as it had come.

'Where did it come from?'

Tommy pointed along the hall. Helen lifted her hand to indicate the general direction of upstairs.

'Right, girls,' Alan called again, this time even louder than before, 'wherever you are, come on out!'

There was a soft knocking sound. Then a drum of little footsteps on a hard floor. This time Helen looked down the hallway, though Alan could have sworn that the sounds came from upstairs.

Another giggle came from nowhere, but again it seemed to be muted, muffled, as if it had travelled a long way. It was followed by an identical tinkling laugh, and then another spate of little footsteps, the sound of small children running on a polished floor.

Alan swivelled and marched down the hall and into the library where the parquet flooring gleamed with old polish. Helen and Tommy were right on his heels.

He strode into the middle of the room. It was empty, apart from the desk he planned to fit into his own little study, and the inevitable boxes filled with books. The twins weren't there.

There was another knocking sound. This time it seemed directly overhead. So they *were* upstairs after all. The tinkling laugh fluttered down again, and Alan felt himself beginning to get angry.

He spun round – and Helen and the boy turned with him – and moved towards the door. Just as they were about to pass through, Tommy stiffened and halted so suddenly Alan almost fell over him.

There was a faint noise, a snick, more felt than heard. It was as if the air had moved, as if a vacuum suddenly ceased to exist, as if the atmosphere in the room had altered. Again Alan felt the hairs on the back of his neck creep, and he spun round so fast he almost tore a muscle.

The twins were standing just beside the big fireplace, smiling up at them. They were holding hands, and their faces, framed by their white silken hair, were dimpled with innocent amusement.

30

'Where in God's name did you two come from?' Alan shouted, a little too loudly.

Helen gasped and crossed the library in quick, rattling steps and grabbed both girls by their shoulders, hugging them to her own body.

The twins seemed puzzled but unalarmed by her reaction. They continued to smile over their mother's shoulder at their father and brother.

'Where were you hiding?' Alan asked, this time, panic over, not so loudly.

Kathryn and Elaine just smiled. Alan knew they understood him, but they couldn't tell him. He went to the fireplace and crouched to look up the flue. There was nowhere the girls could have hidden. He went back to the pile of boxes where he'd stored his books. They must have been crouching down behind them. He must have overlooked them the first time he'd searched the library. It wasn't until later, lying in the dark, waiting for sleep, that he remembered shifting all of the boxes to look behind them.

They hadn't been there.

But in the morning, he'd forgotten all about the thought.

FIVE

Alan wolfed down his bacon and eggs and dipped his buttered bread into the mush of fried tomatoes, finally scouring the plate clean with his crust and washing that down with a mug of steaming, sweet coffee.

'Can we go out and see everything today?' Tommy asked.

'Yeah. Just let me have another cup of coffee, and we'll all go for a look around. I haven't seen everything myself yet, so we can explore and find out what we've come home to.'

Alan had to make short work of his coffee under the weight of the children's impatience. Finally he had to leave half of it and go to find his boots among a welter of unpacked clothes.

At the front door they all paused to take in the spread of gardens, bursting into bloom where flowers and shrubs had been planted, and the long view up the length of the firth where the morning mist was fading to a silver-spangled veil in the bright sunlight.

'Can we go and explore the trees first?' Tommy asked, still stamping his foot to squeeze it into his rubber boot.

'We'll get to them soon enough,' Alan said. 'But first we should take a stroll around the grounds,' he turned to Helen, 'until you feel at home.'

'Like Mrs Robinson?'

Alan's smile froze when he realized his gaffe. Helen had spent long enough in a locked room to be able to see herself as the figure in the song.

'No, just to see what we've got. I've been round a couple of times, but I still don't have a good idea of where the boundary is. I could give you the area in hectares and square yardage, but even that doesn't mean too much to me.'

Tommy had stomped himself into his wellingtons, and on the correct feet too. The twins were decked out in bright anoraks and matching red boots. The morning air was still crisp and there was the merest hint of a dew damping the smooth slope of the lawn. It would fade soon under the sun.

Alan strode down the steps and turned to wait for Helen, proffering his arm. Behind her came Tommy with the girls, holding each by the hand.

They crunched across the gravel at the side of the house, in front of the big window of the sitting-room and round the side of the house where the garage joined it, like a separate block connected by a small passage that also led on to the washroom at the back of the kitchen. It was evident that the garage had first been a stable, built at the same time as the house. Stone-built and set square, some owner had fitted it with up-and-over doors. Inside there was a cold smell and traces of dried-in oil. On the shelves were nuts and bolts, brown and slick with age, and a few old tools.

'Plenty of space here for the flying machine, and whatever car you get,' Alan said. 'You could *live* in this. It's about the same size as our first house.'

'It's the same size as our last one,' Helen replied.

The door at the back of the garage swung out on to a path of flagstones that continued behind the house and into a vegetable garden where the stalks of last season's sprouts were pale green against the burnt-out browns of the dead twine of beans that were looped around a criss-cross frame of canes. Beyond the neat rectangles of the garden plots was a small orchard, with rows of fruit trees in full leaf.

'There's apple and pear trees there,' Alan told Tommy, 'along with a plum, and I think maybe there's a cherry tree too.'

'Can we pick the apples?' Tommy asked, still hauling his sisters along by their hands as if they were his favourite pets.

'You'll have to wait a while for that. They're the ones with the pink flowers. Pretty, aren't they?'

The twins heaved themselves out of their brother's grasp and ran ahead of him on to the short grass, leaving dark green footprints on the lightly frosted dew. Under the trees was a confetti-scattering of apple blossom, like a dusting of pink-tinted snow which the girls gathered up with wide smiles of delight. Alan noticed a hint of a smile play on Helen's lips as she watched and felt a small surge of gladness.

Maybe, just maybe, he thought to himself, this might just be the start of it. A new beginning. All the bad times past. He was never so wrong in his life.

Beyond the fruit trees, under which the twins were showering each other with delicate blossoms, the path ran out of flagstones, but continued as a well-worn track that snaked away towards the belt of taller trees that curved round north of the house.

'Where does that lead to?' Tommy asked.

'I'm not quite sure. I think it goes through the wood and past the stones at the edge of the trees and then down the other side towards the gate.'

'What stones?'

'Great big ones. There's two of them up there. You can just see them from the road. They stand up just at the edge of the trees.'

'Can we go and see them?'

'Sure. We might as well take a look all around. Get to know the place.'

Under the trees, the girls were still scattering blossoms.

Helen said something Alan didn't catch and he turned towards her. 'What was that?'

'They laugh, but they don't speak,' she said. 'God, I wish they could talk.'

'They will. When they're good and ready, everybody says. Probably in their own time, and then they just won't stop. But as long as they're laughing, love, they're happy. Anyway, there's some good people in Edinburgh and Glasgow, who've been recommended. I'll be making some arrangements as soon as I can, and then we'll see.'

'I keep thinking it's my fault,' Helen said miserably.

'I know you do, but it's not, so you might as well just stop thinking it.' He reached across the gap between them and put his arms around Helen's shoulders, giving her a companionable, comforting shake. 'Come on,' he said, 'let's patrol our estate. We've got vast tracts of land to get around before nightfall.'

Under the canopy, the shadows were soft and in constant motion as a light breeze stirred the tops of the trees where the new leaves were bursting into brilliant green. The track continued round the boles of big beeches with bark like smooth grey hide, and gnarled, moss-covered oaks. Further in, they came across the stones, great blue-grey tapering rectangles of basalt standing in a line. They were about twelve feet high and maybe four feet on a side. They were old, the two of them standing close to the edge of the trees like silent guardians. Solid. Set.

'Who put them here?' Tommy asked his father.

'Haven't a clue. But they've been here a long time. They used to put up standing stones like this in the old days, but they were usually in a ring, like Stonehenge.'

'What for?'

'I don't know exactly. Some people think they were like a calendar, to tell the seasons with, but nobody now seems to know how it worked. I reckon we can find a book on it and find out for ourselves, and we can probably check with the local paper to see if there's anything about standing stones.'

Alan watched his son standing in the shadows, dwarf-ed by the massive stones that were rooted in the mossy earth. From where Alan stood, in the sunlight on the grassy slope that led down to the little gully where water tinkled and burbled in a pleasant murmur, the wood looked dark and sunless. He had the twins in his arms and was standing facing the gap between the stones.

Tommy looked out from between the two megaliths and smiled at his father, then turned and stretched his small hand out and touched the upright block.

As soon as his hand brushed the smooth, hard surface, he felt a sudden wrench deep in his stomach, and for a second the world tilted dizzily. It was as if a shock had run through the ground and through the stone, right up his arm, jolting him out of himself. He gave a little cry of surprise and fear as the shocking surge of pure cold sizzled right up his arm. Again there was that sudden tilt, and an inside-out feeling, and Tommy was suddenly alone.

In front of him, the great stone block loomed impossibly high. It was as if it had somehow reared out of the ground, sprouted and stretched itself from the earth like a living thing. Its massive shadow blotted out the sunlight, and the smooth surface of the rock was no longer sanded and polished by the winds and rains of the centuries. Tommy saw carvings etched into the sides of the stone. Not words, but figures, like animals, but not like any animal Tommy had ever seen. And there were lines of strange curved letters that were like nothing Tommy had read in his school-books. But it seemed to him that those lines meant something he could almost see, just at the back of his mind, in that place where his compass was, the one that always *knew* where the twins were.

His hand was still flat against the stone and he could feel surges of cold draining the heat from his arm, in freezing pulses like the beat of a dead heart. It was as if he was holding on to a block of ice that stole his own heat away from him.

And under that cold, he could feel movement.

Under his numbing fingers, there was a slow, writhing feeling, as if the stone was the skin of something alive.

He stared at his freezing hand, and from the corner of his eye he saw something move on the surface of the basalt slab. Then his eye flicked to the left as it caught another shift. Then, with shocking suddenness, like a picture coming into focus, the whole rock seemed to be crawling with life. Tommy's eyes gaped wide as his mind registered that it was the carvings, the little animal-things worked into the stone, that were wriggling and writhing. It seemed they were trying to work their way out of the stone. Out into the air. Out to where *he* was.

With a little squeak of fright, Tommy jerked his hand, trying to get away from that wriggling life, and away from the incredible, stealing cold. But his hand *wouldn't move*.

And the little, horrible things were squirming harder, as if they were getting their life from him.

With a wild surge of panic, Tommy grabbed his left wrist with his right hand and heaved himself back with all his strength. There was a snap, like a rubber band pulled too tight and then let go, as he heaved his palm from the stone, and there was a sudden looping sensation of nausea. Tommy blinked his eyes, and his vision cleared as he held back the sudden tears the fright and effort had brought. He was only a foot away from the strange stone. The movement was still there, but it was slowing down. Right in front of his eyes, one of the little creatures that had been wriggling free slowly turned its head and there was the faintest of stony creaks as it opened two eyes in a head that seemed to be horribly frog-like, with a massive mouth. As the little lids swung up, a pair of black eyes, so dark they gave no reflection, but seemed to suck away all light, glared briefly at him. Then the little mouth opened in an impossible gape, showing an array of spiny teeth that were too big for the mouth: sharp, gripping, rending teeth. Tommy gasped and drew back in case the thing leapt from the stone and bit him with those teeth. But the mouth closed with a barely audible snap, and the eyelids creaked down again.

The creature seemed to subside in slow motion, sinking back into the stone again until it was back in etched relief, not alive at all, just a shape cut in the surface of a stone and then even that faded and the surface smoothed itself out. For a second the rock was strangely still.

Then Tommy felt another lurch, and the inside-out feeling swept through him, carrying him on a wave of dizziness.

From somewhere, deep at the back of his head, but sounding far away, he heard a shrill scream build up. At first he thought it was himself screaming, but the sound got louder and louder, until it rang through his head. Tommy's eyes snapped open and he caught another movement. This time it was a flash of a light colour. His head jerked to the left, and he saw the girl walking along the foot-wide trunk of a fallen pine that had crashed down and was lying at a raised angle against the stone he was standing at.

She too seemed to be walking in slow motion, carefully placing one foot ahead of the other, as she balanced on the log.

Tommy felt a thrill of horror as he watched, dreading exactly what happened. The ground lurched, jarringly, and the tree's whole length shifted with the movement.

Still in slow motion the girl lost her balance and toppled. She was dark-haired and pretty in a tomboyish way, and Tommy saw her pinwheel her arms to keep her position on the tree. She started to fall, and Tommy called out, but no sound escaped his lips. The girl slipped and fell. In that curious slow scene, Tommy saw the leg of her patched jeans rip as it snagged on a stubby dead branch, tearing from calf to thigh, and immediately gouging out a line of red. The scream started – the one that was already ringing in Tommy's head – as she came down, the tree moving with her, tumbling through the air, and landing with a thud that Tommy felt through his feet.

She lay dazed, but probably not badly hurt, but the vibration that had moved the tree went on, and the trunk slipped from its precarious balance on the edge of the stone. It rolled, and came crashing down on top of the girl who lay spreadeagled at the base of the rock. There was another thud, this time a cracking, squelching noise. Tommy saw the sharp dead branch that stuck out from the pine-tree trunk and saw what was going to happen (*again, again, again*). There was a ripping, rending sound, and the rock was drenched with red, all down one side. Great blotches of scarlet, thick stuff splattered up and streaked the stone where the carvings were in shadow. Like a switch being shut off, the scream died in Tommy's brain, leaving him feeling numb. He again blinked back the tears of shock and stared at the girl.

But even the dead tree was not there. There was no girl. Tommy was standing alone between the two stones.

And from just beyond the trees, out there in the sunlight, his father was calling to him.

Alan had watched from the grassy slope as his son reached out to touch the pillar, and even from that distance he had seen a strange, frightened look cross his son's face. Just then, a breeze brushed through the topmost leaves of the big lime trees, shifting the cloud above just enough to lance the sunlight directly into his eyes, and enough to cause the shadows to shift at the edge of the wood where Tommy stood.

For a brief second, it seemed as if Tommy had been swallowed up in the shadow, as if he had just been whisked away by the dark shade that brushed across the space between the stones. Alan shifted position and put the girls down on the grass beside him and turned to raise a hand over his eyes to mask the glare. As he did so, it seemed the shadow in the trees pulled back a fraction, and Tommy was again visible, small and puny against the great bulk of the megalith.

'Tommy,' he called, 'are you all right?'

Tommy stared at the rock as if he hadn't heard.

'Everything OK?' Alan called out again.

The boy turned slowly, and seemed to start, as if surprised to see his father. He nodded, then looked again at the stone, with an expression of bewilderment.

'Yes. I'm coming,' he said, and started out from the trees. As he came across the grass, he kept glancing back, almost fearfully, at the stones.

'What's up, son?'

Tommy looked up at his father. 'The stones. They're . . .' He paused, seeming to grope for the word. 'They're cold.'

'I would imagine they are,' Alan said. 'You would be too, if you'd been standing out all night. In the summer they'll be warmer, just like big storage heaters. We can come up here and have picnics on warm days.'

Tommy nodded, and Alan didn't notice that he wasn't listening to him at all.

Tommy was just about as fearless as any eight-year-old who has been raised on a diet of adventure books and *Star Wars* and who has yet to face the real rough and tumble of the big world.

But he did have one fear. A great big fear that he kept locked up and huddled inside himself, and never spoke to anyone about, for if he did, he was sure that fear would jump out from where it lurked, like a coiled and black spring, and shatter his world completely.

When Tommy was four, and his mother had come back from hospital, he had seen the vast change in her. He had *felt* the changes inside her head. And those changes scared him. It had been like watching his

40

mother drown in quicksand; like watching her sink into a slimy mud-hole.

When Helen had come home again, it was as if she was a different person from the one who had laughed and cuddled him, who had tucked him up in bed at night and planted kisses on his brow. She was different from the one who had tickled him and baked his birthday cakes and sung the nursery rhymes along with him as they watched the children's programmes in the afternoon.

When Helen had come back from *that place*, there had been a coldness inside her, a black space, which she seemed to retreat into most of the time. Tommy could feel it, and he wondered if his dad could feel it too. But it was something he could not bring himself to mention to his father, who tried so hard, and wished so hard, and who played games and joked with him even when he didn't really want to; even when he was so worried.

The strange, cold dark space that seemed to envelop his mother was only part of Tommy's big fear.

He prayed at night, kneeling by the side of the bed the way she had taught him when he was very little, and asked God to make her better again; to bring her out of the dark place and make her *warm* again. There were times when she came closer to that warmth, but never all the way.

But worse was the terror Tommy had that he might be taken to *that place*. He was scared in case he got so cold inside that they would take him to the *loony bin*. In his mind's eye, he saw himself tottering about in a nightgown, gibbering and screaming and rattling the thick iron bars, and jerking around like washing on a line, while on the other side people in white coats grinned and told him he'd never get out.

So deep-rooted was his fear that he'd inherited more from his mother than his bright blue eyes that to mention it would be to give it life. It was something he kept battened down inside and never mentioned to

41

anyone, in case even saying it aloud would cause suspicion. Sometimes at night, he'd have strange dreams that would make him wake up crying, and he always told his dad, who rocked him in his arms, that he couldn't remember what they were. But he could. He would see wriggling things, and hear noises like teeth rasping and rending, and he could see himself running from something big and huge and hungry in long dark corridors that he'd never seen before. And he saw little animals made from stone come clawing their way out of rock, and eating up everything they could. And he saw blood, crimson slashes on a grey surface.

And when Tommy saw the little carved figures writhe on the standing stone, it brought a flood of terror rushing right up from inside him. When he saw the vision of the girl, with that great jagged log twisting and toppling on top of her, spearing her, and sending up those gouts of blood to splash on the grey stone, he was almost sick. Not just with the horror of the vision. But because of what it might mean.

'You sure you're all right?' Alan asked.

Tommy seemed to start out of whatever thought had been running just behind his eyes. He looked up quickly at his father's face and forced a smile. 'Yes, Dad,' he said. The sunlight made the smile easier.

'Good lad. Let's go and see whatever else there is.'

'Watch out for the girls,' Helen called from a few yards away. Father and son turned round to watch the twins, hand in hand again, beginning to trundle down the smooth slope towards the stream. The sight of them just beginning to be overcome by momentum just greater than their little legs could cope with broke the shadow that seemed to have suddenly settled on the man and the boy.

'Quick, catch them before they end up in the water,' Alan said. 'C'mon, TC. Move it!'

Tommy darted down the slope abreast of Alan who

loped on long legs towards the stream, and both of them reached the girls who were just about to lose their balance and cartwheel into the clear water.

Tommy grabbed Elaine's hand, while Alan simply whisked Kathryn off her feet at the last moment and swung her into the air.

'Couple of suicide merchants here,' he said. He hadn't been worried, for the slope of the stream levelled out to a smooth green patch beside a shallow part of the brook. At worst they would have got wet.

Kathryn giggled and Elaine followed suit, as always. Tommy started to laugh too. Already, the weird thing that had happened in the shadow of the stones was fading, shoved as far back as he could push it in his mind.

SIX

'It's just *too* big. *And* too far away from anything. Dear God, Alan, it's almost in the wilds.'

Helen had been sitting at the kitchen table that had fitted snugly into the semi-detached in Surrey, but was dwarfed in the big kitchen at the back of the house. Now she was on her feet, pacing slowly back and forth in front of the big ceramic sink that had been only part of her conversational focus over the past hour.

It was three days since they had moved into Cromwath House. Three days of work cleaning the place up and shifting furniture from one room to another as carpet fitters had pummelled and stretched and tacked their wares on the bedroom floors. They'd had a string of salesmen with measuring tapes and brochures for kitchen units with Germanic names and price tags that smacked of hard currency and made Alan's eyes water at the thought of the equity on their old home being poured down the maw of the garbage disposal that one seller was offering.

The new kitchen hadn't completely appeased Helen. It was plain that she was having difficulty accepting the change in her life, but Alan still thought, still hoped, that she'd come round and really feel at home. He was counting on it.

They'd had the planning, and the move, then settling in and shifting the furniture and having things fitted. Next day Alan planned to knock down the wall that separated the kitchen and the pantry to give them a proper breakfast area with a view to the south-west, and the kitchen was to be fitted too.

Then he had to get back to his office and catch up on

all the things he'd missed. But, he thought to himself, if she keeps on bitching about the house, it's going to be bloody murder.

'Look, the whole thing has been a ton of stress on us all. Why don't you at least give it some time? You'll get used to it, and I'm prepared to bet you'll really like the place when you do,' he said, doing his best not to watch Helen's spasmodic pacing.

'I really don't think so,' she said. 'I mean it's all right for you. You're back in the old country. Back to your roots.' Helen swivelled on her heel and turned to face him directly. 'But what about me? My roots aren't here. And I don't know anybody, and from what I've seen of them, I don't really want to either. Every time I go down to the village, they all want to know my business. Everybody keeps asking what we're doing to the house. They ask all sorts of things about the children. And that old woman at the grocer's kept trying to sell me things I'd never heard of, and telling me they were good for growing youngsters. Dear God, do they think I don't know how to look after my own kids?'

Alan's shoulders slumped perceptibly. 'No, of course not. Don't you understand she's just trying to be friendly?'

'Friendly? Just bloody nosy if you ask me!'

'I wasn't,' Alan mumbled into his cooling coffee.

'What was that?' Helen asked sharply.

'They're not being nosy. It's simple. There must be about three thousand people living here if you put Creggan and Murrin and the other places together. That means people tend to know their neighbours and everybody else, and they like to get to know anybody who moves in, because the incomers become part of the community.'

Helen tried to butt in, but Alan held up a hand to forestall her, and went on, 'It's different here.'

'Too different,' Helen shot back.

45

'That's only because you've just arrived. Look, there must be fifty families from England on the peninsula, and I'll bet they're loving every minute of it . . . including the nosy woman from the grocer's shop.' Alan paused to take a sip of his coffee and made a face when he realized it had gone cold. He pushed his chair back and stood to reach for the filter decanter for another cup.

'And the house is too big and too old,' Helen said in the pause. 'It's creepy.'

'I hope you keep that view to yourself. I don't want Tommy getting ideas forced on him.'

'Oh, don't be so bloody stupid, Alan. I'm not that irresponsible.'

'Right. Let's agree on that. And let's try to think rationally. You always said you'd like to live in a big house and now that you do, you don't like it.'

'That was . . . before,' Helen said. 'Before the girls. It was different then.'

'What's so different about it?'

'I . . .' She faltered, gathered herself, and started again. 'I just don't feel right about the place. It's too much of a change. I don't feel at *home*.'

Helen's voice was beginning to rise in pitch. Alan knew that tears were not too far away, and normally he would have backed down, saved it for another day. But he was angry enough that Helen had been complaining almost non-stop for the past couple of days, and the head of steam that had been building up inside him needed some safety-valve to ease the pressure.

'Well, I don't feel at home yet, but I bloody well will,' he said, a little harshly. 'And I'll tell you why.' Alan felt the pressure rising dangerously high. Felt it in his head and heard it in his voice. He took a slow sip of hot coffee to cool himself down. 'You know where I come from, don't you?'

Helen raised her eyebrows in question, unsure of what he meant.

46

'I'll tell you exactly where I come from. I come from a family of five kids raised in a council house in Corrieside. We couldn't afford to buy a house, so my brothers and I slept in a room you couldn't swing a cat in. We went to school with the arse hanging out of our trousers and had jam sandwiches for lunch three days out of five and lots of porridge for breakfast because it filled us up cheap.'

Alan put his cup down, then sat for a moment, pushing his shoulders hard into the back of the chair.

'My father worked in the shipyards. He was a riveter. Went deaf before he was forty, and because he was deaf, he didn't hear his workmates shouting to him up in the gantry of some oil tanker they were building for the Arabs, and he stepped on to what he thought was a scaffolding plank, except it wasn't. He did the beam-walk.'

He looked up, and Helen looked back at him, again with a question on her face.

'I never told you about that, did I?' Alan asked. 'Must have been a sunny day. In the hulls, they cut holes in the sides for fitting machinery and portholes and what-not. The sun shines through into all the dust, and some-times, at the wrong times, that sunbeam looks as solid as a plank. It happened now and again. You walk on the beam and you walk on air, and if you're deaf from nearly thirty years of pounding hot rivets in a big metal bell, you don't hear it when your mate tells you to watch out.'

Alan's voice had dropped in pitch until it was just a quiet murmur. 'Not much compensation in those days, though. But what I didn't know then was that my old dad had worked every hour God sent, and he didn't blow all his overtime on booze and Woodbines. He'd banked the lot, and to my mother that was a sacred trust. They couldn't give us much as kids, but by Christ they wanted to give us a future.

'This is part of that future. My partnership is part of

it. This is me telling my old man and my mother that it was all worth while. All that hard labour and burst eardrums and red, scadded hands. This is for them, and it's for me, and it's for our kids.

'And I tell you it's for you too. We've had our problems, and we've got over them, so now it's time to start afresh. I know it's not Surrey, and I know it's not heaven, but it'll certainly do to be getting on with.'

Alan paused and looked at his wife, who sat with her arms wrapped around herself, passively listening.

'All I want is that you give it a chance. There's no going back at the moment anyway. We can't just pack up and leave, so why don't you just try to make it feel like *home*?'

Helen still sat, staring at the floor. She said nothing for a moment. Then, amazingly, she looked up at him and said: 'I'll try.'

SEVEN

'Hello. I'm Tom Callander.'

The man on the porch was tall, at least as tall as Alan, with a short-cropped head of thick grey hair. He was wearing a green waxed-cotton coat and an old pair of cords to match were tucked into boots. He was blocky and tough-looking, but even at first sight he had a wide smile that beamed straight out of his lived-in face.

Alan stepped out from the shade of the storm doors and took the hand the man was holding out, felt it shaken in a strong grip.

'I'm your new neighbour. Or I should say, I'm your old neighbour, seeing I've lived here longer. That's my place just across the way. Thought I'd drop by and say welcome to the village, and if there's any help you need, you can just take a short cut over the wall.'

'Come in,' Alan said, gesturing into the hallway. 'I'm just having a break for a coffee. Want some?'

'Love some. My throat's like a badger's arse.'

From behind Alan, there was a giggle, and both men looked down the hallway. Tommy's basic sense of humour liked that one.

'Sorry about that. Didn't mean to talk like that in front of the children, you know.'

'It's all right. He's heard much worse,' said Alan. 'I'm working in the kitchen. Come on through.'

Alan took the man's coat and slung it over the back of a chair. Tom Callander was somewhere in his fifties, but had one of those faces and physiques that make it hard to say exactly whereabouts. He looked around the room: Alan had been plastering the areas where he'd laid extra cable for the new sockets. 'I see you're putting your mark on the place already.'

'Yes. And I'm running out of time, too. It seems the more I do, the more I've got left. I suppose I'll just have to leave some of the major jobs to do them whenever I've got time.'

He handed Callander his coffee and joined him at the table. Helen was in the back garden hanging out some clothes. Tommy stood just outside the kitchen door, examining the stranger.

'Who's this, then?'

'That's the number one son,' Alan said. He called to Tommy. The boy came in shyly.

'Well, Tommy, pleased to meet you. A fine name you have there, son. Same as mine, except you can call me Tom.'

'Tommy, this is Mr Callander, who lives in the next house,' Alan said.

Tommy stuck out his hand and shook.

'How do you like living here, then?' the man asked.

'It's great. Lots of places to play.'

'And have you got somebody to play with?'

'Just my sisters, and they can't play football. But I'll be going to school next week.'

'Well, it's good to have you here. Maybe when you're bored you can come on over to my place. I've got a bit of a boat for fishing in the loch. D'you like fishing?'

'Don't know. I've never tried it.'

'You'll love it. I'll show you how to sail a boat too. How about that?'

'Great,' Tommy replied enthusiastically.

'Right. I'll speak to your dad here, and the first good Saturday we get, you can come out and crew for me.'

When Tommy had bounced his ball out of the kitchen and on to the front lawn, Callander said: 'Fine-looking young feller.'

'Yes, he's a nice lad,' Alan agreed. 'He's loving the space here.'

'Can he swim?'

'Yes, he's pretty good in the water.'

'Well, any time he's fed up he can come along with me. I used to do a fair bit of real sailing, but now I just putter about on the loch and pull in a few mackerel.'

'He'd like that. So would I, if I had the time, but I'm afraid I'm going to be tied up tight with the house, and all the things I've got to get back to.'

Callander asked Alan what he did and listened interestedly to the potted history that came freely as they drank coffee. Alan discovered that Tom Callander was a wealthy man.

'I've got the quarry along at Mambeg. That's the big hole in the hill you can see when you come round the head of the loch,' he said. 'My great-grandfather started it off way back more than a hundred years ago and it's still going strong, especially since they're putting the new face on Glasgow. They can't get enough stone these days. Better than that red brick they're trying to foist on us from down south.'

Alan agreed. 'Miles and miles of that down in Surrey,' he said.

'I'm semi-retired now, but I still keep an eye on things, just to keep my hand in. How do you like living here?' Callander asked, switching the subject.

'So far it's been hectic, but I reckon it'll be just right for us all, when we get settled down. I'm from Leven-ford, originally, so it's as near to home as I can get.'

'It's a nice place, and there's some good folk too. You'll fit in quite well. How about the house? Everything going well?'

'Apart from a few alterations in here, I don't expect to do that much,' Alan said. 'I'm fitting a kitchen, and I'll knock down the adjoining wall to the pantry for a breakfast area. Big job, but I might as well get it over with as soon as possible.'

'Listen. I've got a friend who helps me out with all sorts of jobs. He's a useful fellow to know. Turns his hand to anything. Why don't I get him across to help you out?'

'I don't know I could afford to pay a tradesman just now. I haven't got our finances straightened out yet.'

'Oh, don't worry about that. Seumas isn't a tradesman. He's very reasonable, and about the most reliable man for any kind of work. I'll have a word with him and he'll tackle any job.'

Alan thought about it. 'I suppose I could use another pair of hands in here. And I'd like somebody to have a look at the standpipe out by the garage too. As long as he doesn't cost the earth.'

'He won't. You'll be surprised.'

The two men chatted on for a while and Helen came in from the garden with an empty plastic linen basket. Alan introduced Tom Callander and the older man volunteered that it was a good drying day.

'Just as well,' Helen said. 'This is the first real washing I've managed to do since we arrived. I was beginning to think we'd run out of clothes.'

'I don't want to keep you both back on a busy day,' he said. 'But seeing things are a bit hectic in here, why don't you come across to the house on Thursday evening for a bite to eat? My daughter's staying with me for the moment, and she's a pretty fair cook.'

'That would be nice,' Alan said brightly, at the same time as Helen was saying she didn't know if they could manage.

'What about the children?' she asked Alan, but before he could answer Tom said: 'Bring them along with you. Beth won't mind how many there are, as long as I give her plenty of notice.'

'Fine,' Alan said. 'We'll look forward to it.'

Tom Callander beamed at them both, and moved out towards the door. Alan let him out and the older man strode down the stairs on to the gravel driveway where his boots crunched on the pebbles.

'It's been nice meeting you,' he called over his shoulder. 'We'll look forward to a blether on Thursday.'

Seumas Rhu MacPhee came as a complete surprise to them. He turned up at their door the following morning at breakfast time, wearing an old tweed jacket, frayed in a dozen places, twirling a battered cap between gnarled hands. He was about five foot four and thin as a whip, and he looked about seventy years old. The big black tackety boots he wore looked as if they were made for somebody twice his height.

'Morning, sir. I'm Seumas MacPhee. Tom asked me to come down and see what I can do.'

Alan was slightly taken aback. When Callander had mentioned somebody who was a good worker, a jack of all trades, he'd pictured a big strapping local fellow, maybe forty years younger than the more than slightly weatherbeaten old fellow who stood on the porch, shuffling his boots.

'Oh, hello,' he said, and held the door wider. The old man hesitated.

'I've got my boots on,' he said. 'I don't want to mess up the place.'

'Don't worry. The place is a mess as it is. I'm just getting things fixed up. We're having breakfast just now. Can I get you anything?'

The old fellow shook his head. 'No thanks, sir. I already had something this morning.' He scrunched up his cap and jammed it into one of the slack pockets of his jacket.

'Well, come and join us anyway. I haven't started working yet.'

Seumas followed him into the kitchen, where the family stopped eating in unison to stare at the wiry little man.

'This is Seumas MacPhee,' Alan announced. Seumas flashed a smile that showed a row of strong teeth. Under bushy brows he had a pair of sparkling green eyes that gave him a mischievous, elfin look.

'Morning,' he said.

Tommy said hello, and the twins, yet again streaked with egg yolk, smiled in unison.

Alan brought Seumas over to the table and made him sit down. He pressed a cup of tea on the little man, and watched as he spooned two heaps of sugar into the cup.

'Cheers,' Seumas said.

'Tom tells me you can do most things,' Alan ventured. Helen resumed reading her magazine.

'I reckon so. I've done a lot for him, and everybody else over the piece. Bit of gardening and the odd repair. There's not much I can't figure out.'

'I do have a few things that need to be looked at, and I'm doing some heavy work in here. Knocking that wall down to make more space.'

Seumas caught his thrust immediately. 'Looks like a big job, but I've done heavy work before. You just tell me what needs to be done, and I'll get a start on.'

'Well, I plan to start on that wall today, but there's a standpipe out by the garage that isn't working. I want it for mixing cement – and for cleaning the car. Can you do any plumbing?'

'I'll have a look at that right now.' Seumas made to rise from the table, but Alan insisted he finish his tea.

'Oh, and there's a couple of slates lodged in the gutters. I suppose I should have them shoved back into place.'

Seumas said he'd take a look at those as well. The children watched him curiously, and Tommy gave him a big smile when the old man winked at him over the rim of his cup.

An hour later, while Alan was measuring up the wall and chipping away the plaster to get down to the bricks where he planned to insert a beam, Tommy and Seumas had become friends. They were out in the grounds at the side of the house where Tommy sat on an old curling stone, one of a pair that framed the garage door. He was watching Seumas dig a pit just to the left of the lead standpipe that came out of the ground right against the garage wall on the garden side.

The old man had slung his jacket and his cap on a hook inside the garage door, and now had the sleeves of his heavy checked shirt rolled up. His arms were skinny and knotted, and they looked strong. He swung the spade in easy movements down into the hole, bending low, and scooped out large quantities of earth and gravel.

'We have to find out which direction the water's coming from, and then there's a wee trick I can show you, if you've a mind.'

Tommy nodded pleasantly.

For the past hour, Seumas had regaled him with stories and exploits, and had given him a potted history of the peninsula, and some quickly drawn pictures of some of the local folk. When Tommy had called him Mr MacPhee, the old man had jumped on it immediately.

'It's Seumas to you, and everybody else. Seumas Rhu MacPhee, that's me.'

'What's Seumas Rhu mean?'

'Seumas is maybe just the same as James. It's from the Gaelic, you know. And Rhu, well, there's a couple of meanings to that, but that's not the reason I was called it. You see, my old daddy called all of us after the places around the loch. I came last of the seven of us, and I ended up with Rhu. You'd have passed it when you were coming round the road in that nice car your daddy drives.'

'Yes, I remember it now. That's on the other side of the loch, isn't it?'

'Uh huh. That's the place. I got the short name, seeing I was the runt of the pack.' The old man sat down on the other stone and pulled a ragged cloth from his pocket and mopped his brow, although he wasn't even breathing hard. 'I'm the seventh son of the family, and if I'd been born a girl, I would be so full of Gaelic magic you would see me glow in the dark. But I'm not . . .'

Tommy laughed at the old man's comic expression.

'At least I hope not!'

'I don't think so,' Tommy said, still laughing.

'But I do have some of the sight, you know. I can tell that you're a fine young feller who's got the time to sit and listen to an old man blethering away sixteen to the dozen, and helping him keep happy in his work. And I've got a trick to show you, seeing as you look as if you've got some of the magic in you as well. Have a look at this.'

He gestured over to the hole he'd dug. It was moist and dark, and at the bottom, about three feet down from the surface, the lead pipe took a twist, like a grey snake, with little silvery scales where the spade had nicked the oxide and exposed fresh metal, away from the garage wall, towards the front garden.

'Now it's a shame it's going that way, because it's going to be hard to find.'

'What are we looking for?' Tommy asked.

'Water, Tommy boy. Good clear water. But we won't find it in this pipe, because I reckon there's been a burst somewhere. The water's draining away, I think, and we have to find it.'

'How?'

'Now, didn't I tell you I would show you a trick?' Seumas asked. 'We're going to see if you have any of the magic. Come on along with me and we'll find out.'

Seumas marched, crunching along in his big black boots that were now slick with mud, along the path and up towards the trees. 'It's a shame we don't have any hazel here, but there's one or other that will do almost as well,' he said when they got in under the shade of the trees. 'There's birch, but that's better in the early spring when the sap's just rising. Now hawthorn's pretty good, if we can get a piece just the right shape.

'Good wood, hawthorn. They call it *Uath* in the old tongue, and that had different meanings. The wood is for cleansing, and that's for the water we're going to find. It's also for dreams, and the blue at midnight.'

They strolled along the path through the trees until they suddenly came up against the grey bulk of the standing stone that was nearest the house. Seumas spat out a muted murmur that sounded to Tommy like a curse.

'I'd forgotten they were there,' he said. 'Almost.' He held up his hand, making a quick sign with his fingers. 'That's another meaning of *Uath* too,' he said. He turned and took Tommy by the shoulders, leading him away from the stones, back in the rough direction they had come from. 'It can mean chaos as well as all the others. That's what they called this place in the old days. *Crom Uath.* The chaos stones. The dream stones.

'It was never a good place, you know. There's some fish in that stream that I'll show you how to guddle with your hands, and I'll take you out beachcombing along the rocks, but this isn't a good place for a boy to be on his own, I can tell you that.'

He stopped and turned Tommy round and bent down to look the boy straight in the face. 'You'll remember that, won't you, young feller?'

Tommy nodded, unsure of what it was he was supposed to remember.

'Good lad. Now let's find ourselves a water stick.' He took a couple of steps off the path to where a bush grew in tangles up towards the higher branches of the trees overhead.

'This is what we want,' he said, and, taking an old, worn claspknife out of his pocket, he pushed his way into the heart of the bush. Tommy could hear the thorns snagging the old man's jacket, but Seumas didn't seem to notice, or care if he did. The knife snicked softly a few times, and Seumas came backing out of the thorn bush. In his hands was a small branch, forked near the base and ending at each fork in a bundle of twiggy spines that were shrouded in bright green foliage and flourish.

He deftly cut off the leaves and trimmed the stick down until it was in a rough Y shape, but with the arms much longer than the stem.

'Now we'll see if we can find the leak,' he said, as they walked down out of the trees towards the house. As they were walking, Seumas looked back towards the shady trees, and said to Tommy: 'You'll remember what I said about those stones. Don't be playing up there on your own, now.'

Tommy said nothing. He'd hidden away the incident at the stones, but it was not completely hidden.

EIGHT

Alan chipped away at the plaster on the west wall of the kitchen where he'd marked the outline of the new doorway in chalk. The cold bolster dug into the surface with every stroke of the mallet, sending sharp vibrations through his wrist and up his arm. Dust flew everywhere and the metal on metal clanged loudly as he worked his way through the browning and on to the hard stone underneath. It was hard work, and coupled with the dust that soon coated him and desiccated his throat, tiny slivers kept shooting out of the groove as the chisel bit, and unfailingly lodged themselves in his eyes.

It took him more than half an hour to clear the covering and break through the light wooden strips of lath. Underfoot, the broken pieces of wood and the fragments of old dry plaster were in a heaped mound on the plastic sheet he'd laid down to keep the kitchen tidy. Pieces of the chalky white mortar were strewn in varying sizes all over the floor, and the air was thick with a dust that would no doubt settle on every surface and take days to clean. Finally he was down to the stonework. It was cold and dry and a deep, dark whin that had been carefully jigsawed together and bonded with a light grey cement. The real fabric of the house was exposed, showing the careful craftsmanship of journeymen long dead, but who had left their own epitaph in their work.

Alan thought vaguely that it would be a shame to waste such quality artisanry, but it was too late to stop now. The kitchen units had been bought and designed for the open-plan effect he'd envisaged for the kitchen.

And anyway, once the lath had been stripped, it would be virtually impossible to replaster the wall in the old style. As a civil engineer, Alan's sense of propriety forbade him even to contemplate boarding the wall up with gyprock or, worse still, that cardboard construction the throw-'em-up companies were using for internal walls these days.

It was Helen who'd initially put the thought in his head, as he was stripping the old material. She had come into the kitchen and watched him work for a few moments, before stating that perhaps she didn't want the extension after all.

'I think we should keep the room the way it was,' she said blankly.

Alan's hammer action stopped at the top of the swing, just as he was about to bring the two pounds of steel down in a fast arc. He couldn't believe he'd really heard her properly.

'What was that you said?' he asked incredulously.

'I think I like the room the way it is. Maybe the idea of a breakfast room wasn't so good.'

'But it was *your* idea,' Alan said. 'You didn't like the kitchen being so square, and you said the washroom was just a waste of space.'

He paused to wipe dust out of his eyes with the back of his hand. 'You wanted to be able to walk out on to the garden in the morning. And we bought the kitchen units to fit exactly into the space we're going to have.'

'I just think it's such a nice old room,' she said. 'It's kind of grown on me. Don't you think we should just forget about it?'

'It's a bit late for that, don't you think? I'd have to get this lot plastered up again, then reorder all the units, and frankly I wish you'd suggested that before.'

'I'm sorry,' Helen said, although her tone suggested she was only sorry she'd mentioned it. 'I just think you'll spoil the room, that's all. Can't I express an opinion?' She turned and walked out of the room, leaving Alan standing covered in dust, and with his mouth open so wide he could have swallowed the hammer with space to spare.

He turned to the ripped-up wall. 'I don't believe it,' he said aloud. 'I just don't bloody well believe it.'

Half an hour later, he'd built up a fair sweat. He could feel his scalp itch as rivulets worked their way through the granules of plaster and down on to his forehead. He lifted a hand to wipe it away, leaving a grey smear on his forearm. Standing back, and almost losing his balance on the mound of debris, he surveyed his own work. He marked his other outlines on the stone, with a horizontal above head height, where the H-beam would slot on to the groove he would have to make. The two verticals marked out where the new entrance would be, a couple of inches wider than the final dimensions, just enough to take the finishing mouldings and no more.

Alan brought the bolster up again and held it against the cement between two square stones. He hefted the hammer in his right hand and swung it hard on the battered head of the cold chisel and felt the steel tip bite into the mortar. There was a spark as the blade glanced off the solid stone with a clang that made his ears ring, and the vibration almost numbed his hand. The room seemed to lurch and his foot slipped to the side, throwing him off balance.

Alan worked doggedly, chipping at stone and cement, and using a crowbar to level out the first of the old stones which came crashing to the floor, landing on the mound of rubble. As it came loose and dropped, Alan felt a wrench right through him, a strange, shivery feeling, as if he'd done something wrong. It was the kind of feeling people get when they say someone has walked over their grave. Alan shook his head again, and the feeling began to dissipate. He went back to work.

As he laboured, the dust thickened in the air and the

ringing of steel on stone seemed to get louder until it made his ears crackle. Alan still hadn't shaken off the feeling that he was doing something wrong. Worse, apart from the ache in his hand, there was tension in the back of his neck that was beginning to build up to a taut throbbing in his head.

Alan never got headaches, apart from the occasional dull hangover which was rare enough. He tried to ignore it and raised the bolster again, smashing the hammer on to the shaft. There was another flash of sparks as it struck stone, accompanied by a deep thud on the inside of Alan's skull as the headache notched up a gear.

Without warning, Alan was suddenly swamped by a wave of desolation that washed through him in a bleak, black surge. It pressed on him so violently that he shuddered under its weight. It was as if he realized the total futility of everything he was doing, had done, or would do; as if he should stop right where he was, curl up and cry. The leaden feeling crushed him with such a weight that his knees buckled and he sank to the mound of rubble, staring at the wall.

The bleakness was so vast and so sudden that Alan's breath caught in his dry throat. He sat there, eyes glazing, unfocused on the wall where he had chiselled and gouged. His vision swam dizzily and the bare stones blurred and wavered.

Alan blinked, and in that instant the wall seemed to snap back into focus, every crack and chisel mark sharp. There was a twist in the intervening space between Alan and the wall, as if something had shifted invisibly, wrenching the atmosphere out of the real. Then the stones started to move.

The interlocking blocks appeared to run and drip around the hole like melting wax, widening the space that would lead into the old pantry, and as they did, the shadows beyond seemed to roll and billow outwards in a weird warping. Alan blinked again, uncomprehendingly, still battened down by the black desolation that had floored him, head still thudding from monstrous inner pressure.

The dark shadows flowed outwards, and within them shapes turned and twisted, barely perceptible at first but growing out of the dark.

Alan's jaw dropped slackly as the shapes writhed. It was as if he was looking down into a barrel of snakes and lizards. Here something scaly coiled, there something squatted with an amphibious mouth gaping. He drew back in slack dismay. Inside, underneath the pounding, his mind was telling him that this was not real. But he could no more draw his eyes away from the scene in front of him than he could haul his leaden body off the pile of rubble.

The dark shadows bubbled out into the kitchen. There was a scuttling noise and something that was low-slung and black and blindingly fast scuttled in a blur to the front edge. Alan got the impression of two huge, black eyes that seemed to suck the dim light from the kitchen into them. The blunt head swivelled, left and right. Jaws opened, showing an array of needle teeth that dripped slime. The creature gaped and then was gone in the blink of an eye. Something else that was warty and putrescent lumbered into view. Behind it, behind the scrabbling and scraping and scuttling noises, Alan heard a cry, high and distant. A child's voice calling far off, coming closer, strangely familiar in the echoing dark.

Tommy's voice. It was *Tommy*. In there, in the hole in the wall where the shadows bulged out and into the room. His small voice was high and panicky. When it came again, the slithering, blurring creatures seemed to turn as one, racing back from where they had been crowding in the forefront of the dark bubble of unreality, and vanished down a long black space. There was a high squeal of fright, then a savage chittering screech followed by a snapping sound. The squeal was cut off instantly and Alan's heart stopped dead in his chest as if he'd been punched. His lungs tried to work but a vice clamped them tight and for a few moments the world spun even more dizzily than before. His vision dopplered down through shades of grey, fading in from the edges as if he was falling backwards down a long shaft, and then his heart jolted again so hard that the shock almost threw him backwards. His lungs unlocked, first shoving his breath out in a whoop and then hauling it back in a great gasp. He raised his head, ready to leap up towards the wall for some reason that he couldn't quite remember, and then stopped. In front of him the wall was there, jagged and cut and bolster-scraped. There was nothing else there.

The back of his head pounded violently as Alan struggled to remember what had happened. But despite the shocking vividness of the scene that had unrolled before his eyes, and the utter horror of the scream that had assailed his ears, the memory of it had gone as if it had been plucked straight out of his head.

Alan just sat there, bewildered. His chest was heaving as he panted for air. His hands were shaking and he did not know why.

Helen stood on the cold flagstones down in the cellar. She had been out in the garden, where the shirts were flapping in a gentle breeze, and now she was down in the basement of the house where it was dark and musty. She couldn't remember coming into the house and opening the narrow green door that led down here where spiders' webs festooned every corner. There was a soft buzzing in her ears, a muted rasping that tickled in a vibration that was almost below her threshold. She felt fuzzy.

From up there in the house the hammer struck the chisel and the chisel hit into the stone with a metallic shriek. The sound, sharp and vicious, sleeted through her like a shock wave, causing her to shiver. It was as if *she* had *felt* the blow, running right through her from head to toe. The sound came again, harsh and uncompromising, and the shiver ran through her a second time. Then again, and again, in repeated shocks that she could feel right up her spine. Inside her head, the cracked bell notes crashed in attacks that pounded, then diminished in a high vibrato that she could feel twanging along her nerves and thudding in her brain.

Then the darkness closed in on her and Helen felt herself fade away, withdrawing from the scene. The thudding blows still banged away inside her head, as if the hammer and chisel were working on the inside of her skull, but they too started to fade in intensity as her knees sagged. The darkness seemed to crowd around her, enfolding her in shadow, and she slowly slumped on to the flagstones against the wide stone pillar that supported the roof. She lay face up with her arms spread wide. Her eyes were wide open, but they looked blind.

Out of the swirling darkness that had swallowed her up a figure seemed to form out of a million dots of light that jumped in front of her perception, then coalesced into a shape. The shape moved, and became a man, a figure of light who strode towards her. It seemed he walked forever, striding across a vast distance. She couldn't make out the features as he loomed up over her. The sparkling lights that had swirled and shrunk to form the man faded until he was a grey shadow walking. Across a distance she heard him call, but there were no words, at least not any that were spoken, but she knew he was calling her. Strangely there was no fear in this dream. The dark was warm, and safe, and after the clangour the destruction of the wall had set up in her brain, the dull silence in this place was soft. She huddled into it, watching passively as the figure of light that was now shadow strode across the wide dark, calling her name.

At last it reached her, where she lay. The man stood over her, tall and broad. The shadows played about him, giving the impression of fine, strong muscles, and they flitted across his face so that she could not see it properly. She knew inside of herself that he was smiling. He bent down and reached his hands out to her. She was not afraid. She raised her hands towards him and was swallowed in a warm blanket of black.

At the front of the house Tommy was walking down from the trees with Seumas who was nicking off the thorns and leaves from the hawthorn branch.

'What are we going to do?' the boy asked, and Seumas winked down at him with a grin.

'Just a little bit of magic, Tommy.'

'What, like Paul Daniels?'

'Much better than that. That's just tricks, this is the real McCoy. You'll see.'

They got to the front of the house where the girls were happily bouncing a ball between them. Their laughter spangled the air over the sunny front lawn.

Seumas stopped and watched them, entranced. They didn't notice him for a moment, and continued throwing the large coloured ball to each other with the hesitant co-ordination and joyful ebullience natural to four-year-olds. Then his presence seemed to impinge on them simultaneously, and as one, they turned towards the man and boy. The ball bounded away unheeded. The girls looked solemn for a moment, then both of them smiled broadly, showing pearly teeth.

'Hello ladies,' Seumas said gallantly, doffing his battered cap. 'Sorry if I interrupted the game.'

The girls laughed.

'Come on, Seumas,' urged Tommy, who was standing at his side. 'Let's do the magic.'

Down at the trench the small man had dug, the pipe lay still exposed in the dry hole.

'There's not even drain water here,' Seumas said. 'You'd expect that if the burst was uphill. So it must be somewhere down in that direction.'

He pointed down the driveway towards the gate. The ground sloped gently down towards the road. 'That's where we'll find it.'

NINE

Tommy felt the magic surging through him in a delicious vibration that ran up and down his body in tingling shock waves. When it first hit, it was not unlike the feeling he'd got when his Uncle Tam had bounced his tuning-fork off the table and then held it close to Tommy's ear, letting the resonance twist the air and tingle right inside his head. This feeling was like that, only bigger. It was as if he was being shivered inside, only with a warm buzzing feeling that was so nice.

In his hands, the slingshot-shaped hawthorn branch bucked and twisted slowly as if it had a life of its own. Tommy could feel it move and writhe in his grip, as if it was trying to pull away from him, trying to pull down into the ground.

'What's happening, Seumas? What's it doing?' he cried, excitement pitching his voice high.

'That's the magic, boy. You're chock full of the stuff. Look at that stick *move!*'

'I can feel it moving. But why is it doing it? Look. I'm not moving it. It's going by itself.'

'That's the water, boy. You're right over the top of it. The stick feels the running water and tries to go for it. Now we can follow it back and see if we can't get that pipe hooked up.'

They had started down the slope from the ditch, right down almost as far as the gates, while the girls watched them from under the bay window. They stood there, hand in hand, as the old man and the boy strode down on the grass.

'We can find the burst this way and patch up the pipe and make the water flow again.'

68

'How will you find it?' Tommy asked.

'Well, I was hoping *you* would find it for us,' Seumas replied.

'Will we have to dig up the whole garden?'

'Not if I can help it. I don't like hard work, so we'll try to do it the easy way.'

Seumas had put the hawthorn branchlet into Tommy's hands, and closed the youngster's fingers over the top ends of the Y so that the short joining shaft pointed ahead of him.

'Keep your thumbs out,' he said, 'and then twist your hands together. There. Like that.' He nodded approvingly as the outer twigs bent with the tension.

'Now we just walk along here, one line at a time. And you can let me know if you feel anything.'

'What will I feel for?'

'You'll know it when you do,' Seumas said, and laughed out loud.

The girls were still hand in hand, but they had moved down from the front of the house on to the grass, watching the two of them further down the hill.

Just as Tommy started to quarter the edge of the lawn, a tremor ran through the ground; the kind of shuddering movement that happens when a heavy lorry thunders past at speed. But there was no traffic on the quiet road.

'What was that?' Tommy asked Seumas. 'I felt the ground shake.'

Seumas looked startled. Tommy looked up at him, but the small man had turned away, and was looking at the house.

'What the hell was that?' Tommy heard him mutter under his breath. The blood seemed to have drained out of Seumas's tanned and weatherbeaten face.

'Is something wrong?' the boy asked.

'That I don't know, son. Something's happened, somewhere, but I'm damned if I know what. Pardon my language.'

Tommy looked up at him. There was a frown on Seumas's brow, and the old man's eyes looked distant.

'That's all right. My dad says that all the time.'

'Well, maybe he does,' Seumas said, distractedly. His eyes were still fixed on the house. He was still feeling the aftershock of the tremor that had shuddered through the ground, but the vibration was not in the ground. It was in himself. Tommy heard him mutter something that sounded like the strange words he'd uttered up at the stones.

'Something's *moved*,' he said quietly to himself. Tommy didn't hear it.

The moment passed. Tommy said: 'Am I doing it right?'

His excited yell jerked the strange unreal feeling off Seumas and brought him right back to where he was. In Tommy's hands the hawthorn twig shuddered as if it was trying to pull away and dive right down into the ground.

'That's it, Tommy,' Seumas said, catching the boy's excitement. 'You've got the magic. You've found what we're looking for.'

'It's moving by itself again,' Tommy yelled back at the top of his voice, unable to control his pleasure. 'What's making it do that?'

'It's the water. And *you*. That's the magic, son.'

'It's wonderful. I can feel it. I can *feel* the water.'

'Right, now. What you have to do is walk along in a line, and when you feel it strongest, you're right over it. And if we do it a few times, we can find out the direction of the pipe. Then we can try something to find where the burst is and I can fix it.'

They spent ten minutes quartering back and forth until Seumas established that the main pipe ran in an almost true north-to-south direction, slanting towards the far end of the house. The old man made Tommy search further up the hill where the tremor of the stick grew less in the more sluggardly flow in the smaller, adjoining pipe.

'I expect we've got a good burst that's flowing straight into the field drain, otherwise you'd have a good-going stream right down the front of the garden.'

For another few minutes, they followed the curving path that the weakening pressure in Tommy's hands told them to take until they got close to the azalea bushes that edged the gravel drive. They almost stumbled over the girls who were kneeling beside a low shrub on the grass that had dried from the bright sunlight, and were facing down to a spot between them. When Tommy and Seumas slowly approached the girls didn't even look up.

It was Seumas who noticed what they were doing. He had brought a four-foot length of cane from a stack in the vegetable garden, planning to use it as a gauge when he got close to the burst where the underlying soil would be soft and damp. But the twins had beaten him to it. Kathryn and Elaine were both working at the soil with small sticks, digging in the precise spot where the writhing of the hawthorn faded to a barely felt vibration, showing that the flow of water had almost dissipated completely.

Where the girls were digging, in a little hole not more than six inches across and about the same in depth, a small, muddy trickle of water bubbled up from the earth and slowly filled the cavity with a brown, viscous fluid.

Seumas stood back, watching the girls who were intently working. He took his hat off and scratched his grizzled short hair.

'Well, would you look at that!' he said. 'How the devil did they know what we were looking for, and how the devil did they find it?'

He turned to Tommy and raised his eyebrows so high they almost disappeared into his hairline. 'Looks like your wee sisters have got the magic too, eh?'

He turned back to watch the little girls engrossed in their digging, and rapidly becoming plastered with slick mud.

'And they don't even need the hawthorn neither,' he said. 'I've never heard of that before in my life.'

Kathryn and Elaine both turned as one to look up at him. Then they smiled.

'How did they do it?' Tommy asked. 'I wanted to find the water myself.' He sounded a little bit peeved that his big moment had fizzled.

'Makes no difference who found it. At least you know you've got the water magic. But what kind of magic these little angels have fair beats me.' He bent over the girls, still twiddling his cap in strong, gnarled hands. 'How did you know what we were looking for?' he asked, looking askance from one to the other. The girls continued to smile.

'They don't talk,' Tommy said.

'Sure they do,' Seumas said. 'They laugh, don't they?'

'Yes, but they don't speak to anybody. Except maybe to themselves. I think they *think* at each other.'

'More magic, eh? Looks like they've been kissed by the fairies, so they'll keep their secrets.'

'What secrets?'

'Ah, that's something only your sisters and the fairies know,' Seumas said. 'I don't reckon you nor me will ever find that one out. We've only got a wee bit of the magic.'

He jammed his old hat into a pocket and held out both hands to the girls, who grabbed them with muddy fingers. He eased them to their feet. 'Now we got to do the real work, and there's no magic in that,' he said. 'Did I leave my spade over there?'

Tommy ran and fetched the spade and the three children watched while Seumas dug another ditch. The small man worked quickly and efficiently, first cutting away squares of turf in a line and putting them to the side face down. On top of them he dumped the muddy soil and kept digging until he had a trench a yard deep by several feet long. Water was oozing up, but slowly, through the soft earth. Down another six inches, Seumas hit clean gravel where the silt had been washed away by the water that was bubbling from the pipe and into the field drain a few inches away. The old lead pipe was exposed in a few moments, showing a bulge where ice had blocked it, then expanded and burst a jagged tear in the side. There was not enough pressure to get the flow up the rest of the hill to the standpipe. Seumas hauled himself out of the hole and, like the Pied Piper, was followed by the children down to the water cock just inside the gate. He twisted the jack-handle clockwise half a turn, and then they all marched back up the slope to the hole. Already the hissing of the escaping water had stopped, and the puddle in the pit was diminishing rapidly as the water drained out of the surrounding earth. Seumas gave it a few minutes before getting Tommy to fetch his hacksaw and a spare piece of copper pipe from his old canvas bag which was lying on the gravel beside the garage. The children watched in fascination as he cut the old lead pipe, paring away the jagged edge. Then he hammered the short section of copper into the two ends and flattened the lead all around it. From the bulging bag he produced an old-fashioned pump-up blowtorch and finished the job quickly by melting more lead on to the join. Less than fifteen minutes after that, the hole had been refilled and the turf carefully placed back down on the brown scar. Seumas trod it steadily until there was hardly a mark where he'd been digging, except for the little gap where the girls had torn up the turf. That would heal on its own.

When he turned the water-key and clanged the cover back down again, the little troupe followed him up to the garage for the ceremonial turning on of the water. The tap screeched a little on its dry thread, then a jet of muddy water bulleted out of the nozzle, quickly turning clear. Tommy yelled delightedly and the girls laughed along with him. Seumas watched them all with a grin of pleasure.

TEN

In the cellar, Helen lay on the cold hard slab of stone, glassy-eyed and oblivious to everything except the picture she was seeing in her mind.

The grey man in her dream had lifted her up in his arms and carried her away through the veil of darkness and into a riot of colour in a forest clearing where flowers of immense size and impossibly brilliant hues nodded in a fragrant breeze. Butterflies fluttered in the warm air, sending dazzling flashes of iridescence across the glade, and somewhere in the trees birds trilled, warbling songs of such beauty that she felt the beginnings of tears well up.

The noise and upset were gone. This was a place of peace. A place of beauty. She was alone in the clearing surrounded by a surreal vividness of life, and at long last the incessant anxiety that had become part of her life slipped slowly away, leaving her complete and whole.

At the far side of the clearing she could see the smooth side of a stone pillar reflecting the brilliant sunshine. A few yards away there was another standing stone. And beside that, another. The whole clearing was in the ring of stones, as if they protected an enclave of heart-stopping loveliness.

Behind her, she heard a soft noise, and knew that *he* had returned. A cool hand fleetingly touched her shoulder, drew back, then returned, firm and strong. It moved softly down her bare arm, then slid off where her elbows tucked into her side, and continued down the curve of her naked hip.

(*Naked? I've got no clothes on.*)

The touch was electrically smooth, making her skin

react in a wave of goose-bumps as it passed. Still she didn't turn round to see the man of shadows. She closed her eyes as the hand moved slowly back up her arm, faintly aware of the drone of lazy insects on the warm air, then her breath caught in her throat as the strong hand slowly urged forward to cup her breast. Instantly the nipple hardened and she leaned back against a broad, smooth chest. A small smile played about her lips. On her neck, other lips nuzzled just under her hairline sending skittering little ripples of pleasure down her spine, and the hand that tugged and teased at the nipple drew away and down, leaving it red and swollen and aching for more.

The man's hand left her breast and moved down the smooth curve of her stomach, down to the vee at the top of her thighs. As naturally as breathing, Helen opened them, feeling her hips push themselves forward of their own accord towards the pressure of the hand. Strong fingers teased the fair tangle of hair and she felt a little jolt inside as if something had given way, and then a trickle of slick readiness.

Her hips moved themselves again, insistently pressing upwards against the hand.

The hand that rested on her left shoulder moved down her back, drawing and lowering her to the grass. She could feel every blade against skin that was charged up to an exquisite height of sensitivity.

Helen's eyes remained closed, savouring the moment. She felt his weight against her, then on her, and her legs opened wide. There was a pressure outside, once, twice, then an invasion that launched itself in one amazing thrust that seemed to spear her to the core. And on the point of that invasion, Helen was carried high on wings that beat in the frantic rhythm of her heartbeat, swooping on pulses of the most enormous, unbelievable pleasure.

She thrust frantically to get all of it, to feel everything: to have completion. Again and again she soared on the jolts of pure ecstasy that passed through her entire body like seismic shocks. Somewhere, away in the distance, she heard herself calling out, begging, pleading, demanding. And through it all, a voice in her mind said: 'I am in you, and you are in me.'

And she heard herself cry out: 'Yes. Oh, yes!'

And then came the pain. It came gripping like a fist deep inside her, wrenching and tearing. It was a shard of glass being twisted and dug into the very centre of herself, so shocking and so sudden that she couldn't even draw breath. It rampaged through her in an explosion of such violence that her mind tried to flee from it, trying to blank itself out.

The summer light between the stones winked out in that instant, plunging her into darkness. She was down in the cellar, kneeling on the dusty flagstones, hands up and around the massive stone pillar. She was pressed up against the cold, smooth surface. The pain came again in a lancing thrust. Violent spasms racked her body, thrusting it hard against the stone.

Then between her legs, she felt the terrible oozing, draining sensation. Cramps twisted at her belly and she felt the rhythmic pulses squeezing at her muscles. She pulled back from the pillar with a groan and her weight flopped on to her heels. The stone pillar was splashed with thick, clotted blood. It ran down the stone and onto the floor in a dark, brownish wave.

The pain grabbed at her again with vicious claws, and this time she did cry out, loud and high, into the darkness.

In the kitchen, Alan wondered what the hell he was doing sitting on a pile of rubble holding his head in his hands.

The wave of gloom that had suddenly swamped him lifted so suddenly that it was as if it had never happened. There was no aftertaste. It was gone as inexplicably as it had arrived. And the headache had stopped instantly, at the same moment. The pain vanished so swiftly, it was hard even to remember what it had been like. Alan shook his head, bewildered.

Just then Tommy came bounding in the doorway, with the girls hard on his heels, and Seumas bringing up the rear.

'Dad!' the boy yelled. 'Dad, we did it. I found the water with the stick, like Seumas showed me. It's terrific, Dad.'

Alan almost staggered back from his son's hyperenthusiastic outburst. 'All right, TC, one sentence at a time,' he said. 'Go on, tell me, but slow enough for me to hear.'

'I found the water with the stick. Seumas showed me, and the stick moves in your hand and you get all tickly, and the water's right there in the ground.' Tommy paused for breath and Alan stepped in before he could gun the engine again.

'I didn't understand a word of that, Seumas. Do you know what he's talking about?'

'Dowsing. We had to find the burst pipe with a dowsing rod. I showed Tommy how to do it and it turns out he's an honest-to-goodness water-sniffer.'

'Does that stuff really work?'

'Sure it does, if you've got the right tuning, as my old mother used to tell me. But these two,' he said, pointing at Katie and Laney, standing together at the corner of the table, 'they're tuned up like fine old fiddles. They showed *us* where the leak was, and that was with not a stick of wood. They've got the real talent.'

'I've never really believed in any of that. I thought it was an old wives' tale.'

'No, Dad. It's true. The stick just turns in your hand and wriggles about, and that tells you there's water under the ground.'

'He's right. That's what happens. And I've finished that job.'

'That was quick.'

'We had *magic*,' Tommy said proudly.

'That we did,' said Seumas, with a smile. 'This looks like a heavy job you've got here. Can I give you a hand? These beams are a proper bugger. Pardon my language.'

'Yes, I could do with an extra pair of hands here. I've taken out enough for the lintel, but it's a fair weight, and I want to put those jacks in to take the load before I put the beam in.'

'All right, let's get to it. Now, young ladies, if you'll just stand out there by the door so I don't fall over you,' Seumas said, ushering the twins before him. They did as they were told, as if they had known him all their lives.

Alan and the older man wrestled with the heavy jacks, manoeuvring them into place and slotting batons on their plates to jam them hard against the hole in the stone above the new doorway. They grunted and gasped with the weight of the new steel beam and manhandled it into place. Alan's height allowed him to slot the beam into the ledge and he was surprised at the older man's strength. Though he was small and skinny, he was as strong as an ox. The muscles on his forearms stood out like knots in a rope.

'Right, that's it in place,' Alan said, breathing heavily, and running damp under his armpits. Seumas, who had done his fair share of the heavy lifting, looked as if he could carry on all day.

'Let's have a go at that wall,' Alan said. He picked up the sixteen-pound sledgehammer that had been standing in a corner and hefted in manfully. 'You lot stay over there well out of the way,' he said to the children. 'I don't want you getting hit by any chips.'

He swung the hammer in a low loop behind him, then twisted hard, bringing it up and forward in a high arc against one of the stones he'd loosened with the bolster. It shuddered under the impact, and a spray of mortar fell out, pattering on to the mound below. Alan repeated the motion, and the big square rock was unseated. It rocked, then fell to the floor with a resounding crash. He hefted the hammer again and swung it, and as he did so the room lurched with a tremor, exactly as it had done before. For a second it seemed as if a cloud had passed over the sun, throwing the kitchen into deep shadow. On the upswing movement Alan was unable to stop. He felt the big hammer twist in his hands, the way Tommy had described the dowsing stick. Its haft seemed to squirm with life of its own, bending along its length, spoiling the trajectory. The force with which Alan swung the sledge carried it right round, but not at the point on the wall where he was aiming. It whirled past the stone of the wall and round in a snaking loop and whistled past Seumas, missing the small man by a hair's breadth. Seumas ducked and the hammer twisted again, travelling, apparently, of its own volition, powered by a force that had started with Alan but continuing with an impetus that came from nowhere. The wooden shaft twisted again, seeming to bend like a bow, then the hammer lashed down again as Alan, holding on as tightly as his grip would allow, was spun like a berserk ballet dancer by centripetal force. The big hexagonal head whooped through the air and came crashing down, straight down at Tommy's head.

Instinctively, the boy cowered back and the mallet smashed into the wall beside the door where he'd been standing watching his father. The crash of the hammer boomed out through the house like a gunshot. After the impact the sledge gave a final wrench and slipped from Alan's hand and tumbled to the floor where it bounced once on the solid boards, rolled over, and was still.

'Jesus Christ,' Alan swore vehemently. The blood had drained right out of his face. He was ashen under the powdering of mortar dust. His hands were trembling quite violently. Tommy stood there looking up at his father in shock.

'Are you all right, son?' Alan said in a shaky voice, squatting down to take the boy in his arms. 'Dear God, I nearly killed you.'

'I'm OK, Dad. It missed me. It didn't hurt me.'

Alan clasped Tommy to his chest. He could feel the boy's heart beating fast on the outside of his own ribs. He could feel his own heart pounding away on the inside. It was hammering in his throat.

Alan turned to Seumas. 'Did you see that?'

Seumas nodded.

'I don't know what happened. That thing just seemed to twist itself in my hands.'

'I saw it. Maybe it's out of balance. Or there could be a crack in the shaft,' Seumas said.

'No, there's nothing wrong with it. It just swerved on its own.'

'I think we should maybe take a break and give ourselves a rest,' Seumas volunteered calmly. 'Why don't we put the kettle on and have a cup of tea to get our breath back?'

'Great idea. That's just exactly what I need.' Alan turned to put the kettle on. His hands were still shaking as he filled it.

The two men sat at the table, away from the rubble, and gradually Alan's breathing slowed. They drank a mug of hot tea, and when the children had gone out to the front garden to play, Alan started to tell Seumas exactly what had happened.

Just then the anguished cry of pain came echoing up from somewhere in the house.

'What was that?' Seumas asked, but already Alan was out of his chair and heading for the door. He reached the hallway and the cry, this time more a shuddering moan, came again from somewhere he couldn't place. It trickled off into low notes, like sobbing.

'Helen? Where are you?' he called out, just as he was

passing the cellar door. There was a muted gasp, like a cough. He opened the door quickly, without even pausing to notice that the key was in the lock instead of hanging on the hook by the frame, and flicked on the switch. A thin cone of light spread on to the floor and dissipated into the shadows. Helen was kneeling on the floor, huddled into herself, gasping.

'What's happened?' he asked, taking the stairs three at a time.

Helen moaned again. She pulled herself up from where she'd been crouched just as Alan reached her and knelt beside her to take her in his arms.

'I've lost it,' she said.

'You've lost what?'

Alan followed her eyes. On the wall, where one of the big supporting pillars stood out from the surface like an obelisk, there was a dark splash. It was then that the metallic cloying smell of blood caught in his throat.

'I've lost the baby,' Helen said.

'What baby?' Alan almost shouted.

Dr Docherty, an elderly, ascetic local practitioner, who had been rousted away from sport on television by a breathless Seumas, had given Helen something for the pains that were still pulsing, though now fading, inside her. He left a prescription for antibiotics, told her to get some rest for a day or so, and left Alan sitting on the edge of the bed. He had confirmed that the very heavy blood loss had indeed been a miscarriage, and after a short discussion with Helen had ascertained that she was not much further on than her eighth week. He'd suggested that she give it a couple of months before trying for another baby.

'I don't want one,' Helen said to Alan when they were alone.

'I didn't even know you were having one,' Alan said. He was filled with astonishment and concern, mixed confusingly with more than a little exasperation.

'Neither did I until a couple of weeks ago,' she replied softly.

'But why didn't you tell me?'

'I don't know. It was a mistake. I didn't want it, not after the last time.'

'But you should have told me. We could have sorted things out together.'

Helen turned round on the bed to face him. 'Well, it's sorted out now.'

Afterwards, when Helen was asleep, he was thinking about it. It had been damned stupid of her not to have mentioned it. Pregnancy was the last thing he'd considered, for since Helen's breakdown, their sex life had been intermittent and infrequent. He cast his mind back to the last time, and found he couldn't recall it. It didn't matter. The doctor said Helen was fine and fit. Alan was strangely sad for the loss of something he never knew he had, but as long as it didn't cause his wife more major problems, he could accept the hand of fate.

ELEVEN

'You must have really racked yourself up,' Tom Callander said as Alan eased himself into the old, overstuffed armchair in the drawing-room of the solid Victorian house that Callander had appropriately and humorously referred to as Quarrier's Home.

'Believe it. I think my ribs are facing backwards,' Alan said, letting his breath out in a slow, drawn-out wheeze. He gingerly settled himself back against the comfortable, worn material concave from years of use.

Alan was wrong about that, though he didn't know it.

It was two days after Helen's miscarriage, and she insisted she was well enough to get back to her chores. Over Alan's protests she'd told him that what had happened was just like a very heavy period. She'd agreed to take a nap in the early evening and Alan had woken her with a cup of tea. She looked a little pale, but otherwise fine. She said she'd be fit enough to visit their neighbours, as long as she didn't have to stay too long. Alan knew she didn't relish the prospect of an evening at Tom's place, but since he had been courteous and friendly enough to offer the invitation, she couldn't very well refuse.

'Well, have a quick shower and I'll get the wild bunch spruced up. Oh,' he paused, 'I'd better look out a bottle of something to take over. Can't go empty-handed in this part of the world.'

Helen nodded and yawned widely. Alan left her to it and went downstairs to try to root out the box of bottles he'd brought with them in the back of the car. It took him ten minutes of searching before he turned it up in the little study. It was with a small twinge of regret that he selected the bottle of twenty-year-old malt a grateful client had given him the Christmas before.

The early evening was mild, and Helen was looking chic in a light blue skirt and a finely designed lambswool sweater. The family took the path in the back garden that forked one way to the trees and the other way to the low wall that separated Tom's acres from theirs. At one point it dipped until it was low enough to step over, as their neighbour had suggested, and they took a narrow, winding path, through a large, well-tended fruit and flower garden that seemed a hundred yards long, until they came to the house which was built in a similar style to their own, though maybe just a fraction smaller and perhaps a decade or so younger, but well kept, and four-square to the road in front that gave on to a sharp slope down to the rocky shore.

Beth Callander met them in the garden. She'd seen them coming down the path and came out of her kitchen with a wide welcoming smile.

She was small and pretty in a dark-haired, Irish way, with flashing eyes that looked black under elegant well-shaped brows. Her smile broadened when she saw Katie and Laney hand-in-hand between their parents.

'Hello. I'm Beth,' she said confidently, holding a hand out, first to Helen, then to Alan who found his own being shaken in a strong, soft grip. 'You'll be Alan and Helen. My father told me all about you. All he knows, anyway.' She smiled again, and the row of white teeth split her tanned face pleasantly. Alan liked her straight away.

'In case he didn't tell you, I'm Tom's daughter. I look after him when I'm home, which is more often than not, although he doesn't need it or says he doesn't. Come on in.'

Just at the door, she turned to the twins who clustered behind her. 'You don't mind dogs, do you?'

Both shook their heads.

'We've got an old golden labrador. I'd put him out in the kennel if you were allergic. I had a boyfriend once who couldn't step over the door. It was either he went or we got rid of Gus. Dad decided he liked the dog better.'

Alan responded to her laugh. They all followed her into the house and through the kitchen where a delicious aroma of bread and some sizzling meat competed in the cosy warmth.

Tom Callander was in the lounge, sitting in a big leather chair that was drawn up close to a flickering log fire which obviously wasn't needed during this mild summer spell but threw a rosy glow into the room. At his feet, the golden coat of the dog sprawled on its belly caught the flickering light. It raised its head as they came in and gave them all a lazy, doleful glance before dropping its jaw back on to its paws again. In the other old leather chair sat a striking woman. She turned as they entered and favoured them with a sweep of green eyes and a hint of a smile.

'Come away in,' Tom Callander said, heaving himself to his feet. 'You've met Beth, I take it?'

Alan nodded. 'She took us through the kitchen to whet our appetites. It worked.'

'That girl can cook up a storm, I tell you. If it wasn't for her I'd just fade away.'

The woman in the other chair stood up. Alan couldn't help but notice that she was tall and limber, casually dressed in brown cords and a fawn brushed-cotton shirt. She had a crop of auburn hair that was shading to red, which only accentuated the flash of green in her eyes. She had such natural poise when she arose to meet them that her striking looks could have been intimidating. Then she smiled and Alan noticed the spattering of small freckles across the bridge of her nose, softening the perfectly moulded features, and giving her a girlish appeal.

'Alan and Helen Crombie,' Tom said, 'meet Alex Graham.'

The woman leaned over and shook Helen's hand first. 'Pleased to meet you,' she said in a soft transatlantic accent. 'I've already heard about you from Dr Docherty. Here we call him Doc Doc, but not to his face. How are you feeling today?'

Helen shot her a quick look of interrogation. The young woman immediately caught it and smiled. 'Oh, it's not a breach of ethics. I work with him a couple of days a week at the practice. I'm a doctor too.'

Alan shook her hand. It was dry and warm. 'You're not from around these parts then?'

'She's an interloper,' Tom said. 'At last we've reversed the brain drain,' he added with a chuckle.

'And this is Tommy Crombie.'

Alex bent down to shake his hand, favouring him with a bright smile that he couldn't help return.

'And Kathryn and Elaine,' Tom finished off.

'Sometimes they're Katie and Laney,' Alan said. 'Or Casey and Easy, depending on what kind of mood I'm in. From their initials,' he added.

'They're gorgeous,' Alex said. She went down on her knees in front of the twins who solemnly gazed at her.

'Hello Katie, hello Laney,' Alex said to both. 'Whichever one is which?'

The twins smiled.

'What's wrong? Cat got their tongues?'

Alan felt a quick flush of embarrassment for the woman. 'They don't speak, I'm afraid,' he said.

There was a moment's silence. Alex caught the drift immediately and extricated them all from the situation deftly. 'With their looks they don't have to,' she said, easing herself back to her feet.

Over a remarkable dinner of roast beef in a delicate

sauce and a stack of vegetables washed down with a good red wine, the Crombies got to know the Callanders and their guest. Beth had baked some pies for the children which they demolished with a fervour that brought her obvious pleasure.

Alan and Helen discovered that Tom's daughter was a post-graduate student at Glasgow University where she specialized in history, and that archaeology was her special interest.

Alex Graham was also doing postgraduate work in child psychology at the university. Already she was a general practitioner in her own right, and to work her passage was working second-string for Dr Docherty who ran the practice that covered the peninsula and the whole lochside.

'You must meet a friend of mine,' Alan said when he heard that Alex had studied in Boston. 'He's from Boston. That can't be far from you.'

'Only a couple of hundred miles from Vermont,' she said. 'You guys forget America is a big place. When you live on a small island like this, you don't realize the scale of other countries. But you're right. A couple of hundred miles in the States is nothing.'

She paused for a sip of wine, then went on: 'I suppose you mean Mike Toward?'

Alan was amazed. 'You know Mike? That's incredible.'

'Not really. I know him from here,' she said, indicating Creggan. 'I met him in the bar when he was here looking over the place for you. Two Americans in a small Scottish bar can't miss each other. Anyway, what really *was* the coincidence was that we were born in the same hospital. Different years, of course.'

'Of course,' Alan agreed. Mike Toward had ten years on her.

'But I've spent most of my life in Nova Scotia, which is more like this part of the world than any other,' she added.

The dinner was a huge success. Both Beth and Alex delighted in the children, and Tom Callander kept up a friendly banter that made even Helen seem relaxed. Afterwards Gus, the lazy labrador, allowed the twins to stroke and pummel him mercilessly without complaint, while Tom showed Tommy a marvellous collection of model yachts that filled almost every available surface in the dining-room.

Alex apologized not long after the meal, saying she was on call and had to go. She suggested to Helen that she might want to bring the twins down to the surgery some time in the next few days – 'just for a chat' was the way she put it – and Helen agreed.

Shortly after that, Helen decided it was bedtime for the children. Beth came in with their jackets and when Tom Callander suggested to Alan that he might want to stay for a nightcap, his daughter quickly volunteered to stroll back with Helen and the children.

'I feel like some fresh air anyway,' she said. 'I've been stuck in the kitchen all afternoon.'

'Me too,' Alan said, 'but your results were far superior to mine. I just demolished the place.'

When they had gone, Tom led Alan into the drawing-room, where another fire smouldered in a stone hearth, sending a red flickering glow on to the walls.

Tom poured them both another shot of the malt that Alan had brought, and they sat in the firelight, sipping the mellow whisky.

'It's a good place to live,' Tom said. 'Good for the children, so long as you watch out for them.'

'In what way?'

'Well, accidents can happen,' Tom said, and there was a silence while he took another sip. 'You have to watch them all the time. Sometimes around here, accidents happen. I'm not saying that it's more than any other place, but here, now and again, you get an accident, and some youngster gets hurt. That's all I'm saying.'

'I don't understand you,' Alan said.

'Don't worry. Sometimes I don't understand myself,' Tom replied, smiling. The light from the fire cast shadows on his face, turning the smile into what looked like a grimace of pain, as if he was remembering something that filled him with sadness. 'What I mean is that no matter where you live, something can happen that knocks you for six. Take last winter, with wee Chrissie Watt.'

'Who's that?'

'Oh, I forgot, you wouldn't know her. One of a big family from down in the village. It was just about Christmas time she was playing up at that stand of trees you've got at the top end of your ground. Nobody knows what she was doing up there when it was getting dark anyway, but they found her the next morning. Seems a tree had fallen on her, which was not that surprising after the gales. A couple of pines came down then.

'And a couple of years ago,' Tom stopped and thought, 'maybe three years ago this summer, there were two children just went missing. Only little nippers they were,' he said, indicating with a hand a few feet above the thick rug in front of the fire. 'The MacFarlane boys. They were playing with a bunch of youngsters up there, and they just disappeared. Nobody knows what the hell happened to them. They searched the shore and had search parties all over for days, but there was never a hide nor a hair of them. Pauline MacFarlane took an overdose three months later, and her husband just moved away.'

'What are you trying to tell me?' Alan asked softly.

'Nothing at all, except that no matter where you live, the wee ones always need looking after.'

'Is there something I should know?'

'Not really, but I wouldn't let the wee ones play in the trees on their own. There's always been something funny about that place, and those stones.'

The stones.

Beth Callander had taken great delight in giving the Crombies a potted history of Creggan and the peninsula folk during dinner.

It was Tommy who had asked about the two big stones that stood like dark sentries at the far edge of the copse at the top of the orchard.

'They're what's left of the standing stones that were here until just before your house was built,' Beth had said. 'There was a big ring of them, thirteen pairs in all, one pair for every month of the old Celtic calendar.'

'Are you a Celtic Calendar?' Tommy asked innocently.

Beth looked at him in puzzlement for a second before it dawned, then she burst into laughter. 'No. We're Callan*der*,' she said, chuckling. 'The calendar was to let people know what time of the year it was.'

'Why were there thirteen months?' Alan asked.

'That was the way they worked the seasons. There were five seasons in all, plus the dead days of midwinter, and the months were governed by the moon.

'Professor Sannholm, he was my archaeology teacher at university until a few years ago, he said that most stone circles were positioned so that the moon and the sun would shine on special points at particular times of the year. Hereabouts there are lots of standing stones. Some of them are just on their own, and they were probably used as markers and totems, although there is one down at Westbay point where they've discovered old inscriptions that they're still trying to decipher. And there's others that are like stone tables. They're called *cromlechs*.'

'How old are they?' Alan asked.

'Nobody knows for sure. They brought some of the stones long distances, at least three thousand years ago in some cases, but it could be three times that. The ones here are old, we think, and they did form a perfect circle until they were demolished.'

'When was that?'

'I've got it in my notes somewhere, but it was some-time in the winter of 1887. That was when Andrew Dalmuir came to the peninsula to build his house.'

'Which house is that?' asked Helen.

Beth smiled. 'The one you live in. They started work on it in '88 and knocked down the stones to make room for it. Well, that wasn't quite the reason, but Dalmuir had most of them knocked down anyway. There was a big row about it at the time. The local people were furious, but he had lots of money and influence. Anyway, the stones came down and the house went up, and it's been there ever since. Cromwath.'

'I was going to ask about that,' Alan came in. 'The name Cromwath. It's above the door and on the plaque at the gate. Is that a local name?'

'Oh yes. That was Dalmuir's concession to the history of the area, after he'd vandalized one of the most magnificent megalithic sites in the west of Scotland. The land he built his house on was known as Crom Uath, straight from the Gaelic.'

'What does it mean?' Alex asked.

'*Crom* is the Celtic for a ring, like a stone ring. And there are a number of different meanings of *Uath*. It means hawthorn, but then again it also takes on the meanings of the symbol of the hawthorn, which was one of the sacred trees to the old Celts. *Uath* signified dreams, or chaos, and the magic colour of purple. Cromwath is a corruption of the old tongue, but it means *Ring of Dreams* or *Circle of Chaos*. Or both.'

'We've got standing stones all over our state,' Alex said, 'and there's legends to go with them too. They say the Micmac Indians built stones in rings to keep away the evil *manitou*. And there are stories that the stones weren't there to tell the seasons, but to call up spirits from the underworld. They say the medicine men could travel *between* the stones into the underworld and come out anywhere else in the world, and in other places as well.'

'We've got similar legends,' Beth told her, 'but they're probably not coincidence. They say the old Celts sailed the Atlantic to America long before Columbus, and I think the stories are true. They've found artefacts all over your eastern seaboard that were never made by the Amerindians, and almost certainly originated in Ireland or the west coast of Scotland.

'But as far as the purpose of the rings is concerned, yes, there are many stories about the power of the standing stones. Professor Sannholm, he was a real expert, not only on archaeology, but on the myth and legend of the Gaelic races, which include most of us. He said the old people really did have sacrifices in the middle of the rings on their special great days, and not just to have good harvests. They did believe the rings were gateways to the underworld, places like Tir-nan-Og, the land of the young, and the middle kingdoms.'

'What's the land of the young?' Tommy piped up. The twins were both busy working their way through mounds of mashed potatoes creamed with local butter, and seemingly oblivious to the conversation.

'That was a magical place that was hard to find, but if you got there, you could stay for ever and never get a day older,' Beth said. 'The old stories tell how it was the most beautiful place where it was always summer, and where the flowers always bloomed, and where the animals fell dead at your feet and the fruit fell ripe into your hand.'

'That's the kind of place I want to retire to,' Tom said. He uncorked another bottle of red wine and charged their glasses. Helen put a hand over her glass, protesting that she'd already had two, and another would make her fall asleep.

'I thought you already had, Dad,' Beth riposted. 'Anyway, it's the land of the young, not the land of the cantankerous spoiled elderly.'

'Thank you, dear daughter. Your appreciation is greatly appreciated.' Tom and Beth both laughed together. Alan couldn't resist a smile.

'What do you think about the legends?' Alex asked. 'Did they really believe in all that?'

'Oh, they believed in a lot more besides. Their Druids and bards seemed to have enormous power, and there was great stress placed on the high days of the year. I *love* the legends. It would be nice if there were places like Tir-nan-Og, and magic. I think we all wish for that. It's like wishing you could see the dinosaurs. The world's too mundane without them, and it could do with a little bit of magic.'

'There's something funny about that place and those stones.'

Alan came back to the present. 'I'm not with you. I think they look very impressive. Better than gnomes at the bottom of your garden. It's just a shame that somebody knocked down the rest of them.'

'Oh, they're impressive enough, I grant you. I've always thought that, and maybe I'm just an old fella who's had a glass of red biddy and a shade too much of this fine malt. It's just that . . .' he paused. 'I don't know. Just a feeling. There's a right of way through the trees, as I expect you know.'

Alan nodded. 'Yes, Mike Toward told me about that. It's in the title deeds.'

'Well, I've always taken a stroll up there in the evening, taking old Gus for his constitutional. Most times it's fine, but sometimes, on some nights, I get a shiver. I don't know what does it, but I get a definite shiver. Maybe it's the shadows, but there've been a couple of times I've thought I've seen something.'

'Like what?'

'I've never told anybody this before, and quite frankly I don't know why I'm telling you now, though I've got a good feeling about you, and I think we're going to be good friends, you and me.'

'Me too,' Alan said, taking another heady swallow of the whisky. It burned a dazzling path down his throat and settled in a spreading warmth in his chest.

'A few times I've been there after dusk, I've had a terrible feeling of being watched. Now I know you can get that anywhere, but once or twice, I really had it strong enough to feel it. And at those times, old Gus has been whimpering and whining right at my heel. I kind of saw things out of the corner of my eye, like as if something moved, but when I looked, there was nothing there. Maybe it was my eyes playing tricks on me, but it gave me a hell of a scare.'

'As you say, you get those feelings in the dark anywhere,' Alan said.

'Yes. But there was another time I was going through the trees, and I *did* see something.'

'What was it?'

'Promise you won't tell anybody?' The older man stared at him so hard that Alan could do nothing but nod.

'I promise.'

'I was passing the second pair of stones, you know, where the path takes a sharp turn to the left, when I saw somebody walking between the stones.'

Tom took another drink, a big one this time, then went on. 'I looked around sharply, and there was a figure that was walking towards me. It was in shadow, then it stepped right into the space, and it was David. My son . . . He'd been dead for ten years, but it was him all right.'

Tom looked over at Alan, who tried to look as blank as possible. 'I know what you're thinking, and believe me, it's something I've thought about many a time since. But it was my boy. He had a gash on his head, a deep cut down the side of his face, and he was wearing my lifejacket, the big orange one he had on the day his

95

boat went down, all slick with the sea water. He was limping, as if he'd hurt his leg. I can tell you I nearly died there on the spot. I called out to him, but it was as if he couldn't hear me. I could see his mouth move as if he was saying something, but I couldn't hear it. Then he took another step forward until he was standing square between the stones, and it was as if he'd stepped right into a hole. He just disappeared.'

'Hallucination?' Alan ventured after a pause that stretched for ever.

'I sure as hell hope so,' Tom said. 'I really thought my heart was going to give up on me, and then who would have looked after Beth? But I've thought about it a lot since then, as you can imagine. I just don't have an explanation. For a while, I went a bit crazy. I was up at those stones every night for two months, but I never saw him again. But I'll tell you one thing, and don't take this amiss. No matter how much you love somebody, it's not easy to picture their face in your mind after a while. That's why we have photos. But that night I saw my boy, and it was *him*. Every hair on his head. It was him. And I don't know what caused that to happen.'

Tom looked over at Alan again. 'Yes, I went a bit crazy then. Started pouring this stuff down my throat until Beth took me in hand. She was only thirteen when her brother died, and she's been sorting me out ever since. Her mother died when she was a baby, so she's been the woman of the house since she could talk. If it wasn't for her I'd have drunk myself to death five years ago.'

'She is a lovely girl,' Alan said.

'She's that too. But she's got fire in her eye when she needs it, and a tongue in her head that could cut glass when she's of a mind.'

He reached over for the bottle. They'd demolished three-quarters of it in the last couple of hours while they sat in front of the fire. Beth had come in at some point and had gone to bed. Alan was feeling the whisky.

'One for the road?' Tom asked.

Alan shook his head. 'Better not. Had well over my limit for walking,' he said. 'But it's been a great evening. Thanks.'

'Oh, any time. Just jump the wall when you've a need to get away. I'll do the same,' Tom said, grinning amiably. 'Women. We might love them, but by God we need a bolt hole sometimes.'

Alan laughed in agreement. 'We could dig a tunnel,' he said, as he negotiated the front steps a mite unsteadily.

TWELVE

The night air was refreshing but not cold as Alan skirted the side of Tom's house and took the path that led to the low wall. Clambering over in the dark – and after so much whisky – was not the casual step of earlier in the evening, but he made it without breaking bones. The layout of his own back garden was still unfamiliar, and Alan went off the path twice. The second time he walked straight into the gnarled trunk of one of the fruit trees, smacking it hard with his shoulder and careening off with a grunt. The whisky had a confusingly uncoordinating effect which made him feel as if his feet were hitting the ground a good second before they should have. Despite all that, he made it home without serious mishap. Alan let himself into the darkened hallway, trying to make as little noise as possible, and made his way to the front room, where a small side lamp had been left on, throwing a soft glow over the corner next to the fireplace.

In the slowly cooling room, Alan sat alone, thinking the evening over. It had been a pleasant and stimulating dinner. The kids had been well-behaved and everybody had taken to them, and Helen had been in fairly good spirits too, occasionally taking part in the general round of conversation, and, for a change, smiling once or twice. From their part, everyone had taken a shine to Beth, who was at once entertaining, intelligent and good fun. It was clear from the way she treated her father that they were very close, but it was also clear who was the real boss in the house. Alan felt a mild envy for Tom Callander. Tom himself looked as if he was going to be one of those rare neighbours who very soon become a friend. Alan had few close friends, and those he had he valued enormously. Although he had met the older man only twice, the two had formed an instant liking for each other.

He didn't understand much of what Tom had told him as they had sat over the whisky bottle, but then again that didn't matter too much either. Alan himself was prone to rambling and making little sense after several too many, and there was no reason to suppose that Tom was any different.

But now the memory of the very-close-to-lethal accident in the kitchen came back with a sudden clarity that was enough to make him catch his breath.

In his mind's eye, the image of himself torquing and twisting as the hammer seemed to struggle in his hands came back to him in a playback that brought with it a wrench of shock.

Again the picture in his mind jerked on the strings that worked his stomach and Alan felt the sickening, nauseating lurch deep down inside him. The image stayed at the forefront, no matter how much he tried to dispel it, for long minutes before it began to fade.

'Enough of this,' he said to himself. He hauled himself out of the chair and stood there, half in and half out of the small area of light. He switched off the small light, plunging the room into darkness that was quickly dispelled by the moon that beamed directly into the room, silvering the furniture in muted light.

Alan stood and stared through the glass into the blue-black darkness beyond, seeing the outline of the trees on the hills across the loch limned by the soft moonlight. Quicksilver glistened up from the slow motion of the calm water in the sheltered inlet and dappled the ceiling. All was quiet.

He turned towards the deeper darkness at the far end of the room and opened the door quietly, walking through into the hallway. It was much darker there, a blank space of shadow. Alan took a few blind steps, and came hard up against the wall.

'That's funny,' he thought, though the sudden thud of his heartbeat told him it wasn't really funny. The house, after not much more than a week, was still not imprinted on his mental map. Alan felt around in the darkness, disoriented by finding a wall in front of him. There should have been the whole length of the hallway ahead, straight out from the living-room towards the break where the stairs took a right.

'Must have turned in the dark,' he told himself. He kept a hand on the wall, now sure of his direction, but unsure of where he was putting his feet. Ten steps down the hallway, he almost fell again when his hand encountered empty space along the wall. The momentum carried him forward, and he found himself right up against a door. That really confused him. Surely the kitchen door was on the left?

'Must be going the wrong way,' he muttered to himself, although the mutter seemed louder in the darkness. He stopped.

'Can't be going the wrong way,' he said aloud into the silent dark. Alan had only taken eight steps at the most since he left the living-room. It wouldn't have taken that many to get to the stairs.

The flat panel of the door under his hand swung away, and Alan followed the motion, walking into the room. It was in pitch darkness, an empty void of nothing. His heart still beating uptempo though not quite racing, he edged forward along the wall towards where he knew the light switch to be. It wasn't there. There was a musty smell in the room, not a dusty smell which would have been appropriate after all the work he'd done earlier, but a damp, fusty smell as if the room hadn't been aired in a long time.

Alan stopped dead after a few steps. His heart upped the beat to three-four time. The switch wasn't there.

Behind him the door clattered shut and the beating pulse jumped right up into his throat.

'Steady now,' he told himself. His voice echoed in the room eerily. His hand scrabbled along the wall, urgently groping for the light switch. His fingers found nothing.

Then came the surge of relief when his hand found the cold smoothness of the switch. He stabbed his finger at it, expecting the lamp to come on, before realizing that it wasn't one of the push-button ones he had in the kitchen. It was small and rounded, and stood out from the wall. It was one of the old-fashioned lever ones.

He pushed his finger down and there was a harsh click and the light came full on overhead, stabbing straight into the back of his eyes through night-adjusted pupils that were wide open. Immediately he blinked against the glare, seeing purple spots fuzz the inside of his eyelids. His eyes watered and he brushed the tears away with the back of his hand and blinked again.

Then he opened his eyes and looked around a room he had never seen before in his life.

THIRTEEN

Alan's heart vaulted up into his throat, lodging there in a pulsing lump that he felt would choke him. The shadowy room spun for a moment, then centred itself in his vision. The pounding high in his throat and deep in his chest did not abate.

Shadows played in front of his eyes in the dim light. Alan jerked away from the wall, eyes wide with apprehension. Above him a light shone flickering and feeble. It glowed muted red, not really like electric light at all, casting a strange glow around him.

The room was old. It was like something from an old photograph, and the illumination only enhanced that impression as it tinged everything with a blurred red-brown, freezing the scene in a sepiatone daguerreotype. The air was cloying thick and musty, as if the room had stayed still and closed forever, and it was cold, a deep, damp cold that overlaid everything in a clammy blanket.

Alan felt as if he'd walked into a grave.

Dust laid grey-brown smudges over every surface. There was a big leather armchair beside a marble fireplace that threw out no warmth. The dark hole where the fire should have glowed was a tunnel into infinity, black on deeper black. On the arched back of the armchair was an antimacassar of filigreed linen that looked parched and yellowed in the strange light. There were two more on the *chaise-longue* that bracketed the fireplace beside a nest of small tables that threw back blurred orange from surfaces that were polished between the streaks of dust. On the walls there were serried ranks of books on packed shelves that spanned from ceiling to floor, split only by the spaces for the four doors that led away.

Four doors. Two on the wall to Alan's left and one on the faraway wall beside the window. Another on the wall closest to him. And a fifth had slammed shut behind him.

Heavy patterned curtains fell from a rail to the floor boards, pulled aside in hourglass shapes by sash ties. Beyond the glass, the moon did not shine. The window-space was as dark as the fireplace, a great gaping hole into which the dim light was sucked away into a vast, cold vacuum.

Alan stood, transfixed. He noticed his hand was shaking as he reached out to touch the back of the lounger. The effects of the whisky had been blasted out of his system by the jolt of adrenalin that had first gripped his stomach and then surged through his veins. His breath was a stuttering gasp, the way it felt when he woke up from a bad dream, lungs working like bellows. He put his other hand on the back of the couch to steady himself. A nerve in the back of his leg jittered, making his kneecap jerk up and down, as if the joint was going to give way.

'*This is not real,*' he said aloud. The words came out and were swallowed up by the room. At least his throat was working.

But it looked real. It felt real.

And if it was real, where the hell was it?

The back of the couch felt spongy and cold under his hands, but it was there all right. He took a deep breath, and felt his heart slow down a little.

'There is an explanation for this,' he said to himself in a whisper.

The fright that had iced his limbs and sent jingling impulses down the nerves at the back of his legs loosened its grip, thawing out Alan's own frozen grip on the couch. He moved away towards the door nearest him between the big bookcases. It had a brass handle that at one time had shone but now was tarnished and mottled. He reached out and the handle spun reluctantly under his grip and the door only creaked slightly as he pulled it inwards.

Beyond the door there was a grey haze. Alan stared at it, his eyes wide, trying to see into the gloom. Slowly the grey resolved itself and then jumped into focus as if something mysterious had turned a lens, making the vision clear and sharp.

Alan stood looking into a hallway. At first he thought he was back in the hallway through which he had stumbled before coming into the room because the two doors immediately in front looked exactly like the ones which led off to the living-room and the kitchen. But beyond that, there were another two doors.

His breath hitched up again.

And beyond that, the focus clarified, there were another two. Then another pair, again and again, repeated in a long, impossible corridor to infinity. The perspective was wrong. Nobody could see that many doors in a corridor. But Alan could see dozens, hundreds of pairs, stretching out into the distance, diminishing in size until finally the points converged in a spot in the far, far distance.

'This is crazy,' Alan said, and his voice echoed along that strange tunnel of doors, rebounding off each blank rectangle that opened off the impossible corridor. The echoes trailed away, strangled in the distance.

He stepped back, suddenly struck by the feeling that if he moved through the door, he would find himself in a maze of doors that led on to other corridors with doors that led, for ever and ever, on to others. A surge of panic welled up inside him and he grasped the handle and slammed the door shut. It thudded into the frame and clicked. Alan was back in the room.

He walked, a little unsteadily towards the other door. The hard wooden panels had a fine-textured grain and the mouldings had been carved by someone who loved to work in wood. He reached out and grasped the handle. Like the first one, it turned reluctantly, as if forcing itself back against his hand. Alan doubled the pressure and heard the pin slide back. There was a muted squeak as he slowly pulled it inwards and in an instant he was outside.

He was *outside*. Outside the room. Outside the house. It felt as if he was outside the *world*, in some strange place that did not belong anywhere.

Before him stretched a bleak moorland, grey and lifeless under a roiling sky that was overcast by weird smoky clouds. Rocks grew out of the sparse moss, jutting like rotting teeth, glistening with moisture and festering with slimy lichen. A wind shivered the clumps of brown bracken and tangled heathers, blowing across miles of pitted desolation, whooping down into hollows where stagnant tarns collected the purple-tinged water that oozed down peaty defiles. The wind moaned and howled over the scene of bleak despair. Right in front of Alan, a quick movement caught his eye and he jerked his head. There was a crow, huge and glossy, hopping from one hummock to another. A second great black bird, wings glistening like oily tar, flapped and scuttered to join it. A third pecked nearby. A fourth stood on one of the jagged stones, scrabbling at something pink with its claws, and jerking back with its beak, tearing at a slimy mass.

Alan strained his eyes towards the hummock where the nearest crow pecked violently, lifting its head back and stabbing down in a series of vicious thrusts. The bird was huge, at least the size of a large dog. Its head was flat and reptilian, with a bristling of short snout feathers poking out over the great black beak. Even at a distance of twenty yards or so, Alan could make out the individual scales of its thick legs. Below them the claws were splayed out wider than a man's hand, with the black, curving talons gripping tightly on the mound. Alan looked down.

It was no mound. It was a body.

The great crow was pecking at the riddled, sagging corpse of a man. It was perched on his chest, between splayed arms which held out opened hands with fingers stripped of all but dripping tatters of flesh, curled in agony or supplication. The cadaver's left leg was stretched out, showing the long toe bones like a dog's paw, but grey-brown. The right leg was angled upwards. A knee bone protruded from a tattered legging and the foot was covered with a mouldy leather boot fastened to the gangling shin with strips of leather. The crow bobbed its head, and Alan could hear the thudding of the beak as it hammered deep inside a gaping hole in the man's chest. The head drew back and Alan saw the immense bird tugging at something that looked like wet elastic. The bird's leg muscles flexed and the head jerked backwards, and the slithering rope of intestine came back with it. The crow turned and made an ungainly hop off the body. Behind it, another large bird was pecking away at a head which was matted with tangled fair hair spread out on either side of the shoulders. Alan felt his gorge rise as he watched the black scimitar of the beak plunge down into the eye socket. It opened and closed in a rapid clicking nibble as the crow ate what remained in the deep recess.

'Oh God!' he heard himself say in a hoarse mutter.

The body sprawled in the wet bracken was clutching a sword with a long, straight blade and a heavy golden pommel. Its clawed fingers were still tightly gripped under the guard that was shot with glittering cut stones. Alan started back when he realized that what he had taken for hummocks were all bodies. The moorland was littered with them. Sprawled and slumped in obscene, contorted poses of death. Dead men on a battlefield on a desolate barren plain. There were hundreds of them, decaying into the moss and lichen, being torn by crows and God knows what else.

The golden-haired hero whose eye-juices were being nibbled by the big black bird had been savagely hacked. His sword blade was matted with brown stains that were probably blood. He had fought bitterly. But his left leg was gone, hacked off above the knee in one searing swipe. It lay a few yards off, mouldering, maggot-ridden, with the white bone showing through the grey flesh. An arrow pierced his belly, pointing upwards to the sky. It must have hit him in the back and come right through. There was a hole in his chest from which protruded a broken-off piece of wood looking like an obscene growth, and the man's face was oddly twisted, not grinning like a skull. There was still a lot of flesh there, but the face had an odd shape. Alan stared for a moment before he realized why. The side of the skull had been caved in with an incredible force and the jaw had been hacked right off by another, leaving a grotesque mask that leered at the sky.

A harsh cry rent the air, a gritty, bellowed caw of one of the crows. The big bird nearest left off its pecking at the eye socket and shuffled round to look in Alan's direction.

He felt a shiver raise the hairs on the back of his neck as the bird's head angled up showing him a black cavern where its eye should be.

But there was no eye in that socket, just a hole, jagged and deep.

Alan took a step backwards in fear and disgust, feeling his feet squelch in the dank moss. The crow looked at him again. It had no eyes, but it *looked* at him.

Beside it, the other crow turned in a shambling hop and glared blindly at him from cavernous sockets. All around, the other grotesque birds shifted position to watch.

Suddenly Alan knew they were not looking *at* him. They were staring, sightlessly sensing *past* where he stood. The wind moaned, bringing with it the smell of rotting carrion that clogged in his throat.

There was a faint thrumming in the air, an eerie pulsing that was out of kilter with the pounding of Alan's heart.

One of the crows opened its beak wide, showing a hard barbed tongue. It cawed hoarsely, jerking its body forward and dropping its head. Nearby another took up the cry, followed by another until the air over the whole moor was rent by the rasping cries. The bird that had started the cacophony hopped off the body where it had been gorging and took an ungainly leap, extending glossy pinions that were bigger than condor's wings, and beat savagely at the air. Alan could feel the wind from the wingbeats as the carrion bird rose into the wind and wheeled, pinning him with the ragged socket on one side of its head before banking and flapping away. As one, the whole obscene flock took wing, flight feathers whooping in the air until the sky was black with birds. They flew straight, the way crows do, away from where Alan stood, beating low across the bogland and the rotting corpses of the dead men, gradually diminishing with the distance.

For a few moments, after the earsplitting chorus of harsh cawing, the air seemed silent.

Then Alan felt rather than heard the weird thrumming in the air, a strange tightness that jarred across the moorland and pierced deep into his taut nerves. He stood still for a second, before he realized, instinctively, why the great crows had fled.

Something was coming. Something huge and fearsome and fast was racing across the moor, fleeting over the bog. Something that had terrified the terrifying crows with their dead sockets and ripping beaks. For a moment Alan was paralysed with fright.

Something black and hateful was thrumming in the air; something unnatural and completely evil was racing towards him. Alan could feel it in every nerve, he could sense it in his spine, chittering a warning up and down his back.

He reached behind him, scared to turn and look back in case the door was not there. He knew that if he turned the doorway would be gone and he would be standing defenceless in the middle of this wasteland among the mouldering dead, while the thing he could sense with every jangling nerve bore down on him.

A wave of relief and gratitude washed over him when he felt the smooth hardness of the doorframe. His hand grasped it and he heaved himself backwards right through the doorway and into the room.

He stood facing through the aperture. The moorland stretched into the distance under a threatening grey-purple sky, showing no sign of life. From the comparative safety of the room, the tightness in the air was more muted, but Alan could still hear it. Then a deep shadow suddenly flowed over the land and the massacred bodies, swiftly blotting out the dismal light. The shadow was vast, an immense shape that raced over the bog, plunging the tarns and gullies into blackness. Alan instinctively jumped back and hauled at the door, wrenching his sore shoulder with the force of his panic. The door slammed shut with a thump on the impossible moorland. The thrumming in the air was cut off sharply.

Alan took two steps backwards, facing the well-crafted panels. His hands were shaking again, and his breath was jerky and ragged as his lungs panted for air. He imagined that thing, whatever it was, battering at the door, smashing it down and dragging him, screaming and paralysed with terror, through the doorway into that alien moorland.

The door remained shut. No sound came through from the other side. Alan's panic subsided.

'That was not real,' he told himself. 'I didn't see that.'

There was a third doorway. Alan walked slowly towards it. He stood facing it, an identical one to the previous two, panelled, brass handled.

He reached out with his still shaky hand, then drew

back. His mind yelled at him to walk away. It told him this door too led on to the moor and the great shadowed thing that had scared the birds was waiting, crouched and massive, on the other side, ready to grab.

His hand seemed to have a mind of its own. It reached out and grasped the cold, mottled handle and turned. He eased himself up to the join and pulled the door open a crack. It was dim on the other side, but it was not empty space. It was a room. Alan could make out the blurred outline of a bed. He opened the door further, easing the crack wider until it gaped. He stepped forward into the doorway as the light in the other room increased.

It was his own bedroom.

'I *am* dreaming,' he said, expelling his pent-up breath in a shuddery sigh. His mind told him he must be dreaming (or imagining) for it was impossible to open a door on the ground floor and walk into an upstairs bedroom.

It *was* their bedroom. Alan's eyes gradually adjusted to the faint light. There was Helen, asleep on the bed. The eiderdown had slipped off and was lying in a tangled heap on the carpet. Helen was lying on her side, with both hands tucked under the pillow, one knee drawn up, rucking the flimsy nightdress.

Alan watched her sleeping from the far side of the room. One part of his mind was puzzling faintly over the fact that he could see the bedroom door opposite where he was standing.

Helen moved in her sleep, turning with a soft sigh on to her back. The raised knee gently slipped to one side and as she turned, both arms were spread out beside her. She gave a soft sleepy moan, and a small smile played about her lips.

She's dreaming, Alan thought. He was still standing in the imaginary doorway. Helen sighed again and her smile widened. Her hips moved slightly and her other leg, which had been straight out, drew upwards and sideways, matching the other, giving Alan an inviting view. Helen was nearly naked. He could see the dark shadow between her spreadeagled thighs below the flimsy silk of her nightdress. Helen's hips moved again, and a small moan escaped her lips. Then she whispered something that Alan couldn't make out. He was transfixed, suddenly swept by an erotic surge that was tinged with a shade of guilt as he stood, like a peeping Tom, watching his wife.

'Yes,' she whispered into the darkness. Her hips moved again in an unconscious grinding motion and her hands came off the mattress, raising themselves into the air.

'Please.' The whisper was louder, more urgent. With a strange thrill, Alan realized she was having an erotic dream. He had never even considered the possibility before. Since the twins' birth, Helen had been a reluctant partner, seeming to have almost lost the urge for sex, which was why he was stunned when she'd had her miscarriage.

Now Alan watched as her hips moved in a parody of sexual urging, thrusting upwards off the mattress, and the little insistent voice at the back of his mind started to nag at him, telling him that this was wrong, that the doorway to his bedroom did not exist. That he could not be standing here, watching this.

'Oh yes,' Helen moaned, louder this time. 'Oh please,' she said again. Alan could hear her breathing now, fast and urgent.

Then something changed in the room. Alan sensed it before he felt it. A tightness in the air, as if it had coalesced into something solid. It happened in the blink of an eye, a frigid breath that suddenly *was*. He felt a shock run through him as if he had been riven by a shard of cold metal.

There was something in the room. Alan's eyes flicked from the writhing shape of his wife on the bed towards the far corner on the left, then to the right where the

111

dim light left impenetrable shadows. There was something in the room. His eyes raked backwards and forwards. He could feel something.

On the bed, Helen was now rocking violently, grinding upwards off the mattress, pushing hard and high. And above her, a shadow formed. It was a deep, dark shape that seemed to congeal out of the tense air, elongating, dropping down through the few inches over her body, solidifying, changing.

Alan's breath suddenly caught in his throat. It was a man. Broad-shouldered and heavily muscled, he had his back to Alan. The figure that coalesced out of the darkness was kneeling between her splayed legs. Alan could see the corded powerful bunches of muscle ripple on the man (*was it a man?*) as he moved forward, placing hands on either side of her head. His skin looked rough and granular, almost like scales, a dull grey in the faint light. The figure lowered itself, still kneeling, down on her body. Alan watched in frozen horror as her hands came up and around its broad back, hooked to grip into the skin. From behind he could see the narrow buttocks, and below that a pendulous scrotum, swollen and veiny. Helen's knees rose high and her ankles came right up into the air, clasping around the small of the thing's back. There was a second of stillness, then a sudden, thrusting jolt as the two bodies met hard. Helen's demanding cry, a low upwelling moan of sheer pleasure mixed with need, was matched by a growling grunt that seemed to shudder the room.

Alan's mouth worked open and shut. He was dumbstruck with shock and anger, and behind it all a desperate fear that welled up from deep within him. His feet were welded to the floor between the doorposts and his eyes were transfixed by the sight on the bed.

He could hear Helen grunt fiercely in a duet with the bass visceral snortings of the shape that lunged into her again and again as she tightened her arms and legs around it and bucked again and again.

Still Alan couldn't move. He couldn't speak. His knuckles stood out white, one hand on the door jamb and the other on the handle, like an intruder caught in the act.

Then, on top of the disgust and distress, came a vision so shocking that his heart almost stopped beating. He could feel it lurch in his chest as if he'd been struck on the ribs with the sledgehammer.

For the thing on the bed turned its head. It kept the momentum of the pounding thrust, battering itself into Helen, but impossibly it turned its head. The muscles on its neck twisted like thick knotted hawsers as first the cheek and jaw came into view, then three-quarters of the face, and finally the full front, twisted right around until it was facing backwards between its own shoulder blades.

It was man-like. But it wasn't a man. It was a goblin-like parody of a human. It had a broad face that seemed to ripple and change, becoming at the same time ape-like and dog-like. But it was neither of these. It had a grey, blotched and pebbly skin like a toad's and a wide, thick-lipped mouth. Above high cheekbones two slitted eyes opened and leered evilly across the room. The forehead was low and corrugated in wrinkles on a scaly skin. The creature kept thrusting, extracting a groan from Helen every time it rammed deep.

Alan stared, breathless, scared rigid, almost fainting with terror and panic, and the thing stared back at him with poisonous black eyes.

Then, horror on horror, it grinned at him. The thick lizard lips split along their length, showing jagged stumps of teeth, too many teeth, in a slash of a mouth. The grin broadened and the thundering grunts changed to a deep, animal chuckle. It stared at Alan and sniggered derisively at him. Then it drew itself back on its haunches and slammed itself back into Helen. She let out a low, juddery moan and then was suddenly silent. Very slowly, the head on the thing creaked back, turn-

113

ing the full circle, until it faced her. Alan saw the neck muscles ripple as the head went down, nuzzling into the curve of her neck.

At last the pent-up pressure in his lungs was suddenly released.

'No. *No!*' he exploded. 'Get off her!'

The words tumbled out of his mouth and were swallowed up in the air that seemed to have solidified. Alan's head throbbed with a pounding, erratic pulse and he lurched forward into the room. But he couldn't move. Something was impeding him. It was as if he'd walked into a taut membrane that stretched between the doorposts. He shoved and felt himself being pushed back. He pushed again, trying to power his way across to the bed and grab the thing off his wife. But it was no use. The door was open, but the room was closed to him.

Almost fainting with the panic that sleeted through him, he stood in the doorway, looking stupidly from left to right, then he spun on his heel, slamming the heavy door on the disgusting scene. He dashed across to the far doorway, the one where he'd come in, and scrabbled for the handle. All of a sudden, the lights flickered, dimmed and went out, plunging the room into total darkness.

Frantically his hands rattled against the door as they tried to find the handle. It wasn't there. The panic welled up inside him like a big black bubble and Alan thought his heart was going to stop again.

Then his knuckle rapped against the brass knob. With a whimper of relief, he grasped it hard, twisted and pulled, heaving himself right out of the room and into the darkness of the hallway beyond. He took one step along the corridor and banged sharply into a wall. The thump as his nose met the hard surface almost dropped him to the floor, and a bright light flared in front of his eyes, dissolving into pinpoints that wheeled erratically. He reached out ahead of him and leaned with one hand on the wall. He could see nothing. Under his hand, the light switch seemed magically to materialize, and without conscious thought, Alan hit it. The hallway blazed with light. He wheeled towards the doorway through which he'd stumbled.

Another shocking jolt hit him.

There was no doorway. He was standing opposite the kitchen door, which was half open. The light was there to his right, and on the left there was a blank wall, covered in a rich brocaded wallpaper.

There was no doorway.

Alan's head spun from the shock, and the fright, and the hard thump his nose and forehead had suffered when he'd hit the wall. Bewildered, he stumbled to the stairs and staggered up them.

At the bedroom door he paused, still shaky, wondering if what he'd seen had been real, not knowing what he'd do if it was real, and that horrific creature was still squatted over his wife.

He took a deep breath and opened the door silently. He edged inside holding the breath, every nerve alert. The room was quiet except for the slow, regular breathing of Helen as she slept. His eyes accustomed themselves to the dark, and he could make out her form sprawled on the bed. The duvet was tucked up tight under her armpit.

Alan tiptoed across to her, his mind sending broken-up pictures in a series of images, but Helen was all right. She was sleeping. He *must* have imagined the whole thing, he told himself.

Wearily and unsteadily, he sat on his side of the bed and undressed. He quietly got into bed beside his wife, listening to her breathing in the dark, feeling her warmth. For a while, the images of what he'd seen in the room that didn't exist shunted by his mind's viewer, and then his own breathing slowed down, softened out, and he fell asleep.

FOURTEEN

Alan woke in a ray of sunlight that slanted through the slats of the venetian blinds and laid a triangle of diagonal yellow lines across the bed. He twisted his head out of the glare and sat up quickly, disoriented from the sudden awakening.

A high-octane headache instantly throbbed into being above his eyes, reaching tightly round his temples. He winced, alarmed at the sudden pounding on the inside of his skull, and brought both hands up to cup his face. The edge of his hand brushed against his nose and a sharp pain added to the solid thudding in his head.

He groaned miserably, still fuzzy and bewildered with waking, and knowing that even if he lay down and pulled the duvet over his head he'd never get back to sleep again.

Gingerly he felt around his nose. It was tender and a bit swollen. There was another sore spot just above his left brow that felt raised and bruised. For a moment he sat numbly, fingering the contusions lightly, striving for memory.

Then it came back to him, a startling picture that flooded into his mind, instantly dispelling the dopey blurriness. He saw himself in the strange room, standing by an open door watching as Helen and . . .

He twisted round on the bed and the headache jumped with him to a new, urgent level, making him feel as if his brain was bouncing around inside his head. He spun suddenly, as if expecting Helen and (*what was it?*) the thing still to be on the bed. She wasn't there, and immediately the picture faded, breaking up quickly the way the memory of a dream scatters at the moment of wakening.

'Never again,' Alan said to himself, letting out his breath in a low groan.

He remembered the weird dream he'd had the night before. It had come back to him in an image of shocking clarity that had riddled him through with the same dread feeling of panic that he remembered from the dream itself. That was last night and this was today, and the panic quickly subsided. The headache maintained its regular thudding pressure.

'Never again,' he repeated.

It must have been the drink, Alan thought. He'd polished off a good few glasses of wine at dinner, and then he and Tom had taken their time in giving the malt whisky a fine old hammering. He remembered stumbling up the path with the uncoordinated heavy tread of one who's not quite falling about drunk, but only a kick in the arse off it. He remembered banging his nose somewhere in the dark, and then the dream of the strange room.

He shook his head, which was a mistake because it only gave added bounce to his headache, and he gritted his teeth until the rubber ball inside slowed down its ricochet. Alan was not a great drinker. He'd had one or two hangovers in his life, and this was just as bad as the rest. Normally if he'd taken one too many the night before, he'd be careful to drink a big glass of water and take two Hedex before going to bed. Last night, he told himself, he must have been too rat-arsed to remember. Now he felt rat-eyed.

And the dream. That was more like a dose of d.t.'s. That had been a real psycho-ward nightmare.

But now it was gone, faded in the light of day and the pounding headache and the queasiness Alan felt twisting in his gut. His mouth was dry and his throat was like a barnyard floor, and he didn't have the nerve to look at his tongue. On top of that he'd a sore nose and a bruise on his brow and, oh Christ, it was an abysmal start to the day.

He hauled himself out of bed, taking it easy lest he jar his head which was just settling down under a muffled jackhammer. He crossed to the mirror and looked at the hollow-eyed apparition that faced him. The hair was tousled, the nose was red and angry-looking as if he'd been out in hot sun. There was a greening bruise above his eye. Unthinking, he stuck his tongue out, shuddered at the grey furry coating, and hauled it back out of sight. Peering closer, he prised his bottom eyelids down with both forefingers.

'Definitely never again,' he repeated softly, and right at that minute he meant it sincerely.

Helen gave him coffee but little sympathy when he made it downstairs. He'd come along the hallway towards the kitchen and alongside the wall where he'd thought the door had been. He stood and stared at the dull wallpaper for a minute or two before shaking his head with an irritated motion and continuing into the kitchen.

An eyebath with cold water had helped, and the two Hedex, the ones he should have taken the night before, were arm-wrestling the headache into submission. Alan knew it would be another couple of hours before he felt human again, but the coffee was working its magic, scouring his throat in a strong, sweet stream that fired deep down and seemed to flood through his veins.

'You were late home,' Helen said, 'and you look terrible.'

'I feel terrible.'

'And so you should. Your breath smelled like a brewery this morning.'

'A distillery,' Alan corrected. 'It was malt whisky. Tom and I had a few.'

'And then another few by the look of you.'

'Yeah, probably.'

'Are you going to get this mess cleaned up?' Helen

asked, indicating the mound of rubble that still lay on the plastic sheeting. 'I thought you were going to get up early and finish this off.'

Alan took a long drink of coffee.

'Well, are you going to finish or do I have to stumble around over this lot?' Helen asked crossly. 'Honestly, I can't get a thing done in here with that rubbish underfoot.'

'Yes,' he said drily, irritated. 'Seumas is coming down to finish off the plastering. We'll be finished today. Promise.'

'I really wish you hadn't started this, you know. I did ask you to leave everything the way it was. You just didn't listen, did you?'

Seumas Rhu arrived at the back door a couple of minutes before ten, which allowed Alan to have another cup of coffee and feel the headache fade to a minor irritation.

The small man came into the kitchen, first scuffing his big worn boots on the metal grate outside the door. He accepted a cup from Alan and they stood looking at the wall. The concrete had set neatly, lodging the beam into place. All that needed to be done was to fix up the frame and plaster the spaces.

The two men worked steadily. Alan cut and nailed wood, while Seumas mixed first the plaster, then the browning for the final coat. It took them less time than Alan had estimated, and they completed the job by mid-afternoon. Seumas was a sure, steady worker, and had a fine light hand with the plastering float.

They stood back, admiring their handiwork, watching as the browning gradually changed hue from dark grey to white as the heat in the kitchen evaporated the surface moisture.

'Looks good as new,' the older man said. 'You'll never notice the join once you've put a bit of paper up there.'

'Thank God it's finished,' Alan said. 'I could have done without it today.'

'I thought you were looking a wee bit worse for the wear. You were having a good night then?'

'You could say that. Tom Callander had us over for dinner. I stayed for a blether till late.'

'Ah, he's a fine man, Tom is. Always a good word, and a deft hand when it comes to pouring his whisky. He's richer than all hell, but you'd never know it. He makes no difference with anybody when he talks to them, not like some of these interlopers that have come round to stay in the big houses.'

Alan turned to look at Seumas. 'I take it I'll be an interloper?'

'Oh not at all, not yourself. Sure, you're from these parts in the first place, aren't you?'

'Levenford. That's where I was brought up.'

'Well, there you are. That's only across the loch and round the corner. No, you can't say you're a stranger here. It's the others with their big fancy cars and their boats and their Filofaxes. They've got the airs and graces and their noses in the air. They're not like real people at all.'

Alan smiled at the description. 'It's nice to feel welcome,' he said.

'Oh, you and the missus and the weans will be right at home here in Creggan, make no mistake. And if there's any more jobs needing to be done, just send young Tommy up to my place. I'll be right down.'

Seumas asked for what Alan considered to be a fraction of what the job was worth and wouldn't take a penny more. Alan got his wallet and counted out the notes which the older man crumpled up in his gnarled fist and shoved deep into the pocket of his ragged trousers.

'Do you want something in that coffee before we clean up?' Alan asked.

'Just a wee one, then,' Seumas said immediately. He

grinned mischievously. 'I *knew* you were from these parts.'

Tommy was upstairs in the top hallway, sitting on the carpet with his back against the wall. In front of him lay an upturned box where he kept his model cars. The little steel automobiles, racers and a few assorted transforming robots were in a jumbled heap between his feet.

He was bored.

It was raining outside and Helen had told him he had to stay indoors. The twins were in the dining-room, sitting up at the big table, wearing plastic bibs and sloshing around with poster paints, smearing swaths of colour over sheets of plain paper. Alan was down in the kitchen, working with Seumas. After the accident with the hammer, Tommy had been told he couldn't help them, which was rotten. Daddy always let him help, but this time he said it was too dangerous. Outside, the sky was overcast and the light rain blew in grey veils over the loch and across the garden, pattering on the window at the stairwell.

A darker cloud moved across the sky, shading down the light coming through the window into the hall, making it gloomy and cold. Tommy had a sleek racing car in one hand. He slid down to the left until he was leaning with one elbow on the floor, and started running the car along the carpet. The little black wheels rolled with an easy buzz on their bearings as he shoved the car forward until his arm was at full stretch, then lifted it into the air.

There were fish in the stream, Seumas had told him. You could catch them with your hands, he'd said. Tommy imagined what a fish must feel like as it flipped about, all cold and squirmy, flapping out of the water. He'd much rather be at the stream catching fish.

He rolled the car forward again and brought it up at

the end of its run. The wheels hissed, spinning in the air.

Up at the trees he could be playing soldiers. Darting between the trunks like an SAS man, shooting at the enemy.

Seumas had told him to stay away from the trees.

Or was it the stones? Seumas didn't like it there. Something had happened, Tommy was sure. He could feel it. Something had happened at the stones, and Seumas thought they were bad. Maybe *dangerous*. And there was something else. Tommy had felt it that first time they had walked there, the day after they'd arrived in Creggan. He'd seen something, but he'd shut the sight away where it couldn't be seen again. No, maybe the trees weren't a good idea. At least, not on his own.

Absent-mindedly he zoomed the car and clattered it into the wooden strip of the skirting board as he thought of all the things he'd rather be doing than staying in on a rainy day.

Zoom-clunk. Zoom-clunk. The motion and the noise were hypnotically repetitive. Beyond the road and beyond the trees there was a hill where you could walk up and see the whole firth and the lochs on each side of the peninsula, Seumas had said. The old man lived in a cottage just along the road.

Zoom-clunk. Zoom-clunk. Tommy stretched out and curved in his hand, bringing the car smacking into the woodwork. A little flake of paint chipped off and landed on the carpet. Tommy didn't care.

There was a rumble that felt like deep thunder, shivering the air and sending a tremor through the house.

Tommy brought the car back and repeated the motion, a little bit harder. Another flake of paint flew out.

Another rumble, this time stronger, rattled through the air like a distant shock wave. This time the floor definitely trembled under Tommy.

He stopped what he was doing and looked at the

122

window. There had been no flash of lightning. He brought his hand back and curved the car round in an arc and rammed the skirting board hard.

The angle between the floor and the wall appeared to ripple suddenly all the length of the hall. The movement was so fast it seemed to Tommy that the hallway had suddenly become alive. There was a deep pounding thunder again that seemed to be *inside* the house, and then a loud, tortured shriek.

Tommy froze.

The wall began to pulse and buckle, and the rending, tearing squeal ripped along the hallway.

Something flexed and, before Tommy could move, a massive blow struck right along his side, battering him from shoulder to hip. His head was thrown back in a violent whiplash before smacking into the wall as he was lifted right off the floor and thrown hard against the wall on the other side of the hall.

He hit it with a sickening thump that knocked his breath out of his lungs and made the whole world spin dizzily. He slumped to the floor in a heap.

'What was that?' Seumas asked Alan.

'Did you hear it too?'

'Yes, it sounded as if something fell.'

'I thought I felt the ground shake,' Alan said. 'It happened yesterday when I was knocking this wall down.'

'I felt it too. I wonder what . . .' Seumas broke off in mid-sentence as a wail of pain and fright made them both jump.

'That's Tommy,' Alan said, jumping up from his chair and spilling the coffee across the table. He strode to the door with Seumas on his heels and ran along the hallway and up the stairs, calling to his son.

Tommy wailed again, and the pain was evident in his cry.

Alan found him lying in the top hall, huddled against

the wall. At first he didn't notice the length of skirting that was hanging several inches out from the other side, vibrating like a springboard.

'What happened, son? Are you all right?' Alan's concern tumbled out as he knelt beside the prone child. 'Where does it hurt?'

Tommy moaned. His eyes looked glazed and stunned. The side of his head was matted with fresh blood and there was a red abraded scrape down his cheek. Alan reached out for his son and sat him up. Tommy squealed in pain.

'It's OK, Tommy. I've got you.'

'What happened to him?' Seumas asked. They could hear Helen's footsteps on the stair.

'It was the wall, Daddy,' Tommy said in a high, panicky voice. Tears were streaming down his face and his breath was coming out in great sobbing whoops, as if he'd been badly winded. 'I hit the wall with my car and it hit me back.'

Seumas looked across at the wall. 'Look at that. The skirting board's come right away. It must have sprung out.'

Tommy moaned again. He held tight on to Alan who lifted him up in his arms and carried him through into their bedroom. Helen came striding in, demanded to know what was happening, and when she saw Tommy huddled on the bed she almost knocked the two men aside in her rush of maternal instinct.

She knelt beside Tommy and took him in her arms. He winced with the movement and she drew back.

'What happened Tommy? Where does it hurt?' Her voice was filled with concern. Almost immediately she started taking his shirt off as gently as she could. In moments the small boy was bared to the waist. A huge weal ran from shoulder to hip, red and angry and already turning dark.

'We'd better get a doctor,' Helen said in a strained voice. 'But what happened? Did he fall off something?'

'I don't know what happened,' Alan snapped at Helen. 'But I want somebody to have a look at this. He might have something broken in there.'

He strode off. Seumas was still in the hall examining the skirting board. It was two inches thick and solid hardwood, swinging gently back and forward as the vibration diminished. On the inside, the pointed ends of nails freshly drawn from wood gleamed like teeth.

'The board sprung off and threw him,' the small man said. 'Must have warped.'

'We'll have to look at it later,' Alan said. 'What's the doctor's number?'

Seumas gave him three digits for Dr Docherty. The phone chirruped several times, then a young woman's voice answered in an American accent. Alan told her what had happened and she told him she'd be there in a few minutes.

When she arrived, Alex Graham stripped Tommy completely, and the boy allowed her to probe and palpate without protest. The bruise down his side continued down his thigh. There was a nasty gash on his head that was quickly congealing. Tommy's breath hissed when she cleaned it with alcohol, but he blinked back the tears. Again she asked the boy what had happened, and when he repeated what he'd said when Alan found him, she looked up at his parents, eyebrows raised in question.

Alan shrugged. 'That's what he says. Seumas says the skirting board has sprung off. Maybe he loosened it or something.'

'Well, he's very lucky. He's just bruised, and nothing's broken. I don't want to stitch that scalp cut, so I'll just put a dressing on it.' She turned to Tommy. 'I know you don't feel lucky, but you are. You haven't got anything broken, so you'll be fine in the morning; just a little bit stiff.'

Tommy nodded and let her put a dressing on the cut. He gritted his teeth as the gentle pressure of her fingers sent sharp pain through his head, but he didn't make a sound. One big tear escaped before he could stop it, and rolled down his cheek. The young doctor scooped it with a finger and wiped it on her other hand.

FIFTEEN

Creggan was tucking itself down for the night. Far off across the firth the yellow lights twinkled, throwing a perfect reflection off the water. Across the loch from the Crombies' house the newly built dual carriageway that had been gouged into the rock to cut off a couple of notorious bends showed a string of glowing orange fairy lights, between adjacent patches of black where the lights were hidden by trees. Cromwath was the first house off the Creggan Road, the narrow shore lane that diverted from Peaton Road, the main route down the length of the thin peninsula to the village and the string of tiny hamlets beyond, Corbeth, Murrin, and right at the dead end, Feorlin, where the road took a loop across the Peaton Hill to double back on itself at Mambeg.

Tom Callander's house was in near darkness. A rosy glow from the kitchen showed that Beth Callander was studying there beside the big Raeburn that threw out warm heat to where she sat with books sprawled across the heavy deal table. Tom had gone to his bed just after dark, shoo-ed upstairs by his daughter who had shown him as little sympathy as Alan had got when he had sat beside her at breakfast, refusing everything she'd cooked, looking sorry for himself.

Two houses along, where the narrow road snaked round the hump of Cromwath Point, a craggy promontory that marked the southernmost tip of the peninsula, the Reverend Fergus MacLeod was making his way back to the manse after an argumentative game of chess with his friend Matt Stirling, a young schoolmaster who taught at the academy in Kirkland.

The minister was short and fat in his black coat. He

wore a black felt hat that made him look like a rabbi, especially when he peered myopically through the thick lenses of his heavy-framed spectacles into the gloom. He walked with the paunchy, bumbling gait of the short and overweight. Under his breath he cursed Matt Stirling who had trounced him soundly at their game, checkmating in a surprise move just when Fergus had decided he was on the point of winning.

Fergus walked in the dark. The clumps of elm trees that huddled on the far side of the road were patches of black that cut off the distant twinkling lights across the water, and at his side, where the pavement dipped in worn runnels making him stumble and miss his step, the overhanging branches of the spreading copper beeches and lime trees were eerie reaches of shade. The minister didn't like walking in the dark. The night was not cold, but he shivered, pulling his collar up and tight around his neck, walking a little bit faster. His low-key resentment against Matt Stirling faded to the background as he began to think more warmly of the frosty reception the sour-faced Mrs Smaill would bestow upon him for associating with a Catholic.

He quickened his pace, hearing his shoes scud and rustle in the deep leaf litter that the onshore wind had whirled and heaped close to the dry wall to his left. A twig cracked underfoot, a short, snapping sound that caused him to jump. Already the whisky he'd had at the teacher's house had faded on his tongue and the warm fire had cooled in his belly.

Just ahead of him, thankfully, was the bright light that lit the entrance to the Montagu house, a white beacon set into the stone pillar that held the gate, round and appealing to the minister and the few moths that danced in the glow. As he passed, he looked up at the bright orb and immediately regretted it as the light sent dazzling reflections off the thick lenses. And once he was past, the darkness ahead was even deeper and more impenetrable through night-blinded eyes. He held out his left hand and felt the rough, mossy surface of the wall, and kept walking until his vision returned at least enough to make out the outline of the wall and the trees ahead. His feet crunched erratically in the leaves.

The road took a turn to the left just ahead, where an open patch in the trees let the sky through: dark, but not as black as the shadows under the spreading branches. Fergus kept walking. Ahead of him there was a brief movement, high in the clear patch. Instinctively he looked up and saw the spread of an owl's silent wings flicker whitely as they caught the light behind him. The tawny owl jinked lightly to the side and came flitting, ghost-like, above the road. It must have turned its head in flight, for the light at the Montagu gate reflected back at the minister in two bright yellow circles like glowing headlights. The owl swooped lower until it was only ten feet or so above the pavement, wings broad and silent in the quiet air, questing for small food. The bird was flying towards Fergus and was about forty feet away from him when it banked slightly under the overhang of gnarled and twisted branches looping out from a big beech tree which spread its boughs almost across the road.

Still walking, Fergus watched the bird's flight. It had been years since he'd last seen an owl. The wings came down in a fast, soft sweep, and the eyes again flashed perfect circles of light at him.

Then there was a rustle and a shadow and the owl completely disappeared from the air.

Fergus stopped dead in his tracks. A shadow had flicked hugely from the darkness of the beech tree and had snapped the owl from the air in a sudden lunge. It had gaped widely and there had been a glimmer of something white and then it was gone, lost in the deep shade of the trees.

Fergus stood stock still. He hadn't quite seen what had happened. The bird, seen in the reflected light but through his thick glasses, had merely been a light patch in the dark sky. Only its gleaming eyes, when they turned towards him, had been really visible. And now it was gone.

Fergus was alone in the dark road.

He didn't know what had happened. Had there really been an owl? Was it just a trick of the light and his poor eyesight?

He took a tentative step forward, keeping one hand on the wall. His shoe cracked another twig, making him start, and he felt the quickening of his pulse. Another step, then another. Just ahead was the spreading stoop of the big beech, reaching black, trailing fingers almost to the other side of the road. The minister stopped and stared at the looming shadow of the tree.

Nothing moved in the blackness of the big tree. The minister considered walking out on to the hard metal of the road, out from under the boughs. That would have meant giving up his touch on the wall, which he decided against, because his eyesight wasn't good enough to be stumbling along in the dark with no point of reference.

He shook his head angrily. 'There's nothing there,' he muttered out loud in his still-pronounced island accent, 'nothing at all.'

He started forward again, walking slowly and warily and damning himself for a timorous fool, until he was under the tree.

The old beech had a trunk a yard wide, black and sinewy with thick, muscular forks that jutted at odd angles, twisted and jointed, bearing a mighty spread of boughs. A slight wind coiled in to shake the dry beech mast that hadn't fallen last winter, and the tender covering of summer leaves. Under the branches it was darker than before.

'There's nothing here,' he said again. There was only the dark.

He walked on, still trailing his fingers against the

stone wall, moving quickly, crunching past the trunk towards the lighter gloom ahead. It was past him. There was nothing there. Then something soft and spidery touched his cheek. He jerked his head back with an involuntary gasp, bringing his hand up to his face. Then he let his breath out in a long, relieved sigh. It was nothing. Just a feather, spiralling out of the darkness overhead. The small feather was light and downy. Fergus started walking again, and another feather, then another, slowly tumbled down before his face. Two lazily see-sawed down in front of him, and then a final one, this time a small flight feather that helicoptered down on its vane.

'Just a feather,' he said, almost giggling with relief. For a minute he'd thought he'd walked into a spider's web and that thought was enough to give him the heebie-jeebies. He took two more steps before the significance of the feathers reverberated through him like a shock, sending his pulse stuttering.

'It must have been the owl.'

And that brought the jagged, fearsome thought: *what got the owl?*

The minister was almost garrotted with panic, but his feet kept on walking. He was well past the trunk, coming out of the overhanging darkness, and there was nothing there.

Nothing moved. Of course nothing moved. The owl had swung into the tree, maybe even crashed into a branch. That was it, he told himself.

Except for the soft, gobbling, crunching sound that suddenly came from up there, where the branches forked and twisted in on themselves in the black depths of the tree.

The minister was frozen rigid with a primitive horror. He tried to turn his body away, he moaned with the effort of trying to drag his eyes from the deep shadow. He frantically willed his feet to keep on walking, but for a few seconds his body failed him.

Every nerve was stretched taut and shrieking, but he *couldn't* move. His eyes were glued to the blackest part of the centre of the tree where, quite clearly, there was something rending and crunching with low, shuddering snarls.

Up there something had moved. The slobbering sounds had stopped, and there had been a twist, a change in the utter darkness. Fergus's weak eyesight couldn't make out what it was, but he still couldn't will his body to move. Then the tree rustled. Something scraped, and then a shape leapt out of the black. It was a flitting shadow. Fergus thought, in the fraction of a second that the shape launched itself from the tree, that he could see enormous arms spread wide, impossibly spindly and with spidery fingers claw-like at the ends. Between the arms, he couldn't be sure, there was a filmy membrane that beat down like a huge bat's wing. It vibrated the air in an audible, tingling judder, flicked again round the overhanging branches, and was gone.

Fergus tried to breathe and failed. Inside his chest he felt that everything had swollen up until his ribs were bulging out from the pressure. He was sure something inside was going to burst and a prayer of pure fright shrieked in his mind.

'Oh, not here, dear Lord. Don't let me die out here.'

And as if the dear Lord had suddenly put his hand down on him and patted his back, the stranglehold on his lungs was released and his breath flooded back in a great sweet surge. He gasped mightily, whooping in vast breaths with such vehemence that sparks spun in front of his eyes. The minister scooted along the pavement as if the demons of hell were behind him, shoving his rotund, overindulged body beyond its normal limit.

Past the light, he was in the clear, with no obstacles, no shadows ahead, just the straight road and the turn-off up Murrin Lane, only another forty yards and safe in the street light. His gate squealed on its hinge and snapped shut behind him, jingling the catch. He didn't turn, but kept on, up to the door, quickly turning the latch and almost falling into the lamplit hall.

Mrs Smaill came bustling out of the kitchen. 'Oh, you've decided to come home, have you, Minister,' she said reprovingly. Her shrewish face peered at him over her half-moon glasses. Her nostrils were rucked up on each side of her nose as if she'd smelt something rotten in the hallway, and her narrow mouth was pulled down at the corners in a permanent expression of disdain and reproof.

'Been out having a high old time with that backslider, of course,' she said, and this time the reproving tone was even more pronounced, 'which is better than having him in the house of a man of God.'

The minister was long used to Mrs Smaill's quirks. Most of the time he just ignored them. This time, as he stood panting and dangerously flushed on his own doorstep, he displayed a forcefulness that surprised her into wide-eyed silence.

'Don't just stand there, woman,' he said, almost sobbing the words out of his labouring lungs. 'Drink. Get me a drink, for the love of God.'

'But, Minister,' she began to protest.

'Don't but-minister me,' he gasped. 'Get me the whisky right this minute. I'll be in the study.'

She threw him a venomous look and retreated into the kitchen. He stumbled into his study and flopped into the chair so heavily that the top button on his coat popped off with the sudden strain and pinged on to the low table.

Mrs Smaill came in with a bottle of Grouse and a glass on a tray. Normally Fergus kept his own supply in his room, under lock and key and away from the watchful, predatory eye of his housekeeper.

The minister didn't even take his coat off. He leant forward and grabbed the bottle by the neck and twisted the cap off with shaking fingers. He poured out a measure that gurgled almost to the top of the glass and immediately brought it to his lips. Mrs Smaill looked as if she was in shock as he drained the glass in two gulps and started to pour out another.

'Minister, don't you think you've . . .' she began in her shrill voice.

'No, I don't damn well think. I want a damned drink, woman, and a damned drink I shall have,' he interrupted with unaccustomed venom. 'Now, I suggest you get yourself off to your bed, and leave me to it. And I'll tell you another thing. You can put this bottle in the bin in the morning, for I'll be done with it by then.'

He didn't even watch her stiff back as she marched out of the room.

Matt Stirling had waved the minister goodbye after their game. It was a still night as he stood in the rectangle of light, watching the little clergyman bumble down the pathway to the road.

He liked Fergus, although he was aware of the other man's disapproval of him. It wasn't a deep-rooted thing, he knew, mainly a throwback from the repressive island ways tinged with the inherent dourness of the north-west. Behind the grumbling façade, Fergus was a decent soul, given at times to cantankerous condemnation of all things frivolous, and after a drink, which was more often than was good for him, he became maudlin and stricken with self-centred contempt for the world. But basically he was just a lonely man who found it hard to make friends, but who was, despite his manner, hard-working and generous.

Matt would have preferred to cycle up to the manse on a fine night like this. On the sloping roads he enjoyed scudding along in the quiet hours, headlamp cutting through the dark and giving momentary life to everything he passed. He liked to feel the wind whistling past his ears as he freewheeled down the lanes, and sometimes, especially on good nights like tonight, he'd even taken the ten-speed up to Peaton Hill, taking the long way round by the Finloch and panting up to the shoulder of the conical hill to come speeding down the one-in-six slope towards Feorlin and back again. But that morning, when the teacher had hopped on the slim saddle for the short ride into Creggan for his morning loaf, he'd been forced right off the road by a fast-moving lorry which had honked at him loudly as it nearly clipped his handlebar on a tight bend. He'd careered right against the cobbled kerb and his front wheel had crumpled itself in the sudden hole of a sunken drain cover, spilling him arse over elbow to land, winded but unhurt, in a new clump of nettles.

The wheel was beyond repair. Matt reckoned he'd be able to pick up a replacement on his way to school in the morning. He taught in Kirkland Academy, giving lessons in Latin and French to senior pupils.

Matt Stirling was twenty-seven years old, a tall man with a thick crop of brown curly hair that he tried but generally failed to keep out of his eyes. He mostly wore an old tweed jacket that hung on a gaunt frame, giving him the look of the absent-minded academic which, he admitted to himself, he often was.

When the minister had turned at the gate and had disappeared from view along the darkened road, Matt turned back into his house and closed the door. Upstairs, in his front room, he took out some school papers to correct and spent half an hour marking and crossing. It was getting close to midnight when he gave up and stacked the papers back into his briefcase, and went through to the kitchen. Under the table Morag, the little retriever bitch that Tom Callander had given him a year ago when he'd come to stay in Creggan, lifted her head from between her paws, giving him that half-quizzical, half-hopeful look. She was coming on heat, he knew, and he wasn't at all sure what to do about it. He didn't quite approve of taking her to the vet to solve that problem once and for all, but neither did he fancy having every dog in the village, and all the surrounding farms, sniffing around the door. Nor did he want his image, for what it was worth, dented by having packs of them following him about when he took her for a walk.

Morag sat up quickly and snuffled at his hand. She was eager to be outside. For the last couple of days she had been pawing at the door, a slave to her body clock's imperative, whining softly and insistently. Matt found it comical, and a little sad.

'Between you and me, we've got a lot in common,' he told her with a wry smile. His own glandular demands were not something that would disappear in a few weeks' time. He was a normal male, and they were constant, and all the whining in the world wouldn't make them go away.

'All right, girl, let's go and get some fresh air,' he said directly to the retriever as she sat gazing soulfully up at him. As if she understood every word, she quickly padded out from under the table and stood at the door, her hindquarters swivelling from side to side with the furious wagging of her tail. Matt got his coat and hat and followed the small dog down the stairs. In the garden she bounded about with enthusiasm while he walked down to the gate. In seconds she was by his side as he crossed over the road and on to the tussocky grass that led to the foreshore. It was a mild night. The twinkles from the lights at Greenock and Port Glasgow, five miles away across the water, shone up warmly in reflection. Man and dog walked along the shore path round the piled-up rock of the point, he with his hands deep in his pockets, feet crunching on the shingle, and she roaming around, sniffing every rock and clump. When they reached the first stand of trees Morag, who normally raced ahead into the shadows, held back. She stopped on the track and stared at the dark patch where the elms stood close together. He caught up with her and found her standing stock still. There was something different about her, he thought, then he noticed how

136

the hair on her back, from the shoulders right to the space between her cocked-up ears, was standing on end, almost quivering with tension. There was a low purring noise. Matt thought she had surprised a cat until he realized that it was Morag who was making the noise, a deep soft growl that came right from the back of her throat.

'What's up, girl?' he asked when he hunkered down beside her. He put a hand between her shoulder blades and felt the tingling vibration of tension that was running down the dog's lithe frame.

He stood up and looked ahead at the copse. He couldn't see a thing in the shadows.

Matt reached down again and scratched her under the ear. 'Come on, Morag,' he said softly. 'Let's go.' Normally their evening stroll took them right round the point to where the Finloch joined the firth, then by the rocky path up to the road, and the lane home again.

Morag didn't move. She stood stock still on the rocky path, staring into the trees. The growling in her throat got deeper and louder before it suddenly cut off. Matt looked down at her and she let out a small whine, like a hurt puppy. She was obviously in some distress over something. Maybe, he thought, it's her condition.

'I just hope I don't show it as much,' he said lightly to himself. He looked at the trees, where he could still make out nothing that could have upset the animal, then turned to look back. She whined again and backed down the track, still staring ahead, and her hackles, like a mane, spiked between her ears. She whimpered again, then turned quickly and started trotting, crouched low, and keeping her tail tight, back the way they had come.

Whatever had bothered her, there was no point in calling her back, Matt realized. He sighed, and followed her back to the house. The whining had stopped by the time they got home, and Matt took Morag round to the back of the house to her kennel, fixing her leash to the long running rope that gave her the run of the garden, and let himself in at the back door. Before he closed it he turned to look at his dog. She had slunk into the wooden kennel and was staring at him dolefully from the shadowed opening. He could sense the reproof in her gaze.

Upstairs, he poured himself a small whisky and doubled it with water from the tap, grateful that Fergus hadn't made a real dent in his bottle tonight, and took a book from his filled shelves. He took both across to the fireplace and set them down. He got the poker and stoked the embers of the fire into red warmth, and settled down to read.

The glow of the fire had faded when he woke with a start. The book was lying open, face down on his chest. Beside him, the drink had hardly been touched. He glanced quickly at the clock and realized he must have dozed off for half an hour or more.

Then he heard again the noise that had broken into his slumber. There was a whining sound, high-pitched and urgent, coming from outside in the garden. Over-laid on the whine was a guttural snarling, a deep-throated growl, like an angry animal. It sounded like the kind of noise Morag had made down on the fore-shore, but much, much louder.

Still dozy from the sudden awakening, Matt crossed to the window and peered out. He could see nothing but the reflection of the room on the glass. He stepped to the wall and switched off the side light, then moved back to the window. At first he could see nothing, down there in the shadows, then his eyes accustomed themselves to the dark, and he could make out dim movement.

He peered closer, bending the end of his nose against the glass and bringing both hands up to eliminate all the reflection.

Yes. There was movement. He could see Morag's light golden coat against the dark of the grass. She was standing just behind the kennel, most of her in the shadow. But from the window, he could see her head twisting and turning. There was enough light from the next-door neighbour's window, as his eyes adjusted themselves for night-vision, to see her jaws were wide open, her tongue lolling. As he peered further into the gloom, he thought he could make out her eyes rolling whitely in her head.

All the time, the high-pitched whining continued in waves, and the guttural snarling overlaid the small dog's squeal.

Then he made out the other shape, the one that had cast a shadow over Morag's light frame.

'Damn!' Matt hissed against the window, fogging the glass for a second or two before the misting faded to give him a clearer view.

'I should have kept her in tonight,' he said ruefully. Down in the garden, Morag was getting her chronological imperative attended to. Matt could see it now. The shadow of the kennel was no shadow at all. It was a big black dog that had mounted the little bitch. He could just about make out the shape against the surrounding gloom. It was a huge dog, moving its whole body with every thrust. Immediately Matt thought about the consequences of a litter of mongrel puppies, then dismissed the thought. There wasn't much he could do about it, was there?

At least, he thought, he could break up the party down there, maybe, if he was lucky, before the critical moment.

Morag's squeal got louder, rising high in the night air, as if she was in pain.

Matt thought about the big dog that had invaded the garden. Whoever it was would get a piece of his mind tomorrow. Probably that big mastiff that John Lindsay, the Creggan policeman, kept in the pen behind the station house. The difference in size, he realized, might in fact be painful for the small bitch. Matt wasn't sure of the mechanics or dimensions of the dog's reproductive system, but some things stood to reason.

'*Canis interruptus*,' he said to himself, shoving himself away from the window sill. He kicked off his slippers and put his shoes on. Outside, the whining got louder, matching the force of the savage-sounding growls.

Downstairs, he put his jacket on and went to the back door where the big mortise key jutted from the lock. It twisted in his hand, clicked and spun on. It was an old lock. Matt had meant to have it repaired a dozen times, for often the key didn't catch in the mechanism and needed several twists to spring the bolt. He clicked it again and tried the handle. It was still locked.

Outside, there was a ferocious snarling, and then a screech that was obviously pain. Matt had never heard a dog squeal before, at least not so loudly and continuously. The noise sent his nerves tingling.

'What's going on out there?' he shouted, frustrated at the lock, suddenly worried about his pet.

He gave the key a savage twist and it clicked hard this time, sliding the bolt back with a thud. He heaved on the handle and pulled the door inwards, immediately sending a beam of light out on to the grass.

Morag's head was on the grass, right between her forepaws. He could see her eyes gleam wildly with reflected light. Behind her, forcing her down on to the grass, was the big animal. The light from its eyes shot back at him in green slits. Suddenly Morag's scream was cut off, as if her throat had been cut. There was a snarling growl and then the shadow of the big animal heaved back behind the kennel. Matt hadn't seen it clearly, but he knew that it must have been a bloody big dog. A huge dog. There was a crashing about in the raspberry stalks behind the kennel, then a thump as something heavy hit the trellis fence. There was a scrabbling sound and Matt saw a big black shape scramble over it, landing with a thud, and it was gone. He turned back to Morag who was lying on the grass.

From next door, Ronnie Gordon, who ran the Creggan post office and general store, shouted out: 'What's happening?' Another light came on and Ronnie, a stocky, bald man, came over to the fence.

'Oh, it's you, Matt. I thought I heard something. It sounded like a dogfight.'

'It very nearly was,' Matt said, diverted momentarily from his pet. 'Some big dog must have jumped the fence to get at Morag.'

'Is he all right? It sounded like one almighty scrap.'

'I don't think his intentions were entirely honourable,' Matt said. 'She's on heat, I think.'

'Ah, I see,' Ronnie said as the light dawned. 'She was making a lot of noise about it.'

'Hold on a minute,' Matt called over to him. 'It looks as if she's been hurt.'

The storekeeper stood at the fence, peering into the gloom as the young man walked on to the lawn and crouched down to where the pale coat of the dog showed as a light patch on the grass.

There was a silence for a minute, then he heard the young man groan loudly. 'Oh for heaven's sake,' Matt cried, with a sudden catch in his voice, as if he was about to burst into tears. 'Look what it's done to her.'

'What's happened?' the storekeeper called over anxiously. 'Is she all right?'

'Ronnie, phone the vet for me,' Matt shouted urgently, his voice almost a sob. 'Get him to come right away.'

'But it's after midnight,' the man protested.

'I don't care how bloody late it is,' Matt spat, shocking his neighbour. 'Just get him for me, will you? Please?'

The young teacher's unaccustomed tone made the shopkeeper spin round and dart back into his house.

Matt knelt on the wet grass and cradled Morag's head in his arms. Blood was drooling thickly from her jaws, and the light was reflecting from upturned eyes.

There was a set of deeply gouged bloody lines under her ribs where she'd been raked to the bone by vicious claws. And spreading out from under her tail was a pool of thick blood that glistened blackly in the gloom. In his arms, Matt could feel his pet quiver, and her breath gurgled in a throat that was running with blood, and he knew that no matter how quickly the vet arrived, it would be too late.

His little dog looked as if she had been ripped apart.

SIXTEEN

Tommy woke up suddenly in the welcoming ray of sunlight that was a sharp line of pure white cutting through the narrow space where the curtains didn't quite meet. Today was the day Alan had promised he'd take the whole family out in the car, and from the feel of the sunbeam, it was the perfect day for it. For the last week or so Alan had been too busy working in the house, and Helen had seemed distracted, the way she sometimes got, and it was best to wait until she got better.

He leapt out of bed towards the window and stopped as soon as his feet hit the floor as a pain shot right up his bruised side. He wheezed and caught his breath as the sudden stab peaked and faded, before he gingerly eased himself forward. He pulled one side of the curtains back with his right hand, favouring his aching side, and stood in the sunlight.

The sky was the light blue of early summer morning. Tommy let the light wash over him dispelling the drowsiness, and looked out beyond the wall at the gate, to the hills on the far side of the narrow loch tinged russet and gold.

He had slept soundly after swallowing the painkillers the lady doctor had given him, and he hadn't dreamed. The bump on his head was tender under his gently probing fingers, but otherwise it wasn't painful, and although his side ached when he moved, it was the kind of pain that would fade. He'd been bruised before.

The doctor said that he'd no broken bones, which was something he was grateful for. The thought of spending another day indoors was to be avoided, even if he had to pretend to everyone that he was as fit as ever.

Downstairs Dad was in the kitchen. It looked different with the new opening into the other room, and the plaster was already mostly white.

'Hey, TC, how are you feeling today?' Alan said, looking back over his shoulder from where he stood at the sink.

'Fine. A bit stiff,' Tommy said, making it as bright as possible.

'That's to be expected, as Dr Alex said. You gave us all a bit of a fright, son.'

Tommy nodded and said nothing. He hoped his father didn't want to talk about what had happened because that was one of the scary things that Tommy was trying to bury down at the back of his mind. Every time his thoughts turned towards what had happened up in the hallway when the skirting board had (*hit him*) sprung off, he'd immediately thought of something else, diverting his mind instinctively.

Alan finished filling the kettle, came across the kitchen and gave his son a quick hug. The blood drained from Tommy's face as the pain lanced down his side.

Immediately Alan was contrite, concerned. 'Oh, I'm sorry, Tommy. I didn't mean to hurt you.'

Tommy knew that. And the knowing helped him hold back the tears that had sprung up under his eyelids. 'I'm all right, honest, Dad. Really, I'm just stiff.'

'You're a brave soldier, and I'm proud of you,' Alan said, looking down at the boy, anxiously studying his son's face for further evidence of hurt.

Tommy forced a big smile. 'Really. I'm a lot better. Can we still go out today?'

'Of course we can. Today's a holiday. I've had enough work to last me a lifetime, and I've got to go back tomorrow, so we want to make the best of it, don't we?'

Alan got the cereal out from the new cupboards along

the wall and set out three plates, filling them with crispies. The milk in the fridge was cool and creamy, just the kind of fresh farmhouse milk he remembered and hadn't tasted for years. Alan was tempted to have a plate of cereal for himself.

'Where's Mum?' Tommy asked as he pulled up a chair to get at his breakfast.

'Still upstairs. She's been a bit tired the last couple of days.'

'Is she . . . ?' Tommy's question trailed off.

'Is she what?' Alan asked back.

'I mean, is she OK?'

There was a slight edge to Tommy's question that Alan picked up immediately. He sat on the edge of the table and looked down at his son again, keeping his face brightly neutral. 'You mean, is she feeling better than before?'

'Yes. Sort of.'

'Do you think she's OK?' Alan knew that of all people, Tommy was the best barometer of Helen's fluctuating moods.

'Sometimes I do,' Tommy said from behind a mouthful of milk and crispies. 'And sometimes she's kind of, you know.'

'I do?' Alan asked, smiling, encouraging.

'Well, sort of *sad*.'

Alan paused, still smiling at his boy. Sad was a good word for it. 'I think she's been a bit sad, but I think she's getting better.'

'I hope so. I hate it when she's sad. It makes me sad too.'

'And me, son.'

Helen's erratic recovery from her breakdown had had its ups and downs. There were some days when she was so withdrawn from the family that it was as if they weren't in the same house. At other times, her temper was on a short fuse and she would explode with anger over the most trivial incidents. Alan could cope with those times. But he found it hard to cater for her mood when it swung round to the aloof, sarcastic, intolerant mode. Those times he felt his irritation rising beyond the anger threshold, and at times he felt the blankness of despair.

Since they'd moved into Cromwath, Helen had at first been grumpy, complaining most of the time, irritable with the children.

But in the last couple of days she hadn't been complaining so much, except for her outburst over the kitchen wall which had been *her* idea in the first place. After that she'd seemed withdrawn, remote, and it seemed as if her mind was elsewhere. But she didn't look so down, so flattened by depression. Alan hoped it was the first sign of her settling in.

'I think we'll have a great day today.'

He moved off the table. 'I'd better go and wake the girls,' he said. 'If the kettle boils, stick two slices in the toaster for me, will you?'

Tommy nodded.

Alan almost fell over the twins just outside the kitchen door as they walked down the hallway hand in hand, hair tousled from sleep, and smiling brightly as soon as they saw him.

'Hi kids,' Tommy welcomed his sisters, demonstrating both affection and seniority in the two words. They beamed adoringly at him.

He finished the last spoonful of breakfast and went to the toaster to slide in the thick-cut bread while his father settled the girls before their bowls. Alan made tea and poured two cups just in time for the toast to leap up, golden brown.

'Make sure they don't wreck the place while I take your mother's breakfast upstairs,' he called to Tommy from the door. The boy returned his wink.

Helen had just woken when he backed into the room, holding the tray as level as he could.

'Morning, dear heart, it's a lovely day.'

Helen dopily peered about the room which was still in semi-darkness as the curtains were still drawn. She yawned, stretched and asked: 'What time is it?'

'Just after nine. It's summer outside. The kids are having their breakfast, and they'll be raring to go in about ten minutes.'

'Go? Go where?'

'I thought we'd agreed to take the car out for a run and explore our new territory,' Alan said lightly. He was a past master at the neutral statement, the blithe smile.

'Oh, I really don't think I'm up to that today,' Helen responded lethargically. 'There's a few things I want to get done in here, before you go back to work.'

'Can't they keep, just for one day? I've been so tied up with this place I've hardly had time for anything else.'

'I know, but there's a dozen things that need doing,' Helen insisted.

'I thought you would want to get out. Have you changed your mind about this place?'

'You know, I think I have, really. You were right after all. I *do* think I like the house. I didn't when we came here, but it's sort of grown on me. But that's beside the point. I can always take the kids out at the weekend, but today I'd rather get some things done.'

'Like what, for instance?'

'Oh, don't be a pest,' Helen said crossly, but then she flashed him a bright smile that took five years off her. 'OK, all right. If you insist.'

'I do, I do.'

In half an hour they were all in the car. The tyres spun on the gravel as Alan slid it out of the garage and down to the gate. As they turned on the road, Tommy looked back at the house. The windows looked like black, glistening holes. As he stared, they seemed to flex like shifting, focusing eyes. Tommy shivered and then turned his eyes away. He kept them averted until they were well along the road.

Alan drove them out along the peninsula road in the morning sunlight and took the short cut over the Fruin glen and down to the flat country on the far side of Loch Lomond, heading towards the Trossachs. They stopped for lunch in a converted barn which offered salads and home baking that the children demolished with gusto.

After they left the house, Helen had been quiet for a while, but as the car skirted Gartocharn and Drymen she seemed to snap out of her silence and become, for her, quite animated. She bought Alan a checked hat in one of the small wool shops and treated herself to a fine sweater. She smiled often and joked with the children.

Alan couldn't remember when he had last seen her look so normal. It took a weight off his shoulders.

On the return trip, he thought how good it would be if Helen was at last coming back to normal. They'd had a wonderful day out in the early summer sunshine.

It was the last really good day they would know that year.

SEVENTEEN

By the time John Lindsay got home, his wife was waiting for him with a cup of tea and another message. He was needed urgently up at Peaton Farm. Jack Coggan had been in a panic, Marion Lindsay had told him. Something about an animal at his chickens.

John had swallowed his cooling tea in one long gulp and could have used a second cup, but Marion said Jack had been really upset on the phone and wanted him up right away. He put his cap back on and gave her a peck on the cheek, told her to go back to bed, and lumbered out towards his Land Rover.

Even in the dark of the farmyard, Jack Coggan's face was white when John pulled into the cobbled space. The young farmer was wrapped up in his old coat and his dark hair showed in even greater contrast against the pallor of his skin. As soon as John got out of the jeep, the farmer had turned and indicated the way with a gnarled walking stick. John immediately stepped into a rut that was filled with manure, and felt it squelch up over the sides of his boots. It didn't improve his mood at all.

At the chicken coop, a large, wooden building on a brick base, Jack's two youngsters were standing, huddled in heavy jackets beside the door. Even in the crisp night air, the smell of blood cloyed John's nostrils when he was still yards from the coop. It was maybe half an hour since the animal had broken into the chicken house.

The farmer stood beside the unlocked door which was bowed out and cracked down the frame that sat on the hinges. He said nothing. He simply gestured inside. The coop was a scene of bloody carnage. Some feathers still rocked lightly in the air, stirred by a draught that blew through the gaping hole in the side wall of the coop and out through the door, carrying with it the stench of warm meat, half-digested feed and chicken shit. Out of more than two hundred chickens, big reds, good layers, not more than twenty were left, huddled in a corner, shivering with terror, bespattered with the blood and intestines of their sisters. The whole coop dripped with blood. There were bits of birds hanging from the two smashed fluorescent strips high on the pitched roof. There were heads and half-bodies that had been snapped, torn, ripped. John Lindsay walked gingerly on the joists that held up the tight-mesh flooring wire, trying to avoid slipping on the gory carpet, and looked out of the hole at the far side. The mud there was soft, churned by the feet of Coggan's small herd of cattle when they sheltered in the lee. John shone his flashlight, spreading a cone of brightness over the dark earth.

The living-room in the old farmhouse was a clutter of worn furniture that was solid and smooth and dark with age. The children, looking scared and near to tears, had been sent up the narrow staircase to their beds. Their duffel coats were slung in a heap over the back of one of the chairs that stood off a bit from the table. Beside them, their wet rubber boots slumped amphibiously.

Jack Coggan was rubbing one of his wide, leathery hands on the top of the table, making a scratchy noise as the rough skin on the palms frictioned across the grain. John Lindsay, facing him, could see the raised callouses of old scars on the knuckles, evidence of hard winters and a hard life on a small farm. A wood fire crackled and flickered in the neuk, throwing warm shadows on the rough walls of the room. But the shadows on Jack Coggan's face showed little warmth.

He looks like he's put on twenty years since I last saw him, the policeman thought to himself. Since the last time had only been ten days away at the most, that was some going. The smallholder looked as if he'd just shouldered a huge weight and found that he was buckling at the knees. His mouth seemed to have been clamped and pulled down at the corners, falling into two deep furrows that had been ploughed on either side. His eyes were angry, frustrated, bewildered.

'Tell me it just from the start, Jack,' Lindsay said, softly, almost conversationally, and masking his question by taking a sip of hot tea from a cracked mug that held a full pint. The thick brew helped wash away the cloying after-scent of blood that had settled and congealed at the back of the policeman's throat.

'It's like I said,' the stocky farmer started. His worn cloth cap was riding at the back of his head, peak askew. Lindsay had never seen him without it.

'Just like I said,' Coggan repeated. 'I had been out at the stall checking out my Jersey cross. She's just about ready to drop her calf and the last one was bad, so you have to keep an eye on things.'

Lindsay nodded knowingly, which was not a policeman's ploy. In an area like this, everybody understood the problems farmers faced. The policeman's grandfather had been a farmer, and Lindsay had spent most of his youth ploughing fields and pitching hay and he'd spent cold nights in smelly byres helping distressed, lowing cattle give birth. He'd also sat through the wet dark until dawn, shotgun resting on his numb knees waiting for foxes that had slaughtered chickens. The few dead birds for which he'd sat in revenge vigil could not compare with the carnage that fouled the air in Coggan's coop.

'The cow was all right. She's maybe got a day or two to go. I shut the shed and came back into the house. Mattie was over there by the fire putting a patch on the wee fellow's jacket. She'd put on the kettle and was about to make us a cup when I heard this banging from out there.' He indicated with a sideways jerk of his head. His hands were flat on the table, pressed down on to the surface to keep them still.

'Mattie asks "What's that?" and I said it must be the cow. I thought she must have started and kicked at the stall once or twice. They do that sometimes. I had a cow once that kicked through the side of the pen and we couldn't get her hoof out of the hole until after she'd dropped the calf.'

'But it wasn't the cow, then?' Lindsay asked.

'I truly wish to God it was,' Coggan said, expelling his breath slowly through pursed lips, like a man in pain. 'No. It wasn't the cow. The banging noise came on again. Thud, thud, thud. Like somebody was taking a sledgehammer to the outhouse. You could *feel* the noise. It made the windows rattle. I told Mattie I'd better go and see what was making all the bloody racket and she said to be careful. We had a crowd of them hippie folk up on the hill a few years back, you'll remember, when they had the protest about the defence base. That was the time they used Albert Little's tractor to shove down the dry-stane dike and block off the road, and then some fool set fire to Inverarity's barley and it took the fire brigade all night to put it out before every farm on the Creggan was burnt out.'

The policeman nodded. That had been another long night. 'So what did you do?'

'I told Mattie there was nothing to worry about. I took the gun down off the wall and put my jacket back on. I told her I'd get my tea when I got back. This is it I'm drinking.'

'Go on,' Lindsay encouraged.

'I unlatched the door and went out. That banging noise was even louder from there. I turned to go towards the cowshed, and then there was this awful screech of a sound and all the hens went haywire. It was then I realized the noise wasn't any cow kicking

152

her stall, and it wasn't the bull putting his head up against the wall neither. It was the chicken coop where that racket was coming from, and I tell you it sounded as if all the demons in hell were let loose in there.'

Coggan paused, remembering the scene as if it were rerunning in front of his eyes. 'The gun was in my hands and I broke it and put in two shells of birdshot, 'cause I don't have anything heavier. I was off on the trot, round by the byre and the screeching and clucking was like to take my ears off. Those hens weren't just making the squabble you get when there's a fox or a polecat digging under the wire. They were crying their heads off. When I got round the far side, I saw the hen house. It was *shaking* on its founds. I mean it was moving about, all the walls shivering as if there was a crowd of loonies taking the place apart with sledgehammers. And there was this caterwauling, like some animal, all high and screechy, but growling as well. I could hear things snap, and I thought it was the spars that the groundwire is slung across and I thought to myself it must be the tinkers. They're awful ones for stealing hens.'

Coggan stopped again and looked up from his splayed rough hands, straight at the policeman. 'Now I know you're going to tell me it's not the right thing to do, John, but I cocked that gun and I was going to put an ounce of alpha-max into the first dirty bastard who came out of that door.'

'Understandable, but it would have been a mistake,' Lindsay said agreeably.

The farmer nodded. 'But it weren't no tinkers, though I couldn't see that right away. I got up to the door and the noise was so loud I couldn't hear myself think. All the birds were fluttering around there in a panic, and they were screaming bloody murder, and all the time there is this noise like a big tomcat out on the skite. I reached out and put on the light above the door and it came on right away. Normally it flickers a bit and then it comes on, but not tonight. The light got me right in the eye and nigh-on blinded me. I looked back and I saw that the door wasn't even open. The padlock was still on the hasp, and there's all these chickens, fluttered right up against the wire. I tell you, John, I've never seen anything like it. They were trying to get *through* that mesh any way they could. There was two of them that had pushed their way through the holes so hard they'd stropped their beaks, and one of them had taken its own eye right out with the force. The rest of them were jammed up behind the others, batting their wings and losing feathers, trying to get out. I took the butt of the shotgun and rapped it hard up against the mesh and some of them fell away, but right away they were back up again, squalling and screaming. I swung the butt again, holding on to the two barrels, which was a crazy thing to do, because that gun's got a light trigger and I could have put a hole right through me, but I wasn't thinking straight at the time. I knocked a whole bunch of them off the door and there was enough space to look through the doorway. At first I couldn't see a thing, and the place was covered in feathers. It was as if the kids had been having a right old pillow fight in there and burst a couple. The place was flying with feathers, a whole storm of them whirling about in the air, and there were chickens fluttering and cluttering around all over the place.

'And there was something else. I couldn't make it out, but there was something in amongst them all, moving fast and wailing like a banshee. It was black, or dark grey. I couldn't tell among all the fluttering birds, but it was there.'

'What did it look like?'

'I can't say for sure. It really was hard to see anything, but I could hear it, growling and snapping. Even with the noise of those demented chickens I could hear it tearing them apart. It was moving just like a blur and

154

then another chicken would be gone. One of them came flying back from the middle of the henhouse and battered off the door. Its *skin* had been ripped off with one swipe all down its back along with the feathers. There was hardly nothing left but bones.'

'This thing you saw. What do you think it was? A cat?'

The farmer shook his head. 'I never saw a cat as big as that. If it was a cat, it was black as hell and bloody enormous.'

'That's what I meant. They've had trouble with big cats in a few places. There was that puma down in Ayrshire that was killing sheep for years before they ran it down. And there's supposed to be a black panther up around Sutherland way. I'm thinking it was maybe one of the big ones, escaped from a zoo or whatever.'

'Maybe it was, and maybe it wasn't. I can't say. I never got a good look at it. It was moving so fast I only saw black streaks. I mean, I've *never* seen anything move so quick. Young Willie and Nancy, they watch all the animal programmes on TV. I've seen 'em all too, myself, and none of those cats ever moved as fast as that thing in there. I don't think there's anything that *can* move as quick. It was like watching one of them tornado things they get in the Indies, you know those twisty things that spin. That's what it was like. Couldn't make out an edge to the thing, and it was never in the same place long enough to fix your eye on it. You and me, we've taken the gun to woodcock and duck down on the point at Ardhmor. They can fairly shift, but at least you can *see* them.'

'So then what happened next?'

'I hit the door again with the butt of the gun and some of the birds fell away. They were covered in blood or shit, I can't tell you what. And then I jammed both barrels up against the trigger wire and blasted right into the middle of the coop where I thought that thing was at. I heard the shot smack into some of the birds and some of it rapped up against the far wall. There was another almighty screech, the likes of which I'd never heard before, and a growling noise, like a dog that's worrying at a bone, except this was much louder. I still couldn't see a thing for all the feathers that were flying about, so I put in another couple of shells and cocked the gun. I brought it up against the frame again, and then the commotion started all over again. The hut was shaking fit to burst, and I could feel that thing running around in circles, and then there was an almighty crash and it came straight at the door. The mesh was covered in birds and bits of birds and whatever it was came charging right at me, trying to get me *through* the door, which came bulging out as if somebody had let off a bomb in there, and the wire pinged in a couple of places. Well, that's what happened. The chicken wire spanged apart in the middle, and the birds that were jammed up against it were forced through it, like meat out of a mincer. That fucker was shovin' so hard it was bursting their guts out, and all the time it was screeching and growling like crazy.

'I have to tell you I nearly shit myself into my boots. I mean that thing was *strong*, and if it could squeeze the guts out of those chickens, trying to get at me through the wire, what the hell would it do to me?'

'You've got a point there,' the policeman agreed. 'That's when you shot the gun again?'

The farmer nodded. 'I was scared, sure enough, but I was angry as well. I've got nearly two thousand pounds tied up in those chickens, and getting around twenty dozen eggs a day. At least I did have. And I don't know what the insurance is going to say about this little lot. But yes, I shot again. Both barrels and right through all that mush that was squeezing out of the wire. One-two, and the blast knocked nearly everything off the door. There was a hole about six inches wide in the wire, but it wasn't the gun that did that. It was that thing that was in there, trying to ram its way through, and I'll bet if it had, it would have taken my head off.'

'I reckon you're right enough. D'you think you hit it?'

'I don't see how I could have missed, from that range. Man, I was only two feet away. But I never killed it, that's for sure. There was a quiet, and I thought I *had* killed it. But then I heard this growl. Not as loud as before, but loud enough, and it made the hair on my neck stand straight out. It wasn't a screech, but deep, and scary. And there was me standing with the gun still hot in my hand and no more cartridges. I thought it was going to come at the door again, and I don't think that wire would have stopped it for a minute. I backed off and nearly fell in the mud, for I couldn't take my eyes off the door, and that's why I never got a good look at the thing. I was about ten feet away, and still beatin' a retreat, when the commotion starts up again. There's some thumping and some snarling and some banging, and then everything went quiet.

'I thought I must have killed it. I stood out there looking at the light shining through all the crap on the door, and wondering whether it was safe enough to go and have a look. Mattie came round the corner and shouted something at me and I told her to get back in the house, just in case. Then I got my feet unstuck and went up to the door, but there was nothing in there. Off on the side of the hut there was a big hole, where the thing had broken in. It knocked down nearly a whole frame and, well you saw it, it must have been as strong as a horse. But even though I didn't see it really, it didn't look that big to me. But by God it was faster than anything on this earth.'

'Then what did you do?'

'Then I got on the bloody phone and called you. That's what I did.'

After John had looked again at the carnage in the

chicken shack, he had gone out through the hole in the wall and shone his flashlight over the muddy earth.

'Pugmarks, that's what they call them,' he muttered to himself. He was looking for big tracks, indentations of the pads of a cat, like a leopard or a cougar, something heavy and fierce that had escaped from some private zoo, something large enough to have broken into the coop and gone into some sort of feeding frenzy, destroying more than two hundred chickens.

The flashlight beam showed scrape marks on the wood where something had battered in the side of the coop, using enormous force. And on the ground there were deep gouges as if spikes had been driven into the mud. There was a whole jumbled series of them, making it difficult to identify which mark belonged to which set. Further out, there was a single trail of marks, leading away from the hut across the field to a stand of close-packed spruce. These were easier to isolate one from the other, but that exercise only brought another problem.

For the spike marks were all that there were. There were no impressions of pads or feet. Just deeply gouged holes, as if whatever had been in and slaughtered all the chickens in the space of a mere few minutes hadn't walked on feet at all. It seemed as if its limbs ended in curving claws, and the creature walked on the tip of them.

What was worse, for a country boy like John Lindsay, was that each of the gouged sets showed that the thing had seven claws on each foot, fore and aft. And he knew there was no animal in Scotland – hell, no animal in the *world* – born like that.

In his little office, John stood up and stretched the night's ache from his bones, and picked up his hat from where it lay on the bar. He unslung his jacket from the hook and put it on. He lifted up the swing-top that let him through to the public side and dropped it with a clatter. As he got to the door, he turned and looked at the solitary blank sheet that curved off the top of the typewriter's roller. He just didn't know what to put on it that he was prepared to send down to the divisional office in Levenford.

'Fuck it,' he snorted, and pushed his way through the door.

Alan almost bumped straight into Alex Graham, who was coming out of the grocery shop with both arms hefting a cardboard box filled to several inches above its rim.

Automatically he said sorry and held an arm out to prevent her falling backwards into the doorway. Then he realized the person behind the box was the young doctor.

'My fault, my fault,' she said. 'I just can't see over the top of this thing.'

'Here, let me take it,' Alan said, and grappled the box from the young woman. She smiled gratefully and let her breath out. In Alan's arms, the box wasn't heavy but it was awkward to carry. It was filled with groceries, tins and a couple of loaves which were perched precariously on top of everything.

'You look as though you're trying to feed an army,' he said.

'Near enough. I'm returning the compliment to Tom and Beth, and I've a couple of friends coming across from Edinburgh who've just arrived in Scotland.'

She pointed further along the street to where her car was, a small hatchback, and Alan grappled with the box. He could just see over the top of it, making it possible for him to walk without falling.

'Hey, I should have thought. Why don't you bring Helen along tonight? I can easily make enough for another couple of bodies.'

'Oh, that would be great, but I've got problems. I've got to get back to work tomorrow, and there are some last-minute things to get sorted in the house, and then there's the babysitting scenario. We haven't been here long enough to get that side of things organized. We just don't know anybody yet.'

'Oh, that's not a problem. I can rustle you up half a dozen good sitters any time you like. There's too many young girls around here who jump at the chance of spending a night in a big house away from their younger sisters and brothers. I was a bit like that myself.'

'Well, if you could, that would be great, but really I have to finish some things otherwise I'll never get back to work. And if I don't get there tomorrow, with all the time I've had off, there won't be any work to go to.'

Alex smiled and shrugged her shoulders, sending the light glinting off her red hair in waves. 'Next time, then,' she said. 'Any time, in fact. Don't hesitate to drop in, and by the way I was speaking to a couple of people in Glasgow about the twins. If you don't mind, I can arrange to have one or two of the best to have a look at them.'

'I don't mind at all,' Alan said. 'That's really very good of you, Alex.'

'No, it's no problem. Anyway, I started my career in child medicine and psychology, and I can tell you there's *nothing* wrong with those two ladies. At least, nothing that can't be put right.'

'Well, that's the most encouraging thing I've heard in a long time,' Alan said, feeling a burst of warmth towards the young doctor. 'Listen, I thought you were in general practice. I didn't know you were a specialist.'

'Yes and no. I am a specialist, more or less. But I came across here to find my roots, and the doctor took me on as a locum. I give him a hand whenever I can, but most of the time I'm up at the university or York-hill. That's the hospital for sick kids. We do some good work.'

'I don't doubt it,' Alan observed gallantly. The weight of the box was beginning to make his arms ache. 'So what made you stay after your sabbatical?'

'I found that roots aren't always what you find. I just fell in love with this place. It's as much home to me as anywhere now.' She stopped and looked at him. 'You look as if that's killing you.'

'Quite frankly, it's pulling my arms out of their sockets.'

'Well, thanks for carrying it for me. I would probably never have made it to the car.' She reached for her keys and clicked the lock, flipping up the tailgate on its pneumatic hinges. Alan clumsily dumped the box inside, and felt the warmth steal up his arms as the pressure was removed.

'Thank God for that. I won't be able to hold a pen tomorrow.'

'Oh, while you're there, give my regards to Mike.' She flashed Alan a big smile again and thanked him for his help. 'I must be getting back to start on this lot, otherwise it'll be burgers from the icebox.'

'Have a nice day, you hear?' Alan called in a bad Texan accent. Alex shot him a dismayed look, then laughed. She started the car and drove off along the Creggan Road.

When they had returned to the house, Helen's blithe mood seemed to have sloughed off her within minutes. There was nothing that Alan could define. It just seemed that once in behind the big panelled doors Helen had withdrawn again away from him. She had said she was tired and had gone for a lie-down.

When he'd taken the kids in the car to go down to the shops, Helen, who'd been dozing on their bed, came suddenly awake with a small start. She'd been dreaming again, and while the substance of the dream spilled away from her like water droplets, she was left with that strange warm feeling, that wanted feeling.

She slowly got up and went into the bathroom and turned on the shower. As the steam filled the room, the mirror misted over while she stared at herself, watching her image blur on the glass. Dreamily she felt her body slacken. Shapes moved behind the condensation, her shape, and beyond that another that was coalescing out of the misty surface. Helen felt a small shiver run down her back and felt the warm, needed feeling steal through her again. She closed her eyes and sighed, and the dark came and washed over and within her, taking her over.

She gave herself over to the warm dark, inviting it in.

EIGHTEEN

Seumas Rhu MacPhee fluttered his foot on the brakes
and eased the old Morris Traveller round the tight bend
on the steep dip that joined Creggan Road to Peaton
Road where the way narrowed on the swing down past
the point. He was humming tunelessly to himself, just
loud enough to be heard over the rattle of the chassis
and the clatter of the valves in the ancient engine. The
old van had seen better days. Hell, it had seen better
decades.

But it had done him proud over those years, even
though it could be a bitch to start in the mornings and
shook, rattled and tried to roll now at every curve in
the road. Lashed on top of the scratched and dented
roof, the old wooden shifting ladders jounced and
crumped with every dip. Seumas could see the first four
rungs swinging down into view every time the old
shock absorbers spanged with the judder of the wheels.
The extra weight made the back wheels skitter on the
corners, reminding him to be doubly careful with his
feathering on the brakes. It had been a murderous job
getting the big old ladders up on to the rack. He didn't
fancy hauling them out of a ditch and doing it all again.

The final bend he took at five miles an hour, feeling
the ladders slither against the clothes rope that held
them on the roof, and then he was on the gentle curve
that led down to the Crombies' house. He sat on the
edge of the seat with his cap turned back on his head
like a rally driver of bygone times. Half a cigarette was
jammed behind one of his jug-handle ears and his big
working hands were clamped in a killer's grip on the
big black wheel. At the driveway at Cromwath he eased

the old Traveller through the gateway and willed it up the incline on the pebbled curve towards the house.

Alan Crombie's car was gone. Seumas remembered that the new owner of the big house had told him he would be away for the day, but just to carry on with the work on the roof. There were a couple of slates down, probably from the gales that had swept up the firth during the winter, those cold wet winds that batted spray from the tops of the big grey waves which seemed to blow up from the Irish Sea in a dead straight line towards the point. The slates were no great problem for Seumas who had been up on every roof in Creggan, Corbeth and Murrin, and just about every other place on the peninsula, in the last fifty years. He'd already had a look at the strongly pitched roof with his expert's eye and worked out there might be a dozen or so slates that had slipped out from under and skittered down to crunch into the guttering. Earlier in the morning he'd taken a turn down to the council's works yard on the edge of Kirkland where he'd been able to talk Sam Galbraith the gateman into letting him have a pile of good Ballachullish slates in usable condition for a quick backhander. Sammy had made the three pounds disappear into his big old jacket with the practised speed and ease of a conjuror. All gatemen have the knack.

Seumas parked the Traveller at the garage side and walked round the front of the house. The windows were black and opaque, dead square holes that showed only shadow, as if they were tinted to keep the light out and the dark in. As he passed the front door where the steps led up towards the porch with its two pillars, Seumas heard a noise, faint but definite, from inside the house. A small hiss. The sound of water running. He walked around the path to the back of the house and peered in the window at the kitchen, thinking that perhaps a tap had been left on. Up against the window, shading his eyes against the dim reflection of his own face, he leaned forward until his nose was right up against the glass. It was dark in there, so dark he could barely make out the shape of the taps at the kitchen sink which were only inches from the window. Behind the glass, the darkness seemed cloudy and thick as if all the light of the morning were being sucked away from the window and broken up into shadows. But although Seumas couldn't see a thing, there was no noise from the kitchen.

He leaned back and walked backwards on to the grass on the drying green and looked at the upstairs windows. The small one in the middle that jutted from the slates in a dormer triangle was slightly open. There was a light on, and through the small gap in the open frame Seumas could just make out a faint sheen of steam. That's where the noise was coming from. Someone was in the bathroom, or had been, and was either having a shower or had left the hot tap running.

Seumas had just about decided to slip the window latch and crawl through a downstairs window when he heard another noise above the hissing of the water. Someone was talking. He could hear the murmur faintly through the half-opened dormer. At first he couldn't decide if he'd just imagined it, the way he'd sometimes heard voices from around the corner in Glen Peaton where the narrow valley dog-legged and zigzagged down to the loch. Sometimes the echo of the tumbling water sounded like mumbled conversation.

But no, the sound came again. It was definitely someone speaking. A woman's voice. Seumas couldn't make out the words, but once he'd identified the sound, he felt a small relief that he wouldn't have to break into the house. It must be Mrs Crombie, he thought to himself. No danger of the bath flooding. He shrugged his shoulders and walked round to the front of the house. He struggled to get the ladders off the rack and managed to swing the double span on a slant against the stonework. That done, he paused for a breather before hauling the slates, heavy and awkward in their wooden boxes, out from the swung-open tailgates, and dumped them below the rungs.

The ladder swayed under his weight as he stood eight feet up. He swung back to pull the tip away from the wall, shoving with his hands gripped palm upwards to raise the ladder higher. This was always the difficult part. Seumas didn't have enough weight really to swing the big double out and slide the top ladder higher with every jerk. But eventually the extension moved up until it clattered on the gutter, relieving the friction on the top and allowing the small man to slide it higher, giving him access to the roof. When it was set in place and he had jounced it from side to side to make sure it wouldn't slide he eased himself down the ladder, counted out ten of the big slates and slung them into an old canvas shoulder bag. This done, he hitched on his heavy carpenter's belt with the leather slots for the hammer and the deep pocket for the nails, and slung the coiled nylon rope over his shoulder. Back at the top of the ladder, he scrambled on to the steep slate pitch and gently scaled the incline to the ridge next to the chimney. He looped the rope, swinging the heavy knot round the massive block like a lasso and catching the end which he deftly tied in a double-hitch, then locked the knot with an extra one. From his pocket he pulled another piece of rope which he threaded through the heavy belt. Then he cinched it tightly before joining it to the finely braided main nylon length in a climber's safety-hitch which would slide up and down the line allowing him to move about the roof, but would lock tight if he slipped. It was a long drop to earth from the top of the roof. Seumas had no great fear of heights, but he took no chances. So far he'd been lucky. He'd also been careful.

The morning sun was bright and beat straight down on to the slope of slate which was just at the right angle to take the full heat. The blue-black roof was warm to the touch and even the slick mossy algae had dried out, making it easier for Seumas's big boots to get a purchase on the smooth slates.

He worked steadily for an hour, scrambling about on the warm roof, feeling the sun on his back and smelling the dust of old stone that swirled up when he hefted one of the big dark rectangles and punched a nail-hole through with an expert whip of the wrist. From the ridge where the flashing was the dull red of landpipe clay and humped in smooth half-circles like the back of a dragon, Seumas could see far out on either side of the peninsula. To the east the rising sun, now higher in the sky and shifting its beams to rake the south corner of the big house, had burned off the early morning sea mist and spangled on the silver water in a coruscation of white daggers.

Much closer in, to Seumas's left as he faced south, the water of Finloch, the narrow strip of water that formed one side of the finger-like Creggan peninsula, was half in shade, a deep grey-blue that showed the glacial depths of the loch. On the Shandon side north of Rhu, the white sails of the dinghies of the Northern Yacht Club signalled morse as the little boats yawed and heeled. To his right, almost behind him, Loch Creggan on the other side was a lighter blue where its sheltered, calm waters reflected back the cloudless sky, and mirrored, on its far side, the serried ranks of sitka spruce that marched up the Cowal hills to the tree line nearly two thousand feet up, just below the grey rocky crags that towered over the calm waters like jagged teeth.

The villages of Corbeth, Murrin and Feorlin, connected by the grey string of the twisting Creggan Road that snaked round the headland, nestled side by side in their sheltered coves, diminishing in size in direct proportion to their distance from Creggan itself. Feorlin, huddled in the outcrop that formed the narrows where the hook on the Cowal side swung across the loch nipping it in a tight cinch that was less than fifty yards wide, was only a dozen or so white-stone houses crowded round the small jetty just outside the throat of the narrows.

Seumas surveyed his handiwork from the perch which gave him a vantage of the entire roof from gable to gable with the exception of the small turret on the north corner. The new slates were snug and flat on the slope, chipped and finished to the same size as their fellows, but contrasting darkly against the grey of the old shingles. Given a month or so, the airborne lichen spores would settle on the damp of the next rainstorm and film down the dark to match the rest. There was a piece of ridging that had weathered off but would have to wait until Seumas found a match for it to make a proper repair. He had worked steadily all morning and either slope was littered with the blue-grey debris of small chippings which would eventually slide down into the gutter. They were too small to bother brushing off, or to lodge in the roan-pipe, so he left them for the next rain to disperse. When he finished his cigarette, Seumas gingerly swung himself around and scrabbled across the roof to the chimney where he unhitched the rope. Below him, the voice he had heard from the open window was now silent.

Seumas thought he'd best go down and tell the lady of the house that he'd finished. Probably she'd heard the noise of his scrambling across the slates, but since she hadn't been out to check, he assumed she'd know who it was clambering above her head.

The rope drew back easily once Seumas slipped the lock knot and the two hitches, then he hauled it from the chimney stack. He wound it round in loops, using his elbow as a catch, and tied the loose end around the coil in a neat pack. The climber's stay he just jammed in one of the big, saggy pockets of his jacket, and he started back from the chimney, gingerly watching his footing, until he was above the point where the ladder leaned against the guttering. He turned to sit on the slope, preparing to ease himself down to the ladder, when there was a sort of hitching sensation under him, a tremor that seemed to throb through his boots and up through his palms where they were flat on the slates, meeting in a weird lurch in his stomach.

He stopped moving and the tremor dissipated.

Seumas looked around him. The roof was still. The vibration felt something like the trembling of a building next to a main road when a juggernaut roars past.

He started down again, carefully edging down, feet first with his hands flattened for stability on each side.

Suddenly there was a dizzying lurch, as if the roof had *tilted* first one way, then another, like the deck of a boat in a heavy swell.

The small man's breath jacked in sharply in fright. The lurch of the roof had made his hands slip out on either side and he had come down spreadeagled on the slope. Above him the sky wheeled in a disorienting see-saw, while under him the roof pitched and yawed crazily. It was as if ripples were starting at one gable end and wavering right across the surface to bounce back from the other.

'What the hell . . . ?' Seumas started to say.

For a scary moment, he thought he might have had some sort of stroke that had smacked him down on to the roof. Underneath him he could feel the tilt and sway and his eyes and ears were thrown into such confusion that he didn't know which way was up.

Were his feet pointing down towards the ladder or up towards the ridging? He couldn't tell. His eyes bugged out as another lurch shot through the roof and slid him several feet. It *felt* as if he was sliding upwards, and he knew that was impossible. Inside, his stomach reneged at the inside-out looping that sent instant waves of nausea through him. Frantically he tried to scrabble a hold of the slates and felt his nails catch on the sides of the cut stones, then pull free as he slipped another yard. He rolled with the next lurch, coming face down, panting, on to the shingles. His arms and legs were wide apart, every part of him screaming for purchase where there was none. He realized his eyes had been tight shut and he opened them again. The roof lurched and he *saw* a wave rolling across the surface, like a big comber driving up the firth. He could see the slate edges separating as they went up the wave, spreading wide at the top, then closing like clams as the wave passed underneath them. He heard the snap and rattle as the flat stones were shifted in a jangling rhythm under the bore of the tremor.

That was bad enough.

But what was worse, much worse, was the immense *size* of the waves. The roof seemed to stretch for ever in a great grey expanse that went from horizon to horizon. Seumas was like a fly stuck and exposed on that great rippling desert. The chimney stack seemed miles away, a tall monolith of stone that reached for the sky under the four round towers of the chimneys. Seumas almost broke his neck, still skittering his nails under the edges of the rippling slates, when he jerked his head around to look in the other direction. The other chimney pile was on the far horizon underneath the distant shadow of the conical turret. It looked as if he could walk for days before he reached it.

A rolling wave of the roof passed under him. He could feel the lurching dip that hit first, sending his stomach swooping up, then the slow lift up to the apex.

Time seemed to stretch into infinity. Inside his head Seumas knew that what was happening couldn't possibly be happening.

Up, up and upwards he felt himself on the edge of that crazy looping wave while around him the slates were rising edge-up, opening their carapaces like scales on the back of some monstrous lizard, the mother and father, the great-great ancestor of all lizards.

He could feel it. He could see the waves rolling down in ranks across the impossibly vast roof. But his mind

170

yelled out to him that it wasn't happening. Because even in the midst of this sudden terror, it didn't feel *right*.

His mind held on to that thought in the crazily stretched-out seconds that felt like hours while his fingernails ripped at the undulating, snapping slates.

'It's not happening.' He heard his own voice, hoarse above the clattering scaly slates.

The roof tilted again, curved up, spun, and suddenly Seumas was looking down into an immense depression, a slate ladle, a caldera of shingles. It was like looking down into a whirlpool. He was flattened against the side, looking downwards to where the serried ranks of slates dwindled away in perspective to a black hole. He felt his hands, pressed and hooked on the surface, begin to slip. His boots clattered against the smooth edges, scraping for purchase.

And he felt himself slide.

The cone that minutes before had been the pitch of the roof dived steeply down at an angle that swiftly became perpendicular, like a funnel stood on its end, like a whirling tornado of stone.

Something at the back of Seumas's mind, something from way back when he sat at his mother's knee, clicked into clarity.

He felt his fingers slip and he shuddered down ten, twenty feet and grazed to a stuttery halt, head down, facing the black maw in the centre of the maelstrom.

'Don't believe you,' he grunted through his teeth. 'Hear me? I don't believe you,' he bawled, and his words were flipped and carried across the undulating stone.

And even as his mind forced the words from his throat, another part of that mind, the part that had listened at his mother's knee long ago, knew that something was putting that nightmare vision in his head.

For in the split second that he looked into the black hole at the centre of the huge funnel, he had felt something cold and alien, felt the touch of something dank and scaly flitter right through him.

'Get out,' the small man yelled. 'Get you out of my head.'

There was a slip, a sliding sensation, and he skittered another twenty, maybe thirty feet down the incline towards the dark. From the corner of his eye, he could see the ridging of the roof, now vast and plated like the humped back of a stegosaur, like a *dragon's back*, piked up against the skyline. He opened his hands up and completely let his grip go.

He shut his eyes tight and wiped out the picture of the rolling waves on the vast plain. He shut out the image of the great dark funnel into the black pit. He refused to *believe* it.

Instead he pictured the roof. The chimney stacks, the turret at the far end. The old double-extended ladder propped up against the gutter. He held on to that thought like a pit bull, for dear life.

And the cold, shuddery feeling that he had felt passing through him abruptly recoiled from him.

There was one more lurch and he slid forwards, jerked to a halt and opened his eyes.

He was on the roof. Only the roof. He had come down maybe twenty feet in all from the ridging. Two feet before his eyes was the propped-up end of the old ladder, splintery and grey and solid. Beside that there was a thirty-foot drop on to the rockery at the corner of the house.

Seumas slid himself down the last couple of feet and reached out with shaky hands to grip the ladder posts. Gingerly he eased himself over the gutter, hooked a boot around on to the rung and let himself descend to the ground. Once his feet were on the pebbles of the path, he turned around on jittery legs and promptly ejected his breakfast into the azaleas.

This done in two wrenching heaves, he forced himself across the path to the lawn where his legs suddenly lost their strength. His small wiry frame just seemed to go loose, and he sat down on the lush grass with a slight thump. His hands were shaking as he reached into a pocket for a cigarette from his battered pack. They continued to quiver like a drunk's as he made several attempts to light it with his ancient Zippo before being forced to use both hands to keep the blue flame steady. Even then the shakes were so strong that he had to concentrate hard to join the flame to the cigarette long enough to light it, and then he drew in long and hard, pulling the smoke right down into his lungs, feeling the instant hit as the nicotine launched itself into his bloodstream.

'There's something not right here at all,' he said aloud, blowing out a plume of blue smoke. Beside him a bee buzzed on an embroidered patch of daisies, and a small, practical and involuntary part of his mind noted the fact that he would have to come and mow the lawn in a week or so. Over at the hedge against the wall, a blackbird warbled its liquid notes, and out over the loch, herring gulls wheeled and squalled. From any vantage-point it was a bright, early summer day.

But Seumas could feel the beginning of some dark, wintry shade. He wasn't sure what it was, but he knew if he thought about it long enough it would come to him.

'Something definitely wrong all right,' he said out loud again.

There was something. A memory that nudged away insistently but wouldn't come out into the open. Seumas chased it instinctively.

There had been something. A year or two back, maybe more. More like twenty years. The year Tom Callander's boy had gone missing. The year his old mother had suddenly gone blind. Something had happened that year that gave him the same creepy feeling that now jittered around on the inside of his skull.

It would come, he told himself. I've felt this before.

The sun beat down on top of his cap and seeped warmly through his tattered jacket as he sat there on the grass, thinking.

In the bathroom Helen listened to the hiss of the shower spray while she got her towels together. The sunlight didn't reach through the small dormer window at this time of day and already the small strip light over the oval mirror was competing with the steam.

The bathroom was certainly one of the main attractions of the house for her. It was wide and spacious, and the central heating boiler was big enough to ensure an endless supply of hot water for either a bath or a shower. Helen liked a soak in a bath so hot it turned her pink, but since Alan had fitted the power motor to the shower supply and connected the wide rose that gave a selection of water flow from needle spray to pulse jet, she loved to stand in the scalding steam and feel the rivulets of liquid heat.

The drizzly rumble of the water pounding on the floor of the shower cabinet was a steady welcome. Helen slid the panel and a grey-white cloud of steam billowed out. She stepped inside, dropping the big towels in a heap on the carpet, and gasped when the hot jets riveted her skin with a searing tingle.

Under the rose she stood with her eyes closed, face tilted to feel the hot pressure beating down on her forehead and cheeks. She could feel the pulse on her mouth, almost tickling, like a weird kiss. The steam built up all around her. Helen breathed in, feeling the hot, vapour-laden air slide down into her lungs, catchy velvet at the back of her throat.

She soaped herself all over, then reached up to the high shelf for the shampoo bottle, squirted a viscous green puddle on to her cupped palm, and began to massage the frothy bubbles into her hair.

The steam billowed, coiling grey-white and dimming the little strip light to a small hot fuzzy spot on the far side of the translucent panel. The shower cabinet was a warm cocoon of dim wetness that slicked around Helen's body as she luxuriated. A feeling of well being flitted through her and she welcomed it. It had been so long since she had felt *good*. So long. Too long.

Dreamily, she let a series of thoughts flitter through her mind. The bad ones she jinked and swerved from, allowing them to slide past her, bouncing off her mental filter. Those were the dark thoughts from back *then*. They had been dreary, black days, woeful times when Helen walked in a world filled with only shadow and deeper shades of dark. And after that had been the strange days when she ran away from the black, from the dark, and stayed still and quiet in a world of grey where no colours could intrude.

Then she had been hauled, screaming and crying, back into the other world and held there despite her panicked attempts to retreat to that place of no pain.

There was the slow, agonized, resentful return to life of a sort while they forced her to go through the motions of what they called normal living. They kept her chained and bound with their presence, their demands, their solicitude.

And in all that time they didn't know that inside her, a part of her had rejected them and everything else. And that sometimes her mind slipped down that crack and into the world of oblivion.

Oh yes, she bore it. She played it. She *did* what they wanted. But even after a while, when they said she was *fine, oh so fine*, there was still the niche at the edge of her mind, where the real Helen cowered from the light.

But now, she was better. She could *feel* it inside herself. Something had changed. Under the hot drizzle she could feel the fine surge through her in a soft wave of pleasure.

Something had changed. It had clicked inside her, like a vital piece of a jigsaw puzzle. It had slotted into place with a soft, subtle snick.

She couldn't recall exactly when it had happened, or how or why.

It was as if she had just found herself; had been lost and alone and scared, and now she had found the place where she should have been. It gave her a warm feeling of being alive, of being in *control*.

Oh, she had hated the house, hated the place, the peninsula, the whole damned country when they had arrived here. The resentment she felt against Alan had been poisonous and hot and overwhelming. It had sat inside her like a branding iron, red and shiny and ready to be launched in a blistering sizzle at anything and everyone. Alan and his back-to-his-roots notions. He had simply gone ahead and made his decision with little or no consultation. He'd dragged her away from everything she had known and bundled them off to this backwoods island and this crumbling old Wuthering Heights where she was certain she would cave in and falter and fail.

She had hated him for that. She had hated the children too, for their obvious delight that excluded her. Tommy had been so excited he hadn't slowed down for days. His hyperactive energy had left her feeling so drained that she wanted to grab him by the ears and shake him until he stopped.

And the twins. The twins had that placid, happy acceptance of everything that happened to them. They never cried. They never knew what it was to cry. It was as if they had left her womb without taking with them their share of the normal misery and anguish of the world, giving her a double, a triple share.

Helen tried not to show it, but she resented the twins for their shiny joyful happiness. She had been unable to cope with their wriggling warmth after the birth, and had been away from them in the ensuing months. She felt she didn't really *know* them. Oh, she washed and bathed them, and she fed them and she kissed them goodnight.

176

Nobody knew that she didn't feel they were a part of her.

They never spoke. Not once. And they never cried. Not once.

It was as if they were playing some baby game, a joke on her. There were times when she had thought *they* were the joke on her. The times when people cooed and aaahed over their gold beauty in the big double pram or when they were sitting sidesaddle on the buggy, and people would ask her if they couldn't speak. Helen would tell them that they were just a bit slow.

In the grey place where Helen's mind still clung for shelter, she could peer at her children, her husband, and feel nothing. The other part of her mind had tried to accept, to cope, but the split, the chasm, had stretched her abilities to the point where she often did not know where she was, how to think, how to cope.

But now she was better. Inside, her resentment dwindled. She could feel the warm internal sparkle as clearly as she could feel the hot pressure of the shower on her skin. The clouds of steam billowed around her, enclosing her in a suffusing blanket of warmth.

She felt so *good* about the house. She felt so welcome here. And after the barren years, with one foot on either side of the chasm in her mind, she felt complete.

There were so many things to do to the place. She wanted to take it over and make it even more perfect. She felt safe and wanted.

Here she had slept so well, and when she awoke she had felt refreshed. Only in the last few days the feeling of well being had enfolded her like a lover.

She stood with her face up into the flow, washing off the mass of suds, and the memory of the dream came back to her, sharp and aching through her loins.

Helen gave a sharp intake of breath, feeling the humid air slide on the back of her throat as a sudden shock of pleasure ran through her. The surge of the pulse rocketed upwards, beaming through her. She almost staggered with the force of it, as if the floor had suddenly lurched.

The shower jetted down, achingly, wondrously warm, and the clouds of steam thickened sharply until they were palpable, wrapping their grey wings around her.

Helen could feel the gauzy billows on her skin, feathering her between the beating drops of water. Another longer wave jolted up, and she held on to it.

How she was doing this she did not know, but she held it, savoured it, and still the mist thickened, blotting out the now dim and distant light.

'Oh, oh,' she gasped, and the small, whimpering noises were swallowed in the mist and the beat of the water. Right from her core, as if she had been stroked, came a shuddering, expanding pulse of ecstasy.

'Oh please,' she said even louder as the floor of the cabinet seemed to wrench again. She took her hands down from her face and planted them wide on the tiled wall.

The buzz came again, rolling up from between her legs, juddering into her brain.

It was happening. Whatever it was, she was going up and over and through. And it didn't matter why. She felt the touch again (in her mind, surely) as clear and as clean as a soft hand.

'Oh!' she mouthed, feeling her hips buck, once, twice, hard and fast against the pressure.

Then they came, the big waves, the great blue rollers that carried her way up and up. Her eyes were screwed up tight, holding on, and she didn't see the mist coalesce, become darker, become almost solid. She didn't care. It felt as if warm, tender hands were all over her slick, smooth body, sliding and easing. She felt pressure, not from the water this time, but like arms enfolding her, and she didn't care. This was the feeling, this was the *wanting*. She could feel it through her feet and through the hands that were almost clawing at the tiles. She felt it course through her and gave herself to it, willingly.

Above her head, Seumas Rhu MacPhee was scared for his life as he looked into the maw of a black funnel that went down a million miles into hell.

But Helen knew nothing but the pleasure that coursed through her body and she gave herself to it, wholly and completely. And something looked into the chasm inside her mind and a cold thought sleeted up and outward.

The almost hidden door in Helen Crombie's mind opened a fraction and welcomed. And other doors elsewhere creaked open.

The moment went on and on and on as Helen's chaotic mind collapsed in on itself and sent her thoughts careening into a maze of tunnels and caverns, and she was gone.

Some time later, outside on the grass Seumas Rhu MacPhee stirred as if waking from a dream. It was not a dream that had fuzzed out his conscious perception of his surroundings, but the concentration of his mind as he searched for the memory. The thought had slid away from his grasp as he tried to remember when he had felt that odd, *invaded* sensation before.

But Seumas, the runt of the litter, had a little of the speciality that had made his mother special. He had the touch, the dowser's touch, that streak of old knowledge and old lore that even in the west coast was a rarity.

The feeling on the roof when he knew that the picture of the world that he was seeing was not a true one, that it had been *put* there by another mind, had come to him with such certainty and clarity that he knew he had experienced it before. He was about to give up chasing the elusive memory when up it came and smacked him on the back of his head.

It had been way back, oh, twenty years or so. It *had* been the year when his mother had gone blind, suddenly, utterly and incurably stone blind. Seumas had insisted on getting the doctor to see her over his mother's protests of 'Never bother, it won't do me a damned bit of goodness no matter what they say.'

She'd been right. Old Dr Patterson had come round and had a peek into his mother's green eyes, flicking on and off a little flashlight, and then he'd sent round a specialist as old Mrs MacPhee had refused to leave the house. He couldn't find anything wrong and suggested a hospital visit, but still the old woman had refused to be budged. 'It's nothing I've got that you nor anyone else can fix, so there's an end to it. I'll be here in the dark till the day I go, so there's no use in saying I won't be.'

The old woman had said that and she'd smiled a smile that sent a chill through the eye specialist who was young and good-looking and obviously a little pissed off at travelling forty miles to see an old ragbag of a wizened woman with perfectly withering eyes and no faith in medicine.

'What I've got, nobody can help,' she'd said in a whisper that Seumas, in the kitchen of the little cottage, could barely hear. 'And maybe you should be thankful for that, young doctor.'

That was the year Tom Callander's boy had gone out in his dinghy and come on to the rocks just down from Cromwath Point and had never been seen again, though they found his jacket up in the trees just behind where Seumas now sat, torn and dishevelled. But there had been no sign of the boy, who was about twelve or thirteen or so. Tom Callander had been a wrecked man at the end of that week when they'd searched high and low, from Rhu right round the loch and up to the hook at Feorlin, thinking he might have been washed ashore on the high tide. How his lifejacket had got up to the old Dalmuir house nobody knew. Some said that maybe some children had found it and had brought it up from the shore, but old Gilbert Neil who'd been the policeman in Creggan for nearly twenty years until he'd retired to his cottage in Murrin had gone round and spoken to every boy and girl on the peninsula, painstakingly asking them what they'd been doing and where they'd been and what they'd found. He'd drawn a blank. And young Tom Callander had never been seen again.

It had been a hot summer night with no wind, and Seumas and a few of the men from Creggan had been combing the Corrie hills just up from the main road without hide nor hair of the boy being found. They were working on the possibility, the remote possibility, that maybe the boy had been hurt when his boat had hit the rocks, and again maybe he'd been wandering in a stupor on the hills. It was late and the light was fading, although right on the midsummer the sky would never be completely dark unless you were in the trees, when they called the search off. Seumas had come down to the road and was taking a shortcut through the trees. It was dark under the tall branches. He'd jumped the low dike and got on to the pathway, saving himself maybe five minutes by walking as the crow flies.

Then he'd passed by the standing stones and he'd looked between the two immense blocks into a shadow that was inky black. There was little enough light in the copse, but between the stones was a dark so unnaturally black that it seemed like a great big hole in the centre of the world.

Seumas had stopped and looked, a little puzzled.

Then had come a scream, a human scream, so piercing in its intensity and so filled with pain that his hair had stood on end right up on the crown of his head.

The small man had been rocked back with the intensity of it, shaken by the terror and agony that was encapsulated in that one, shuddering scream.

And then, as he'd stared into that rectangle of purest black, he had felt something scrabbling at his brain. It was as if his thoughts were being nudged aside by another mind that was trying to force its way in between them and scatter them. It was as if some mind-thief had slipped a thin larcenous hand inside his head and was rooting about trying to steal his very self.

Seumas had felt the scabrous tingle of something very cold and alien, and had cried aloud in disgust. Actually he swore eight times without repeating himself once, and though Seumas was never given to strong language, it had seemed the right thing to do at the time. He had felt the weird inverted feeling of the *other* thing scurrying backwards and there was an even weirder strum *inside* him as the intrusion suddenly ended.

Seumas had stared into the black rectangle and had seen a dim shape in deep shadow. Something moving. He couldn't tell exactly what it was and he really didn't want to know, but it was big and black and monstrous. It seemed to scramble at him, humping and lurching between the stones. He tore his feet from where they'd sprouted roots among the pine needles and went scurrying down the path, smacking in the darkness into the rough bark of a tree and winding himself badly. Behind him, loud but fading fast, as if retreating at a huge speed into the distance, came the cry again. This time it sounded like a cry for help. Maybe it was a cry for help.

But Seumas Rhu was on his way. He didn't want to hear it. And he didn't stop until he got to the Harbour Inn where he drank himself into oblivion in the space of an hour and a half and stayed that way for two days until he'd numbed out the fear and disgust that had surged through him and left him contaminated. He never told another living soul about what he'd seen. Not that anybody would have believed him.

But now. Now he had felt the same thing again. The same scaly, disgusting intrusion of a mind that was horribly alien, horribly insane. And he knew that something bad was going to come of it.

NINETEEN

John Lindsay looked at the reports on his desk. The vet, Sandy Tate, had sent him his findings from the post-mortem he'd carried out on the dog that had been killed. It made gruesome reading. Tate had done a very thorough job.

But even Tate couldn't begin to imagine what could have caused the shocking damage to Matt Stirling's dog.

The policeman hunched himself up on his seat, pulling closer to the desk. The five sheets, stapled at one corner which was bent and curled from the several rereadings, looked like any other vet's report.

Lindsay had seen dozens. If any farm animal died suddenly a copy always came to his office. It was a matter of form. There were always sheep worryings, mostly in the summer when the tourists brought dogs that had never seen livestock. There had been a case of anthrax only a couple of years back that had caused a whole flock to be wiped out, and old George McGlyn who shepherded up on Dumbuie had caught it and had died a terrible purulent death after lying for five days in his croft before anyone found him.

This report was different because it was wildly inexplicable.

Oh, the damage, the horrendous, savage destruction, was easy to describe, and Tate had taken pains to put down every contusion and laceration.

Something had taken hold of the little dog in a crushing grip and had squeezed it so hard that almost every rib on each side of its chest had been cracked and crushed, sending massive shards of bone into the lungs.

One splinter had been pushed so hard that it had gone right into the dog's heart. There was a ragged gash on the dog's neck just above the shoulder blades where it had been held in a bite-like grip that had been enough to crush two of the vertebrae into fragments. The enormous pressure on the chest and neck had swelled almost every blood vessel above the lungs like balloons. The vet had found burst aneurisms in the ears, eyes and in the brain itself. It was as if the dog had been run over by a steam-roller.

And the internal damage, that was what made the policeman squirm in his seat. For he couldn't imagine, no matter how he tried, what could have caused it.

To a certain extent, Matt Stirling had been right when he'd thought that his dog, which had been coming into heat at the time, had let nature take its course. The bitch had been mounted, but it hadn't been any kind of dog that Lindsay could identify. Not even Luath, his big mastiff which was probably the largest dog on the peninsula, could have wreaked such injury on another animal.

But something had gripped Stirling's little retriever and had penetrated it with something so huge that the vaginal and anal walls had been burst asunder. It was as if she'd been impaled on a thick, jagged pole, an enormous sharp spike that had ripped its way right inside and had torn almost every organ in the body to pieces. In his straightforward style, Tate had identified rupturing of the liver and spleen, massive perforations of the intestine, a kidney that had been punctured so savagely that it had been torn loose.

In a most prosaic note, added for the policeman's sole attention, Tate had said: 'I can't imagine *what* could have done this. There is no animal I know capable of inflicting so much internal damage. The crushing to the ribs and the neck could possibly have been achieved by an immensely powerful animal, maybe something like a very large bear, which is unlikely in the extreme. But the pulping of the organs is beyond me. Having seen the extent of the damage, I tend to think that this was perhaps not an animal after all. I think perhaps that someone, or maybe several people, attacked the dog. It looks as though an iron bar or a sharpened pickaxe handle had been hammered right inside her, for there is no animal with anything *that* big. Maybe you should think about some very sick human rather than a wild beast. Is there anybody with that kind of grudge against Stirling? And should we tell him any of this?'

Everything in the report gave John Lindsay a headache.

No, he did not know of anyone with that kind of grudge against the mild-mannered teacher.

No, he didn't believe it would be a wonderful idea to suggest to him that some maniac had grabbed his dog and crushed the life out of it and had raped its innards with a spike. Best let dead dogs die quietly, if they could.

But despite the vet's note, there was a nagging doubt. The policeman threw the sheets down onto the desk and let out an exasperated sigh.

If it had been a sick, crazy nutcase, then how had he managed to inflict such damage in such a short space of time? Lindsay went over his own notes. Stirling had looked out of the window and had seen a dark shape on his dog. He'd gone downstairs to the back garden and the dog had been dying. Whatever had done it had gone. Lindsay had a problem in imagining how the hell *anybody* could have done all that in the two minutes it had taken. Either Stirling had made a mistake, or the vet was hopelessly wrong.

And apart from that, it had certainly been no crazy man who had rampaged in Jack Coggan's chicken shack. Nobody could have torn all those birds apart, no matter how much time he'd had to do it.

The big policeman pushed his chair away from the desk and stood up, stretching until his knuckles almost hit the ceiling. He hauled his tunic off the hook and wriggled into it, grabbed his hat and squared it on his red hair, and went out into the daylight. He tried to dismiss the thoughts that were rolling about on their own, and failed.

TWENTY

Mike Toward's boisterous bear hug had left Alan almost gasping for breath when he finally made it to his new office on the second floor of MacKenzie-Kelso in the city of culture.

'Good to have you back, little buddy,' Toward twanged. Alan was a shade under six feet tall, but by comparison to the American's massive frame he looked slight.

'Little *boss*,' Alan said, returning Mike's exuberant handshake and smiling at his associate's ebullient good humour. 'I hope you've kept everything ship-shape for me.'

'Aye aye. And I believe it's time I was piped from the bridge. Way over time.'

'It's good to be back, for a rest. I've been putting in a sixteen-hour day since I started on Wuthering Heights. If there's anything left to do, it'll have to wait until next year.'

'Not much to do to that old place,' Mike said. 'I went over it with a slide rule and a flashlight. I reckon you've made a pretty good buy there.'

'Me too, but you know what it's like getting a place liveable. It's been empty for six months or more . . .'

'More like five,' Mike interrupted. 'Look. I got you a present,' he said and drew Alan across to his desk. On the shiny flat surface was a bound folder that had been slickly done in MacKenzie-Kelso's red and black colours. On the cover was one word in bold letters: Cromwath.

'We got the Sasines check done through the legal boys and ran off a copy for you. Gives you the whole history of the place from day one. It still knocks me out how you Scots have everything written down that anybody has ever done. That old place of yours was built way back more than a hundred years ago. And guess what?'

'What?' Alan said. He'd picked up the slim folder and was thumbing through it.

'It only cost sixteen hundred sterling. Foundations, bricks, stone, the works. Those were the days, amigo. You could have bought the whole country for twenty grand.'

'You still can, just about, the way everything else is being sold off.'

'That Dalmuir fellow, he sounds like a real old character.'

'Who?'

'The guy who built your house. Sixteen hundred pounds! When you think of the budgets I've got to work with, it sounds like heaven to me.'

'Polarized society then, Mike. Not like the good old US of A where everybody's equal by law. In fact, it looks as if we're getting back to that now.'

'And which pole are you at?'

'Who knows?'

Alan looked up from the booklet. The Register of Sasines report, he knew, would show the whole history of his house, land rights, boundaries and borders. It was something he hadn't considered before when he'd bought the place. He knew from the style and construction that it was about a hundred years old, but he hadn't considered who had built it. He knew the register would list everybody who had owned the house since then. It would be an interesting file to read.

He held it up to Mike. 'Thanks a lot,' he said. 'It's a nice touch.'

Mike waved his hand deprecatingly. 'It was nothing, and the firm paid for it anyway.'

'No. I appreciate it. Now I can find all the skeletons in the cupboards.'

'No luck there, compadre. All you get is prices and owners. The skeletons you got to find them yourself.' Mike threw him a wide grin and a mock salute, and left him alone in the bright executive office.

Alan didn't manage to read the report until the weekend. He didn't have time for anything but work after the first hour in the office where he was introduced around by Tony Kelso, the number one partner. Most of the people he'd met before, and the others' names and faces he filed away. The first meeting gave him a picture of company operations in the various locations in the UK, and Alan was able to compare them with his picture of the state of the game a month before. There were a few areas that needed attention, but by and large Mike Toward had kept his seat warm for him. There were no major problems.

But Alan got his new secretary to haul out the files on all the projects, and examined them minutely. He called for a list of all the contracts, and then the contracts themselves, refreshing his memory, giving himself the picture. Then it was down to work, an endless initial round of meetings and discussions and site visitations. At night when he drove along the Peaton Road towards home, he was washed out from the unaccustomed effort of using his brain. He didn't even notice, not that first week, that Helen had become more and more vague and distracted.

At the weekend he had to go back to the office to put in a morning's work on last-minute details of a contract on the new jetty on the Moray Firth, and it was only when leaving the office just before lunch that he came across the report on the house. He slipped it in his briefcase and forgot about it until later that afternoon when he was sitting in the garden enjoying a cool beer. The children were playing around in the orchard, the high-pitched tinkle of their laughter echoing from under the spreading boughs, and Helen was somewhere in the house, beavering away as usual. Alan thought she was overdoing the house mother bit but refrained from saying so.

He went into the house and fished the booklet from his case and took it back out, along with another can of beer, to the garden table, and sat down to read.

The report had been copied from the old register in Edinburgh where the details of every land transaction since the days of Alexander were kept in the huge vaults. Scanning quickly through the pages, Alan screwed up his eyes against the glare of the sunlight reflecting off the page and shifted position so that the writing was in shadow. The first entries were in a fine copperplate script that was ochre with age, detailing the purchase of the land known as Cromuath from the estate of the late John MacFarlane, farmer, of Corrie in the Parish of Creggan. That had been in September of 1887. The eleven acres had cost Andrew Dalmuir four hundred pounds cash, and the parcel had included a strip of the headland off the point, some forested land, paddocks and grazings to the south and east of the old Corrie farm. That same month Dalmuir, listed in the Sasines as an ironfounder, of Glasgow and Lanark, had been given consent to build a home on the land and had spent a good part of his fortune on constructing the house, finally completing it eighteen months later. He sold off one plot of land in 1889 to a Dr Kintyre for a three hundred-pound killing, and a further two parcels, each for four hundred pounds, six months later to a Gregory Callander and a Wallace Macleod, still keeping the bulk of the land for himself, but shrewdly obtaining the money to build virtually the whole of his house.

The record showed that for all his wheeling and dealing, Dalmuir did not enjoy the house for long, for in 1895 there was a new owner, listed as Alan Laing, who bought Cromwath, as the house was now known, from the estate of Dalmuir. He paid a mere thousand for the whole, showing that property values had fallen off a little in the course of seven years or so.

Laing stayed in the place for thirteen years before selling it in 1908, twenty-one years after Dalmuir had started building.

The new owners, the John Davidsons, he a solicitor and notary public, stayed a little longer, enjoying the life on the point until 1929 when again Cromwath changed hands. This time another medical man took over the pile, paying out the vast sum of two thousand pounds and loose change for a home in what was becoming a sought-after retreat for the comfortably off. His daughters, Jessica and Philippa Kinross, inherited the house in 1951 and lived there until about the middle of 1975, probably at some ripe old age, when the executors of their estate sold it off again for the huge sum of forty thousand pounds.

The penultimate owner was a Gerald McGrath, a haulage contractor, who took over that autumn and occupied the house until the new year before Alan brought his family north. He had left the sale in the hands of his solicitors. They had accepted offers through the estate agency who showed prospective buyers around the place on request.

Alan smiled wryly when he considered Dalmuir's land dealing and his building price for the house. He and Mike Toward had appraised the building and the stonework with their professional eyes and they had noted the fine oaken joists, the teak banisters, the close-grained, finely masoned facing stones. They had pointed out the blue, almost purple edgings with which the doors and windows had been bordered, along with the cornerstones of the gable walls, which threw the other stone into contrast. They had checked out the fine plasterwork, and the high-quality slating and lead flashing, which, but for a few windblown shingles, was as good today as it had been more than a hundred years ago.

Both men knew that you couldn't begin to build an old house of those dimensions and with those materials for much under a quarter of a million at modern prices. Alan thought he'd got a bargain in keeping the price down below one-forty, and that was only because of the relative isolation of the place.

But if he'd been able to buy it at the original price, it would have been like a pools win. Old Dalmuir, he thought, must have been stinking rich.

On his way to the office the following day, Alan dropped Tommy off at the gate of the little primary school at the far end of Creggan where the children from all over the peninsula were taught.

Since Tommy had started there, shy for his first few days, he'd begun to get used to the idea and was already making a few friends. Mrs Ross, the headmistress, was a friendly and outgoing young woman and seemed to run a good school in the little old Victorian building.

Alan watched his son disappear beyond the heavy cast-iron gate and merge himself with a crowd of boys his own age. He waved automatically, not noticing whether Tommy waved back, and drove off up the Creggan Road.

At home Katie and Laney were playing their *game*.

The house was a wondrous maze of rooms and passages, and places *between*, where they could run and play and hide. Their tiny sandals pattered on the polished wooden floor of the top hall as the pair chased each other through the house. Downstairs they could hear the hoarse drone of a vacuum cleaner from the front room. Overhead there was a soft bubbling hiss as the hot water tank slowly filled. Katie ran ahead and swung herself into their room, skidding momentarily on the polished floor, two yards ahead of her sister. She could feel the laughter of the *game* bubbling up inside her. Her

192

little knees pumped as she ran towards the cupboard set into the wall, and the *between* opened and she ran through into the warm, echoing silence.

She giggled to herself as she ran down the slope, hearing the patter of her feet reverberate softly from the far wall. Behind her she could *feel* Laney close by, on the *outside*, not yet *between*. There was a little pulse, a twist in the air, a change of pressure that was like a tickle, and Laney was *there*, hard on her heels, chuckling. Katie ran down the slope, hearing the paired footfalls, almost in unison. When she came to the warm wall at the bottom she turned left and opened the kitchen cupboard and stepped out into the sunlight that slanted down through the window. The kitchen was the *right* place. If she'd turned right she would have come out of the door that opened into the front room, where the whine of the vacuum cleaner, now loud, showed that was where their mother was working.

It was a game they'd discovered on their very first day. The *between* places were their own, places to go and play. They could open the doors and walk through. It didn't occur to them to consider that neither of their parents, nor even Tommy, who was always a warm red buzz at the back of their thoughts no matter where he was, not even Tommy went into the other places. It was their own space.

Katie barged out of the kitchen and along the bottom hall, turning right again for up the staircase.

At the first landing, still chuckling to herself and to her twin, she called: 'Come on, slowcoach. Hurry up!'

'I'm coming. Race you to the top,' Laney called back.

If their mother had been in the hall, she would have heard nothing but the clacking of tiny heels.

Helen had worked steadily since she'd arrived home. Normally, at least for the past year or so, she'd have treated herself to a break from housework (for which she'd never had any enthusiasm anyway) and had a coffee and a biscuit in the mid-morning while the twins, and Tommy if he was home, would have a glass of milk. Now she just didn't want to stop. She felt fired up, jittering with energy, moving in top gear.

There was just no time for anything else. The housework, *her* housework, had to be done. She had never felt like this about any other place, even as a child. It was as if she and the house had been made for each other.

Helen vaguely remembered her arrival at the place, when she was still dark and fuzzy and unsure. It was hard to recall how she'd looked at the house and disliked it on sight. She couldn't remember when that feeling had changed, suddenly, when she realized that this was *the* house. This was *her* place.

She only knew that now she belonged. When she closed the front door behind her and stepped into the wide hallway, she felt the warmth, the comfort, the need steal around her, enfolding her in a glow. And the insistent voice in her head, the soothing whisper, urged her to care for the house. In the night she dreamed wonderful scenes and the same voice told her they were *together*, and the warmth snuggled her and carried her away until she forgot about everything else.

Down in the front room Helen vacuumed and dusted and polished, and then moved on to the drawing-room with its big open fireplace and started again. Soon she would move on to the kitchen where she'd scrub and shine until her hands were red and scadded.

She didn't hear the skitter of her daughters' feet on the stairways and in behind the walls. She didn't notice them when they came into the drawing-room where she was busy waxing the polished wooden floor to a gleaming shine. They'd stood, hand in hand, watching her, not smiling, just watching, unable to tell her they were hungry. At three o'clock in the afternoon, they reappeared, clutching a box of cornflakes, standing in

194

the open doorway, unable to realize why their mother hadn't fed them.

She only noticed them when she started on the kitchen and found them at the table, each crunching her way through a bowl of dry cereal. But it was the scattered cornflakes on the floor that she noticed first. She'd crunched them underfoot when she'd walked into the room, and felt the instant fury boil up inside her at the mess on the floor, a soaring high-pitched wrath that surged behind her eyes, momentarily fierce, before snapping off suddenly as the insistent tugging in her brain withdrew into the shadows.

And then, for a while, she was herself again.

'Oh dear,' she said wearily, 'I didn't even realize the time. Here, let me get you something proper to eat.' She rummaged about in the fridge and began preparing lunch. The twins watched her, blankly, curiously.

Later, when she and they were fed and they'd gone back to playing out in the garden (*and sometimes in the house*), that the shadowy insistence came back again, tugging gently at her will, feeling for the weak spot, the flawed part of her mind that was still tender, still wounded, still dark from the difficult times of the past. It *oozed* inside and whispered softly, and Helen went back to work.

TWENTY-ONE

'I just don't believe it,' Alan said very slowly, every word an enunciated hiss through teeth that were clenched right up to the molars. 'Look at this place.'

In the doorway of his little study, Helen stood, facing him, eyes flashing in righteous indignation. 'But it was such a mess. It was like a pigsty.'

'And it was *my* pigsty,' Alan bawled back. 'I had everything where I wanted it. Everything . . .' He spread his hands and looked around the small room that he'd set up as an office. It was shining, polished, neat. All the documents that he'd had spread on the old rolltop desk were gone. Even the Texas calculator that the London office had given him as a farewell present had disappeared.

Alan gestured around the room, demonstrating unnecessarily to Helen who stood defiantly with her hands on her hips. Then, as he turned, a grey shape caught his eye. It was a folder that jutted out of a slick black bin-bag leaning against the door. Helen had been hauling the bag out of the room when Alan came upstairs and found her in his sanctuary.

'What the hell is *that*?' He virtually leapt across to the doorway and grabbed the bag, spilling the papers that were on the top of the rest of the rubbish. They cascaded on to the floor. 'It's the Moray contract. What in God's name is it doing here? I've spent five days working on this.' He stopped and straightened up, running the fingers of his right hand through his hair in frustrated exasperation. They were trying to curl themselves into angry fists.

'I didn't know they were so important,' Helen shot back sullenly.

'Important?' Alan could hear his voice rising up an octave as simple disbelief and frustration competed for pole position. 'They're so bloody important that if they had gone to the bloody rubbish dump I'd be out of a bloody job. There's near enough ten million in paperwork there. Jobs depend on it. The clothes on your damned back depend on it. Just leave me alone. And leave this room alone. It's my office. It's out of bounds. *Verboten.* Understand?'

Helen spun round on her heel and strode along the hallway. He could hear the angry clack clack of her mules on the floor, then the heavy staccato on the stairs. Alan started to riffle through the papers that had spilled on to the floor. He was still in a state of panicky disbelief at the sheer stupidity his wife had demonstrated. He did not understand it. He opened the glass door that fronted the shallow cupboard and threw the papers inside, making sure that nothing important had been left in the bag.

Still angry, he slammed the cupboard door hard enough for the glass to rattle. There was a little thump as the books and documents banged against the back of the wall.

TWENTY-TWO

Alex Graham stood on the steps under the stone porch and waited for a moment, watching the evening sun strike red highlights on to the smooth hills across the loch. Far out on the water the faint cries of wheeling gulls came wavering in, thin and mewling. Overhead the moon was a pale half-disc, not yet night bright.

The garden of the old Dalmuir place was looking neat and well tended on the slope of the lawn as it curved down towards the gateway. On either side the clipped balls of rhododendron were bright with pom-pom clusters of opulent pink flowers. A warm breeze eddied and trailed on the deep blue waters of the loch, spangling the water. Alex took a deep breath, taking in the honey scent of honeysuckle. Just at her right, where the vine mixed its blossom with the broad green leaves of Virginia creeper, a late bee hummed tiredly.

Alex thought the whole peninsula a beautiful place. She didn't mind the drive to Glasgow where she spent half her working life, for Creggan, that long arm of rock and tree and heather that separated the two deep lochs, was in her mind a part of paradise.

This was where her people had come from, way back a hundred years and more. This was home. In some ways it reminded her of her other home, across the Atlantic, although the coast was more like the land around St John in New Brunswick, or better still like the fiord that ran up to Truro on Nova Scotia. The Creggan peninsula wasn't so cold in winter, of course. Here the sea never froze, despite being much further north than any of those places, and those banks of fog, grey and swirling damp from Boston to Newfoundland, could not exist for long in this clear air.

At first it had been strange and exciting. Her mother and grandmother had told her tales of the old place where the Grahams had come from, stories handed down for a couple of generations, romanticized perhaps, even nostalgic. But none of them had prepared her for that wonderful feeling of *belonging* when she drove round the head of the loch and down the stretch of the peninsula.

Working with Dr Docherty (she had laughed aloud the first time she heard one of the local children refer to him as Doc Doc) wasn't onerous and it allowed her ample time for her research in Glasgow's Yorkhill Hospital, which even in the States had an almost unrivalled reputation for its excellence in child medicine. Both fields also gave Alex enough time for her research on her family history, on finding her real roots. After almost two years on the peninsula, the plans she'd had of flying back across the Atlantic had faded to maybe, might be, to perhaps. Recently she just hadn't thought of it at all.

Alex pressed on the old doorbell again. From deep within the house came its muffled sound, and she waited a few moments longer, watching the shadows lengthen on the other side of the loch. A noise behind her made her turn. The door opened an inch or two. In the shadow she saw a figure behind the edge, peering from within, only an outline. Then the door opened further and Helen poked her head, almost warily, past the jamb.

'Hi, I thought I'd drop by tonight,' Alex said, smiling. 'I should have done it sooner, but I've been kept busy this last week.' She stepped forward and held her hand out to Helen, who seemed confused, as if she hadn't recognized her. She looked as if she was still drowsy from sleep.

Helen peered out, not opening the door fully, screwing her eyes up uncertainly.

'It's me. Alex. Don't you remember we met at Tom's place the other week? I came round to have a look at Tommy's bruises.'

Helen stared at her, making Alex feel uncomfortable.

'By the way, how's he coming along? I expect he's up and running again.'

Helen nodded vaguely, still holding the door half-shut.

'If you'd like me to come back another time,' Alex ventured, and made to step back. Helen's expression went blank for an instant, then she seemed to start, as if she'd been thinking about something else and had suddenly come back to the present.

'Oh, no. I mean . . .' She paused and shook her head. 'Sorry, I didn't recognize you. Wait. I'll put on the light.'

She reached to the side of the wall and clicked on the porch light which illuminated the doorway and right into the hall. Alex smiled and stepped forward, and Helen opened the door to let her past.

'Oh, my, you really have done this place up.' The last time Alex had been here, that time Tommy had been bruised when the skirting board had warped off the wall, the house had been just like any other old place, faintly gloomy, in need of a late spring clean. Alan Crombie had been working on some interior building, and there had been dust all over the place. Now the hallway gleamed. Every smooth surface shot back the light in a rich glow. There was not a speck of dust. The air was heavy with the scent of wax polish.

'This place is transformed,' Alex enthused. Helen shot her a faltering, embarrassed smile that disappeared as quickly as it had come. She looked at Alex then looked away, casting her gaze all around, as if searching, or even inspecting.

'And how have you been?' Alex asked when they

were in the kitchen. This room sparkled too, although the smell of wax polish was overcome by the tingly harsh smell of bleach. The kitchen looked like something out of a magazine. Every surface was clean. There were no dishes or cutlery on the draining board. There was not a crumb on the floor.

'I've been fine. Busy getting the house ready. I mean tidy.'

'I can see that. What a difference you've made. The whole place is looking terrific. I just haven't got your touch. I keep promising myself I'm going to give my place a real working over, but I never seem to get round to it, and it's only a quarter the size of this house.'

Helen asked if she'd like some tea and Alex agreed. The electric kettle boiled within minutes while Helen sorted out some cups and saucers and set them on little doilies next to a matching sugar and milk set.

'Just a spot of milk and no sugar,' Alex said. 'I have to watch my shape. I go on a binge every now and then and I have to pay for it by weeks of dieting.'

As Alex spoke, she watched Helen pour the tea and add some milk to her cup. She thought Helen looked as if she'd been on a crash diet. Her face was tight and drawn and she sat with her shoulders hunched, wound in on herself. But it was her hands that Alex noticed most. The first time they'd met, at Tom Callander's, she had seen Helen's hands and admired her long, narrow, red lacquered nails. They had looked like the hands of a lady of leisure, smooth and delicate. Now they were red and scadded-looking. The nails were broken or chewed down to the quicks. The backs of her hands were roughened and the knuckles stood out in ridges.

'You've not been overdoing it, have you?' Alex asked. Helen caught her looking and drew her hands back quickly, furtively, making them disappear from view under the edge of the table.

'No. It's been all right.'

'Good,' Alex said lightly. 'And everybody else is well too, huh?' She bent to take a sip of tea, then almost recoiled at the taste. She looked into the cup and saw pale blobs of cream floating on the surface. The milk was sour, adding a bitter taste to the tea.

'Anything wrong?' Helen asked.

'No. It's just a bit hot. I think I should leave it for a bit. Actually, I came round to see the girls. I spoke to some people at the hospital. Professor Royston, you've probably heard of him, he said he'd like to see my initial report on them. He's got the file from Mr Jamieson who did the neurological examination. He's very interested.'

Helen nodded distractedly. Her eyes had started flicking around the room again, as if she was looking for something.

'We'll be able to get the records from the other specialists, and of course we'll be going over some old ground, but the people in Glasgow, and there are one or two in Edinburgh, are real experts in this sort of field. If anybody can help, they can.'

Helen nodded again, not looking at Alex. She rose from the table and went to the sink, and brought back a small square cloth which she folded twice into a smaller, neater square, and started to wipe up a smattering of sugar crystals that had fallen on to the table.

'Do you mind if I have a look at the twins just now?'

'Pardon?' Helen asked, still wiping the now spotless table-top.

'Maybe I should give the girls a check-out while I'm here.'

'Oh, yes. I'll get them.' Helen got up and crossed to the sink where she rinsed the cloth and folded it neatly before turning to lead the way out of the kitchen.

In the front room the twins were kneeling on the floor playing with an enormous set of Lego building blocks which were scattered in a kaleidoscope of colours across the carpet. They looked around as Helen and

Alex entered the room and simultaneously beamed their unfathomable smiles.

'What a mess!' Helen cried as soon as she saw the profusion of little bricks. 'I *told* you to keep this room tidy.'

The smiles faltered as the twins watched their mother stride across the room to where they played. They gazed up at her with identical expressions of bewilderment on their faces.

'Just *look* at this place. I did this room only this morning, and as soon as my back's turned it's a pigsty. I'll have to do it all over again, you *naughty* girls.'

Watching from behind, Alex could see the tension in Helen's back. Her arms were straight down at her sides, anger written in every line of her posture. 'Come on,' she said, crossing over to the little confrontation. 'I'll give you a hand.'

'No. Please.' Helen turned, lifting her hands up in a warding-off gesture. 'I can manage. Come on, girls, you go with the doctor into the other room.' She turned to Alex again. 'Will that be all right, Doctor?'

'Just fine. It won't be too long anyway. And please, just call me Alex. Everybody else does.'

Helen nodded, as if dismissing them all, and turned to bend down towards the pile of bricks. Alex took both girls by the hand.

'OK, kids, let's see what you can do.' They smiled up at her and went through the door, one on each side. Behind them came the sound of the plastic bricks being gathered from the floor and dropped into their box.

Forty-five minutes later, Helen still hadn't shown up in the lounge where Alex sat between the twins with her books and files on her knee. Kathryn and Elaine had giggled when she'd given them a brief check over using only her stethoscope and optical light. The children were healthy enough, although the doctor noticed that they weren't just as clean as the house was. They were wearing little summer frocks that had dried-in stains down their fronts. There was grime under their nails and on their knees. They looked as if they hadn't been washed for a couple of days.

Alex depressed their tongues and checked out their throats. There was nothing obvious there. In fact, the girls could laugh normally, just like any other children, except they seemed to laugh more often, so there was evidently no physical damage to the vocal chords. If there had been, Alan Crombie or his wife would have told her in any case. Alex had an idea that the twins' lack of speech was more psychological, perhaps some form of autism, although she knew that in the truly autistic there was a severe retardation of emotional ability and perception of relationships. And the girls didn't appear to have suffered any major trauma. There were none of the classic symptoms of withdrawal or nervousness that would normally be associated with either condition.

She had sat on the couch with the picture book and had got the girls alternately to point to the animals she had named. They had a wide range of knowledge for their age. They understood every word she said.

But when she asked them to say any of those words, they just smiled at her.

They didn't even make an attempt.

And they looked so pleased with themselves that had Alex not been a highly trained professional, she might have thought they were playing an elaborate practical joke on the world.

When she was ready to go, she had to look for Helen whom she found in the dining-room adjacent to the kitchen where a big dark mahogany table dominated, surrounded by a set of six ornate chairs. Helen was on her knees at the far wall, panting with effort as she rubbed away at the dark wood with a cloth. The smell of wax polish was strong in the air.

'That's me finished for the moment,' Alex called across.

Helen kept on rubbing earnestly, her shoulders swaying with the motion. She was humming to herself. Or was it talking to herself? Alex couldn't quite hear, but over in the corner Helen was definitely muttering something.

Alex called out again, and Helen jerked back, almost guiltily, as if she'd been caught doing something she shouldn't.

'I've had a look at the girls, and they're both fine. I'll make out a report and Professor Royston will probably want to see them himself.'

Helen nodded. She was still on her knees, twisting the polishing cloth in her hand. Alex got the impression that she just wanted to get back to her work.

'Are you sure you're all right?'

Helen nodded blankly.

'Well, don't overdo it, huh?' Alex said, as brightly as she could. There was definitely something *wrong* here. There was something about Helen, and her distracted manner, that was strange. 'By the way, how is Tommy?' she asked, trying to dismiss the thought, and aware how obviously forced her question sounded.

'Oh, he's fine,' Helen said, pausing briefly at her work and leaning back from the wall, letting her heels take the weight. 'He's out somewhere with his schoolfriends.'

'And Alan, he's well too?'

Helen's expression clouded over. It was as if Alex had mentioned the name of a stranger, and Helen was trying to remember the face. Again she started, as if stumbling upon a memory.

'Busy. Very busy. Just like me. Except he's up north. One of his big projects. He's had to go away for a few days. I expect he'll be back tomorrow. Or maybe the day after.'

'Well, give him my regards, and say hello to Tommy.'

Helen nodded absently and half turned, back towards

the wall. She looked as if her hands were itching to get back to work again. Already Alex could see the distraction on her face, as if the small talk was fading from the forefront of her mind.

'OK, I've got to go now. Thanks for the tea, and I'll let you know as soon as I hear anything. Take it easy.'

Alex let herself out. As soon as she had turned from the door she knew, without looking back, that Helen had gone back to work with the polishing cloth. From the other side of the room, she could hear the squeak of the cloth as it rubbed the wood.

On the way home, driving her little hatchback round the shore road at the point, Alex realized what had been so strange about the woman's behaviour.

The fidgeting and anxious manner, the distraction and the fixated concern with housework, told her that Helen was becoming obsessively houseproud. Either that, or she was heading for a nervous breakdown. Maybe, she thought, she should have a word with Dr Docherty about it.

'Maybe I should mind my own business,' she said aloud as she rounded the point and headed for the west side of Creggan.

But even after she arrived home, she couldn't dismiss the nagging thoughts. There had been something odd, something *weird* about the way Helen Crombie had been acting. Her house was bright as a new pin, but her children could have done with a good soaking. Dazzling though their identical, silent smiles were, their blonde hair looked as if it hadn't been washed, and their clothes certainly could have used a session in the washer. The kitchen too, it was as clean as an operating theatre. Alex recalled the nervous way the woman had picked, the finicky, irritated way, at the few sugar crystals that had scattered on the table-top. But the milk she had poured in the tea must have been several days old.

It was strange, sure enough. Alex wondered if all

was well in the Crombie household. She wondered if Alan Crombie was aware that a problem might be developing while he was away. The thoughts nagged at her for a while, but in the end Alex thought that she couldn't do much about it. Maybe she was just reading too much into a situation into which she had already intruded more than she ought.

Tom Callander met Alex in the lounge of the Harbour Inn when she arrived shortly after ten looking flushed and breathless. She walked through the doorway and stood looking around for a few seconds, then spied Tom sitting at the bar. She came across in a few strides, dressed in a faded working shirt and a pair of even more faded Levis. Her chestnut red hair was pinned up in a mass of waves showing a slender neck that matched the rest of her frame. As usual, a few of the men at the far end turned to have a good look, and a few of the women caught their men at it and glared at them. Tom gave her an up-and-down glance and a soft, mischievous whistle.

'That'll be enough of that from you,' Alex said with mock sternness. 'You're old enough to be my friend's father.'

'Ah, but not too old to appreciate a good pair of pins, speaking aesthetically, of course,' he replied, grinning.

'Of course. You know, you could be in danger of becoming a dirty old lounge lizard.'

'I *am* a dirty old lounge lizard. I've had my backside stuck in a JCB digger all day. As we say here in the west, my bum's numb.'

'Where I come from, a bum's what you look like. Haven't you been home yet?'

'Oh, get away with you. You're beginning to sound more like Beth every day. She nearly refused to come down here with me because I was wearing my working gear.'

'Well, I can't say I blame her. And anyway, where is she?'

'In there,' he said, indicating the door at the far end of the lounge with a nod of his head. 'Powdering whatever it is young ladies powder these days, if they still do that sort of thing. What'll you have?'

Alex slid on to the seat beside him and settled for a gin and tonic which arrived with Tom's whisky and another gin for Beth who came through the lounge and joined them.

'I thought you weren't going to make it,' Beth said.

'Me too. I was going through some paperwork and didn't realize the time.'

Tom enjoyed a few whiskies, letting his thoughts wander and hardly noticing the buzz of the girls' conversation. It was close to ten and twilight was just beginning to set when he left the girls in the lounge and sauntered homewards, allowing them an hour or so of women's talk. Alex and Beth had become close friends over the past year, and shared an interest in the history of the area. Beth's own career stemmed from a lifelong interest in the subject. Tom remembered how she had been fascinated with dinosaurs and fossils as a child, and then had become interested in palaeontology. He had not been surprised when she had chosen to specialize in history and archaeology. Alex's interest in the history of the area had started with her fascination with the land that had been home to her several times great-grandparents who had left for Nova Scotia at the beginning of the nineteenth century.

Tom strolled up the road, a little stiff from the hours in the cabin of the big digger, but glowing from the internal combustion of several whiskies washed down with cold beer chasers, and the knowledge that he'd done a good day's work. It was only work from the point of view that he had been doing a particular job. From Tom's semi-retired position, it had been more like play. Maybe he did need a bath and he would have one later, but he took pleasure in the fact that he smelled like a working man, and that took him back twenty years or more, when he used to handle the big steam digger every day. Already he could feel the old callouses coming back on the palms of his hands where they joined his fingers, giving them once again the feel of a working man's hands. His shoulders might be a bit stiff, but he could feel the muscles harden up again. They would never be what they had been, but it was good to know he wasn't getting soft.

Up at the house he grabbed an old walking stick from the umbrella rack and whistled softly. He heard the sibilant scrape of a claw on the old stone hearth in the living-room and seconds later Gus padded through the doorway, tail thumping furiously.

'Come on, boy,' Tom said, waiting until he came right up to him before bending down to scratch behind an ear. 'Ready for a walk, eh?'

The labrador's tail beat an enthusiastic arc. Tom held the door open for him and they strolled out into the gloaming. The night was warm and no wind blew.

Along from Tom's house, the road took a left turn along the shoreline where the big granite rocks, scraped off the highlands and shoved down the vast grooves that became Finloch and Loch Creggan in the last ice age, were humped and tumbled, smoothed with thousands of years of wind and rain and tide. Past the old Dalmuir house, now the Crombie house, the road turned again, following the curve of the shore for a little way before joining on to the main Creggan Road. At this time of night there was little traffic. Man and dog ambled in the deepening twilight for half a mile before taking the farm track that led a little way up the Peaton Hill towards Jack Coggan's farm. Up there was a favourite spot where two tracks converged and the dry-stane dike formed a natural seat with a view over both lochs right and left, and the whole of the firth to the south. Tom whistled to Gus who was sniffing in a hedgerow, letting him know he was stopping for a while although he didn't need to. Any time they came up this road he would sit on the dike for maybe half an hour if the weather was right, just appreciating the view.

The dog ambled off into a stand of saplings and Tom heaved himself up on to the stone seat, using his heels as levers. He shifted his backside a couple of times to get comfortable on the rough stones which were still warm from the day's sun. He pulled his pipe out from his pocket and lit it with an easy flick of his lighter, drawing in the pungent smoke and savouring the flavour. All he needed now was just another whisky, maybe a fine Strathisla malt, and he'd be the king of all he surveyed.

It was a wonderfully quiet night, only two weeks away from midsummer. The air was clear and warm, and despite the shadows that gathered in the hollows and runnels, it would not be complete night. Behind him, the north sky still glimmered red that would remain until dawn. Due south the half-moon was high and torch-bright in a sky that merged black and purple in a velvet mix. The moonlight caught the contours of the land, limning them with silver blue. Far out across the firth, the lights of the southern ports glistened like frosting. To the left Finloch was black as night, for there was no wind to stir the water and catch the moon, but down on the firth the reflection sparkled in a blazing path that was almost breathtaking in its purity. Up on the hill a curlew piped. In the hedgerow, something squeaked and rustled through the stems. Down at the edge of the Finloch, an oyster catcher whistled a piercing cry and was answered by another further along the rocks. Tom drew in on his pipe and looked out over the water. He felt at peace with the world.

For half an hour he watched the land grow darker, the shadows in the hollows and dips spread and flow into larger patches, the moon shift in the sky until the path of light thrown up from the firth caught the roofs of the Creggan houses.

Reluctantly, he called softly to Gus who appeared from the shadow, a silent silver ghost, then heaved himself out of his stone seat on the wall.

'Come on, lad, it's time we were getting back,' he said. He scratched him behind the ears again, feeling the simple depth of affection for him emanate from the warm body. Then he and his dog set off down the hill.

Down at Cromwath House the twins were asleep. Tommy lay in the darkness of the room with his eyes wide open, catching the glimmer of the half-moon which had moved further west until it no longer shone directly through the crack in the curtain on to his bed. A silvered blue line of light split the wall, and the reflection illuminated the room enough to see, although the chair in the corner and the racks of toys on the shelves were just grey shapes with fading, wavering edges, only sharp in wide-eyed peripheral vision, and merging back into the dark again when looked at directly.

Downstairs, Tommy could hear his mother moving around. He knew she would be working at something, cleaning or polishing. The night before he had been awakened, deep into the night, from a dream that had ended with the howling of something huge and shadowy that had flitted after him on immense wings. He had started awake to the sudden realization that the howling was only the far-off whine of the vacuum cleaner downstairs. Relief had flooded through him, and the terror of the chase, the breathless horror of being *prey*, had drained away, leaving him weak and washed out.

Tonight he hadn't quite gone to sleep. The moonlight had slanted across the bed and Tommy had been watching the thin, misty clouds pass in front of the shining half-disc, fading it down behind their gauze, then passing slowly until it flared clean again. He had dozed, listening to the house settle. The hot water had gurgled briefly in the pipes inside the walls, and then the radiator had pinged and creaked minutely as it contracted. From up in the loft something rustled, maybe a bat, or a bird that had got in under the eaves, and then the house had gone quiet, letting him drift off into a semi-slumber that wasn't quite sleep. The noise below had twitched him awake. He heard his mother's soft footsteps in the hall fading away as she walked, he was sure, into the kitchen. A faint sound of running water, a brief following hiss in the pipes, confirmed it, and a bump, as if a chair had been moved. The footsteps came padding back again, muffled staccato. A door opened, closed, and then the house went quiet.

Tommy was worried. He didn't know what was happening, but he was sure, dead sure, that something was wrong. He wished his dad were back home. *He* would know.

There was something wrong with his mother. That much he was sure of. And he was scared that it was getting worse.

Long ago, he recalled, his mother had gone away, and his gran had come to mind him. She had been away a long time, and he had only been taken to visit her once, in that scary place where the strange woman that had been his mother had stared at him with dull, sleepy eyes and had smiled, tired and wan, from the big bed in the small room with the tiny windows.

(*The loony bin.*)

He remembered the distant woman who had come back from there, vague and strange, lost and trying to find her bearings. Tommy remembered her eyes, wide and uncertain, and behind those eyes he could sense the grey space that was another *place* inside where her thoughts were dark and fearful.

Now there was something wrong with his mother, and again her eyes were wide and deep, but he couldn't read what he saw in them. It was as if, sometimes, she just wasn't *there*. It was as if the grey place had opened up and she had gone in there again. For the past week, since his father had gone away (*just a couple of days, TC, way up in the frozen north*), his mother had faded into the woodwork, and that strange woman, the one who had come home from (*the loony bin*) hospital, had returned again, to wash and clean and wipe and scrub. That woman, the other one, seemed at times to have forgotten about Tommy and the twins. As she bustled about in the house, working steadily from room to room, it was as if she *was* in another world, only occasionally and distractedly coming back again to the real one, as if waking from a dream.

Tommy was glad to be at school, where he had friends to play with. In the morning, he would get up and pour out the cornflakes for himself and the twins while his mother bustled about between the kitchen and the other rooms. After school, when he came home, he would have to ask her for something to eat, and she'd open a tin of spaghetti or beans and make some toast and leave them to get on with it. The twins didn't seem to mind. Tommy would wipe their chins and wash up the plates the way his mother said, and they'd go and play together. But he was getting awfully fed up with toast. Round in the garage, his mother's little red car sat gleaming and new-looking. She had only used it once since his dad bought it two weeks before. Now she never seemed to go out, and she never seemed to have time for any of them.

She just went about cleaning and scrubbing, ignoring everybody, at least until they left something lying about (and then they were for it) or when they trailed dirty footsteps into the hall. Then the angry look in her eyes would come back and she would shout at them and wave her hands about in the air.

And the worst thing was that after a week Tommy

wasn't sure if he didn't prefer her like that. At least, on those occasions, she noticed them.

The house was quiet again, a big, vast place of shadows and corners. A cloud passed in front of the moon, cutting its light out as if a switch had been thrown, and the room was pitched into darkness. Tommy's pupils dilated as his eyes struggled for light and gradually his vision adjusted to the gloom. He could make out the big black rectangle of the cupboard door against the grey of the wall. He kept his eyes fixed firmly on that, snuggling himself deeper under the covers.

TWENTY-THREE

'Dishy? Is that what you said?' Beth Callander snorted. She was sitting in the big leather armchair, feet drawn up under her, and with both hands cupped round a cut glass that tinkled with ice and threw back reflections of the small lamp glowing in her corner of the room.

Across from her on the other side of the empty hearth, Alex raised her eyes over the rim of her glass. She too was curled up comfortably, wedged in the corner of the chair with one leg crossed over the wide arm, letting her foot dangle.

'Yes. What's wrong with dishy?'

'Nothing wrong with the sentiment. It's just that I haven't heard that word outside an old romantic novel. A *very* old one at that.'

'I thought that's how you Brits said it.'

'Us *Scots,*' Beth corrected with mock seriousness. 'Dishy was a swinging sixties word. Positively medieval. Like debonair and gay.'

'Oh, he's definitely not *gay,*' Alex said emphatically.

'No. Of course he's not. He's married.'

'Where I come from, that means next to nothing. No. What I meant is that he's *obviously* straight. Just a shame that he is married. It's the story of my life. All the best ones are, and time's pushing on.'

'You're the last one to be complaining about the lack of men. You attract them like flies,' Beth told her.

'Yeah, and I wish ninety-nine per cent of them would buzz off like flies.'

'I thought you fancied that friend of his, what was his name?'

'Mike Toward.'

'Yes, him. The American. Didn't he take a shine to you?'

Alex sipped her drink and twinkled a smile across the room at her friend. 'Oh yes. He thought he'd found a soul-mate, just because I spoke with the same accent. But it was the same old story. You know, I don't mind the fact that they're married so much as the bullshit they try to con us with. I mean Mike's an OK guy. He's smart and he's good-looking, and he dresses not too bad for a New Englander. And I don't mind an excess of male hormones now and again, which I can assure you Mike *does* have . . .' She nodded knowingly at Beth who returned the look with a smile. 'But I can't *stand* it when they come out with the "*my wife doesn't understand me*" routine. It makes me mad when they butter you up with all their flattery, then insult your intelligence with that crap.'

Beth chuckled. 'Did he really give you that line?'

'Sure he did. Otherwise, I might have been tempted. I mean, if he'd come straight out and said his wife was four thousand miles away and he was in dire need of a good time, between consenting adults, as you *Scots* put it, then I could have thrown the idea around at least.'

'And would you actually have . . . ?'

'No. But for different reasons. He just wasn't my type.'

'And you think maybe Alan Crombie *is* your type?'

Alex shifted her gaze and took another sip from her glass, musing on the question. 'I'd say, under different circumstances, he could have been. I think he's pretty OK.'

'Dishy, even?'

'Yeah, that too,' Alex agreed with a rueful laugh. 'But that wife of his. Her I *don't* understand.'

'*That's* a new angle,' Beth said pointedly.

'How do you mean?'

'You were complaining about men telling you their

wives don't understand them, and now you're complaining about not understanding the *wife*.'

Alex caught Beth's mischievous wink and laughed again. 'Another blow for liberated women,' she said. 'But seriously, I think that woman's got a problem. And there's something odd between them.'

'How so?'

Alex stretched back in her chair and looked up at the picture on the wall above the fireplace. It was an old print of the view from Creggan Point west on the firth to the old harbour at Murrin. The sun was setting over the hills on the far side of the loch, catching on the topmasts of the old fishing boats and casting long shadows on the water. It was an idyllic scene from the turn of the century when the peninsula was a remote outpost on the west coast, a scattering of crofts and tiny harbours, sparsely populated by fishermen and farmers, Gaelic-speaking folk who had worked on this land since the dawn of time. Alex thought the picture beautiful and evocative of a quieter, more *worthy* time, when the pace of life was slower, when the roots of the people were deep in the land and washed by the sea. It was that elemental feeling, an internal calling, that had summoned her back across four thousand miles of ocean and a vast span of time to the land where her people's roots had once clung so tenaciously, until they were twisted and hauled in turn by the clearances of the avaricious feudal landlords, by poverty and hunger, and by the invasion of a southern culture that had squeezed and pushed and worn down the heart and soul of the old people. Now the peninsula was still a haven. There were still many families here who could trace their line back to the old fishing people and crofters, and there were some clan names that went back even further than that, to the days when the whole long arm of land was covered in trees, and to the days when the standing stones that lined the spine of the peninsula were fresh-cut.

Alex knew her wistfulness for the tranquillity of times past was only a romantic notion. Beth was the expert on history, and the way she told it, this west coast had never been as tranquil as the sunset picture would suggest. Clan wars had raged and blood had been spilt in red rivers. Famine and war had riven this part of the country, and in between times the life on the croft, or in the fishing boats, or in the cottages where the women waited for their men and the return to the raw-handed filleting that ensued, was hard and often dreary. But still, even though Alex knew these things in her mind, the old picture above the Callanders' fireplace evoked that feeling of a slower, less frantic life.

Now the peninsula was a dormitory for some of the professional people who could afford the large stone villas that had been built on selected spots overlooking the twin lochs. Good roads led to the straight arrow of the Kirkland and Arden bypáss that had been built to service the Trident base, and carried people quickly and easily to the offices in Glasgow. The local people still worked the land and worked the boats, but most of the smallholdings were market gardens specializing in vegetables for the supermarkets and chain stores, and the boats the sons of the old fishermen worked on were the smooth white dinghies and yachts owned or hired by summer visitors who tacked out on the deep sheltered waters of the lochs, or the sleek black Polaris submarines that prowled under the surface, traceless except for the displacement waves that mysteriously curled on the rocky shoreline long after their passing.

'How so?' Beth asked again, and Alex's gaze snapped away from the old print.

'How *what*?'

'The Crombie woman. Helen, isn't that her name? What's so odd about her?'

'I saw her today and she gave me the weirdest feeling,' Alex said. She went on to tell Beth what had happened when she called at the Crombie home, recounting how unkempt the little girls had looked and how Helen had acted as if the only important thing in her life was keeping her house clean.

'The first time I met her, she couldn't get me up there quickly enough to give my professional opinion on the twins. When she heard I was a child psychologist, she almost wanted me to examine them on the spot, but when I got there today, she didn't seem to want to know.'

'What do you think is wrong with her?' Beth asked.

'I'm not sure. But from the look of her, there's almost definitely an incipient neurosis. Her behaviour had all the classic symptoms of obsessive fixation and repetition, and her seeming lack of interest in the children's welfare only helps confirm that. You know I shouldn't be telling you any of this, and I don't know why I am really. It's a total breach of ethics.'

'I'm no gossip,' Beth said flatly.

'I know that, so I won't worry about it.'

'What are you going to do about her?'

'Nothing for the moment,' Alex said after a pause. 'First of all, I saw nothing that caused me really great concern. It could be only temporary. After all, she has just moved in to the house, and she's living in an unfamiliar area. She could be under some strain, and with having the problem with the girls, maybe you can't blame somebody for being just a bit flaky.'

Alex paused. She looked thoughtful and serious for a moment then she smiled. 'But those two girls. The twins. They're absolutely gorgeous.'

'I know,' Beth agreed. 'They're lovely.'

'There's something almost magnetic about them. When I was talking to them today, I just wanted to cuddle both of them. Their eyes are so huge you could drown in them. Maybe they don't speak, but they're the happiest-looking babies I've seen in a long time.'

'Why don't they speak?' Beth asked.

'I dunno. Alan said they've had every possible test, from EEG, CAT scans and brain scans, and nobody has come up with anything. It's possible that they just don't want to talk.'

'Maybe they're telepathic and don't need words like us mortals.'

Alex quickly looked across at Beth. 'What makes you say that?' she asked.

'There was a programme a couple of months ago about a pair of identical twins. They were black girls living in England somewhere, Birmingham, I think. They never spoke to anybody, and they had their own language that they used between themselves. It was the weirdest thing you ever saw. They did everything together. I mean *exactly* together. If one lifted her hand, the other would do the same. It was like watching one person. It was creepy.'

'But there's nothing creepy about Katie and Laney. There have been a number of studies on identical twins, there is some evidence that points towards some level of mutual understanding, a sort of empathy. But it's strange that you say that. I was doing a spatial co-ordination test on Katie, you know the one where you get them to spread their fingers and then join each hand at the fingertips. I was sitting with Katie to the side, with my back to Elaine. I turned around and there she was, doing exactly the same as her sister. It gave me the strangest feeling.' The ice rattled in the bottom of the glass as Alex took a final sip of her drink. It was mostly meltwater. 'It was impossible for her to have seen what I was doing.'

'Maybe she heard you telling her sister what to do.'

'She couldn't have done that either. I demonstrated what to do, without actually defining it in words.' Alex put her glass down on the little table beside her, which supported a lamp identical to the one on Beth's side of the room. It cast a warm glow over one half of her face and her auburn hair spangled in deep red highlights.

She held out her hands and spread her fingers. 'I just said: "Can you do this?"' Alex brought her hands together in a slow movement. Beth watched her friend as each finger moved towards its counterpart, and touched at the tips. 'I still can't figure out why she did it,' Alex said.

The light had almost completely faded from the sky, leaving it deep and blue-black straight ahead as he walked south on the farm road. Out to the west the half-moon was scraping the top of the Cowal Hills on the far side of Loch Creggan, spilling silver across the heather and the bare rocks that pushed their way through the bracken. Behind him a band of pink and mauve held the last of the day and would remain until dawn this close to midsummer. To his left was the pitch darkness of the clump of trees that crowded on to the farm road and continued their march, unbroken, save for the grey ribbon of the winding road into the village that cut through the copse at its narrowest part. Tom took the left fork and ambled slowly downhill, then turned right along the road. Beside him Gus padded close to his thigh. In the quiet of the evening, there was little sound, save the regular crunch of Tom's walking shoes on the grit of the roadway and the occasional tap of his stick on the hard surface. Gus panted softly, and now and then there would be a scrape as one of his claws skittered on the metal.

Five minutes along the road there was a thinning of the clump of trees, and Tom angled between two wide rough Scots pine trunks where the path had been well worn in a regular short cut. There was a track that led down to the other road which serviced the big houses, including his own, on the shore front. And there was another that skirted the houses and led right along to the huddle of houses in Creggan itself. A third took him straight down towards the dry-stone wall that formed the top boundary of the old Dalmuir place. 'The *Crombie* place,' he mentally corrected himself.

There was a dip on the wall, where a couple of the top stones had been rolled off, probably by the careless children who had used this stand of trees as a play-ground for as long as anybody could remember, despite the express forbidding of every parent who lived in these parts. Here, the wall was low enough for Tom to step over. Gus followed with a scrabbling of paws on the smooth stones, and the man and his dog walked into the deep shade of the thick stand of trees.

It was dark in there.

The moonlight glimmered in between the trunks for a few seconds as Tom walked away from the wall, a flickering silver strobe that was quickly dimmed and then cut off as a cloud passed, borne on the west wind that swept over the Cowals and flowed over the now black face of the loch to hiss through the pine needles high overhead, making them sound like coarse sand on the beach.

A deeper dark blotted the path through the trees.

Tom walked more slowly, despite his familiarity with the route. Underfoot the dead pine needles crunched and skittered. Gus stayed close.

The narrow track wound between the pines and then broadened a little where the big beech trees, smooth and massive, reared up from the crunchy carpet of beechmast and dry broad leaves. Tom's eyes accustomed themselves to the darkness so that he could make out the looming shapes of the boles as he skirted them. Overhead the wind sighed and soughed, rattling the fine topmost twigs, dulling out the sound of Tom's footsteps and the dog's paws. Further from the wall, the copse was much darker as shadow piled upon shadow, and even Tom's peripheral vision blurred until he was walking by memory alone.

It was here, right in the centre of the trees where the dark was thickest, almost palpable, that he paused. The wind had risen, changed up a gear, moving the tops of the trees. From ahead came a deep creaking sound as one thick branch sawed against another, squealing eerily over the moan of the wind. The noise was a sudden startle which jerked Tom's eyes to the right and made his heart take an extra quick beat before he realized what the sound was. The dark had closed in entirely, and in turning round Tom had almost lost his bearings. He turned back and moved on, heading round to the north of the Crombie land to where he could get to the low wall that bounded his own garden.

The beeches gave way to another stand of pine trees that were close together. A few had fallen in the gales of previous years and leaned drunkenly against their neighbours. A couple had crashed to the forest floor leaving a tangle of roughened trunks that were ridged with jagged branch-stumps. Here the going was more difficult, but Gus kept close and slightly ahead. If the dog had not been with Tom, then he would have taken the road rather than the short cut through the trees.

'Good boy,' he said, into the dark. His words were lost in the wind that blew between the trunks, but he knew that Gus heard. 'Not far to go now.'

They were in the middle of the tangle of pines when Gus stopped suddenly. Tom almost fell over the dog before he realized it. 'Come on, ye daft bugger. Let's be getting home,' he said affectionately.

Gus stood stock still.

'What's the matter, lad? Did you smell a rabbit?'

Tom peered ahead into the darkness. Ahead there were more pines for about twenty feet or so, and beyond that two great black shadows. Between them he could make out the sky, just a shade lighter. 'Och, we've come the wrong road,' Tom said aloud. 'I thought you were supposed to be taking me home, old feller.'

In front of him stood two of the great megaliths that remained near the edge of the Cromwath grounds.

Tom started to walk forward, but Gus stayed where he was, his stocky legs held stiff and planted straight in the leaf litter. Tom felt rather than heard, at first, the low growl that seemed to come from deep in the dog's belly. He bent down to ruffle the hair behind its ears and stopped when he felt the hackles, stiff and bristly, ridging its back.

'What's the matter, boy?' he said in a whisper, before he even realized he *was* whispering. Through the stiffened bristles he could feel the dog's skin tight against the underlying muscle, and under the skin he could sense the body shaking with tension. Gus was vibrating in there like a regular tuning fork. Still the low growl continued, winding up like a motor.

Tom felt the hairs on the back of *his* neck prickle in a tight little wave. He felt a light shiver skitter up and down the nerves of his back, and when he felt it his heart thudded, once, twice, hard and fast against his ribs, seeming to flip inside. It gave him an alarming jolt, and his breath hitched in a gasp to compensate.

The dog's growl wound up a degree, louder, more menacing. Tom was still bent over the animal, and could feel the bunched muscles rippling spasmodically, hard and tight. The growl deep inside was vibrating through bone and muscles. It was a sound Tom had never heard before. It was full of menace, full of warning. Suddenly Tom felt a twinge of alarm for himself. He wondered if there was something wrong with Gus. Maybe he was sick or something.

He wondered if perhaps the dog had eaten some tainted meat left by one of the farmers to kill off stoats and foxes, or maybe even been bitten by something in the hedgerow. There were still a few adders about the peninsula, basking on the rocks to catch the last heat of the day.

Suddenly from ahead, with startling, shocking loudness came a cry which tore into the dark. It was a hoarse, high screech of fear, or pain, or terror that split the night. Tom's head jerked up so quickly he felt a pain rip through his neck and into his head. Under his hand Gus was wound up like a wire hawser that had gone way beyond its breaking limit.

The scream reverberated off the trunks of the trees, reaching a crescendo, then fading into a harsh sob.

'What in Christ's name was *that*?' Tom blurted out. His eyes were staring straight ahead into the patch of gloom between the pitch black of the standing stones.

There was instant silence as the wind faltered, leaving only the deep vibration of the dog's growl, a shocking, old, fearsome animal sound. Then, as if it had been pausing before a renewed onslaught, the wind howled in again, buffeting the trees and raking the high branches.

Then came the cry again. This time louder and closer. It wasn't the loudness that was shocking, but the intensity of the pure *terror* that the scream encompassed. It was a primitive wail of fear and anguish that was unmistakable.

Gus jerked back, quivering. His growl instantly became a snarl, ferocious, almost slavering.

In front of the man and his dog there was a movement, a fluttering motion, dim, barely visible, but a movement none the less.

The cry swelled. Came closer.

Tom peered ahead, his heart now fairly scudding away in there. He could feel the pressure in his throat and temples.

Something was coming towards them, running from out there in the distance between the stones. It was difficult to see what in the gloom. The hairs on the back of his neck seemed to take on a life of their own as the atmosphere of this place that he had avoided for years jangled in the air around him.

The cry came again, high and rasping, and suddenly Tom didn't know whether it was animal or human. Then the shape materialized as if seen through a dark membrane. It was a small boy running and stumbling, one leg of his jeans flapping raggedly. The shriek came again, from behind the running boy. Tom couldn't see his face properly, but there was something in the way he pumped his legs that told the man the child was terrified, running for his life.

A shape bobbed into view behind the fleeting figure. Another one joined it. It seemed there were trees out there, although Tom knew there were none in the sloping field. They crowded in, massive and jungly, festooned with black creepers. Something small and many-legged scuttled down a hole with a clattering of armoured joints.

The boy raced forward, heading for the gap and safety. His eyes were rolling wildly. And just at the last minute he jinked to the left, on the other side of the big stone. Tom swivelled his head, about to call out to the lad, and then stopped. The boy had disappeared. The sounds of his flight, which should have continued through the ferns and bracken, had been cut off instantly. Between the stones the two loping shapes charged straight forward. Tom jerked back. One of the things, blurred in speed, oddly jointed, leapt for the gap.

It was like something from a nightmare. It had a long spindly neck and forelegs to match with two sets of elbows and grasping claws. But its eyes were what transfixed Tom Callander. They were blacker than black, empty and hungry, huge in a gargoyle's wrinkled face. The scream that erupted from its throat was shattering in its intensity. Jaws opened and snapped shut again with the sound of a gin trap.

Tom staggered back, tripped and fell over Gus as he watched the thing hurtle towards him.

Gus snarled again and Tom felt the dog's muscles bunch under his hand. It felt as if some internal explosion had taken place deep inside the animal's body as it coiled, then erupted forward, the snarl suddenly a

226

wild spitting screech that sounded like no dog Tom had ever heard, although at that moment he was unaware of it.

The dog bulleted forward, snarling like a demon. In the slow-motion adrenalin burst that was pumping speed into Tom's arteries, he saw his dog surge towards the black rectangle where the light seemed to have been sucked out of the world. There was a rustle as paws dug into the leaf litter, a sound separate from the spitting snarl that burst in one continuous rasp from the dog's throat. Tom saw the shoulders hunch down, then come up again, a lighter shape against the dark, hackles rigid as a razorback boar's, and Gus was in the air. The initial rush had pitched Tom forward in a stumbling sprawl. As he went down, eyes still staring forward, and wider probably than they had ever been in his life, he saw the dog sail up and *into* the black space.

Then, in the fraction of a second before the man overbalanced and pitched headlong into the undergrowth, he saw the dog *connect* with the darkness, as if it had hit a wall just as the nightmare shape struck. It was as if the two creatures had collided in mid-air.

There was a spongy thump, as if a weight had hit a membrane stretched between the stones, a deep *infra-*sonic boom like a vast drumbeat. Gus seemed to push through, his body bending as the momentum of his leap curved his spine up against whatever had blocked his leap. In that split fragment of time, the black space seemed to give a little, then bulge outwards like a mal-evolent bubble.

The blurred thing twisted and turned, eyes dead black and jaws snapping as it tried to bite through at the dog. Both its clawed hands came up and raked at the air so blindingly quickly that Tom expected to see the dog torn to shreds. Then the creature simply disappeared as if it had been sucked out of existence.

The snarl cut right off as Gus literally bounced back-wards. There was a muffled snap that sounded like a bone breaking (but was in fact only the trap-shot of the dog's teeth as the jaws clamped together, putting one large canine right through the middle of its tongue) and Gus spun, paws over tail, flipping twice in mid-air, to land on his back right beside his master.

Tom's stumble had skidded him forward on his face for five feet and punched the wind right out of his guts. He shook his head and his breath hauled itself into his lungs in a whooping gasp. The spinning sensation faded almost instantly, although it took another second or two before the tiny pinpoints of light stopped orbiting like shooting stars in front of his eyes. Beside him, Gus was trying to scrabble to his feet for another go and Tom almost instinctively clamped his hand on the dog's neck. Just as instinctively, Gus arched his back and snapped at him, nipping into the fleshy part below his thumb before realizing the enormity of what it had done.

'Easy boy, easy,' Tom said, without conscious thought. His mind was still focused so intently on the black, the bulging black square between the standing stones that the rest of him was operating on automatic pilot, on another level altogether. He craned forward, feeling his heart pounding painfully somewhere inside his barrel chest, building up the pressure on the big arteries on either side of his neck. He was in a state of shock although at that moment he didn't realize it. He felt as if in the middle of a dream, the kind of nightmare where everything is real and unreal simultaneously, and the mind goes into overdrive to compensate for the loss of reason. It was as if he'd been turned inside-out by the blast of one of the five-pounder Semtex charges they laid into the quarry face.

Then there was a twist in the night, a shudder that seemed to rumble through the earth (a silent, motionless shudder that could be felt only on the level of the long neurons that run down the length of the spine), and a looping, wrenching sensation that made his vision flicker out of focus. The two stones seemed to lean towards each other as if they had been bent by an impossible force. A crackling rumble seemed to come from their very roots, deep inside the earth, and then the darkness winked out. It was as if something black and solid had been taken away, leaving a pale sky in the vacant space. Between the megaliths, Tom Callander saw the far-off, glittering lights of the ports on the far side of the firth. Gus whined softly.

Tom hauled himself to his feet and a tremor shook him, the aftermath of the adrenalin jolt. One of his knees was shaking and threatening to spill him down again, but he managed to stumble forward, walking shoes snagging on the fern tufts until he was right up against the stone. It was only then that he realized that the ground on the other side sloped *down* the hill towards the stream. The apparition he'd seen had been above his eye-line, running down towards him.

It was impossible.

TWENTY-FOUR

On the night that Alex Graham confessed to Beth Callander that she was attracted to Alan Crombie, and only half an hour after Tom Callander had seen the nightmare creatures between the standing stones (and he had been tempted to follow the same whisky route as Seumas and the minister), the Rev. Fergus MacLeod was sitting hunched over the wheel of his ancient black Austin that had been bequeathed to him by a lady parishioner some ten years before and was still going strong. The springs creaked and jostled as he eased the little bull-nosed car round the bends on its narrow cross-ply tyres, belly pressing into the wheel. He peered myopically along the twin cones of light that grey-misted the road for twenty yards ahead and petered out any distance beyond that on the straights.

The minister was on his way home after the monthly presbytery meeting that was held in Kirkland Parish Church Hall and attended by every minister in the district to help upgrade the strength of the church physically, financially and, if time allowed, spiritually. This had been a long meeting, some of the debates heated and enjoyable, punctuated by the strange rumble of the presbytery's voting system in which the winner of some particular obscure point would know his success by the loudness of the foot-tapping applause of his assembled peers. As assistant to the presbytery clerk, the minister had remained in the empty hall collating the minutes and finishing off minor paperwork details before heading for home. As he drove down the last mile on the peninsula road towards the manse, the moon was just a horn of light goring a black sky above the hills on his right. Ahead of him awaited a warm house, a hot cup of tea, and afterwards a burning sensation of Drambuie liqueur.

'Maybe even two,' he muttered to himself, 'no matter what Docherty says.'

The doctor had warned the minister about more than just fatty foods. The cleric's rotund figure and florid complexion spoke as eloquently about his cholesterol level as had the blood test he'd had only six months before. Docherty, who was maybe a year or so older than Fergus's fifty-six, had told him in graphic detail about the strain on his heart and liver and kidneys, and had insisted on a strict regimen which precluded all things saturated and most things liquid. Fergus had wholeheartedly agreed, given a staunch and steadfast assurance in his slow, highland lilt, and he'd gone out and carried on as before.

The thought of a neat Drambuie was uppermost in his mind when he turned the second to last bend that would take him down the shore road to the manse. As the car rocked on its hard suspension, the minister hauled the wheel round the tight curve, and the narrow twin beams panned the stand of hawthorn hedges that crowded densely to the edge of the road. On the near-side, a few bramble runners that reached out from the verge scraped the wheel arch, telling him he was too close to the edge. His attention was diverted for a second, then the car straightened up on the road and something came whirling right out of nowhere, zipping into the light from up ahead, and moving with enormous speed. The minister instinctively jerked on the wheel. The car wobbled and veered into the verge again, lashing against the brambles, before the minister over-compensated, sending the little Austin curving to the far side.

Whatever had appeared in front of the lights was hit again by the full beam as the Traveller swerved, giving Fergus a brief, almost subliminal glimpse of a grey shape that bounded on impossibly slender legs and leapt up and over the rounded bonnet. There was a hard, chitinous scutter, another scrape on the roof near the back of the car, and then it was gone. Without thinking, the minister instinctively jerked around, trying to see what he had nearly hit. His eyes still held a shape, an outline that was so unlikely it couldn't have been real. But because his attention had been diverted at precisely the wrong time, when the little car was curving across the wrong side of the road, Fergus, whose reactions at the best of times were slow, failed to steer away from the thick hawthorn hedge in time.

The car crunched into the close-backed branches and the front wheel bounced in the high verge. It veered again as the minister's grip was jarred off the steering wheel and it skidded left, cutting straight across the road in a spin, balancing for a long moment on the two left wheels before mounting the opposite verge and crashing backwards into the ditch with an enormous crump as three yards of bramble tangles were crushed. If the car had hit head-on, Fergus would probably have had his ribs staved in on the steering wheel which was in any case jammed up against his belly. But his considerable weight was pressed right back into the seat with the force of the impact, winding him slightly and whipping his neck back hard enough to make him see stars.

The car's little engine whined, coughed twice, then sputtered into silence. It sat at an awkward angle, tilted over on one side with the front end pointing up and out of the shallow ditch, headlamps angled into the air, catching the undersides of the hawthorn leaves on the tall hedge opposite.

The stars whirled, then began to fade out and Fergus shook himself, struggling up from the angled seat, but finding it difficult to shift his weight in the bulky overcoat that he wore winter and summer. He grunted with the effort and finally hauled himself forward, hanging on to the steering wheel for support, his breath coming in a series of raspy wheezes.

'Just terrible,' he was muttering to himself. 'The damned thing nearly had me killed, whatever it was.'

The force of the accident and the wrench on his neck had jolted away the vision of the thing that Fergus had glimpsed in the headlamps. He held on to the steering wheel and levered himself towards the door, scrabbling for the little chrome lever that would open it. He found it, pressed it down, and the door catch popped. He shoved and the door opened an inch, then bounced back towards him, forced by the tension of the bent saplings and bramble branches.

'Dammit to all hell,' the minister swore softly. He gave another shove and the door opened maybe another inch, and then stuck on a broken branch. He heaved twice, three times more, but because of the angle of the seat which sloped down away from the driver's door he didn't have enough purchase to force it further. Instead, he gave up and swung his weight down to the other door, grunting as he clambered with cumbersome difficulty over the knobbly gearstick. There was a faint acrid whiff of something burning behind the dashboard although it was too dark inside the car to see if there was any smoke.

The uncomfortable thought struck him that he could be stuck in the car when it went up in flames. He'd seen that kind of thing on television, and while he was not sure whether good old British cars exploded into flame with the same frequency and regularity as the American cars seemed to, the thought of being trapped inside this one sent his heartbeat into a higher gear. He reached the other side of the car, suddenly acutely aware of the bitter smell of smouldering plastic, and pulled down on the other handle.

There was a click and he overbalanced as the door opened and his weight carried him forward, but the movement stopped sharply as his nose cracked up against the small side window when the door swing was abruptly halted by the pressing undergrowth on this side. Because of the tilt of the car, the nearside door was dug even further into the briars in the ditch. The door was opened only six inches. Fergus threw his weight against it and there was a tinny squeal as the bottom edge rasped against the pressing branch. His nose was numb where he'd banged it against the glass, but not numb enough to kill the smoky smouldering smell. There was another rasp and one of the broken branches gave way, spanging under the metal lip, and the door jolted open another couple of inches before it butted hard up against an old deadfall trunk that had been slung into the ditch.

'Dammit to all hell,' Fergus muttered again. He swung himself round and put a foot against the door and kicked it hard. It didn't move. 'How the devil do I get out of here?' he said into the darkness.

It was rare for the minister to be out at this time of night, so he didn't know how much traffic there would be on the Creggan Road.

After a couple of vain tries at both doors, he pondered winding down the little side window and squeezing out on the high side. But he was realistic enough to gauge the space against his own girth, and the thought of being stuck half-in and half-out of the car, with his head pressed into thorny brambles, was just as bad as the thought of being trapped inside.

The burning smell diminished quickly, and the minister's heart stopped pounding in panic. This was just as much of a relief to him because the thudding inside his chest was becoming painful, making it difficult for him to catch his breath. He calmed himself down and surveyed the situation.

'Somebody will have to come along,' he said aloud. 'They can't fail to see the lights here, and they can get help.'

Having thought that, the minister smiled to himself.

It was simple. All he had to do was wait. He pulled his coat around himself and after a few fumbles, gave up trying to find his plain black brimmed hat which had fallen off when the car started to spin. He settled back in the seat, watching the road, waiting for headlamps to beam round the curves in either direction. In front, his own beams angled up to the opposite side through the sea mist that billowed up from the loch and snaked through the saplings.

Fergus folded his arms, leaning them on top of the steering wheel, and thought longingly of the glass of liqueur that waited for him. He could almost taste it; could feel the tight hot burn of the first sip.

It was the movement that startled him out of that thought.

He almost missed it, just catching the slight flicker out of the corner of his eye when his head was turned to the left, peering into the darkness, longing for the twin beams that would mean rescue. His head automatically whipped round and he craned forward over the wheel, eyes big and frog-like behind the thick glasses. The movement was gone.

Then from the side, the up-side next to the driver's door, came a noise. Bramble runners snapped once, twice, as if they had been crunched underfoot. The bulk of the minister's coat, and the fact that he was jammed against the wheel, prevented him from easily turning round to look out of the window. The noise came again. Quick treads, five, maybe six in succession.

'Who's there?' he called out. 'Is there anyone there?'

To the right, a figure moved out of the shade into the misty grey area just outside the twin cones of light in front of the car. Fergus jerked forward, peering myopically through his lenses, trying to make it out. Then again from the right there was the sound of movement as twigs crackled, snapped.

'Come on now,' he called out. 'Over here.'

The figure moved further away from the light.

'I'm in the car, dammit. Down here in the ditch,' Fergus shouted. He struggled with his weight and shifted enough to push at the door again. It opened a fraction and the minister yelled through the space, 'I need help. I'm stuck in the car!' His voice reached out into the night and was quickly lost in the mist. There was silence.

'Can you hear me?' Fergus called again, feeling the tightness in his temples that always came when he was annoyed with something, sending the internal pressure rising. 'I'm in the car and I need help. I've gone off the road and I can't get out.'

There was another silence as his voice faded. Then, from just outside the car, on the dark side, there was a noise. Twigs crackled and then there was a sound like a low cough followed by a snuffle, like a dog on the scent. It stopped, then came again, a watery, raspy sound of rapid panting.

The minister's heart skipped a beat. 'Who's there? Come on, show yourself.'

The snuffling sound, accompanied by the crunch of dry undergrowth, came suddenly closer and a shadow barged through the tangled foliage. Fergus caught it out of the side of his eye and jerked round. There was something there, but he couldn't make it out. Then another movement danced in his peripheral vision at the side of the car. He snatched round to look, rocking the car, and the headlamps flickered and went out, plunging him into darkness. A shadow flowed round to the front of the car and moved from side to side in a motion that was fluid yet clumsy. Fergus craned forward and the shape suddenly lunged down towards him.

His heart seemed to freeze like a seized engine inside his chest as the thing loomed right in front of the bonnet, swung its head round at Fergus. He jerked back in great alarm, rocking the car again; then something under the bonnet connected and the lights flickered on again, dimly beaming through the sea mist that had crept over the road.

The shape swivelled in front of the windscreen and glared straight at Fergus with huge, protruding black eyes that were set in a grotesque gargoyle face. A mouth like a frog's opened in a gape a foot wide, showing twin rows of teeth that caught the dim light like shards of jagged glass, while the black, dead eyes pierced the space and locked with the minister's. His heart suddenly leapt back to life again, punching against his ribs in a quickfire series of thuds. His lips mouthed out: 'Oh dear Jesus'; but no words came, for his breath was locked in his throat.

The thing swivelled to the left, then to the right, on what seemed an impossible number of legs, but it moved with such spider-like speed that the motion was blurred. It had a glistening, warty hide that looked wet, amphibious. But in the dimness there was no reflection from those eyes. It lifted its head and the back rippled with muscles crossed and latticed to serve a body that could not have evolved in the same world as any of the animals on the peninsula (*or anywhere for that matter*).

The creature crouched, bunched on the bonnet. Its feet scrabbled on the metal and it thumped up against the windscreen. To the side, something hit the door, hard, popping the latch back in again as it slammed shut.

The minister's eyes were opened so wide they almost bulged out to touch the lenses of his glasses. The snuffling sound was inches away from his right ear, a terrible, threatening, *hunting* sound. Fergus rocked back against the seat, trying to push as much distance between himself and the thing that crouched, obscenely toad-like, on the bonnet, a dark hunched shape that pressed right up against the glass, blocking out the light. He cringed away from the door where something else sniffed and growled, forcing its weight against the metal.

'Oh dear sweet Lord. Please God,' he squeaked in a high-pitched whine of pure terror. The car rocked with the weight and Fergus slid in a sprawl to the passenger side, banging his meaty thigh hard against the gearstick. He hit the other door which was still open about six inches and butting against the deadfall. It was with a sudden shock that he realized that those things (*those nightmare shapes*) could get *into the car*. His fearful, prayerful litany never stopped as he scrabbled frantically for the little leather strap which served as a handle. From in front came a series of scraping thumps and the shape moved off the bonnet, rocking the car on its springs. Fergus found the strap and hauled hard.

The door stayed open. A crash came from just outside and something heavy flattened the bushes. The sound galvanized Fergus to huge exertion. The door whipped back and forth twice, held open by the stump of a smashed sapling, then the greenwood bent under his frantic haul. The door juddered as the thing hit it from the side. A grey, scaly hand with long skeletal fingers snaked under the bottom edge and flexed more fingers than any hand had a right to have. They rasped against the metal lip in a horrible, horny way, then disappeared back out of the space as the combined weight of the thing and the spastic haul that Fergus jerked on the handle swung the door over the stump with a quivering *spang* and it thudded shut.

The minister screeched out loud in fear. The car rocked again, and the thing at the side, the thing that had tried to *get inside*, loomed up against the window. A vast black eye speared him with dull hunger. It was like looking into a gravity well where no light existed. The thing grinned what looked like a huge, hungry smile. Scaly lips pulled back over the barbed glass rows of teeth and ropy saliva dripped out to sizzle on the glass.

Inside Fergus's chest his heart was chugging like an overheating steam engine, fast, too fast, punching around, out of control. The thing at the other side hit the door again, tilting the car still further. Fergus felt a great scream of pure fear build up inside him, but there was nowhere for it to go. His throat had closed right over. Something thumped hard under his jawline and pulsed frantic in his temples. There was a popping sensation deep inside, as if an inner tube had just blown under pressure, then a pain exploded, right in the centre of his chest. It felt as if he had been struck a massive blow right on his breastbone and the pain soared up and up, crashing deep into his head.

He was swept up on the crescendo of pain, higher and higher, electrified with the agony of it, then the sensation just seemed to burst asunder into whirling jagged edges of hurt that began to fade. The thudding in his chest was gone, the pounding faded in his ears. Fergus let out one long sigh as his throat unlocked, hitched in two small breaths. 'Oh sweet Jesus,' he said very softly, and everything went dark.

The thing at the passenger window swung its head from side to side then pressed up against the glass, its wide amphibious lips plastering outwards with the pressure. Two of its snaggled teeth rasped against the pane and scratched parallel arcs as it twisted away. A trail of liquid dripped from each tooth and ran along the scratches, hissing as they scoured the sharp twin lines into fogged ruts.

Inside the car there was a twitching movement followed by a judder that shivered the old Austin, then a silence. The creature nudged the glass again and sniffed the air; wide nostrils set between its two blank black eyes fluttered open wetly. It turned away and moved back up the bank. From the other side of the car the bracken crunched and a shape joined it from the gloom. It too snuffled raspingly. The first one, smaller in bulk but longer in limb, whipped out a spidery arm that seemed to have too many joints in it. Claw raked thick skin. A gurgling scream rent the air, seeming to freeze the mist. Something small scurried, panic-stricken in the tangle of hawthorn, and the first creature scuttled, insect-like, almost flowing in a blur of speed, towards the sound on an improbable series of claw-like hands and dived into the darkness of the thicket. There was a crackle and a snap as wide jaws closed.

It was after three in the morning and the skyline, never quite completely dark in the north, was tinged pink with the prospect of high summer dawn in the east over the hills on the far side of Loch Creggan, when Archie Calvert wound his way down the peninsula road and came across the now faint beams of the Austin headlamps angled up and across the road. Archie had inherited his father's boat-hiring business only a couple of years before and could have made a good living from the dozen or so fibreglass twelve-footers with their putt-putt seagull outboards. They were in steady demand from the weekend anglers who dropped their hooks way out in the deep firth water near the gantocks, hauling for the big cod.

If Archie had been as steady a businessman as his father Henry had been, he probably wouldn't have been out so late, and the body of the Rev. Fergus MacLeod would have lain, contorted and stiff, jammed up against the steering wheel in the tilted car until Hector Lawrie came trundling around the bend at the head of the loch, bringing the early morning post.

But since his father died eighteen months before, Archie had found himself with pockets full of ready cash, which was like a dream come true. A tall, whip-thin man in his twenties, with a huge beak-like nose and a stilted walk like a west-coast Ichabod Crane, Archie found himself freed from the drudgery of haul-ing boats and outboards out of the water every night. Now he had a boy from the village to do that work on the shingle beach at Murrin, while the money, which had always been doled out sparingly by old Henry, now went straight into his pocket.

From there it went straight into the ringing cash registers of every bar on each side of the two lochs where Archie spent most of his time. Tonight had been no exception. In fact, when he drove round the corner between the high hawthorn and the bramble stand, he had seen two pairs of lights beaming across the road. This was because his vision was switching from single to double with every movement of the old Vauxhall he'd inherited along with the business. His car wobbled to a halt and Archie heaved himself out on to the road, lurching a little unsteadily.

'What's the score here?' he called out, more than a little slurred. 'Somebody have a wee accident then?'

He wove over to the side of the road and peered down, straight into the nearest beam of light. He lifted a hand up to shade his eyes from the glare and leaned forward, trying to see further. He didn't have the wit to move out of the light.

'Hey there. You OK?' he shouted. 'Anybody in there?'

There was no reply. Archie moved closer and accidentally walked outside the cone of light. He could see the car there. It looked familiar. He was about to scramble down to where it lay at an angle, when a demanding pressure below his navel diverted his attention. He crossed back to the other side of the road, weaving an interesting pattern on the tarmac, and when he was close enough to the bushes he stopped, unzipped his fly and just managed to get it out before the floodgates opened. He stood there, breathing a sigh of relief, enjoying the blissful *draining* sensation as the day's takings were sluiced into the verge. That done, his head felt just a bit clearer and he walked with hardly a stumble to the crashed car. He teetered on the lip of the ditch trying to decide what to do when the decision was taken from him by the force of gravity. His scuffed shoe caught in one of the twisted stalks and Archie overbalanced, arms pinwheeling to regain equilibrium and failing miserably. He skidded down the slope and barked his shin against the angled bumper, feeling the pain bite hard enough to make his eyes water.

'Bastard,' he grunted. 'Nearly took my fuckin' leg off.'

He sat down heavily and a broken-off sapling stump did its best to puncture the seat of his pants, giving him another dagger of pain on his right cheek.

Archie yelled meaningfully. He hauled himself to his feet, rubbing both sore spots with either hand in an awkward mime. When the sharp pain diminished, he edged round the side of the car and peered in. He could see nothing in the darkness. He grabbed the door handle, tugged it down, and gave it a hard yank. It opened, stuttered briefly over the stump, and something rolled clumsily towards him. Archie yelped and jumped back, almost landing on his backside again. His hand was still on the door and it swung wide. There was a flowing, rustling movement from the dark well of the car, and then the shape tumbled out. Something hit Archie hard on the knee, giving it an awful thump right on the bone and making a pain worse than the other two shoot in a blue bolt right up his thigh. He gasped in pain and fright and staggered back, catching his heel on a runner. This time he did fall, but his backside was spared any further damage for he landed on a soft clump of bracken. The light in the sky was just enough for him to see what had hit him. It was the minister's head.

The rest of the man's body was sprawled and humped half inside the car, and his head lolled right out on to the trampled bracken. Archie saw that his glasses were dangling from one ear. The man's face was black and swollen and his tongue was sticking out in a horrible parody of an insolent child. Archie gasped again in fright. He scrambled backwards, crab-like, shoving himself away on his hands, using his heels for traction. He didn't even notice the line of bramble thorns that dug into the heel of his hand, rasping the skin and leaving the thorn tips broken off just under the surface. Archie hauled himself to his feet and clambered out of the ditch. He didn't look back. Instead he got straight into his car and started up the engine, much more sober now than he had been on the drive round from the late-night bar in Kirkland.

That's not how John Lindsay perceived him when Archie pounded on his door just after three in the morning. The lanky red-headed policeman had only crawled under the duvet two hours before, after having driven round to Corbeth where a couple of the tinkers had got themselves into an argument with some of the young men from Murrin, and the argument had escalated into a roly-poly tussle with fists and feet flying but nobody greatly injured beyond a bloody nose or a scraped knuckle. John had read the riot act and threatened them all with a night behind the steel door in Creggan's single jail cell. Annoyed at having been dragged out at such an hour, he was in the mood to sling them all in and leave them to cool their heels until morning, but he was a practical man. That would only mean more paperwork, and God knew he had had plenty of that in recent weeks one way and another, but it would also mean that the fight could erupt again, maybe even several times, between lock-up and breakfast time, and he was not prepared to lose any more sleep over it. Besides that, he wasn't sure whether the travelling people smelled worse than the Murrin long-liners who had spent the day gutting haddock. He just didn't fancy having to aerate the cell in the cold light of day.

John Lindsay was in no mood for any nonsense when Archie banged on his door. He cursed under his breath, very quietly so as not to disturb Marion, who had the remarkable knack of being able to sleep through the sound of a massed pipe band but waking like a cat at the slightest sound if he'd been out for a late one at the Harbour Inn and come home in the early hours, leaving his big, black policeman's boots at the bottom of the stairs and tiptoeing up to bed.

He pulled the door open and stood in his vest and old serge trousers, peering at the figure who stood in front of him, gasping for breath and holding hard on to the lintel.

'This had better be bloody good, Archie.'

'It is. I mean it isn't,' Archie said in a rush. He was out of breath. The policeman could smell the whisky and beer on his breath from four feet away. Just along the road John could see the old Vauxhall. Its lights were still on and one door hung open.

'Well, that clears the whole matter up,' John said with heavy sarcasm. He looked over Archie's shoulder towards the car. 'You been driving that thing?'

Archie turned to look behind him then turned back. 'Sure I have . . .' He stopped in mid-sentence. 'I mean, no. I didn't. I mean, I . . .'

'Oh stop your babbling, man, and tell me what makes you come knocking me up at this time of night. And if I don't hear something good, you're going to spend the night in there,' he said, cocking his head backwards ominously, 'and you won't be driving your dad's old car for a while either.'

Archie stood and looked at him, catching the drift. Then he leaned forward, wafting the policeman with a fresh bouquet of beer fumes.

'It's the minister,' he blurted out. 'He's dead. I saw him. He fell out the car and hit me with his head. Here,' he said, bending down to pat the knee which was still throbbing and on which a large bruise would flower before the morning was really begun.

John Lindsay held his hands up, stopping Archie's rush. 'Hold on a minute. Just hold on, son, before you wake up the whole village. And if you wake up the missus, I swear to God I'll kick your arse so hard my boot'll get stuck.'

Archie started to say something when, from upstairs, a tired woman's voice called down: 'Is everything all right, John?'

The policeman turned and transfixed Archie with a glare. The skinny man backed away from the lintel, eyes wide. 'Honest to God,' he wailed in a whisper, 'it's not my fault. It's the minister, Mr MacLeod. He's dead. In his car. He must have crashed or something.'

'All right, but you had better not be spinning me a fanny, Archie. I suppose you'd better come in. But remember,' he paused, and fixed his eye on the other man's, 'keep the noise down, or I'll get you to blow into one of these wee bags. Catch my drift?'

Archie nodded. He went in. It took John Lindsay only five minutes to find out enough. He made a call to Dr Docherty, got no reply, and rang Alex Graham. She answered sleepily, asked a couple of questions, then told him she'd be there. He made another call to the ambulance service down at Kirkland, having ascertained from Archie that the fire service with their cutting equipment would not be needed. Then he found his shirt and tunic, hauled them on, and sat and pulled his boots over his thick socks.

'OK, Archie, you can go now. Come on, I'll be on my way, and you'd better be on yours. I'll want to see you in the morning,' he said, opening the door to let Archie past, again wrinkling his nose at the sour smell of stale drink. 'Oh, and another thing. You'd best leave that car there. I'll expect to see it when I get back.'

'But it's nearly two miles,' Archie protested.

'All the better to sober you up,' John said with a wide, satisfied grin. 'And if I catch you coming round that Creggan Road three sheets to the wind again, you know what'll happen.'

He clapped his hat on his head and walked round to the garage. Archie moved off. The engine on the

Landrover coughed into life and the big white jeep nosed out from under the aluminium door. Archie watched as it swung out on to the road, heading towards the lightening sky. When it was maybe fifty yards away, he glared at it, then swung his hand up and over into the crook of his right elbow, snapping that arm hard into the time-honoured two-finger salute.

In the rear-view mirror, John Lindsay, who had been waiting for just such a gesture, chuckled to himself. That one was marked.

Dawn was light and pale on the far side of the loch when he got to the scene a few minutes later. The sun would not peek over the Carman Hills for another two hours, but already the promise of day was in the far sky. The lights of the Austin were still angled up, dim and watery in the disappearing mist. John braked his car right on the edge of the road. He looked down from the height and saw it just as Archie Calvert had told him. The minister was lying half in, half out of the car, sprawled and ungainly in death. His face looked bloated. His eyes, lodged deep between the sagging cheeks, were staring at the sky.

Alex Graham arrived within minutes, screeching to a halt in her little red hatchback. She left the door open as she came scrambling out and ran towards where John stood.

'Doesn't look as if he needs a doctor,' John said matter-of-factly. He had liked the rotund little minister, pompous and irascible though he might have been.

He turned round to watch Alex Graham scramble down towards the car. She moved well, agile in a pair of faded Levis and scuffed Nikes. Down at the body, she dumped her bag, pulled out her stethoscope and placed the flat end under the minister's jaw. Then she pulled open his shirt and did the same again. It was obvious that there was no life there. John had seen the man's face, the protruding tongue. He had seen dead men plenty of times. Like him, Alex Graham was a professional. He waited, silent, while she went through the routine, flashing her light into eyes that were glazing over, feeling for non-existent pulses, checking reflexes that would never flex again. He saw her shake her head. She stood, heaved herself up the steep short slope, and joined him.

'I'm afraid you're right,' she said.

'I've got the ambulance coming round from Kirkland,' John said. 'They can take him to the hospital. What do you think happened?'

'I'm not sure. I've made a brief examination. I can't find any major injury, but that doesn't mean to say there isn't one. The PM will show anything.' She paused and fiddled with her bag, cramming the stethoscope inside. 'How about you? Any idea what might have caused it?'

'Looks like he hit the verge there,' John said, pointing along the road. 'I reckon he bounced over, then back again, and went down the ditch. It doesn't look as though he was going too fast.'

The policeman moved away and went back towards the car again. He looked round it, noting where the tough thorny branches had scraped the paintwork and taking in the gleaming metal that was exposed by the stumps of saplings scouring off the paint on the sills and the bottom half of the doors. He came round to the front of the car, stepping over the body carefully, not wishing to move it yet. On the window, there were two long curving marks. He touched one with a forefinger. It felt like a gouge in the glass, a little worn gully, as if it had been etched by something, then smoothed down. He raised his eyebrows, faintly puzzled. Round at the front of the car he looked over the bonnet. There were scrape marks here too: two sets just between the lights at the front end, then a series of deeper indentations right up at the windscreen as if hard hooks had been pressed into the metal. He looked them over, then moved away, thinking about them, not reaching any conclusion. Round on the other side of the loch he could see the blue winking light of the ambulance as it speeded along the low road.

TWENTY-FIVE

Other things were happening on the night that Fergus MacLeod's heart burst in his chest when he saw something that could not exist scuttering across the bonnet of his old car. After the moon dipped below the Cowals, washing the rest of the real light from the sky (and plunging the stand of trees where Tom Callander had stood, heart pounding and horrified, into darkness), shadows moved in the darker places on the peninsula.

In that night, things moved and slid and snaked, wraith-like, humped and strange, through the trees and along the sides of hedgerows and dry-stane dikes. They squeezed themselves through black gaps and into the gloom of the summer night, snuffling and searching, outrunners of the other thing that waited patiently for the gates to open fully, for worlds to join.

The time was coming closer. Things had happened, keys had been turned in doors that only one person knew existed; others could have known about them but would never have given them any credence. They were, however, to find out.

It watched from the far side of the reflection, from that *other* place, as Helen Crombie strode through the doorway in a swirl of pink. It was a shadow in the corner of the identical room, smoky and dark and unmoving. The thing that watched with hungry senses was not truly aware in this world. *Not yet.*

But it would be. Oh yes. It would be aware of everything soon. Its time was coming.

It was old and it had many names. In times past it had been known as *Glae-gruamach*, the *Gleidhidh*, the keeper of the ways, the black guardian of the narrow thin place that joined the path of this world to the trails and paths of other places. In this world it had no life, not yet. But things had happened.

It sensed life and rebirth in the timeless, ponderous way that an ancient oak senses the spring and the pulse of life, that sends the stirrings into its buds; the tremulous sproutings of its acorns that have been buried far from its roots by the autumn jaybirds.

The *Gleidhidh*. It was older than the stone gate built by those beetling little people whose life forces flickered past its slumbering, dull awareness, like the brief light of August fireflies. It was much older than that. The gate had been built in the twink of an eye only twenty-five of its spans past; that was six thousand years to the hot, frantic creatures whose lives flashed and guttered in the space of one short, cold breath.

Even then it was as ancient as the paths that plunged through the darkness and radiated from the centre of things to the other places. It had been there when those ways came into being, and they had been there for so long that their creation was lost in the unplumbed depths of its memory. Its mind was creaking stone, cold with age. It knew no beginning for it and its kind, only *being*. And it had waited for ever.

And now, something almost new. It hungered for it; grew impatient for it. Already the doors were creaking open, blowing winds over the crossroads on the paths as the great year, the cusp of the great lunar year, approached again, and the rules that turned the runes clicked the tumblers on the lock that joined times past to times present, and places here to other places that were not part of this universe.

The crossroads, where all paths from all doors met, was a place of no time and no light. It existed only as the maze of darkness without dimension, and at the centre of it sat the *Gleidhidh*, the guardian of the roads, compelled by the only law in this state where the concept of any law was unthinkable: to let pass that which had the power and no other.

And now, something almost new.

It could feel the warm life through the crack in the doorway; the one that had been left unlocked *then*. It could feel the pulse of life and hungered for it. It could sense that life drawing it upwards and out and towards. Already its hungry instinct had sent out a part of itself, a shade of itself, only a tiny, spinning thought, and had found another thin place, a crack in the real doorway. A way through a flickering mind; a fault line in the walls of the prison that kept it at the crossroads, for ever and ever.

Almost new. It had felt life before, but not so close, not so ready.

And it would have it all.

Tommy thought he was dreaming, but he felt as if he was awake. Nothing had moved in the cupboard as the last light of the moon faded from the sky and cast the room into gloom. The sound of the water hissing and gurgling in the pipes had made him drowsy. He had lain huddled in his pyjamas and the little check dressing gown with the fancy silk cord just like his dad's that he had got at Christmas. He was jammed up against the pillows, with the light quilt hauled up to his neck and tucked under his chin, listening to the sighing of the old house, drowsily trying not to think of it as *breathing*.

The next thing he knew, he was standing in front of the set-in cupboard door which yawned agape in the wall.

(It was closed, *it was closed!*)

It was dark there. He could make out the inside panel of the door which was swung right back until it pressed up against his pine chest of drawers. The window was a paler rectangle on the wall which let in just enough dim light for his wide eyes to make out smudged, undefined shapes. He reached a hand forward, despite a buzz of panic that told him to stand still, to get back into bed, but his hand moved away, of its own volition, towards where his clothes hung on the brass rail.

There were no clothes in the cupboard. No jeans, no school trousers folded over their bright yellow plastic hangers. His shirts were not there.

Tommy felt his breath catch. A little shudder passed up from the fingers of his outstretched arm which he tried to pull back from the dark, but he seemed to have no control over it at all. Involuntarily (*I don't want to go in there*) he took a step forward. On either side of him, the door frames were grey pillars. Another step and he was inside the oblong of black. His fingers were stretched in front of him, questing with their own need to know. They should have hit the back of the cupboard by now, should have touched the wall.

He was inside. Another step, another, and still, dragging his feet, not wanting to, trying not to, a third, a fourth. And there was nothing there. He was in a tunnel of blackness. He was *in the cupboard*. Again his ribs gave a heave, short and sharp, and dry air swooped into his lungs.

'Wake up. *Wake up now!*' His mind yammered at him in a high panicky demand.

But he couldn't wake up, couldn't stop himself. Tommy walked down the long cupboard tunnel, eyes wide, heart hammering, breath coming in short, shallow pants; his outstretched fingers tingling with apprehension of cobwebs and spiders and things that scuttled and scurried and scuttered in the dark.

Then he touched something. A hard, flat panel. His fingernails bent back, scraping on the old wood as the momentum of his step carried him forward. A tight little sliver of pain arced up his arm and was gone to numbness in a second. The whole of him seemed a-quiver. He brought his other hand up hard against the wall in front, feeling it with fingers and palms. Around in the dark, the gloom was filled with an ambience that crowded in, whispering and echoing in the cupboard.

Gingerly he turned his head around, still with his hands flat on the wooden wall, feeling the far-away vibration that seemed to be coming from the very fabric itself, listening to the almost inaudible rasping sound that came from deep within the walls. Behind him, far behind him, the closet door was a pale shape in the encompassing black. He turned back to face forward and felt his hands push. There was a resistance, then a small click, and the wall ahead swung forward under the pressure of his palms, and a door opened. Momentum carried him onwards and through into a purple-grey light that came from all around without an obvious source.

Walls loomed up on either side. Stone walls that seemed to go on for ever in the strange purple light. The rasping sound was louder here, as if there were *things* inside the walls, chewing and boring their way behind the surface. On the periphery of vision he saw a jumble of boxes and two broken chairs. There was a dimly perceived set of shelves that seemed to be suspended in mid-air and shimmered into vague outlines when he looked at them directly.

'It's the cellar,' Tommy said to himself, almost matter-of-factly.

It was the cellar, and yet it wasn't.

Those shelves, they were the shelves where his father had put some of his tools. Yet the wall on which the shelves were hung on old, rusty, paint-peeling brackets was filmy and indistinct. Behind them was the real wall. A massive, blocky stone wall that stretched up and away. Between the rough-hewn stones was a pillar of smooth rock that seemed to carry a vast weight. To the left of that was another, a massive block that sprouted from the earth as if it had rooted down there in the bowels of the world and had pushed its way through and under the house. Yards to the right was another.

Tommy turned back towards the doorway he'd stepped through and his heart leapt right up in his chest, hammered two or three times like blows against the inside of his ribs.

For the doorway was gone.

Where it had been was another massive stone pillar a yard wide.

And Tommy was down here in the cellar where his father had told him never to go.

Alan had said it with stern warning in his eyes. 'There's a lot of rubbish down there, Tommy. Whoever had this place before us threw all their old stuff down in the cellar. I don't want you going down there. You could break a leg.'

And Tommy never had been there. He'd never even had the normal curiosity about the cellar that he had about almost everything else. His father had shown him the old wooden stairway that led down into the gloom. It was painted a sickly green and between the uprights of the banister (one or two spars were broken) he could see the fluffy grey smudges of old cobwebs, dark triangles where fat spiders lurked, waiting to pounce.

'You could fall down here, or something could fall on you,' Alan had said. 'I don't want you getting hurt.'

'I won't go down, Dad,' Tommy had promised, and his dad had ruffled his hair the way he always did when he was pleased with him. Tommy never had any intention of going down into that dark well. From the top of the stairs, he had peeked down just as his father had switched off the single light bulb that dangled from a braided cord, plunging the cellar into darkness. He had imagined sneaking down there, down the wooden steps, and had pictured *all* of the scenarios. Falling through a crumbling tread and crashing down on to the old chairs and bric-à-brac where he would lie in agony with a broken leg (or unable to move because his back was broken) while the door clicked shut and nobody heard his cries for help. He had pictured himself lying crumpled in the dark, while things crawled over his face, things with many legs and pincer jaws that could bite and nip. He had imagined just being down in the cellar when the dim bulb blew, dropping him into the darkness and leaving him to grope around for the stairs, which in his vivid imagination he would never find. Alan had hung the old tarnished brass key on the hook beside the door and Tommy had let it hang there. The cellar was the kind of place that he didn't want to explore. No way.

And now here he was. In the cellar. And yet *not* in it.

The vague outlines of the *real* cellar wavered like some odd double vision, like the shimmering reflection of water on a dry, dusty road in summer that his dad said was a mirage. And behind the wavering shelves and jumbled junk were the real cellar walls, hard and cold and stone.

Tommy whirled round, away from the pillar where the door had been. To his right was another, and further on another big block. Five in all, set in a curious pentagon. Even with his heart beating its panic inside his chest, and even though he didn't know what a pentagon was, Tommy could see the shape and sense that it was right in all the wrong of his dream.

The purple light seemed to ooze out of the walls between the stone pillars, casting an eerie glow around him. Unbidden, feet dragging, he walked forward into the big cellar.

Shivers trickled coldly up and down his spine and he could feel the soft, short hair on the back of his neck crawl as his skin tightened.

Then there was a vibration that coursed through the flagstones and right up through his feet, as if something had shifted and changed. He looked ahead into the middle of the cellar, and the floor was suddenly gone. In its place there was a hole, a wide black crater with crumbling edges.

From within, the rasping, crawling sound came echoing. Tommy's feet took him forward three slow steps although he didn't want to go anywhere near that hole. He stood there at the lip and his eyes, still wide and staring in the strange light, peered down into the purple depths.

His eyes darted down into the chasm and then widened even further in a jolt of terror. For down there in the dim purple light a shadow was rushing upwards like a black gusher spewing up a well; a roaring, surging wave of shade that came swooping up from an infinite depth towards him. And in that instant Tommy realized that whatever *it* was, it was coming to get him.

A wave of revulsion jittered through him, so strong it was like a physical blow. He scrabbled back from the crater, feet sliding on the flagstones. One of his slippers flipped off and tumbled out from the edge, heel over toe, and plummeted down towards the rushing shadow. The rough stone scraped against Tommy's bare sole as he shoved himself back from the lip, skittering crab-like on hands and backside, before he turned, got to his knees and then lurched to his feet. The roaring sound whooped up like a storm from the chasm in a deep thunder, that made the stones shudder.

He almost sprawled forward, caught his balance and ran from the lip, one bare foot slapping the floor. The cellar seemed vast, a massive vault supported on five tremendous pillars. The wall was far away, and behind him the midnight express was rushing and sizzling up for him. Terror clamped his throat like a choking grip and a little wail tried and failed to get through. His dressing gown flapped behind him, trailing a long tassled cord like a tail. He made for the wall that was suddenly away in the distance across an expanse of wide, square flagstones. Then his shin clipped something hard enough to rivet a fiery explosion of pain into the bone and the world took a little flip and the shimmering, insubstantial jumble of objects that faded away in direct vision twanged into reality (*oh but the pain was real, it was one hundred per cent real*) and Tommy went crashing in a forward sprawl into the tangle of odds and ends and broken chairs. Something slammed into his hip and he bounced hard into an upturned table leg that caught him right in the midriff and socked his breath away. The momentum carried him towards the wall in a tumble and his head jerked forward. In the fraction of a second before he hit, Tommy's eyes squeezed shut and he had a flash preview of the sickening thud that would happen when his forehead met the stone wall and then . . .

He was through the doorway and landing with a soft thud on a wet hummock of heather. The air that had been punched out of his lungs in the cellar came whooping back in an almighty, desperate gasp. A wind ruffled the back of his head and Tommy lifted his face from the slick sphagnum moss and looked up into a sky that was grey and tinged with a thundery orange. The wind moaned across low-lying purple-clad hills. From the right there was a harsh cry, but from where Tommy lay sprawled in a shallow dip he couldn't see what had made the noise. He crawled forward on his elbow, trying to lever himself to his feet, and felt the damp through his dressing gown. He managed to get up, still winded, sides heaving. A wave of nausea swelled as the stench of the rotting moss caught in his throat. His vision blurred for a moment and Tommy thought he saw a black shape spread wings and swoop towards him. Without thinking he pulled his head backwards and the hoarse cries and the moaning wind and the smell were gone and he was back in the dark again, in a tunnel of stone.

He was somewhere under the house. Not in the cellar but close to it, he knew. The arched passageway was dry and dusty and festooned with old, decaying webs. From behind him, somewhere in the distance, he could hear the roaring noise that had terrified him into flight.

For a second he was numbed with the dread, then his muscles unlocked and he took off down the dark tunnel. He raced down a long straight, seeing ahead in the dusty gloom the passage dwindle into the distance in a long straight perspective. There seemed no end to it. Tommy ran, panting, and his strides seemed enormous. The lines of stone on the wall whipped by in a blur as he sped, impossibly quick, blindingly fast, while behind him the sounds of black pursuit were thrumming between his ears.

It was as if distances here were all wrong, as if they were somehow compressed and squashed. The far end of the tunnel which had seemed miles away raced suddenly towards him as his feet took their seven-league strides with a hollow pattering that drummed on the flickering walls. The end of the tube came to meet him, a solid dry wall. Tommy skidded to a halt, while behind him the noise increased and solid shadows loomed. On either side, the tunnel branched. He swung first left, then right, in urgent indecision, chose the right and clattered along. Another ending brought him up short within a hundred steps. This time there were four choices, each radiating at odd angles. Instinctively he went to the second on the left and found himself on another long straight. Again, the perspective seemed wrong. He was moving much faster than he knew he could, and it was taking him nowhere. In the distance the tunnel was foreshortened and the walls seemed to curve in towards him as if, in the dimness, the little light left actually bent to meet him.

Another hundred sprinted paces on, the passageway ended. This time there was no fork, no branching escape. Tommy slewed to a stop just before he caroomed off the hard stone, holding his hands out in front of him as buffers. He turned left and right seeking a way out, then spun round and his jaw dropped slackly. For the tunnel was closed off. He was in a cylinder of stone, boxed in and trapped. And from somewhere he could hear the roaring sound as the dread passage of his pursuer squeezed and ripped the very air. It was coming. He didn't know from where.

As he stood there, at bay, panting for breath, the other end of the tunnel darkened as shadow enveloped the stone. It was as if the blackness were pouring through, flowing between the cracks. Above the rasping, crushing noise, the boy could hear a fierce thudding sound, and dimly realized it was his own heart, hammering like a bird's.

Then above that, he heard a clear note. The sound wasn't in his ears. It seemed to come from all around, and yet, strangely, *within* him, echoing at the back of his head.

Behind the sweet, pure sound that cut through the cacophony of noises, there was a whispering, gentle and persuasive.

The wall beside him shimmered confusingly and suddenly Katie was there.

'Come on, Tommy,' his sister said in words that were music, though her lips never moved.

'I . . . I . . .' Tommy's words backed up in his throat.

Katie shook her head and pulled him until he faced away from the rolling dark shadow. His feet moved of their own volition. Laney, from nowhere, stood on his left and grasped his other hand. It felt warm and dry and tingly in his own.

Insistently, they drew him back past the shimmer of stone and into another dark (but not a black dark) where the echoes died away and where the shadow did not follow. Tommy felt his head spin dizzily as the soft dark closed in on him in a protective wave and he simply gave in to it.

He woke with a start not long after the sun rose over the Carman Hills across the loch to the east and flooded the room with light.

Gasping for a breath that at first refused to draw itself

in, he scrambled to a hunched position, like a small, frightened, cornered animal. He jerked his head to left and right, eyes darting in confusion and alarm around the room. The cupboard door was closed, as it had been when he went to bed the night before. He scrambled across the bed, tangling himself in the duvet, and fumbled with the handle. The door swung open silently. His jeans and school trousers were folded over their plastic yellow hangers. His shirts were lined up in a colourful row. Behind them he could see the old dark wood panel of the back of the closet. The big breath that had taken so long to muster expelled itself in a long, relieved sigh. Tommy felt his whole body sag as the initial panic drained away.

'It *was* a dream,' he said. 'It really *was* a dream.'

Suddenly the day seemed ten degrees brighter. Tommy felt his breathing slow down to near normal. He had dreamed the whole thing. He had dreamt that it had hunted for him, and that down there in the dark, little Katie had spoken to him. Spoken into his head.

He sat down on the bed and pulled on his jeans and picked out a T-shirt from his drawer. He pulled on his scuffed Nikes and then folded down the duvet as his father had shown him. This he did almost absently. He did not notice the slightly muddy patch where his elbow had been pressed against the sheet.

Today was Saturday. The horrors of the night and the terrible dream were fading fast, fragmenting in the light of day. Today his father would be coming home from up north and that would be the best thing to happen to him all week.

Already it was starting off to be a good day.

TWENTY-SIX

Helen was up and about by the time Tommy got downstairs to the kitchen. He looked along the hallway at the bottom of the stairs to where the cellar door, narrower than the others, stood at the end of the lobby. The big brass key hung from the hook. If Tommy had wanted to use it (*oh no he wouldn't want to do that*) he would have had to pull a chair out from the dining-room and clamber up to reach it. He walked slowly down the hallway and stood looking up at the door. Down there behind its blank face it was dark and filled with spiders.

And *nothing else*, he told himself.

There was only old junk down there under the weak light of the naked bulb, nothing more. But still he didn't want to go down there and find out, not down the creaking staircase and into the corners where the fat spiders lurked and wove their dusty grey webs.

He backed away from the door and kept facing it until he got to the kitchen, then turned and walked into the bright room.

'Hi, Mum,' he said to his mother's back. She was bent over the sink, filling a bucket with hot water. She looked round and stared at him almost dreamily, before she gave a small start and came to herself, as if her mind had been on other things.

'Oh, Tommy, it's you,' she said. A weak smile flickered across her face. Tommy thought she looked *awfully* tired.

'Yeah, it's me all right,' Tommy concurred agreeably.

'Can you fix yourself some cereal?'

'Sure I can,' he said. *I do it every other day*, he thought. Tommy couldn't remember the last time his mother had actually made them a breakfast. She used to make them toast and marmalade with good wholemeal bread with the chewy bits of corn in them. Other times she'd fill them up with bacon and eggs, or she'd flip pancakes or serve up scones dripping with golden butter. That had been so long ago that he'd almost forgotten what a scone tasted like. It seemed he'd had rice crispies or cornflakes with cold milk every day for weeks, except for the weekends his father was home and they'd enjoy a giant fry-up that would leave Tommy feeling as though he'd burst.

'Sure I can, Mum,' he said resignedly.

Helen went on filling the bucket and then heaved it out from the sink. A small drop of water lapped over the rim and spattered on the floor. Helen dumped the bucket on the draining board and wiped the spillage with a cloth, then hefted the load again and carried it out of the kitchen. Tommy watched her as she went, her back arched to take the weight. The scary thought came to him: *she doesn't care.*

In fact, it seemed as if Helen hardly noticed any of them at all. All she cared about was the house. All the time.

Tommy poured his cornflakes into a bowl, then went to the fridge for milk which was still in its carton. He sniffed it first, having had a couple of nasty surprises in the last few days when the milk glopped out of the hole in a thick, sluggish stream, sour and bitter. Helen hadn't been out of the house for days, and she didn't seem to realize when they ran short. Now Tommy just took enough from her purse when they needed milk or bread, and brought it home with him on the way back from school. Helen never even noticed, and that was the most scary thing of all.

He was half-way through the bowl of cereal when the twins came pattering into the kitchen on bare feet, golden hair awry from sleep. Tommy stopped in mid-spoonful when he saw them at the door, and the memory of the strange, terrifying nightmare he'd had came zooming back with shocking force. He gulped on the cereal, rasping his throat, and the resultant coughing fit spun the vision out of his thoughts as he gasped for breath.

Katie and Laney's smiles vanished when they saw their big brother gagging over his breakfast bowl. They came across the kitchen and stood on either side of him, staring up with blank seriousness until the tickly cough stopped. Red-faced, he shoved himself back from the table and when his watering eyes cleared, he saw his sisters on either side. He grinned, sheepishly.

'S'all right now. I'm fine,' he said and raised his hands up to ruffle their hair, just as his father did. The twins gazed up at him, their expression of mute concern transforming into pure hero-worship.

'All right now,' Tommy said in his best imitation of his dad's jocular way. 'What'll it be ladies? Cornflakes with milk, followed by more cornflakes and with cornflakes to follow?'

They smiled delightedly and nodded in unison.

'A very good choice, ladies,' Tommy continued, getting into the swing of it. 'If you just sit yourselves down, I'll be mother.' As he said it, he felt a brief chill at the thought. *I'll be mother because I have to be mother.* He suppressed it quickly, shoving it down where he couldn't hear the little voice with the edge of fear in it.

'And if we eat any more of this stuff, we'll crunch when we walk,' he finished.

The girls eased themselves up on to their stools and Tommy pushed their bowls in front of them, edging them on to the mats that their mother insisted they always use at the table. He poured the milk in and sprinkled heaped tablespoonfuls of sugar on the cereal. His sisters beamed their thanks at him more eloquently than words could have done, and bent to their breakfast.

Later, after Tommy had got his sisters to change into their matching corduroy dungarees, their out-to-play gear, he rummaged in his play-box for his football. It was Saturday. In the afternoon, he and Bobby Lindsay and Jim Rodger were going to have a kick-around and maybe play commandos up in the trees beyond the road. His father would be back by lunchtime after his week up north, and he'd be home for a few days, and then, fingers crossed, touch wood, everything would get back to normal.

When they came downstairs again, Tommy bouncing the ball on the steps like a basketball player, trying to make it land square on the treads and failing, Helen was working in the dining-room. The three of them went in and saw their mother polishing the shutters that framed the window, burnishing them to a deep lustre.

'We're just going out to play in the garden,' Tommy said for the three of them. Helen stopped what she was doing and looked round at them standing in the doorway.

'What was that?'

'Me and the girls are going to play ball out the front,' Tommy said.

Helen looked blank, as if he'd spoken in a foreign language. 'Outside?' she said slowly.

'Yes, just in the garden. I'll watch out for them.'

Helen paused, seeming to think about this weighty proposition, then she seemed to get all the facts aligned in her head and came to a decision. 'Oh no, you can't go out today.'

'But it's Saturday, Mum,' Tommy immediately protested. Beside him the girls moved closer together and their hands automatically clasped. 'I've put away all the breakfast things and I've folded down the bedclothes. We're just going out in the garden.'

'But it's . . .' Helen said. The glazed look filmed her eyes over, passed and then her look became sharp. 'It's raining. You can't go and play in the rain.'

'No it's not,' Tommy shot back. 'It's sunny,' he said simply.

Helen's canny look shot across the space between them. 'I don't want any backchat from you. It's raining out there and that's all about it. You'll have to stay in the house.'

Tommy's heart sank. When his father was away he didn't like staying in the house a moment longer than necessary. He didn't even like leaving the girls here when he went to school in the mornings. The house made him feel strange, uncomfortable. And the way his mother seemed to think about nothing else these days just accentuated that feeling.

'But Mum, it was bright this morning. The sun was shining in the kitchen window.'

'Tommy, I told you I don't want any backchat. Watch my lips, young man. It is raining outside, and you are to stay in. I don't want you catching your death of cold.'

Tommy opened his mouth to start off another protest, but Helen cut him off, holding up a hand which was still clenched around a dusting cloth. 'The sun might have been shining in through the kitchen window, but if you care to look through the dining-room window, you can see it's raining buckets out there. Now have I made myself clear?'

Tommy shifted his eyes from his mother and looked through the pane of glass. It was grey and murky. There were big drops of rain sliding in wavery lines down the glass.

The brief argument with his mother had centred Tommy's attention on her. He could have sworn the sun was shining when he'd walked into the room, but he couldn't deny that from where he was standing, it was definitely raining out there.

'Shit,' he whispered very softly. It wasn't a word he normally used, but Jimmy Rodger said it so often that Tommy had picked it up by contagion.

'What was that?' his mother called from across the room.

'Nothing,' Tommy said. Beside him his sisters cupped their hands over their mouths and they giggled in conspiratorial silence.

'That's fine then. Just go and play in the front room, and don't make a mess,' Helen called, accentuating the last part.

Tommy turned and shepherded Katie and Laney out of the door. They crossed the hall and he swung the door of the big room open. Sunlight flooded in, reflecting off the wallpaper nearest the door. Tommy walked over the threshold and the brightness dimmed as if a switch had been thrown, making the room instantly dull. He took two steps forward and turned towards the window. It was spattered with rain which ran in rivulets to the bottom of the pane. Outside it was fairly *shoving* it down. A wind whipped the cypress trees at the bottom of the garden, making them shiver violently, and across the loch it was so heavy that it looked as if grey veils had been hung over the water. The far side of the loch where the Carman Hills reared up was completely shrouded. The water out in the loch was grey slate flecked with the white of spume as the wind caught the tops of the waves and whisked them into froth. It was not a day to be out.

The three of them looked out through the big bay window where the drops were rapping against the glass, fuzzing vision in wavery runnels. The room was now dark as big thundery clouds piled up overhead, making the summer morning sky bleak and wintry.

'Shit, shit, shit,' Tommy hissed vehemently, and immediately felt the guilt of using swear words. He let the plastic football slip from where he'd tucked it under his armpit and it bounced twice on the carpet and rolled lazily under the settee.

Alan arrived home just after one in the afternoon. The children heard the crunch of tyres on the smooth driveway chuckie-stones as the BMW swung up through the gates and along the curve towards the house. The three of them dropped what they were doing, Tommy leaving his array of transformers and the girls letting their dolls flop to the floor. They pressed their noses up against the glass, Katie and Laney on either side of their brother, standing on tiptoe to peer out through the rain. The car crunched to a halt just outside. Alan waved and smiled at them, then reversed back in a neat loop and disappeared from view round the side of the house. He'd been gone for nearly a week. Tommy felt a strange, strong, surge of relief to know his father was home.

'Well, hello you lot, how's it going?' Alan bellowed happily, his face split by a big grim. He hunkered down and swept them all into his arms in a tumble. Squashed between Katie and Laney, Tommy could feel his dad's big strong arms around him. He could smell that hard-to-define *dad* smell that was warm and dry and slightly smoky. His cheek was rasped by Alan's roughcast and it was the best feeling in the whole world. In an instant, he felt safe and secure.

Alan released them almost reluctantly, giving them all a fond final squeeze before he did so.

'So what are you all up to then?' he asked, swinging his gaze over all three.

'Nothing much. I've got my transformers and the girls are playing with their dolls. It's a bit boring.'

'Sounds a *lot* boring for a Saturday,' Alan said, straightening up. 'You should be out in the fresh air, running around mad, as usual.'

'We can't. Mum said we have to stay in.'

'Why's that? Have you been up to something while I've been away?'

Tommy was about to reply when Helen came out of the kitchen and proffered a cheek. Alan kissed it resoundingly. 'Had a good week?' he asked.

'Busy,' Helen replied. 'You?'

'Busting a gut the whole time. God, it's good to be back. I've been up to my oxters in problems and up to my ass in mud and crap. But the job's going all right.' He turned to the upturned faces of his children. 'But enough of all this. I've been driving all day and my backside has gone to sleep. Your ole dad's got a numb bum.'

They all sniggered.

'And he's starving. I could eat a mangy horse. Just show me where it is and I'll eat it raw.' He made to walk away from the door and down the hallway.

'Could you take your shoes off, Alan. I've just done the carpet.'

Alan stopped and looked blankly at Helen. Tommy watched him standing there with his briefcase in one hand and his light raincoat slung over the other. There was something about him that was odd, but it didn't strike Tommy until later.

'What was that?'

'I've just cleaned the carpet. If you put your slippers on it'll save me having to do it again. Look. I've left them there on the rack.'

Alan let out an exasperated sigh. The good feeling of being home again evaporated a little. Helen just looked at him from a few feet away.

Some welcome, Alan thought.

'Oh, all right,' was what he said. He dumped the briefcase on the carpet and hooked his coat on the polished bentwood stand and shuffled with his feet, easing his shoes off without loosening the laces the way he'd told Tommy a million times not to, and slid his blue slippers on.

'Okay?' he asked almost challengingly when he had done it. Helen simply nodded and flicked him a small smile. Alan sighed, then gathered himself in an almost visible effort, determined not to argue. He followed Helen into the immaculate kitchen, smelling the polish as he entered.

'Well, you *have* been busy, haven't you? The place is bright as a new pin. You must have used a ton of Mister Sheen.'

Alan sat himself down heavily on a chair which he slid back from the table. He swung both legs up and plonked his feet, one crossed over the other, on the pine surface. He looked incongruous in his sports jacket and slacks and blue slippers, but he didn't give a damn. Slippers or not, it was good to be home again.

'I'd shoot my granny for a cup of tea,' he said, stretching the long drive out of his back and arms. 'If I knew where they'd buried the old lady, that is. Be a dear and stick the kettle on, would you?'

Helen nodded. The water splashed into the upright kettle. She flicked a switch and then started absently wiping at the surface next to the sink.

Alan rambled on about his work, getting the week out of his system as he normally did after arriving home from a site job. Helen pottered about until the kettle boiled, then made a pot of tea. She unhooked a cup from under the cupboard shelf and brought it to the table with the carton of milk. She poured a cup for Alan and put the pot back at the sink.

'Aren't you having one with me?' he asked.

'Maybe later. I've got too much to do.'

'Oh, come on. Take the weight off your feet. Anything that needs to be done can wait until tomorrow. I reckon we both need a weekend off.'

Helen stood against the sink, eyes shifting around the room almost anxiously.

'Here,' Alan said. 'I'll get it.' He unslung another cup and poured one for Helen. 'Come and have a break.

And let's have a Kitkat too. Where do we keep the biscuits?' He swung open the cupboard door and brought out the biscuit barrel, popped the cork top and delved a hand inside. Down at the bottom there were a few crumbs. There was a slightly stale smell coming from the earthenware jar. 'What? No biscuits?' Alan said.

'I didn't get a chance to buy any today,' Helen said.

'Never mind. I'll have a sandwich. I really am starving. That's a long trip from the Moray Firth, and that road's a killer.'

Alan crossed to the fridge and swung it open. The little light shone bluely on the interior surface. There were two eggs nestled in the recesses near the inside top of the door. Down in the vegetable compartment something green and limp was draped next to a squashed tomato. A couple of tupperware bowls with press-down lids were sqeezed to the back of one of the plastic shelves. He opened the green one with a pop. A small square of hard corned beef rattled around like a mottled brown dice. It looked as dry as a nut. The other bowl was empty. On the lower shelf there was the remains of a loaf of bread. It wasn't quite biscuit-hard, but it was heading that way.

'Where's the bread then?' Alan asked reasonably, although he could already feel irritation rise.

'I told you I didn't manage to get to the shops today. I had far too much to do.'

'But the fridge is *empty*,' Alan said. 'I mean, there's nothing in there to eat.'

'I meant to go down and get some things, but I just didn't have the time.'

Alan felt the pleasure of homecoming fade further. Inwardly he sighed, trying not to show it, trying not to let his exasperation and disappointment bubble up to the surface.

'Well, I suppose I'd better get down to the shop

before it closes,' he said as agreeably as he could. 'I'll take the troops with me.'

Helen nodded. 'Thanks, I appreciate it. It's been non-stop for the past couple of days.'

Inwardly torn between his annoyance and his appreciation of the fact that Helen had obviously made an effort in one direction, even if it had led to the neglect of others, Alan hauled himself to his feet.

'I need to stretch my legs anyway,' he said. He bent down and gave Helen a small kiss on the cheek. 'See you later.'

She nodded again.

'Tommy,' he called from the bottom of the stairs. 'You too, you two. Want to come to the shops with me?'

The three children came out from the front room.

'Wait till I get my coat, Dad.'

'What do you want a coat for, son?'

'It's raining out there.'

'Where?'

'Everywhere,' Tommy said. The twins nodded in agreement. Their bright faces did a great deal to evaporate Alan's tension. He could feel the internal valve open, venting off his emotional steam.

'Don't be silly,' he said lightly. 'The sun's splitting the skies.' Alan remembered Tommy had said he'd been forbidden to go out to play that morning. The problem with the slippers and the food had arisen too suddenly for him to have considered that, but it was odd for the children not to be out playing, at least on the rolling lawn, on a weekend morning. He opened the front door and hauled at the storm door, flooding sunlight blindingly into the hallway. 'Show me,' he said, holding the big door wide.

Tommy and the twins wandered forward and peeked past their father. The smell of summer wafted up from the lobelias and the little white alyssum flowers that alternated with the blue all along the front of the house.

The honeysuckle that looped around the Virginia creeper sent its bouquet whirling along to mix with the rest, a high-summer, lazy smell that was redolent of hazy days. Down the driveway the azaleas and fuchsias shot up colour from masses of flowers that were motionless in the still air. Out on the loch, the water was like glass.

'But it *was* raining. It was pouring, and you couldn't even see the hills over there. Mum said we'd get soaked.'

'Sure it was today, TC?'

Tommy nodded.

'Don't think so, m'boy. Looks like it hasn't rained here in a month of Sundays. I'll have to get Seumas to put a sprinkler on the lawn.'

Tommy looked agog at the expanse of lawn. It had the dry, dusty look of parched earth. The big, smooth stones that had been hauled up to line the gravel drive were light and hot-looking.

But I saw it, he told himself.

That was when the thought struck him. The odd thing about his father when he had come in and wrapped the three of them in his arms. Alan had smelt *dad*-like. Hard and dry and with a faint hint of tobacco.

And he'd been dry!

The memory hit him. The three of them had been standing in the front room, jammed up against the window where the rivulets of rain were running down the glass in such torrents that everything outside was warped and fuzzy. He remembered feeling the chill of a summer storm inside the room, as if the air pressure had changed, making everything grey and cold. He remembered peering through the running water at his dad, just a featureless shape on the other side of the window, waving a white blob of a hand at them. He saw with clarity how the backlights of the car had twinkled through the raindrops which magnified them and broke them up into dozens of little sparkly stars.

It had been *bucketing* down. And when his dad came in two minutes later, his hair was dry and his clothes were warm.

Not for the first time, Tommy thought: There's something funny going on around here.

They walked together down the narrow shoreline road towards the centre of the village where Alan spent as little time as possible buying groceries. They went to the little butcher's shop where the children watched the big bacon slicer in action, hissing through a boulder-sized slab, cutting it to fine sheets. The thought of one of his dad's fry-ups made Tommy's mouth water.

Instead of going straight home, Alan took the three of them into the little coffee shop on the corner of Firth View where they sat in wicker chairs and enjoyed ice cream and cokes for a treat. Alan savoured a coffee and watched as the kids demolished the lot.

A half-hour later he herded them out into the sunlight and turned to go home, almost bumping into Beth Callander who was walking along the pavement towards them with Alex Graham. Both young women were wearing cotton-print dresses that reflected the high sun almost blindingly.

Beth whispered into Alex's ear, just one word: 'Dishy.'

Alan didn't even notice it but Alex blushed rosily.

'Hello, you two, how are you?'

Alex stammered with embarrassment. Beth's eyes twinkled mischievously. '*I'm* fine,' she said archly.

Alan turned to Alex. 'And you? Got a day off?'

She nodded. 'For once.'

'Me too. I'm just back.'

'Yes I heard you were away. Up north, wasn't it?'

They talked for five minutes or so. Alan gleaned that Alex had got the girls' records transferred and that the professor at Edinburgh was very interested in having the twins across to examine them, if he didn't mind.

'No, of course not. I'll bring them myself.'

Alex ventured that she thought there wasn't anything wrong with the girls and that there was every possibility, no, *every probability*, that the Edinburgh people could achieve major results. She said it with such genuine enthusiasm and obvious honesty that Alan was mightily cheered.

As they were talking two of Tommy's school pals came along, each with a plastic bucket and each armed with a long branch that had been cut off just below a fork so that it formed a hook. 'Are you coming down?' Alan heard one of them say.

'Dunno, I'll have to ask,' Tommy replied. Alan felt a small surge of pride in the way that Tommy was already picking up the accent, his own accent, from his schoolfriends in a way he'd never acquired it when they lived down south.

'Ask what, son?'

'Bobby and Jim are going down the shore. There's pools down there.'

'And what do you do there?' Alan asked the boys who were looking up at him earnestly.

'We're going to catch crabs.'

'Catch crabs?' Alan felt a smile try to force itself on him. Behind him one of the girls, either Beth or Alex, chuckled lightly.

'Yeah. There's some real big ones down at the rocks. You have to get the tide right out.'

'Well, can you wait till Tommy's had his lunch?'

'No bother. That OK, Tam?' the dark-haired boy asked Tommy, who nodded enthusiastically.

'All right, so long as you all take care down there.'

'Och, it's all right. The water's dead shallow.'

The boys, with their pails and their sticks, sauntered along the pavement. Just before they turned the corner, Alan heard the smaller one tell his red-haired friend: 'He was right. His dad sounds just the same as us.'

Tommy heard them and blushed. Alan smiled and ruffled his hair.

TWENTY-SEVEN

Alan took the girls for a walk after lunch. Tommy had wolfed everything that had been laid in front of him, while Helen, who had been annoyingly distant, favouring him with an aggressive silence, had only picked at her food, refusing to meet his eyes. Alan bit down on his annoyance. He'd had a hard week, one hell of a hard week, if you came right down to it. He'd made up for much of the time he'd had off, and he'd justified MacKenzie-Kelso's confidence in him. He'd worked his butt off, and then he'd come home to a bare fridge and a frosty reception.

There had been times, oh, many times, in the course of the past couple of years when he'd been on the point of despair. It was hard enough raising a family and at the same time carving out a career in the ruthlessly competitive world of civil engineering. He understood, logically, mentally, that Helen's troubles were a medical problem; at least he had done up until now. He'd battled for her and helped her over the years, hauling her to her feet and giving her every support. He'd bust a gut on that job too, wearing himself down, stretching his resources so thin they could snap.

And now what? Now what?

He felt like a stranger in his own house. An intruder. Someone who'd barged in and upset the routine, the established way of things.

And yet, he knew he hadn't done that. He'd only come home after a long, exhausting week of working round the clock, just looking for a warm place to rest and be at home.

'Put your slippers on.' That's what she'd said. He

was just in the door and all she was concerned about was that he should take off his shoes and put his slippers on. And then the scene with the empty fridge.

'I was too busy. I was working in the house.' That was another thing she'd said. Alan could remember it, could picture the look in her eyes when she said it. He felt something cold and undoing sluggishly creep in his veins. Helen was sipping at her tea, the bacon and eggs that he'd made congealing on her plate. She appeared to be reading a magazine, but Alan couldn't tell whether she was just using it as a barricade. As if they needed any barriers. They were there, crackling the air between them.

Suddenly, all he wanted was for her to reach out to him, to make him feel welcome, to tell him that he was wanted.

But that would never happen. Not now. With a click of insight, like a camera shutter snapping, Alan abruptly realized the truth of it. He'd spent four years keeping the family together, keeping the clouds at bay as best he could, making sure the sun shone. He'd done it in the hope that they would *be* a family, a team. The realization that hit him like a physical blow was that Helen had given up.

She didn't want it.

And the past four years, from Alan's point of perspective in that instant as he sat at the end of the table, surreptitiously sneaking glances at his wife's stony face, had been just a waste of time. The effort he'd made bringing her back to normal had been fruitless and futile. She just didn't want to know.

The cold thoughts sleeted through his mind like a chill current of wind. No, he wasn't angry. That emotion was too positive for the way he suddenly felt.

Instead, he found himself being swept along on a wave of sadness and loss. Gloomily, he stood up from the table, pushing his chair back squeakily on the smooth tiled floor. The noise made Helen twitch with irritation, although she still refused to take her eyes from the magazine. She hadn't said a word to him since he'd come back from the shops.

Alan washed the dishes in the sink by hand instead of stacking the dishwasher, frothing up the bubbles and feeling the warmth of the water soak through his hands. He wiped the girls' faces, first Elaine, then Kathryn, and helped them down from their stools. He took them upstairs for their jackets and then came back down with them into the kitchen. Helen looked carved from stone as if she hadn't moved a muscle in the past ten minutes.

'I'm just taking the girls out for a stroll,' he said from the doorway.

Helen shrugged. She stared at the page.

'We won't be long,' Alan ventured again.

She nodded, almost imperceptibly. Alan stood and looked at her for several long moments. Then he too shrugged and closed the kitchen door softly. As he did so, he felt that he was closing another door, a final one, on part of his life.

He hauled on his Reebok trainers in the front room, looking through the window as he did so. The clouds seemed to be piling up over the hills on the far side of the loch, reflecting gloomily from the grey surface. Alan thought their walk wouldn't last long by the looks of things. He remembered that when he'd arrived Tommy had said something about it raining. Maybe he'd had *déjà-vu* or something. By the shade of the clouds that were rolling up, blue-grey and heavy, rain wasn't far off.

He got his casual jacket from the little cupboard in the hall just opposite the cellar door and slipped it on. Katie and Laney stood together beside him. He looked down at them and winked. They threw him back their immaculate smiles.

'Very well, ladies,' he said, suddenly overcome with a compensating love for them that overwhelmed the dismal feeling that had drowned him only minutes before. 'It's just the three of us. Let's go and have fun before rain stops play.'

He held out both hands and they put their tiny ones into his, nestling soft and warm and fragile between his hard fingers. They walked down the hallway and out through the storm doors into the sunlight. They went down the steps, he walking and the girls bouncing as he swung each of them, giggling, into the air to land gently on the stone treads.

'At least you laugh, you two,' he said, matter-of-factly, 'and I can tell you it warms my heart, you pair of beauties,' he concluded, softly, almost inaudibly.

They do laugh, he thought to himself. They smile and giggle and they laugh a lot. *They're happy*.

Alan looked down again at the girls. Their golden-white hair fairly shot back the sun.

He could *feel* their innocent joy of life. They could respond and they could join.

The thought that he wanted them to speak riffled guilt through him, but oh, he wanted that very badly indeed. He was prepared to move any mountain for the priceless gift of his babies *talking* to him.

He wanted to hear them call him *Daddy*.

They walked down the pathway, having fun with the crunching of their feet on the stones, he deliberately missing his step, and the girls trying to keep pace. The sun shone down on them and it was just as they got to the gate that Alan realized how summery it was. He turned to look over at the loch and the hills beyond. The water was a deep, inviting blue, reflecting back a sky that was clear and clean. Away in the distance a couple of high nimbo-stratus clouds looked as if they were fighting a losing battle with the sun. The rolling thick threatening rainclouds had disappeared.

Alan stopped and stared up over the Carman Hills, puzzled at the sudden change in the weather. He thought back to only five minutes ago when the sky had been dark and heavy. Now it was light and airy. In his mind, he had difficulty matching the two pictures.

'That's very odd,' he said.

The girls stopped and looked up at him, each standing hipshot, putting weight on opposite legs. They couldn't ask.

'One minute it looks like we're in for a right miserable rainstorm, and the next we're sunbathing. I've never seen the weather change so quickly in my life,' he said.

He walked on a few steps, holding his arms out wing-like until Katie and Laney pattered up behind him and grabbed for his fingers.

'Unless you take the flash flood out in Colorado. One minute the sky was blue and the next it was black, and your dear old Dad was up to his armpits in mud and all sorts of things you can't hear about until you're much older.'

Kathryn looked across at Elaine on the other side of her dad and flicked her a glance that Alan caught and interpreted as: 'Here we go, *another* tall tale.'

He laughed out loud. It was such an adult expression on the innocent face of a four-year-old. There was no doubt about it. The girls understood every word, and probably more. Unexpectedly the feelings that had been rolling inside him smoothed themselves out. For the first time since he'd come home, Alan felt himself getting back to normal. Oh, there were things he'd have to think about, things he'd have to face head-on. Decisions he'd have to make.

The realization that he'd lost the battle with Helen was still with him; the knowledge that despite the past four hard years she didn't love him any more, didn't seem to want him any more, that was still there. But he'd face it, and he'd deal with it, and he'd go on loving his kids and making a life for them.

That, Alan realized with instant clarity, was the bottom line.

'Let's go down to the shore and see how Tommy's getting on,' he suggested to the girls. They nodded delightedly, pulling on his hands in their haste, as they strode down the path that led to the foreshore.

TWENTY-EIGHT

The book would have remained unread if Helen hadn't tidied up Alan's little study on the north side of the house. That time he'd lost his temper when Helen had shown impossible stupidity in trashing some of the papers he'd been working on. He couldn't understand it then, and he still found it difficult to believe that she'd been so short-sighted. The house seemed to have taken her over, as much as she'd taken over the house. He remembered thinking that then, and the scene of the morning when he'd arrived home merely served to convince him. She was becoming houseproud, plain and simple. Caring more, like a broody hen, for the nest than for those in the nest.

That day Alan had rescued his papers from the waste-basket and he'd slung some books in the wall cupboard. He hadn't noticed then that the momentum (he'd been angry and had fairly *slammed* the books onto the shelves) had forced the back panel inwards, revealing a smaller cupboard within the main one. It would have gone unnoticed for long enough had Alan not decided to sort out some paperwork early in the weekend so that he could clear his plate and relax for the rest of the break. Tommy had come in briefly after his crab-hunting expedition with the other two small boys and had disappeared again, telling Alan they were going to play soldiers up in the trees. Alan had told him to be careful and Tommy had said he would. Alan had been pleased that his son was making friends and having fun. Katie and Laney had parked themselves together on the settee to watch a children's programme that would keep them amused for the next hour. Alan decided he could use the hour.

When he opened the glass-fronted door he thought at first that the panel had just slipped. He cleared the books off the shelf, thinking that he'd manage to slip the wooden facing back into line; after all, it was an old house, so you had to expect a few things to come loose, like the skirting board that had hit Tommy a smack.

When he looked more closely, he noticed that the wooden board had slipped backwards and to the left. He pushed it lightly, expecting it to fetch up against lath and plaster or bump against the stone of the wall behind. There was some resistance, then the panel just slid on a groove, exposing a small cavity within the cupboard. Alan crossed to the desk, switched on the swan-necked reading lamp and swung the head so that the light beamed directly on to the shelf. The space was about the same depth again as the bookshelves, about a foot deep, and when the door was closed it was perfectly hidden. It was dry. There was a small, ancient, crumbly spider's web. Below it, the dry husk of the long-dead arachnid, paper-thin and curled. To the right was a small wooden box which rattled as Alan reached in and lifted it from where it must have sat for a long time. There was a thin coating of dust on the top, which was dry enough to blow off into a light cloud, revealing a smooth surface unmarked except for a monogram, the letter D, set in darker wood in a cursive script. Inside were a pair of cufflinks and a matching stick-pin that were obviously rose gold. Each piece was set with small diamonds. There were some tightly folded old banknotes, almost as big as the pages of Alan's notebook, and a pair of half-moon reading glasses with gold frames.

Fascinated by his find, Alan went back to the cache and reached in again. The door only slid back half the width of the shelves, so he had to crook his elbow round the edge and feel in the dark. His hand came across something heavy and oblong, dry with dust. He hefted it and brought it out into the light.

It was a book. The kind you might see in an antiquary shop, bound in beaten red leather with gold piping. The gold lines showed through in only a few places under the grey film.

Alan took it across to the waste-basket into which he lightly blew the bulk of the dust; then he pulled a tissue from the box on his desk and flipped the rest off, wiping the surface until it was clean. The read leather looked none the worse for the wait in the dark. It was carefully tooled and bound. On the spine were a pair of entwined letters: A.D.

On the cover, in the same style as the marquetry on the old box, was a single name in a large, imposing script, embossed deep into the surface. It read: ANDREW DALMUIR.

Immediately the name came back to Alan. Beth Callander had mentioned it on the first night they'd met down at Tom's, when she was telling them of the history of the peninsula and a bit about their new home. He was the man who had built Cromwath House. And again, in the extracts from the Sasines that Mike Toward and the guys in the office had prepared as a welcome-back gift, he'd seen the name again. Dalmuir was the one who had first bought the land and started building the houses that told of the wealth of the industrial revolution and its barons.

Fascinated, Alan gingerly eased the book open, careful in case the years in the dark behind the panel had made the material brittle. On the inside, the name was repeated on the first page in the same lettering. The text was handwritten in a bold hand, the letters brown and faded with age, but clearly legible.

The page was headed with a date: 'January first, 1888.'

Fascinated, Alan sat down and began to read the diary of Andrew Dalmuir.

TWENTY-NINE

I have not kept a diary before this, having neither the time nor the inclination for such things. To date, my life has been one of business and manufacture, and, thanks be to God, it has until now been a successful one.

I write this, the first entry of my account, to which, as time progresses, I will endeavour to make such additions as I am able, from the vantage of the cottage which I have taken on this Creggan peninsula, which gives the finest of aspects south over the Firth. My view here, on this clear day, the first of the New Year, allows me vantage over the water to the Gantocks on the far side, and down the whole of the wide gap mayhap as far as Arran. It is a fine view. It is one that I wish to make my own, for my wife Margaret, and my sons John and James, who will be the better for the fresh and bracing air here in these rural parts.

This is the place to which I intend to bring my family, and to build our house. For my purposes, it is not far from Glasgow where I need to be from time to time to ensure the good and continued success of my foundry, but far enough away to make this almost another world.

I have bought from the MacFarlane estate a parcel of land of some eleven acres which includes, very nearby this cottage, a remarkable ring of standing stones, which, the Reverend Jamieson of Rhu tells me, are the artefacts of heathen folk long since gone. They are of considerable interest, mainly because of their great age, which I am told is possibly before the birth of Christ, suggesting that they are indeed of heathen construction. I am impressed by their grandiose stature. They stand in a perfect circle at the point of this peninsula, on the flat land, and give view on to either loch. In the centre is a second circle, this time a mere five large stones set in a dip or depression.

I put no stock in folk tales. I have decided to build my house within the circle of stones. For me, it will serve as the most imposing of perimeters, as grand as if I constructed the house within the Colosseum. My house will be far enough away from the grime and fogs of Glasgow, yet the road between here and Rhu is of good construction and from there I can take the railway to town.

So I have decided. Here I will build a house that I can pass on to my sons. Already there is no small interest, now that I have shown my intent, from others who may wish to build here. I have sold a small parcel to the quarrymaster Mr Callander, whose stone I have arranged to use in the construction. Doctor James Kintyre has offered me three hundred for the low pasture to the south, and he can have it. The price is eminently fair, and I shall want to have good neighbours. There is fishing in the streams and, in season, sufficient deer and grouse to keep a man happy in his free moments. This will be a good place to bring my sons.

Alan read on, as fascinated by the stilted language, the pompous and grave expressions, as he was by the very fact that he was reading an account of the decision to build *this* house.

The diary, a long introduction and then a series of sporadic notes over a considerable span of time, showed that Dalmuir had been the pilgrim father of the Glasgow business gentry, the prime mover in the exodus from the city to the sedate and genteel dormitory towns that were just beginning to spring up in what, until then, had been the remote countryside. Alan read a description of the peninsula. There were farms strung along the spine and on each side of the low-lying Peaton Hills. There were descriptions of Creggan, Corbeth, Murrin and Feorlin, tiny hamlets clustering against the westerly wind around small harbours where the fishing boats jostled for space.

He read a detailed entry about the giant standing stones, twenty-six in all, that spanned the north section of the five acres in a wide flat circle, with the five monstrous megaliths in the centre.

'Where are they now?' he wondered. He remembered the stroll through the woods on the first day. There were only two of the great stones still standing at the edge of the trees. The rest were gone. Alan felt a twinge of regret for that. They must have been impressive.

He read on. Andrew Dalmuir had run two foundries, one in the south side of Glasgow, close to the shipyards which were beginning to spring up on the Clydeside, building iron boats to carry the wealth of an empire. His business had gone from a manufacturing blacksmith's and ironmonger's to a full-fledged foundry that made steel for the new constructions. Business was good. His other foundry, in Lanarkshire, served to make machinery and cables for the coal mines throughout the central belt. Dalmuir was one of the new rich, and he had money to spend.

The next account in the chronicle was of his discussions with Kenneth Adams, one of the new young architects who was already achieving a reputation for his designs for buildings in the merchant city centre of Glasgow.

Adams had dissuaded Dalmuir from building in the baronial style that the ironfounder had envisaged. Dalmuir told how he had been at the Whites' country house at Overtoun, overlooking Levenford, and had been greatly impressed with the new Lord Overtoun's stately pile. The young architect had convinced him that such a monstrous castle would look completely out of place on the point of the peninsula.

Dalmuir had allowed his grandiose ideas to be whittled down to something a little less ostentatious. Adams presented him with plans for a smaller, but still spacious, country home. He cut Dalmuir from two towers to one, but, with his fine perspectives on paper, convinced the ironfounder of the final balance of the design shown in a setting of cultivated gardens. Dalmuir had obviously taken a shine to the architect. They had arguments frequently, and Dalmuir was often vitriolic about his designer when it came to describing those differences of opinion in his chronicle, but the admiration for the young man shone through.

Ruefully, Alan realized that his position was very similar to that of Adams a hundred years before, but in his case there seemed to be less admiration and more aggravation. These days, cost was all and time was money. Civil engineers now worked to hairline tolerances.

The change in the account came in November of 1888 when Dalmuir finally agreed on the plans for the house. He had been staying at the cottage for a week, enjoying the grouse shooting in Glen Peaton, and Adams had come from Glasgow, taking a buggy from Rhu on a fine early winter morning when a sea mist covered the whole loch in a white gauze. Dalmuir had looked over the plans and drawings, and Adams had shown him the estimates for materials. He had with him a book showing every room in detail, some with cornices and ceiling roses intricately depicted in colour. The woods of the banisters and stairways were specified. Even the large bay-window panes were to be specially ordered from the glassmakers in Edinburgh who were the finest in the country.

Then came the work on getting the house started, and Dalmuir found that the standing stones were not just of great importance to long-dead heathens:

I cannot understand these people. For them, the construction of my house will bring much-needed industry to these villages, and those which my neighbours intend to build will only serve to ensure that prosperity continues. Yet they have raised objections to the construction of my house on my own land. Preposterous. Ridiculous. I have already told them so. The

Rev. Jamieson has taken pains to tell me of the interest these people have in the standing stones. I would dearly like to know why they have expressed no such interest heretofore. The minister tells me that there is a certain symbolism in the stones which is held very dear in the hearts of the people of the four villages, and indeed, on the whole peninsula. Never heard of it, I told him, but he seemed to feel it would perhaps be better if I built elsewhere, in the interests of goodwill. I told him there and then that I would build where I please. I have spent hundreds already, and will be spending hundreds more, and I will not be dictated to by a collection of barely educated crofters, some of whom haven't taken the trouble to learn the Queen's English. As for the stones, they were built by heathens long since dead. What importance can they have for Christian folk? That is exactly what I said to the Reverend, and I appear to have silenced this argument. It would be a sad day for any gentleman to be cowed by opinion such as that when he knows he is in the right.

That was not the end of it. Far from it. Work was delayed during November when the local workers refused to set foot within the ring of stones. Dalmuir was forced to bring in squads from Glasgow where Irish labour was still the cheapest, forty years after the potato famine which had brought thousands of starving peasants to Scotland. The ironfounder was then obliged to build shanty huts for the workers because none of the local families would accommodate them. Even supplies had to be shipped in by ferry, or brought round the loch by horse and cart.

On 26 December the first turves of the green flat land in the ring of stones were cut. And the next night, the trouble started:

I have had to call the constable to keep the peace. And I have told him that I will brook no interference or trespassing on my land. Today I was visited by a deputation from the villages, led by a tinker fellow by the name of MacFie, who seems like a rogue if there ever was one. They demand that I desist from building my house within the stones. They tell me that my family will suffer misfortune. This MacFie said that the stones are part of his people's heritage, their birthright, and have been for generations. To this I replied that his people should have bid for the land before I did, but he paid little notice to that. My wife was distressed by the disturbance. She cares little for the solitude of the cottage, and she was concerned for our sons who were asleep after our Boxing Day celebrations.

MacFie told me that I must not disturb the stones, especially on these nights at the end of the year.

I asked him why, and he mumbled something that I did not understand in that gutteral tongue of his. Farlane, the crofter, told me that the tinker folk held a ceremony in the stones on the five dead days of the year, and had done so for as long as anyone could remember. What these five dead days are, I have no idea. MacFie was vehement that the tradition be allowed to continue. I told him to be off, in no uncertain terms, and I informed him that the constable will be called if there are any more such disturbances. He glared at me and made a sign or gesture with his fingers, and the men with them turned their heads away, as if afraid. Then this tinker fellow told me that if I interfered with the stones, it would be the worse for me and my family. At this I was incensed and told them to be off. When they had gone, I put on my coat and boots and took my walking stick as a precaution and walked to the constable's house to tell him what had happened.

Despite the holiday, work started on the foundations of the house. The builder James Latta had marked out the lines with pegs and twine about twenty yards from the central ring of stones, which Dalmuir fancied as an arbour in the centre of his garden. The squads got to digging. Later in the evening one of the Irishmen arrived, breathless, at Dalmuir's cottage further up the hill to tell him there was a commotion down at the site.

The ironfounder pulled on his boots again and went striding down the path.

When he arrived, there was a circle of lights in the centre of the ring. All of the foundation markers had been torn up. The Irishmen stood to one side, watching nervously, and held back from the inner circle by a crowd of villagers. Inside the pentagon was a ring of tallow torches flickering brightly, casting shadows on to the sides of the stones.

Dalmuir shoved his way past the workers, and the villagers tried to bar his way. Farlane, who crofted up from Corbeth, seemed embarrassed but adamant.

'What's to do here?' Dalmuir demanded.

'It's the old ways, Sir,' Farlane had muttered. 'Best to let them be.'

'Best to get off my land this instant,' Dalmuir replied abruptly. 'I know you all, and you will all have to pay for this outrage.'

'You don't understand. It's the old way. The tinker folk come every year for this. And at Samhain and Beltane and midsummer's night.'

'What gibberish is this?'

'They have their ceremony. It has always been.'

'And now, no more, I tell you,' Dalmuir stormed. 'I will have no heathen blasphemy here, d'you understand?' He turned to the foreman of the work crew. 'You, man. Go and fetch the constable immediately. Bring him straight here without delay.'

A hush ran through the crowd. The Irishmen, corralled next to their tents, made signs of the cross and muttered under their breath.

Dalmuir shoved his way forward, forcing the crowd to part. A hand landed on his shoulder and he rapped it sharply with the silver knob on the top of his cane. It withdrew quickly. He shouldered through and strode towards the five stones. The torchlight showed a crowd of figures moving silently inside the ring.

The silent crowd followed behind the ironfounder

until he got to the space between the nearest pillars. He stopped and stared into the lit interior.

There were maybe forty people, all dressed in long robes of a dark blue homespun cloth. In the centre, on a flat stone that was sunk into the earth, stood a tall man who was swathed in a deerskin. The pelt was complete, even to the forelegs which dangled over his shoulders. The skin of the head covered the man's face, making him look like some grotesque two-footed animal. Crowning the whole array was a spread of antlers that were more than a yard wide: huge branching curves of a magnificent stag.

The man was making gestures over the stone. He turned slowly and stopped when he saw Dalmuir standing there in the light. In the jagged eye sockets of the deerskin, something glittered.

'You come to Crom Uath this night?' the man asked harshly. Dalmuir couldn't make out the face under the skin mask.

'I ask the same thing,' Dalmuir responded. 'What do you mean by this?'

The man let out a bellow of laughter. 'This has meaning that is older than you would comprehend. Go now. Leave us in peace.'

'You are on my land. I demand that you leave and take this rabble with you, or it will be the worse for you.'

'The worse for me? You don't even know what you are saying.' The man's voice, even behind the mask, was strong and hard and clear in the night air. All around, the blue-cloaked figures stood silently watching the interchange. 'We do as we have always done in this place. Do not interfere. This is not for you, but for this land and this people.'

'I have called for the constable. I suggest that you take your leave immediately, or there will be trouble,' Dalmuir replied.

'Interloper,' the tall man called out. 'You interfere in

that which has been for more generations than you can count. Go now and let us be about our business.'

'I will have no heathen nonsense on my land, d'you hear?' Dalmuir shouted. He stepped forward and reached his hand out to grasp the antlers, pulling hard. He expected the whole skin to come off, exposing the man's face. Instead the big man swivelled, pulling Dalmuir round. It was as if the great spread of horns were fixed on to his head. Dalmuir felt as if he'd grabbed a bull by the horns. He stumbled to the stone. A hushed murmur went like a wave through the crowd who watched from outside the ring.

Dalmuir hauled himself to his feet, and it was then that he noticed the wicker baskets hanging from every stone. Each one held a white cockerel, except for the one which stood on the flat centre stone. Inside that was a small white goat. Its yellow eyes flickered wetly in the torchlight.

The ironfounder suddenly realized what the ceremony was. 'Damned blood sacrifice. You pagans!'

He launched himself upright and raised his stick into the air, crashing it down on the light wicker cage. Inside, the goat bucked in alarm. The cage overturned and the animal scrabbled out when the lid flew open. It was little more than a kid, its short horns just beginning to show through the skin on its head. One of the blue-robed figures made a dive for it. It jinked left, then right, and made a bolt for the nearest space and shot through into the darkness. Somebody shouted and a hand grabbed Dalmuir. He spun and raised his stick and smacked someone hard on the shoulder. A woman screamed. Dalmuir lashed out at two figures who moved in on him, then the whole site became a battleground. One of the torches fell from the wall and set fire to a small basket. Inside, the cockerel screeched in terror. A fist caught Dalmuir under the jaw and he went down.

There was a blare of noise from outside the ring, and

then the Irishmen who had been standing further back rushed in to help the man who was paying their wages and feeding their large families. One of them waded in with a pickaxe handle. Another ran to the hut for his shovel. There was another almighty scream, this time from a man. Somebody grabbed a torch and swung the firebrand around in a rippling circle of light to keep the crowd at bay. There were yells and grunts and thuds as bodies whirled in the half-light. The tumult went on for ten minutes or more, with Dalmuir lashing out in righteous fury at anything that moved, until the constable and two other men arrived with lanterns and whistles. Then the fight went out of everybody. The villagers who had been at first just observers didn't want to be observed. They melted away. The Irishmen, who realized their vulnerable position in Presbyterian Scotland, moved back to their tents.

Constable McAllister, a big, beefy man with mutton-chop whiskers, came rushing into the circle where Dalmuir stood, panting, against one of the stones.

Around them stood the tinker folk in their blue robes. The man in the deerskin loomed over the flat stone. Where the goat had been caged, the tattered remains of the wicker box was scattered all around. And on the stone a young woman lay spreadeagled. A great gash split the side of her head to the jawline. Blood pulsed from the wound on to the stone.

One of the robed figures moaned and ran to where the woman lay. It was another young woman. She lifted up the injured girl's head, yammering something frantic and guttural. The robe's hood fell back and the girl turned dark eyes on Dalmuir. Between her fingers, blood poured out of the deep wound and dripped on to the stone.

Constable McAllister stood taking in the situation, his brass buttons gleaming in the flickering light of the two remaining torches.

Before he could say anything, the man in the deerskin

came striding forward and bent over the spreadeagled woman and the other girl who was rocking her in her arms.

The big man reached down into the pool of blood and scooped up a thick handful, cupping it in the palm of his hand. Without a pause, he walked to the first stone and left a bloody handprint on the flat inside face, head-high. He walked round the circle, slapping the red print on the stones until he got to the one where Dalmuir stood. Then he paused and grabbed the torches from where they were angled into the soft ground. He held them up high and stared at Dalmuir.

'Build then, and be done,' he said in a clear voice. Then he stabbed the flaming ends of the torches into the ground, snuffing them out instantly, and plunging the circle into darkness. There was a scuffling noise. The constable called to his man outside the ring to bring the lantern. He came sprinting up waving the light in front of him, stepped between the two stones and shone the lamp. McAllister stood there next to Dalmuir. There was no one else in the ring.

All this was told in the pedantic language that Dalmuir affected in his diary. Alan realized he'd been reading for more than an hour, and hadn't managed to do any of the work that he had intended. He was about to close the book, and put it down on his desk. Instead, he decided to read just one last page.

In it Dalmuir described the thunderstorm that had erupted just as he and the constable and his men left the circle. Lightning had streaked across the sky and the thunder had crashed all around without warning. Torrential rain lashed down into the dry earth. When the small group of men reached the perimeter circle, there was one vast peal of thunder and a simultaneous crash of lightning that forked down from the black sky and exploded in the centre of the stones, sending blue fire dancing up and down the great pillars of rock. The earth beneath their feet trembled and shuddered. It seemed to buck hard, and one of the men was thrown to the ground and cracked his head on a rock.

The group fled for their lives. The storm roared the whole night on the peninsula. Up in the cottage, Dalmuir could feel the earth tremble as lightning hammered at the ground. His wife was petrified and the boys were shaking with fright. In the morning the storm was done. Dalmuir went down to the site where the foreman told him some of the Irishmen had decided to pack up and leave. In the centre of the five stones, where the flat rock had lain the night before, the earth had sunk into a crevasse, as if shoved down by a monstrous weight. Latta told him there must have been an old digging in the spot before, and the night's rain had washed away the sub-surface.

Dalmuir made an instant decision. 'This is where I want my cellar,' he said. 'Confer with Adams, but I want the house centred here. And we'll put an end to this nonsense once and for all.'

THIRTY

After dinner the night was still warm and dry. The air was heavy with high-summer pollen. Out on the loch, the sun in the west caught the wings of the wheeling gulls, sending a morse code of spangled white light back over the smooth water.

Helen had been mute at dinner, although she had condescended to make something to eat. There was an atmosphere across the table, which the twins with their customary sunny innocence failed to notice, although Tommy could feel it stretched between his parents like taut wires. He didn't know exactly what was wrong, but he could make a fair guess. It was something to do with the way his mother didn't seem to care any more; something to do with where she went inside her head. To him, all of eight years old, it was as if she was lost.

Alan mopped up his salad cream with fresh buttered bread, trying to maintain conversation. Helen responded with nods and shrugged shoulders. There was nothing for it but to talk to the kids, which was no hardship for him anyway. Alan felt Helen's withdrawal was almost absolute. When he'd come down from his study, two hours after picking up Dalmuir's account of the building of Cromwath, he was fascinated by the unfolding story. He had read just another couple of pages, and then he'd lost himself in Dalmuir's narrative. The jumbled tale was still whirling around in his head when he'd come downstairs. Helen had been working at something in the bedroom and when she came down, the blue plastic bucket where she kept her sprays and wax polishes was slung over her arm. She had met his look with a blank return, a depthless stare

297

that seemed to go right through him and past him as if he wasn't there.

'Anything fancy for dinner?' he'd asked as lightly as he could. Helen had looked at him blankly, then had given a start, as if she had just realized his presence.

'What was that?'

'Dinner,' Alan repeated. 'Got anything fancy planned?'

'I hadn't thought about it. I don't know what there is.'

Isn't *that* a fact, Alan thought. 'There's a fridge full of stuff,' was what he said. 'Lettuce, tomatoes and whatnot. I got some cold meat as well, and there's some cheddar.'

'Fine. Salad then,' Helen said, as if dinner was the least important thing in the world. 'I'll fix it.' She turned into the kitchen, walking slowly.

Up in the trees on the far side of the road Tommy was lying behind a moss-covered deadfall that bore a spike of ferns along its spine. Beside him Bobby and Jim were sprawled lethargically. They'd been playing soldiers in the trees for the past hour or so, but the game had palled.

'Let's go up Peaton Hill,' Bobby suggested. 'There's gun huts from the war up there.'

'Nah, too far,' Jim said.

'Back down the shore?' Tommy chipped in. 'See what's on the beach?'

'We did that today,' Bobby said. 'And I cut my hands on the barnacles.'

'OK,' Jim said. 'How about bird-egging in Corrie Glen?'

'It's against the law,' Bobby said loftily. 'My dad says you can get done for it.'

'We don't have to take any,' Jim said with exaggerated exasperation. 'But it's good fun finding them. How about it?'

Bobby looked at Tommy, who nodded. 'All right then, but no taking eggs. It's a sin anyway.'

They came out of the copse on to the road and headed north, sauntering, hands in jeans pockets, together in the evening sunlight.

It was close to nine when they decided to get back home. The air was still clear, but the shadows were beginning to lengthen. None of them had a watch; they all operated on boys' mean-time, that body clock dictated to mainly by the stomach and always an hour or so behind the rest of the world. It's the main reason why small boys are always late, and have their futile excuses ready when they arrive home to worried parents.

They were up at the top end of the Corrie Glen, which was a shallow gorge with sweeping sides crowded with trees and hedges. Already they had found a dipper's nest behind the spray of the small waterfall. Bobby had scaled an oak trunk that had been broken off in a previous gale maybe twelve feet from the ground and had discovered a nest full of fledgling starlings that gaped their beaks in a yellow and red semaphore as the boys took turns to peer down into the nest.

On the way down the cattle track that had been pounded into concrete hardness by the hoofs of generations of Andy Noble's herds, the three of them were rounding a bend on the path when Tommy, slightly in front of the others, stopped suddenly, causing the others to halt abruptly.

Jim started to say something, but Tommy waved him to silence. A movement from off the track, hidden from plain sight by a mass of brambles and bracken, flickered in the shadows.

'What is it?' Bobby asked.

'An animal, I think. Look there.' Tommy pointed into the hedge. There was a wavering white patch and a rustling sound. Jim edged past him and shouldered his way through the runners and branches.

'It's a rabbit,' he called over his shoulder. 'It's caught in a trap.'

'Let me see,' said Bobby Lindsay, who was a bit taller than the others and was craning forward over their heads. The three of them barged in to where there was a space between the hedges. As soon as the rabbit saw them, it started to haul frantically away from them, legs pumping desperately but futilely against the wire around its neck. There was blood at its mouth.

'It's a snare,' Jim said.

'I can see that, smartass,' Bobby retorted. 'It's choking to death.'

'Can we let it go?' Tommy asked.

'What for? There's good eating in a rabbit.'

'No, let it go. The poor thing's going to kill itself if we don't.'

The rabbit scuttered its feet against the ground. The eye on their side seemed to be popping out of its socket, and its neck, caught in the wire noose, looked as if it was being squeezed hard enough to cut it in two. The trapped animal looked pitiful to Tommy.

He crouched down beside it and grabbed it in both hands. It kicked against him powerfully, so hard and frantic that he almost dropped it. Once its feet were off the ground, the animal went still. Tommy could feel it shivering, and deep inside the warm bundle, its heartbeat was a furious, fluttering pulse. Tommy drew it back from where it was pulling against the wire and Jim hunkered closer. He tried to loop a finger between the noose and the fur which was already ragged from the friction of the animal's exertions.

'It's awfully tight,' he said. Then his finger slipped under the wire. It caught, and then started to pull back as he hooked another finger under and drew both apart. The wire rasped against the little lock loop until the noose was big enough to draw over the animal's head.

The rabbit kicked twice in Tommy's hands, but he held it tight, feeling the thin ribs bellow in and out as the tiny lungs pumped fresh breath.

'Set it down now,' Bobby said and Tommy knelt on the short grass of the rabbit run and put the freed creature on to the ground. It toppled on to its flank. He righted it with his hand and it sat there, crouched and shivering.

'Will it be all right?' he asked.

'Dunno. Maybe, maybe not.'

Tommy straightened and the rabbit cringed from the movement. Its ears, which were flat on its shoulder blades, twitched, and it took a little shuffling few steps forwards. Then it seemed to come to. It twitched again, then with a sudden dash it was gone, tail flashing a wink of white, into the hedges. They could hear the rustle of its passage for a few seconds, then silence.

'Hey, you boys there. What're you doing?'

The bellow made them all jump about three feet into the air. About thirty yards away a man was lumbering down the slope through the trees towards them. He was big and heavy, wearing a tattered jacket and big black boots.

'What the hell are you up to, eh?'

The man had a gnarled stick in his hands. He swung it twice, hard against the bracken to clear a way, and barged through.

Jim was first to move. He jinked past Bobby and was out through the gap in the hedge like a dark ferret. Bobby was next and Tommy followed on their heels, filled with sudden alarm.

'Come back, you wee bastards,' the man shouted hoarsely behind them. 'I'll put my boot up your arses.'

Tommy could feel his sphincter tighten. In front of him Jim gave a small cry of dismay and fright, and the three of them were off down the track sprinting fast, each trying to get in front, feet drumming on the hard earth.

Behind them they could hear the crashing as the man followed. He was shouting angrily and cursing non-stop. The boys' panic accelerated their flight and they came scooting out of the glen at top speed. Bobby hit the wooden gate first, taking it high on the bar and was over like an athlete. Tommy was next. He scrambled over, hitching his hips at the last minute and tumbling on to the hard earth on the other side. He scrambled to his feet and was off behind the red-haired boy. Jim Rodger missed his footing when he reached the gate. He slipped on the second bottom bar and the momentum carried him forward and down. His chin hit a spar, clicking his teeth shut over his tongue. An instant metallic taste flooded his mouth and he sprawled heavily, jamming himself under the lowest bar. From down the track, he could hear the pounding of the big man's boots and panic flared so high it shut off the pain that filled his mouth.

'Oh-mi-god. Oh-mi-god,' he spluttered. A thin drool of blood came out with the words.

Down the track, Tommy skidded to a halt when he realized that Jim wasn't on his heels. Without thinking, he scurried back up the path to the gate. Jim was scrambling to his feet. There was blood all over his mouth. Along the glen the big man was running towards them, bellowing hoarsely at the top of his voice and waving his stick.

'Come *on*, Jim. Get over the gate.'

Jim seemed paralysed. He just stood there, looking at Tommy. 'I fell,' he said.

'Get over the gate, come on, Jim,' Tommy yelled, darting his eyes from his friend to the figure who was looming closer. The big man had long dark hair, almost like an Indian's. He looked big and fierce and very, very angry. 'Get a *move* on, you idiot,' Tommy heard himself shout.

Jim seemed to come out of his paralysis at a dead run. One instant he was standing looking dazed, and the next he was in mid-air, leaping over the gate. He didn't falter this time. He landed like a cat, and without any break in his stride he was off along the path with Tommy right at his back. Forty yards further on there were two trees and beyond that the dike which bordered the road. Bobby was already on the other side, urging them over. Both boys scrambled over the dry stones of the wall and all three headed for home at a sprint. They made it without incident, earlier than they had originally intended.

Later, when Tommy was asleep, Alan tried to talk to Helen, and found he wasn't getting very far. He had put the girls to bed before Tommy had come home, and he'd watched some television. Helen was elsewhere in the house. She never seemed to sit still. Finally he had to find her and tell her it was time she gave herself a break. He made a cup of tea for them both and she sat in the opposite chair in the living-room. Her eyes were on the television, but she didn't seem to be taking it in. It was as if her mind were a million miles away.

She had drunk her tea methodically. She had accepted a biscuit from the plate when he'd offered it, nodding her thanks, and later, when he used the zapper to switch channels from the hospital series, which he hated, to a snooker match, which he enjoyed, her expression didn't change.

After they both went upstairs, Alan pulled his clothes off and slung them on a chair. He showered and shaved quickly and went back into the bedroom. Helen was lying there staring at the ceiling. He clambered in on the other side and pulled up the sheet.

'I think maybe we should have a chat,' he said, keeping his voice calm and reasonable. 'Otherwise there might be a problem.'

Helen slowly turned her head until it was facing him. Her short, dark brown hair framed a pale face. Her eyes looked huge and sunken. It was strange that he hadn't really noticed how haggard she had suddenly become. 'What problem?'

'I'm not sure exactly what it is,' Alan said, automatically playing for time after she wrong-footed him by actually replying to his words.

'What problem?' she asked again, distantly, her voice almost a whisper.

'Well, I think there might be one between you and me, and that means it's something that affects us all,' Alan started. 'I mean, we haven't spoken more than two words since I got back. It's as if you just don't want to know me.'

'Oh?'

'That's the way I feel. I had a nearly two-hundred-mile drive this morning and when I got here after a week of busting my backside, I didn't get much of a welcome. Unless you consider telling me to take my shoes off in the hall a fanfare.'

'I was busy too,' Helen said. She had turned away from him and was staring upwards again.

'OK, I can accept that. But you can't be busy every minute of the day. There must be other things than housework. There wasn't a thing to eat. Nothing in the fridge, nothing in the pantry. I mean, what have the kids been living on this week?'

'The house *is* important,' Helen said. It was the first time she'd sounded in any way animated. 'It's *my* house.

'Yes, it is important, I'll agree. It's *our* house. Our *home*. And I'm glad you finally like it. But it isn't the be-all and end-all. There's more to a home than just a house,' he said, feeling trite as he did so.

'That's what you think,' she replied, almost dreamily.

'What's that?'

'The house. It's more than that.'

'I just said that. It's a home. A place to bring up a family. And if we're going to be a family, we've got to talk about it when there's a problem.'

'You don't understand. I *love* this house. And it loves me.'

'Don't be so daft. It's a good place, a great place even. But it's still only bricks and mortar.'

'Stone,' Helen replied forcefully. 'I have to keep the house.'

'But not to the exclusion of everybody and everything else.'

'You don't understand,' she repeated.

'So tell me.'

'You'll find out.'

'Find *what* out?'

'Nothing.'

'Come on, it can't be nothing,' Alan protested, again feeling his temper beginning to rise out of his frustration. Helen was talking riddles.

'It's none of your business. It's got nothing to do with you.'

'Anything that happens here has something to do with me. Now I'm just about fed up with this claptrap. This is *my* house and *my* family, and you're behaving as if you just don't give a damn. So it's time you started talking, if we're ever going to have anything to talk about.'

'Is that a threat?' Helen asked. 'You want to threaten me?'

'If you don't get your act together and let us communicate like two adults, I don't know what I'll do.'

'I don't need you,' Helen said blankly, coldly. That stopped Alan right in his tracks. Those four words hit him like a blow between the eyes.

'You've got someone else, is that it?' He'd never considered that before. He didn't even know what made him ask.

Helen suddenly brayed into the sudden silence. Shrill and high and almost hysterical. Alan recoiled. He stared at her lying there with her eyes wide open, staring up at the ceiling with her mouth gaping. Her whole body was vibrating with the spasms of that odd-sounding laugh. He reached across and grabbed her by the shoulder. The laugh didn't stop. It sounded like a wail. Looked like a scream.

She shook his hand off and suddenly Alan's temper got caught up with the shuddering alarm which surged through him as he watched his wife spasmodically quivering on the bed beside him. He hauled her roughly up to a sitting position and for the first time in his life, he hit a woman. His right arm came up from the side in a big roundhouse and his open palm met her cheek with a resounding crack that jerked her head violently to the left.

The strange laughter cut off immediately. Alan saw his handprint blossom rapidly across Helen's cheek and instantly felt a powerful wave of self-disgust run through him. He had hit her so hard that the individual fingermarks were clearly delineated on her face, disappearing into her hair.

'I'm sorry, Helen,' he started to say, then stopped suddenly. Helen lifted her head and looked at him with eyes that were wide and dark and coldly empty.

'Don't ever hit me again,' she hissed in a low voice. There was no malice, no anger, only a dreadful desolate coldness.

Alan was about to continue his apology, while inside him he felt more revulsion in the look on her face and the sound of her voice than he had when he heard the chilling, hysterical laughter. But suddenly there was a flash outside in the night that shot blue flickering light into the room, and an almighty crash that made the window-panes rattle in their frames and rumbled around the house with such force that the floor shook. Alan jerked around, startled.

The big bay window was awash with a strange purple-blue lightning that seemed to fuzz out the outlines of the stone pillars that separated each pane. St Elmo's fire raced up and down the stone in streams of unearthly colour while the thunder lashed the house, drilling deep into the foundations.

'What the hell was *that*?' Alan said when the thunder began to fade, rolling off into the night. The flickering light dopplered down, leaving an after-picture the shape of the window dancing in orange in front of Alan's eyes.

'Don't hit me again,' Helen said.

He started to speak, but Helen just stared at him for a second, and turned away from him. Her arm snaked out from under the sheet, reaching out towards the wall. Helen's fingers brushed against the surface gently, feeling the smooth contact. Under her fingers, the light blue patterned wallpaper was worn from where her touch had rubbed it. Outside the lightning had gone, but rain started to pour down in the darkness. It drummed against the windows as the wind rose, lashing it against the glass.

Eventually Alan's breathing evened out. He felt drained and helpless, as if his world had suddenly taken a spinning t.'+ out of true. He fell into a fitful sleep.

In the darkness of the room, Helen's fingers kept stroking the wall. Through them she felt the deep, vibrating pulse that sent the feelings of belonging course through her.

And when she felt that, nothing else mattered.

Much later in the night, Alan woke up with a start. He was alone. And he wasn't in the room where he'd fallen asleep.

THIRTY-ONE

A tremor shivered the floor under his feet, rippling across the smooth boards, causing him to swing his arms to keep balance. At the same time, the walls bulged and seemed to shift and that made Alan's stomach swoop sickly.

The room was not quite dark. A weak light outlined the window with purple-green (*I've seen this before, I've dreamed this before*) and the pane shimmered elastically, like the surface of a scummy stagnant pool in some wet woodland hollow. Beyond it, thunder lashed and crashed with such violence the air sang with vibrations that could be felt. The purple-green light was flooded every few seconds by a shaft of orange that streaked sizzling baleful fire across the window pane.

Alan rocked backwards on his heels as the floor shuddered again like the nerves in some monster's skin. That he was bewildered was no surprise, but this time he realized he was in the middle of a dream.

Orange lightning? Moving floors? Oh yes, a dream all right.

It was the same room he'd dreamed of before. There were four doors and they were all warping and bulging in time to the insane heartbeat of the walls, the way cartoon doors bulge crazily, surrealistically. The deep drumbeat sound was so low it crackled in his ears and in the back of his head, numbing down his thoughts.

It was the same room, except for one thing. His bed was there, hard against the wall to the left, between two of the stretching doors.

Alan turned to stare at it. It was *half* of their bed, *his* half, jammed headboard to foot lengthwise against the wall. Not *jammed* against the wall. Growing out of it. It was as if some big bandsaw had ripped it with a fine blade right down the middle, separating his half of the bed from hers. Either that, or Helen's side of the bed was *through* the wall, and that wasn't something he wanted to think about, even in the crazy rationality you could sometimes have in a dream.

Alan wasn't scared. Surprised, bewildered and maybe befuddled, but not yet afraid. Because the good thing about dreams is that you wake up. Maybe sweating and panting for breath, but there is always a morning on the other side.

He looked down at himself. He was wearing the slacks that he'd folded and slung on the chair. He was even surprised at the dream detail that showed him his fly was undone. He reached down and caught the zipper and hauled it up. It made a normal zipper buzz. His shirt was buttoned up to two below the collar. On his feet were the running shoes that he'd had on that morning, tightly laced. But he'd forgotten to put his socks on.

The floor rippled again, buckling the floorboards in a wave. Alan stepped to catch his balance, went down on one knee, steadied himself and stood again with his feet planted wide. He looked around for something to grab hold of if it happened again, but before he did so there was a sudden, screeching ripping sound and the skirting board spanged off the wall, swiping out like a springboard across the room. Alan caught the movement out of the corner of his eyes and jumped instinctively. The board, about a foot high, whacked across the floor. If it had hit, it would have broken his legs. When it reached the end of its arc, instead of springing back, there was another wrenching noise and the whole thing flew off the wall with a noise like a gunshot. Almost in slow motion, Alan saw the long plank spin crazily in the air, showing him the jagged-teeth row of nails that had held it on to the battens in the wall. The plank bounced and flipped, scything through the air, twisting and turning, right at his head. He ducked and it whistled past him with a whooping sound and crashed on to the far wall above head height. It vibrated violently and smashed to the ground. Then came another screech of nails being torn violently from wood, a noise like a pig dying down in the slaughter-house.

Alan snatched a look at the far wall where the skirting board was lying teeth-up on the floor. Its opposite number was still firmly fixed to the wall beside his half of the bed. There was a tremor against the wall, then one of the floorboards seemed to curl right up like a clock-spring. The one next to it popped and leapt up, then the next. It was like the rippling of piano keys, only on a monstrous, terrifying scale. Fright hit Alan just above the solar plexus and his heart lurched crazily, stalled, then hit the pedal again.

The floorboards whipped towards him in succession. He ducked the first as it looped up from the floor, then the next. By the time the third hit the air where he'd been standing, Alan had taken off towards the far wall, with the ripping, rending sound tearing in his ears.

And that's when everything leapt right out of true.

The floor itself tilted as if someone had lifted the entire room at one corner and heaved it into the air. Alan's stomach lurched again in an instant of motion sickness, and he was veered by his momentum and the shifting gravity to stagger left towards one of the puls-ing doors. He was only a few feet away from it, arms pinwheeling, when it gave an almighty surge and spat itself open with such force that it whipped on its hinge and hit the wall with a jarring thump. Alan, still caught off balance, lurched over the threshold and in an instant of pure terror caught on to the door jamb.

The room turned itself almost upside-down. Alan was caught in the doorspace that looked straight *down-*

wards, right down into a gaping hole filled with unearthly light and movement.

A wail of fright and pain came out as his weight carried him over the threshold. His hands gripped the moulded doorframe on either side, wrenching his shoulders cruelly, and his feet slammed against the upright jambs at floor-level. He hung there like St Andrew on his cross, spreadeagled over the vast chasm that stretched into infinity below.

Like the walls of the room, the sides of the pit seemed to heave and shiver and Alan knew he couldn't hold on for more than a few moments longer, that he was going to slip and fall, tumble into that unearthly light and whatever waited down there. In an instant of clarity he realized that there was *something* down there, something grotesque and inhuman and terribly blankly evil. Panic surged through him along with the pain of his stretched muscles and tendons.

This didn't feel like a dream. The pain felt too real, too natural, in this frightening and unnatural place.

Alan's foot slipped and with the jerk his other toe which was hooked round the frame came away and he swung wildly downwards, his body a small pendulum high over the chasm. Alan grunted in alarm as his outstretched arms took the sudden weight. He felt the fingers of his left hand begin to slip and dug his fingers into the smooth surface, automatically trying to gouge his nails into the wood. From below came a roaring noise that reminded him of a night express steam train that used to rumble and rattle through Levenford station on its way down from the north, sending sparks from its funnel. It sounded like that, without the clatter of rails. Alan had to stretch his neck to look below his dangling feet. There was a dark movement way down there in that hole that was drilled right into the core of the earth. A vast shadow was spilling upwards, cutting off the baleful light as it came from far below, fast and roaring, surging to where he hung like a fly.

'Oh Christ,' Alan heard himself groan.

Without thinking, he swung his body forward, back and then forward again, bringing his knees right up to the wall from where he was suspended. Using all his strength he coiled himself and got one heel high over his head and on to the doorjamb. With another immense effort, all the time listening to that whistling roar as whatever it was shot up from down below, every nerve stretched like a bow-string, he heaved himself upwards, levering with his leg and hauling with both hands. He got an elbow on to the horizontal jamb which should have been vertical, and eased himself out on to the flat surface of the door which was lying against the wall which was now the floor. He skittered away from the gaping hole and, still lying sprawled, he got both his hands under the door-panel and heaved. It took every ounce of his strength to raise it from the flat. It was as if he was working against a huge tide, a foreign gravity, but it began to swing, inch by ponderous inch until it was upright, until Alan could get a shoulder against it and slam it shut. He lay for a moment, breathless and sore, his heart still jackhammering so wildly as to blur his vision.

The roaring sound with its dreadful threat was cut off. The room went suddenly still and dim. Alan caught his breath in a grateful swoop of air and sat up on the flat, closed door, aware that he should move away, but so drained of energy that even the thought was an effort. He shook his head slowly from side to side.

'It's just a dream,' he said aloud, and some deep part of him wondered that he was able to think that.

Before he could think any more, the room tilted again and he rolled along the wall to crash into the far side. The big breath that he'd hauled in was punched out again and his chin cracked into the surface with enough force to stun him. There was another lurch as the room spun again. It felt as if he was in a big square rolling box. He bounced across the wall, right over the

312

window, and hit the other side with his feet which helped to deaden the impact. Then again across the other wall, tumbling and rolling and bellowing with anger and fear.

Then it stopped completely. Alan slid to a halt, looking down (or up) at the opposite wall. There was a trickle of blood running down from his elbow where he'd given himself a friction burn that had abraded the skin in a six-inch path on his arm. He lay there panting heavily, trying to wake himself up and failing miserably. There was a strange quiet.

He started to crawl across to the door that he'd dreamed he came in by that first night, the door that didn't exist anywhere in the house but would take him into the bottom hall, when the room seemed to leap again and he was thrown right off the flat surface and across the room, dropping like a stone. The opposite door swung open like a huge mouth and he went whizzing through, too quickly even to think about grabbing the jamb. He landed with a thump that winded him yet again, on something soft and wet.

He was in trees. He could smell them, green and resinous. It was dark, but not night. He raised himself up from a scummy pool of mud and looked around him. On every side, trees stretched upwards from monstrous, contorted boles, their trunks swollen and warty, riddled with boreholes. All around was the sound of water dripping from wet leaves. The air smelled green and damp, cloyingly sweet with the scent of unseen blossom. High overhead in the canopy, something shrieked. A movement caught Alan's vision and his eyes flickered towards it. Something slithered down a trunk and was lost in a clump of dripping ferns that sprouted from the nearest tree and had long, trailing and almost threatening roots dangling almost to the ground.

He was on a path which curved between the boles. He walked forward tentatively.

This was a jungle.

- He had gone maybe twenty steps, feeling a sense of vertigo, dwarfed by the vast trees, when there was a flutter in the air, just at head-height. An iridescent butterfly danced in front of his eyes. It was huge. The passage of the plate-sized wings through the air was a thrum that tickled inside Alan's ears.

Another huge insect joined it, then another. They were peeling off the trunks of the trees where they had been camouflaged against the wrinkled bark.

The butterflies were so large that Alan could make out their antennae as they fluttered, almost lazily, around him. They had long, narrow bodies from which trailed slender legs. Almost child-like, he held out a hand towards one of them. It flickered back a foot, then came forward. Air fanned his hand and then the insect gently alighted.

Alan drew his hand in, fascinated, as the butterfly folded back its wings. There was something strange about its eyes. They were dark and shiny and clear, not faceted like normal insects' eyes. He could see two small reflections of himself in the wet orbs and bent down for a closer look.

Just then the butterfly's tongue uncoiled like a dark spring. It looked exactly like the ones he'd seen in nature programmes, a long coiled tongue for sipping nectar. The organ unpeeled and straightened out, gently probing at his arm. Another butterfly landed on his shoulder, its velvet wings stroking his ear.

Wonderingly, Alan peered at the immense, gentle insect as its tongue palped his skin, vainly probing for sweet nectar. Then the thin, wire-like legs spasmed on his hand in a crushing grip. The movement was so sudden that at first Alan couldn't comprehend the pain that accompanied it. His arm muscles locked with its startling abruptness. On his shoulder, steely joints that felt like talons crushed into his collarbone.

Eyes wide with alarm, Alan tried to pull back his

314

arm but the grip seemed to have frozen it in place. As he reached forward with his left hand to tear the thing off he saw the long slender tongue elongate further, then snap into a straight, rigid black line. The creature flexed its legs, loosening the grip slightly, raising up its chitinous body, then clenched again. The tip of the needle-like tongue went into Alan's arm just above the wrist, and as the legs gripped tighter it lanced right under the skin, piercing muscle and scraping off bone, right up to the crook of his elbow.

An *insane* river of pain flowed upwards as if sulphuric acid had been injected into every vein in Alan's arm.

He screamed out loud and the sound echoed off the trees.

On his shoulder, the grip loosened momentarily and even through the red mist of agony Alan instinctively twisted in fright. Another bolt of mad fire drilled into his shoulder and burned its way down the back of his ribs. He screamed again, and his anguish was answered by something high in the treetops.

Alan's feet jittered on the soft earth as his body convulsed under the overload of pain. He felt as if his body was expanding on a bubble of *hurt*. He whirled frantically, his free hand grabbing at the thing on his shoulder. His fingers hooked around the slender body, tearing through papery wings, and he squeezed. Something cracked and then popped and a sticky wetness splattered on his neck. He pulled hard against the resistance of the grip and felt the skin on his shoulder rip as he dragged the thing off. Then he felt the sickening slide of the long needle tongue right down his back as it withdrew from inside him like a stiletto, burning like lava as it came.

Almost fainting, Alan tottered to the nearest tree. In one hand the crumpled body of the huge insect pulsed redly with Alan's own blood. On his other hand the monstrous predatory butterfly hung on, belly swelling purple as it fed. Alan swung round in terror, clubbing his hand on the tree trunk. There was a wet cracking sound as the insect burst. Its gripping legs sprang open and the thing flopped, suspended by the long tongue that was still drilled up the length of Alan's forearm. He battered it again on the tree, seeing his blood splatter the warty bark. From one of the holes in the damp wood, something flicked out like lightning. Alan got an impression of legs and pincers. There was a snap and a wrench and the thing was gone, along with the insect. Alan leapt away from the tree, riddled with fright. From his arm, the broken-off black needle jutted out. He grasped it with his fingers and pulled it out of himself in one quick yank. The pain was awesome.

All around him the butterflies darted and danced, trying to land on him. He windmilled his arms and knocked one from the air. Another landed on the back of his neck and he reached round without looking and crushed it in his fingers. It broke drily.

Then he simply ran terror-stricken along the path. Something long and snakelike reared from the undergrowth, but he was moving too fast to see its strike miss him by inches. He powered along the trail and a butterfly swooped in front of him and clamped its legs around his face. He felt the joints contract and then, blinded by the broad wings, he ran smack into a tree with a thud that sent him reeling. The blow flattened the butterfly to a papery ruin.

Alan spun and took off again. The track narrowed and darkened. Around him he could hear the tickly fluttering of the huge insects. It sent him haring down the track, mouth gaping for breath. Ahead of him the passageway between the trees narrowed even further into a shadowy tunnel. Alan saw dimly right in front of him a shimmering patch in the air, like the mirages you see on a dry road. He tried to stop before he hit it, mistaking it for a spider's web, failed, and went right through. There was a soft, popping sound as the jungle disappeared in a wink and he emerged somewhere else.

He came through about three feet above the ground and landed on both feet on a dark roadway. The sky was pitch dark but on the other side of the water, through the driving rain, the lights of Rhu and Shandon twinkled distantly.

He turned round, hauling his breath, and discovered where he was. Facing him was the gateway with its two stone pillars on the gravel path that led up to the house.

Through the rain that was lashing down in torrents and being thrown on the wind right up the loch he could see Cromwath, big and dark and looming. The fright and alarm that had riven him almost from the moment he'd found himself in the strange moving room started to fade instantly in the cold. But they were replaced by something else that made him shiver inside.

For Alan realized that this was no longer a dream. He was awake, and standing outside the grounds of his house. He could feel the rain on his face, and he could feel the cold wind that tried to sleet through him. He walked through the gateway and he could hear the gravel crunching under his feet as he slowly made his way up to the house. Behind him, a car passed on the road, wheels kicking up spume, headlamps flickering in the rain.

For the first time, he wondered if maybe the problem was not only with Helen. Maybe it was with *himself*. He'd gone to bed and had found himself in the most realistic nightmare he'd ever experienced, and he'd woken up in the middle of the road in the pouring rain.

Alan mumbled to himself as he crunched painfully up the sloping path. 'Either I'm going out of my mind,' he said, 'or there's something funny going on around here.' And he remembered the other things he'd read in the diary that Andrew Dalmuir had hidden away in the false cupboard.

When he got to the front door he found it was open,

although he remembered locking it after he'd stood in the porch enjoying the last few calm moments of the summer night. That seemed a lifetime ago. He walked in to the darkened house, shivering with the cold, and into the kitchen where he'd felt that tremor when he'd first taken the big sledgehammer to the wall. Up at the back of the cupboard was a half-full bottle of brandy that hadn't been opened in an age. He hauled it out and unslung a cup from where it dangled on a hook. Alan was not in the mood for niceties. He poured himself a large one, raised it to his mouth and tipped it straight down his throat. It burned him clean and hit his stomach in a fireball that seared its way right through him.

Then he sat down at the kitchen table under the rise-and-fall light, and poured himself a real drink, filling the mug to well over half-way. There was no way he was going to get back to sleep this night, and no way he wanted to either.

What he wanted to do was pour brandy down his throat and think.

Matt Stirling had got caught in a sudden thunderstorm when he was freewheeling down the Peaton Hill Road where it veered sharply to the west taking a dog-leg to the right at a one-in-seven gradient which needed a hair-trigger brake finger and a faster sense of balance. The night had been warm and sultry after the sun had gone down beyond the Cowals, and Matt had pumped hell for leather, fairly building up a summer-evening sweat, along the winding road through the glen.

The young teacher was heading south, maybe two miles up from Creggan, when the first flashes of lightning streaked down from a sky that was cobalt overhead. The lightning danced and forked, streaks of silvered blue venom that bounced from high and seemed to jitter between the earth and the sky way down there at the point. Matt travelled about a hundred yards or so before the first shock of thunder shook the ground below his hissing tyres. The air crackled with the shock, a brittle, hard judder that seemed to stun the atmosphere rather than roll in a wave up the glen. He was left with a fuzzed and streaky after-image flickering on his retinas so brightly that he almost veered off the road at the turn but managed to stay on the saddle by dint of luck and a fast reflex. When his vision came back he noted that the sky over Creggan had gone from inky blue to coal black in an instant.

'Fireworks tonight,' he said into the wind that was ruffling his cheeks. He pedalled harder, heading for home and into the summer storm that was ripping the night apart.

He went left at the fork that could have taken him to Murrin and Feorlin half a mile down the road when he ran into a wall of water that simply fell from the sky. It was like running into a tropical rainstorm, a monsoon. His tyres hissed through the surface slick for ten seconds, and then they were ploughing through an inch of run-off as the rain spun its coin-splashes. The little front lamp shone a beam maybe ten yards into the rain as the dynamo from the rear wheel fed it power. At the speed Matt had reached, the lamp would be juiced up enough to throw a cone of light forty, maybe even fifty, yards ahead, but the blanket of rain swallowed up the light in a grey miasma.

Matt realized he was going faster than he could control his racer down the hill. He had never actually aquaplaned on a bike before, and it was one of the things he had never had a notion to do, especially on a night like this. He came to the bend that sloped downwards, sensing rather than seeing the hawthorn bushes whizz by on the left, and the stone dike flicker a dark morse on the right. He touched the brakes for the downturn and felt the rear wheel slip, taking his stomach with it in an instant jolt of over-reaction. He tried to compensate by shifting his weight and nosing the front wheel into the skid, slackening the brake to get better traction on the slippery road. He got himself back again just on the bend and hauled his weight to the other side to let him arrow close to the grass verge for the drop down on to the straight when the whole bike just went from under him.

There was a flash that lit the whole sky in front of him and a bolt of lightning smacked down into the stand of trees ahead. The rain instantly killed any chance of a fire. Matt saw it happen with that distant interest in detail that comes with the chemical blood-surge of sudden alarm. There was a clatter as the bike scraped itself across the road. Matt hit the road metal with a jarring thud on his hip, bounced and tumbled after the spidery bike, and crashed into the low bushes at the side of the road. Something socked him on the back, flipped him over, and he landed face down among the saplings that ran next to the dike with a thud that was hard and dull enough to send his mind floating, stunned, up and out.

THIRTY-TWO

Matt slowly hauled himself out of his daze. The rain was drumming hard on his back. He opened his eyes and the world swam darkly and giddily in a nauseating swirl which slowed, then steadied and jumped into focus. He was lying face down in the tangle beside the dike. He remembered skidding and tumbling across the road, a punch on his back and a blow to his middle, then nothing. He was sprawled with one foot up in the air, high behind him. It was sending electric messages down his leg. He moved and the pain screwed up a notch across his ankle, so he moved back again, this time gingerly turning his body round without putting pressure on the leg. It felt as if his ankle was broken. South of him, the air arched and sparkled with pyrotechnics of the thunderstorm. The rain was a cataract of incessant drops that splashed from the leaves of the tangle of small birches and gorse into which he had tumbled.

Matt raised himself up on his elbows, feeling the pressure on his ankle abate a fraction. This allowed him to turn awkwardly and face backwards. His foot was caught in the fork of a sapling, the bones of his ankle forced into the narrow grip by the weight of his plunge. It was difficult to move. If he turned, it put stress on the leg. He tried it and fell back, gasping.

'Bloody hell,' he gasped to himself when the pain receded. 'It's another fine mess you've got me into, Matthew.'

Beside him, the buckled wheel of his bike was a close approximation of a Möbius strip, folded in on itself with the force of the clattering impact against the dike.

It was going to be no damned use, even if he did manage to get his ankle out of the footlock wedge.

Matt waited until he got his breath back and tried to stand, bracing himself gingerly to keep his balance. Despite the pain, he was aware of how ungainly he looked, standing in the middle of a rainstorm with one foot in the fork of a tree and the other trying to keep his balance. If someone were to pass by now, he would probably keep moving.

Just as that rueful thought struck him, Matt saw the movement ahead, maybe twenty yards further down the slope of the road. Had it not been for the streak of silver-blue lightning that danced down on top of Creggan he would have missed it.

Something had come over the wall, fast and dark. Like a big dog prowling the night. There was another movement on the road. Something squatted there, shifting slightly in the strobe-effect flashes. As the lightning tailed off, there was another scuttling motion, and two other shapes came loping over the low dike. Matt screwed his eyes up against the rain, peering forward into the darkness ahead. He could make out dim forms, but the rain was so heavy that they were just blurred images. If they were dogs, there would be a farmer with them most likely, even on a night like this. He was about to call out when he heard a low growling sound that was unlike any dog he had ever heard before.

Instantly he froze as a sudden fear slicked up from his belly. Under him his knee started to give with the pressure of his weight and he slid to the ground, catching himself on outstretched hands.

The sound came again, deep and slavering. Hungry. There was a quick, scuttering movement, and the sound of trampling in the bushes at the far side of the road. Matt heard the heavy panting of a big animal, then the click of teeth and jaws opened, then closed.

'What the hell *is* it?' he asked himself. The strange, unnatural fear started to inflate inside him again. There was something unearthly about the noise and the movement.

His ankle was still caught in the fork of the sapling. He couldn't move and that made him feel completely helpless. Even if it was a pack of big dogs, there was nothing he could do to defend himself. But something inside him said this was no pack of big dogs. Shivers ran from the base of his spine right up the bones of his back, and the skin of his neck puckered strongly enough for him to feel his hair move.

From just ahead in the patch of gorse there was a crackling noise. Then the branches parted and something shoved its face right up close to where the young man was sprawled in the dark. It was a shadow. Then the lightning flickered and Matt saw its face and let out a cry of pure fright.

It turned a flat, wide face on him. Great saucer-like eyes that were so black they were like huge circular wells sunk deep into space. They didn't blink, reflecting dully on each flat surface the jittering, forked lightning. Matt instinctively recoiled in horror and fright. Pain shot from his trapped foot, but it seemed far away. In the corner of his vision, he saw another of the things lope up towards the first, scrambling on the road surface on spindly, many-jointed legs. The scrabble of claws clicking against the surface could be heard over the noise of the rain.

The lightning died in a wink leaving Matt for an instant in total darkness. There was a snuffling sound ahead, and when his vision returned the first gargoyle had moved in closer, savouring his scent. A musty smell like rotting toadstools suddenly emanated, and the thing put forward a clawed hand that had too many long, spindly fingers and curved talons. The hand came down, grey and scaly, right in front of Matt. He felt his breath back up in his lungs, cutting off the bellow of fear that was trying to get out. The thing leaned forward and he got a whiff of breath like the stench from something that had rotted on a hot beach. A wide mouth opened and there was a glint of long shards of teeth. Matt cowered back, ignoring the drill of pain that had gone from sporadic bolts to one continuous pulse.

Then from behind the first creature there came a snarling grunt as the second tried to squeeze past. Matt knew in an instant that this was the noise he had heard in his garden on the night that his dog was savaged.

The first grotesque thing snarled back in a deep gurgling threat. It arched its neck impossibly, lifting its head up and over on a strangely scrawny neck until it was parallel with its spine, and snapped, still facing upside-down, at the nearest one. Behind them both, there was scrabbling and panting as others loped forward, attracted by the noise.

The thing settled its staked claim and swung its head up, then down to face the trapped man, its huge, black and blinkless eyes sucking in what was left of the light. It was a face from hell, a living gargoyle that radiated such cold hunger that Matt felt himself shake with fright. His heart which had been pounding away seemed to freeze inside his rib-cage. Again the mouth opened and the row of glass needles glinted wetly.

'Get away from me,' Matt shouted helplessly, pulling himself back as far as his trapped leg would allow.

The creature's head darted forward, like a striking snake. The jaws opened in an immense gape as it lunged. Matt jerked back and another bolt of pain socked out from his ankle, far away and distant. The jaws snapped shut, a mere inch from his eyes, which felt as if they were bulging out so far they'd roll down on to his cheeks. There was a grating crack as the row of spines clamped together with enormous force. A wet drip of spittle splashed out from between them and the droplet landed on Matt's chin. Instantly an excruciating point of agony flared under his lip like molten metal and the young man yelped with the sudden intensity.

The thing's head drew back on a strangely articulated neck. The jaws started to open again as the neck flexed. Like a slow playback, Matt saw the stringy muscles bunch under a knotted skin and ripple as the head started on its strike. Two pinpoints of light switched on in the sucking depths of the vast night eyes and sparkled poisonously over the needle array of teeth. It looked as if something had sparked into life within the depth of the dead eyes. Matt did not know that they were just the far-off reflections of John Lindsay's Land Rover which was breasting the Peaton Hill Road two miles behind.

He cringed, unable to move, and in that moment of paralysing fear his bladder simply let itself go.

The thing whipped forward and the mouth opened in a flashing gape. Matt's head twisted to the side and the creature's mouth clamped shut on his jaw with a crunch of rending bone. It shook its head from side to side, like a terrier with a rat in its jaws. Under the wave of pain that instantly swamped him Matt Stirling felt his jaw pop out at his ear. His neck muscles felt as if they were being torn from the ligaments as his head was whipped back and forth. He was dimly aware of a far-off wrenching pain as the force of this movement snapped his ankle in the sapling's fork, forcing the bone through the skin.

The vile thing's jaws tightened like a vice and it pulled. Matt felt himself falling as his broken ankle was dislodged from where it had been trapped. His leg and hips hit the ground and bounced. The creature pulled back and Matt felt a horrible scraping sensation above the pain that tore across the front of his face. The thing shook its head once more and the young teacher's own jaw came ripping away. His chin, tongue and seven of his upper teeth were gone in an instant, leaving him with a red, gaping hole from which blood simply poured. He tried to cry out, to scream for help, and from his larynx came a reedy, gurgling noise that sounded like a distant cry. But there was no mouth to magnify it; nothing there to make that sound into a human voice.

The creature's jaws worked twice and Matt heard the sound of his own bones crunching inside its mouth. There was a gulp and half of his face was swallowed quickly. It swung round on him again and he tried to scramble backwards, still unable to comprehend that he was dying. Its spindly legs carried it forward with spider-like, scuttling speed and its head dipped again. It grabbed Matt by the shoulder, tore through T-shirt, muscle, sinew and bone, and clamped so hard that on either side ribs collapsed. Another of the creatures scrambled over the first, chittering frenziedly. It landed on Matt's back and sank its head into his side.

Something grabbed at his leg and chewed. There was a shocking wrench from his side as one creature hauled, and a corresponding pull in the opposite direction as his leg was twisted at right angles to his body. Something howled in fury. Another grunted and chewed and swallowed and bit. In the fading fuzziness that quickly drained his senses, Matt felt something give at his hip. The last thing he felt was a sudden creak as his thigh was pulled from its socket and the whole limb torn away.

And after that he knew nothing as the snarling pack gulped and chewed. In minutes there was nothing left on the verge but a trampled, bloodied carpet that was already being washed into the ditch by the pounding rain.

By the time John Lindsay's Land Rover turned the corner on the slope that swooped towards Creggan, the creatures had disappeared in a scuttling blur over the dry-stane dike and into the belt of trees.

In the driving rain, the big policeman failed to see the bike that had skidded for twenty yards round the bend until his nearside wheel had clipped the handlebars and sent it clattering further along the road.

Cursing under his breath, he floored the brake and

brought the jeep up sharply. He clambered out and found the tangled frame lying in the middle of the road. Flicking his torch on, he swept the light over the bike and then on to the verge. There was nothing to be seen. If the sleek, now crumpled racer, hadn't been carried by its own momentum down the hill, and if the Land Rover hadn't knocked it even further, then John might have seen the mess of blood that was trickling down into the run-off. It was washed down at the side of the road along with the rainwater, turning it pink, and falling straight into the drain that ran at the side of the road.

John Lindsay picked up the bike, noted the bucked wheels and twisted frame. It looked like the kind of hot rod the young teacher with the dead dog was scooting about on, but he couldn't be sure. He hefted it and slung it into the back of the Land Rover. No doubt it would be claimed the next day or so, he told himself.

Now thoroughly wet, he got back into the driver's seat, started the engine and carried on down the hill, completely unaware of the carnage that had obliterated Matt Stirling from the world only moments before.

He drove down to Creggan, taking the shore road that was just as quick as the main way over the back of the village. When he got down to the first big house on the point, the headlamps picked out a man standing by the gateway of the old Dalmuir place, standing in his shirtsleeves in the pouring rain.

He didn't seem to notice the jeep as it roared past. His attention seemed to be fixed on the big stone house up at the end of the drive.

John Lindsay's unofficial night shift had started just after midnight when he'd been watching the second to last frame of the snooker final on television in the living-room of the police house. Marion had taken a book upstairs and the policeman had sat with his long legs crossed in front of him, lazily enjoying the tension of the game. It had been a fairly quiet day. He'd gone along to the tinkers' field at the far side of Corbeth close up to Murrin, and had talked with Jake MacFie, a big, wide-shouldered bull of a man with deep-set dark eyes. Some of the locals had been complaining about the fights that had broken out after closing time down at the Creel, which was the pub in Murrin where the farm hands and everybody else went to drink. Andy Noble up at Corrie Farm had lost a couple of sheep, and across the Peaton Glen just up from Creggan where Sandy Farquhar raised pheasants and grouse for the autumn syndicate somebody had broken into the cages and made away with two hundred birds. While there was no evidence to suggest that the tinkers had been in any way responsible, John took it as his duty to have a quiet chat with Jake MacFie, to all intents and purposes the leader of the tinkers. They were all MacFies or MacPhersons or MacFarlanes, descendents of the old west coasters who'd been displaced in the highland clearances, but to John Lindsay's point of view, the remnants of the nomads who'd been wandering Scotland since before the old Caledonia Forest was cut down, and that was back a while.

They'd had words before, and had learned a grudging respect for each other. When the policeman strode up the lane from where he'd parked the jeep, the camp went silent. Grizzled women gathered their shawls round about themselves where they sat on upturned plastic milk-crates round a big fire. Children, fair-haired and blue-eyed mostly, but some with traces of the old dark-haired Celt showing on their fine-boned features, stared distrustingly. It was ever thus.

Jake MacFie came out of the rickety caravan that seemed to be rooted in the long, dry grass. He stood with his hands on his hips and watched as the policeman came through the camp towards him. Then he stepped on the plank that was slung across two short pillars of bricks to act as a doorstep, and walked forward.

'Mornin' John. You're well?'

'Well as ever, Jake, and yourself?'

'Same as ever. Good summer helps.' He looked around the camp, which had gone back to normal as soon as the introductions showed there was no immediate trouble.

'Getting the work then?'

'Aye, picking the totties up the top end. It's been a good year for that, and old Donald isn't the curmudgeon he was last time. Here, will you have a cup with me?' He looked across to the fire. John nodded and followed him. The women got up and separated, gossiping quietly but looking over their shoulders at the man who was, to them, a stranger. Both men eased their big frames down on the crates. An old black kettle was hanging on a chain over the fire from a central cross-pole. Jake reached and gripped the handle with a big, hard hand and hoisted it off the heat. There were several mugs hanging from cut-off twigs on a stick that was jammed into the earth. He took two and poured tea into them straight from the kettle. It looked dark and thick.

'You want anything in that?'

'Just the milk. A wee spot of colour,' John said. Jake called out something and a girl of about seven came shyly across with a metal jug. He thanked her and poured enough to take the tarry look off the tea. Both men drank, letting the silence settle down between them.

'And yourself, John. You've been kept busy?'

'It could be quieter,' the policeman said, savouring the brew.

'Trouble?'

'Here and there. This and that.'

'Go on,' Jake said, staring directly, almost challengingly, at the policeman.

'Well, there's been one or two breaches. But you'll

know about that. I had words with a couple of your boys the other night. Drink was talking.'

'Aye, well there was drink talking in a few folk that night.'

John nodded agreeably. 'There's been a couple of farmers complaining, you know?'

Jake raised his eyebrows in question on the far side of his cavernous mug.

'Couple of sheep gone. And a few young game birds. And there was a lot of chickens killed up at Jack Coggan's place. Some animal, I think.'

'Not ours. We keep them tied up at night, which is more than I can say for the folks around here. The farmers aren't the only ones. We lost a goat, on Thursday. It was tied out by the fence,' he said, indicating the far-off edge of the camp, under a spread of oak tree. 'Somebody came in the night and killed it. There was blood all around, but they took the beast. It was a fine wee white billy.'

'You didn't see who it was?'

'No, but if I had done, he wouldn't have come back to make mischief again.' He looked over at John, and again that calm challenge was there. Lindsay ignored it.

'About these other matters.'

'They've got nothing to do with us.'

'Aye, well, that's as maybe, Jake. But I'm here to keep the peace and to try to get some sleep at night if I can. I think we both want a quiet life, so if any of your boys have maybe been doing any night fighting in these hereabouts, I'd be obliged if you can maybe have a word yourself. Not that I'm saying they have, mind you, but just in case.'

'If they had, I would know about it, so I can tell you now, John Lindsay, that you're looking in the wrong place.'

'I have to look everywhere. As I said, I just keep the peace.'

'And so do I,' the big tinker replied. 'But you can sleep easy. We're just about finished up at the top end. We'll be moving on to the Stirling Flats for the main-crop the day after the midsummer.'

John drained his mug and put it upside-down on one of the warm stones that encircled the fire. 'I'll ask about your goat,' he said.

'Aye, well if you find it you'll be the fine detective,' Jake said, and he laughed.

John stood up and grinned. 'Well, you take care of yourself, MacFie. I'll be seeing you next year, no doubt.'

'Sure as day dawns, Lindsay. And keep your peace now, eh?'

John smiled and walked out of the camp, feeling the eyes of the children on his back.

It was after midnight when the phone rang, right next to where he sat sprawled on the sofa. He snatched it up quickly before it woke Marion. The line crackled for a bit and somebody bawled down the line, forcing John to hold it away from his ear.

'Calm yourself down, man,' he said into the receiver. 'I can't hear a damned word you're saying.'

The voice dropped fifty decibels to a mere roar. It was Henry MacLeish, who raised stock on the border ground above the Peaton Glen where the valley gave on to upland grazing.

'There's something after my beasts,' Henry roared. 'Them tinkers have been in at my sheep. I'm going to take my gun to the lot of them.'

'Now hold on, Henry,' John said quickly, halting the man in mid-splutter. 'Just slow down a bit and tell me what's happening.'

'It's my sheep. They've been at the flock, damned bastards. There's near a dozen of them lying in the field, cut to bits. It's like a fucking slaughterhouse.'

'Right, I'll be up in five minutes. Just stay in the house until I get there,' John said. Then, almost as an

331

afterthought, he added: 'And you keep that gun on the rack, Henry. I don't want you running around and blasting at everything that moves. Not over a few head of sheep. And remember, it'll be me that's knocking on your door and I don't want to be looking down any barrels. You understand what I'm telling you?'

MacLeish allowed that he did. John could heard the man's heavy breathing mixed with the static on the line.

'Right, stay put and I'll be there.'

On television, the tall, poker-faced man at the table had taken his break into the nineties with clean, robotic efficiency, guaranteeing a tense final frame. John got his tunic and cursed to himself as he pulled on his boots. He was going to miss it.

If Jack Coggan's chicken shack had been a scene of carnage, this was a battleground. There were more than a dozen carcasses lying on the small pasture, and blood was everywhere. If it hadn't been for the woolly fleeces, either man would have been hard put to identify the bloody remains as sheep. They had been mauled, savaged, slaughtered with such ferocity that their bodies had been torn to pieces. One sheep, a big, black-faced tup, looked as if it had been completely chewed from behind. From the head to the chest it looked normal. The rest of it looked as if it had been put through an industrial grinder. Entrails and chewed limbs strung out behind. It was obvious, even in the light of the torches, that it had dragged itself across the field. Dragged itself and whatever had been eating into it as it went.

'Did you hear anything?' John asked the ashen-faced farmer.

'I was watching the television, me and the wife,' he said. 'She's a bit hard of hearing, so it's always turned up and it wasn't until I heard a bit of a commotion that I came out for a look. I never saw anything though, bar a couple of shadows. When I put on the outside light, there was nothing. Only this,' he said, indicating the mutilated carcass of one of his prize tups. John could hear the catch in his voice that showed the man was close to tears.

The policeman was about to say something when there was a huge clatter and a bellow coming from a pitched-roof stone building that ran at right angles to the farmhouse.

'My God,' Henry shouted in sudden alarm. 'It's the Prince.'

John looked at him blankly for a second before he realized what the man was talking about. The Prince was Henry's pride and joy, a huge black Angus bull that the farmer had bought for a fortune two summers before at the Perth fatstock auctions. Henry started forward, raising the shotgun up from the crook of his arm into a shooting position. John reached out and gripped the barrel, twisting it out of the man's hands.

They ran towards the outhouse. From inside there was a screeching cacophony, and the wild, furious roaring of a bull. John got to the big byre door first but because he had the gun in one hand and the flashlight in the other, he had to wait until the farmer caught up with him to open it. Henry hauled on the handles, pulling each of the doors outwards, and followed as John stepped in, both men swinging their torches forward.

At the far end, there was a churning commotion of black shadows. Then there was the enormous noise of the bull blasting out from the end stall. The Prince was struggling and hauling at the chain that held it to the concrete pillar. Its huge bulk was rearing up and down. On it, under it and behind it, shadows seemed to move with blurring speed.

John slid the torchlight over it, walking quickly up the central aisle of the short bull-byre. Then he stopped dead on his tracks. The big bull was lathered in blood, spattered over its back and down its broad flanks. Half of its face was torn away. The policeman could see its eyes rolling in terror.

And on the animal were things that moved in a scuttling monkey-like way. They were the size of dogs, but humped and hunched and moving faster than the eye could reasonably follow.

'What the fuck is that?' Henry shouted hoarsely.

'Only Christ knows,' John came back. It was impossible to see clearly what the hell it was, but there were a few of them, scuttling and swarming over the terrified animal's back. The bull screamed and Henry flicked the beam of the torch right along it. There was a screech of pain, but this time not from the bull. A big flat eye seemed to draw the torchlight into it without reflection. Henry looked with horror and saw that the bull's dangling testicles, the real reason he'd spent all those thousands, were a bloody, chewed mess hanging down between its thighs.

'Oh no!' he wailed. John arched his beam across and one of the shadows recoiled with a screech. There was a sudden flurry of movement as the stall exploded in a twisting black mêlée. Then there was a crash of glass and a scrabbling at the small metal-framed window on the wall. John brought the shotgun up one-handed and squeezed the trigger. The hy-max hit with a thud, the spread rapping through the glass and into the wall. Another high-pitched caterwaul, and the thing was gone. Another shadow, then another, and a third scuttered for the window. John let them all have the other barrel. They lurched, blurringly screaming their dreadful wails, out into the night.

John whirled and ran to the door, swinging the torchlight beam in front of him. He sprinted round the side of the byre to where the window faced on to the lane. There was a small verge of grass growing between the wall and the cobble. He shone the torch down on to it and saw the dark splashes of blood dripping from the wall on to the stalls. There was a bitter acid smell that burned in his nose, and a sizzling noise. John peered closer and saw the stone of the wall steaming under the viscous black fluid. He stepped back and panned the beam over the grass. It was already black and shrivelled.

'What the hell's going on here?' Henry asked, his voice trembling with despair and anger and frustration.

'I haven't a clue, Henry,' John said. 'But I'm sure as hell going to find out.'

Just then, there was a flash of lightning from down at the point, and a few moments later the boom of thunder rolling up the hill. As Henry and John walked round the side of the byre, the rain hit, lashing down in a sudden torrent. Henry took the shotgun from John's hand, broke it and thumbed in two shells. Both men walked up to the back of the byre where the bull was still rearing in pain and panic, its hoofs drumming a heavy, ragged beat on the hard floor. Henry reached for the wall switch and felt his stomach heave when he saw the dreadful injuries on his prize animal. It was hard to believe that it was still alive, never mind on its feet.

'I can't leave it like this,' he said, looking at the big animal. It was covered in blood. Great chunks of flesh had been torn from its back and sides and head, exposing muscle and bone. Underneath, the scrotum dangling into the straw was a wet, bloody mass that dripped obscenely.

Henry put the long barrel up against the thick neck behind the bull's wasted head. He pulled the trigger and the animal dropped to the ground instantly with a crashing thud that shook the byre.

THIRTY-THREE

Alan woke with a start, stiff and sore and damp in his shirt and jeans. He opened his eyes and the room danced a little, and when he moved his head up it danced a little more, blurred at the edges, and swinging in time to the pressure pain just above his eyes. His throat felt dry and tight and there was a rank taste between his tongue and palate. Beside him, on the coffee table, the brandy bottle swam into focus. There was half an inch of amber liquid lying shallowly on the bottom. He grunted, peeling his tongue off the roof of his mouth with an effort. He stood and stretched, feeling unkempt and dishevelled and more than a little hung over. He could also feel the raw bits at the back of his knees where the wrinkles of his wet jeans had been digging into the skin, rubbing them red.

Just at the peak of the stretch, the events of the previous night came lurching back into his memory. For a second he could remember the tumbling of the room where the floorboards snapped up in succession like crazy piano keys. Then the doorway where he'd hung over the black infinite pit, and then the jungle and those fluttering horrors.

He shuddered, and again the thought came back to him, the one that he'd had before making his heroic plunge into the brandy bottle, that maybe he was beginning to crack.

Through the window, the sky was black and thundery still. Alan shook himself, or rather an early-morning shudder riddled through him. He shoved the picture of the nightmare (*it must have been a nightmare!*) away from him and went through to the kitchen. He turned the cold tap on, absently looking out of the picture window on to the back garden, and further out at the small orchard. There was a rattling in the pipes and a far-off hissing sound. The tap spat a couple of times, coughing a weak spray into the steel sink, then a dribble of dirty water, more dirt than water, splurged out to splat sickly in the bottom of the basin.

'Damn, that's all I need,' Alan muttered. What he did need was a large mug of coffee, as black and as strong as he could make it, to get rid of the night shakes that were hovering at the edge of his mind, and to ease the headache that was pounding dully behind his eyes. He thought that maybe one of the water mains had burst in the storm of last night. Maybe the pumping station along on the Mambeg shore had been hit. That didn't help his predicament in any way. What did help was the fact that the upright electric kettle on the work surface was filled with water. He poured some on to the cupped palm of his hand and splashed his eyes. It helped a little, more from the shock of cold than anything else. While towelling his eyes, he flicked the kettle switch and sat down to wait for it to boil.

The coffee did help. It scalded and scoured the scum that was congealing the inside of his mouth. The second one, black as tar but heaped with three spoonfuls of sugar, helped him feel more human. While he drank, Alan tried to puzzle out the meaning of the previous night's misadventure. On his third cup, this one with milk to help ease the bitterness that he knew would plague him all morning if he drank any more, he came to some conclusions.

They were these: if he thought he was going crazy, then he couldn't be; but having said that, there *must* be something wrong with him if he had dreadful nightmares and went sleepwalking out of the house into a summer storm. Having reached what to him seemed a logical conclusion, he put his clearing mind to the reasons. By the end of the third cup, he had come to the decision that the agglomeration of problems and stresses, including moving house, taking the big promotion that doubled his responsibility at MacKenzie-Kelso, the strange blank aloofness of his wife (and her other attendant problems), had been building up to such an extent that he had reached the limit of his ability to cope. That in itself was a surprise to Alan Crombie who had always managed, or at least tried to handle, any problem or difficulty that life threw at him, and so far he had done reasonably well.

The alternative thought, that actually he had been in a room which didn't exist, and through doorways to places that couldn't possibly exist, was one which he was not prepared to dwell on, even for an instant.

Alan Crombie was only human. Somewhere between opening the bottle of brandy and the cold, stiff awakening in the grey morning, his mind had sorted itself out in the way that the human brain can. It accepted as true the most likely scenario, built up its unconscious arguments for it, and believed it as the only possible truth.

Alan Crombie was to learn the real truth of it, but not yet. Not quite yet.

The twins were still fast asleep when he checked on them. Tommy was stirring dozily. In their room, Helen was lying spreadeagled on the bed. It was solid and square against the wall, not cut in half.

Alan quietly took his jeans off and bunched his shirt on top. He considered a shower, remembered the water was off, and had a quick wash, using what little water he could from the tank up in the attic. There was an abraded scratch up on his arm that nipped under the hot flow. He remembered getting that in the dream, but again his mind flipped that thought out and rationalized the injury. He must have cut himself while wandering around in the garden.

The wash and a fresh pair of cord trousers and a thick

338

checked shirt went a good way to making him feel more human. The coffee had faded down the dullness of the headache. Alan went downstairs, opened up the storm doors and stepped out into the brilliant sunshine of an early summer morning. The surprise of it almost took his breath away. The grey, gloomy clouds had dissipated. Above was a blue sky that fairly zinged with the promise of a hazy day and temperatures zooming up through the seventies. In the honeysuckle that wound itself around the Virginia creeper on the wall, early bees were already humming busily. Out on the loch, the mewling cries of the diving sea birds came floating on clear air, faint and high. It was too early to wake the family. Alan went for a walk down by the foreshore.

It was there that he met Beth Callander who was wandering along the high-tide mark, hands deep in the pockets of her jeans, eyes fixed on the flotsam tangled in the dark line of wrack and kelp. She looked up, surprised, when he said hello.

They chatted for a few minutes and Alan took the opportunity to ask her if Alex could be contacted that morning.

'Nothing wrong, is there?'

'No, I just fancy having a chat about the girls,' Alan said, and although he wasn't telling the complete truth, he wasn't sure what he wanted to talk to the doctor about. She wasn't even their family doctor, but he felt that maybe the auburn-haired young American might be able to help him in some way.

'I'm having a coffee with her at ten at the Gossip Shop,' Beth said. 'Want to come along?'

'Yeah, all right,' Alan agreed. He had decided in any event to take Katie and Laney for a walk by the shore to make up for the lost time over the past week. By ten o'clock, the black coffee he'd poured down his dry throat would have worked itself out.

Back at the house, Alan walked around the property

starting with the garage side, round the back where the garden was still in early-morning shadow, dew still damping the short-cut grass, and back round the top end and into the sunlight at the front. It was then that he noticed the line of shingles that had slid down from the roof, big grey axeheads of Scottish slate that had skittered down from the pitched slope and sliced themselves right into the lawn at the front. They must have come down with some force in the storm, for they were buried to half their depth in the turf. Alan wondered what would happen to a human, *to the children*, if one of those deadly sharp stone blades had come schicking down. It would have cut them in half.

In the kitchen, Tommy and the girls were demolishing cocoa-pops with gusto. Alan squeezed them some orange juice and then made a fourth for himself.

'Any plans for today, Tam?' Alan asked. Tommy blushed at his father's use of the name his school friends had called him, then grinned to match his father's smile.

'Me and Bobby and Jim are going to make bows and arrows,' Tommy said. 'We were playing commandos yesterday.' He thought of it, but didn't mention the big raggedy man who had scared the daylights out of them in the Corrie Glen.

'Sounds like fun. I suppose I'll be left here with the womenfolk while you go and do something manly.'

Tommy's face took on a serious look. 'I'll stay if you want me to,' he said loyally.

'And be bored stiff? No, you go and have fun. I'm going to take the ladies walking,' he said. After the big change in moving up from Surrey to the west of Scotland, Alan considered that Tommy needed friends more than he needed his father, on a day-to-day basis. 'But before you go, I'd like you to do me a big favour.'

Tommy's bright expression collapsed a little. Normally when his dad wanted a favour, it was something that was going to severely curtail his playing arrangements. Alan noted the look immediately.

'Oh, don't worry, it's not a big job. I just want you to go to Seumas's house for me while I'm getting the girls ready. Tell him there's something wrong with the water pipes, and there's a couple of slates that have come down off the roof. Just say that if he's got a minute, I'd like some extra work done this week.'

This job was no problem to Tommy. Seumas was a regular in the garden. He was there once or twice a week, mowing the lawn with the big petrol machine that chugged ferociously, belching a plume of blue smoke across the wide slope of turf. A few times he'd let Tommy hold on to the widespread handlebars that almost came up to head-height on an eight-year-old, and the boy had felt the delicious vibration that shook his whole body as the mower pulled away, dragging him behind it in the close-shaved path that its blades cut.

'Where does he live?'

'Just go up the road on the left, and watch out for any traffic. Stay close to the verge,' Alan started with his list of directions. 'Then take the left again at the main road. His house is the first white one at the edge of the trees. It's got a chimney at each end and a greenhouse against the wall.'

Tommy nodded. He'd seen the little, deserted-looking cottage. He had never thought about who might live there.

'OK,' he nodded brightly and got down from his chair, dutifully taking his cereal plate to the sink. From upstairs, the sound of the vacuum cleaner burred a low howl. Helen had started work immediately she woke. She hadn't bothered to join them for breakfast. Alan tried not to dwell on that.

Tommy skittered out of the front door on fast feet, his Nikes pattering on the stone steps, and he was gone into the summer morning. Alan wiped the girls' chins automatically and looked out their sandals from the bottom of the cupboard. They were a bit scuffed from the week's wear, he noted with another little surge of annoyance, unlike the house which was cleaner than any lived-in home had a right to be. He brushed them with Kiwi and didn't even bother to work out which might be whose. They were identical. As long as Katie and Laney had a left and right, it would make no difference. He didn't even notice the K and E written in black ballpoint on the inside of the heel, and if he had done it would have made the cloud of unease that bit darker in his mind. Helen had made those marks before they'd moved north. They would only have shown him the difference in her between then and now.

Down at the Gossip Shop, a little teahouse right on the front of the village beside the small harbour in a position that looked out across the firth, Beth and Alex were sharing a pot and buttered scones fresh from the oven, warm and light. Both of the women looked up and smiled as Alan walked in with the girls in tow. Beth's attention was on the girls. Alex coloured slightly, remembering what she'd confided in her friend. Alan didn't notice.

He allowed the girls a small cola each. They knelt up on their chairs, sipping contentedly while Beth made a fuss.

'What happened to your arm?' Alex asked immediately. Alan's shirtsleeves were rolled up, and the long abraded weal showed on the side from elbow almost to wrist. She automatically reached across the table to take his hand and turn the arm around. Her touch was warm and dry.

'Haven't much of a clue, to tell you the truth,' Alan admitted.

She looked at him sceptically. 'That doesn't look like the kind of scrape you'd get and not notice.' His hand felt strong, like a working man's hand without the callouses. The touch of it gave her a small tingle which she tried to suppress. She felt her colour rise again and let Alan's hand go almost abruptly. The release was unexpected and his arm slipped and hit off the edge of the table.

'Ow,' he said softly as the cut rasped on the wood. Instinctively Alex reached and grasped his hand again, raising and turning it as she had a moment before.

'Oh, I'm sorry. I didn't mean that,' she said. Inside her she felt a small surge of warmth looping like a wave. This time she just rolled with it.

'Well, I just hope I'm never really ill,' Alan came back, smiling to show her he was kidding. 'Then you might really bump me off.'

'I leave that to Doc Doc,' Alex said, returning his smile. She was still holding his hand and hadn't noticed yet. 'I just mop up and do the paperwork.'

'For which the whole community will be grateful,' Alan continued in the same vein. For some reason, and if he'd cared to analyse it he could have come up with several realistic and probably true conclusions, the feel of her hand on his, the gentle pressure of her fingers, was tremendously welcome. Alex was a striking girl, long-limbed and slim, with her auburn, shiny hair caught up in a chignon, showing a graceful neck. She had a wide, open smile and green eyes that gleamed with friendliness under naturally shaped eyebrows that gave her a girlish, unpretentious look. Added to that was the fact that Alan was pushed to remember the last time he'd had any contact with a woman, at least any contact that wasn't a conflict. Deep down, so deep that it was a mere whisper, there was a tickle of guilt, because he was a *married man*, but it was so small and so far off that it was easily ignored.

Beth said something that neither of them heard.

'Pardon?' Alan asked, jerked away from the moment.

'Are you planning to take the girls down on the shore?'

'Yes, we're going beachcombing,' Alan said. Neither noticed, although Beth did, that Alex was still holding his hand. She carefully didn't look.

'Well, why don't I take them on down? You two can catch up.'

Alex noticed the diplomacy of her friend, as well as the twinkle in her eyes under the wavy luxuriance of her black hair. As casually as she could manage, she gently let Alan's hand go. Fortunately it didn't drop to the table for a replay.

'Is that all right with you girls?' he asked. They nodded, sucking hard until their straws gurgled at the bottom of their small empty tumblers.

'Right, I'll catch you along at the point. Don't worry, I won't let them get wet.'

'I'm not worried about them. I'm worried about *you*,' Alan replied. 'They'll run you off your feet.'

'No chance of that,' Tom's daughter shot back from the door. The girls were each holding a hand, looking as placid and contented and happy as they always did. The door swung closed, and the little bell above it tinkled. The tall, middle-aged woman with the blue rinse and pearls who ran the shop popped her head through the serving hatch, checking for new customers. Then she quickly withdrew, leaving Alan and Alex alone in the corner of the tearoom.

'How *did* you do that?' Alex asked, indicating the scrape. 'You should have a dressing on it, you know.'

'Yeah, I suppose. Maybe later.'

'Maybe later tetanus, or septicaemia.'

'OK Doc,' Alan protested. 'I'll do it.'

'That's better. And how did it happen?'

'Honestly, I haven't a clue. I think I went sleepwalking last night.'

'That's a bad sign,' she replied quickly.

'Don't I know it. I wanted to ask you about that, and a couple of other things.'

'So this is a consultation? On a Sunday?' Alex asked, but her smile belied the serious tone.

'Hell, I don't know. I don't know what to think.'

Alex reached out her hand and clasped his again, this

344

time deliberately, almost reassuringly. Again the warm feeling rolled gently inside. It was as if their hands met and fitted. 'Have you got a problem?'

'Yes and no. I don't know exactly if the problem is with me, or with . . .' he paused, reluctant to say it, '. . . with my wife.'

'I know she had difficulties before,' Alex said. 'Postnatal depression. It's a lot more prevalent than people imagine, and that's both here and in the States. I've seen some case histories. It can be very serious.'

'I know that. I've lived with it for the past four years. I thought she was getting better, but since we moved here she's got a lot worse. But she's not like before.'

'Stress can do that, and you know that moving house is one of the biggest.'

'Yes, I *do* know that. But it's, well, *different*. Listen, can I talk confidentially with you for a minute?'

'I'm surprised you have to ask that. I thought we were,' Alex said, and for a second her eyes flashed with fast irritation.

'I'm sorry. Yes, of course you're right,' Alan said and squeezed Alex's fingers to emphasize his point. 'What I'm trying to say is that she seems to have given up on everything. All she cares about is the house. Now, it's a fine place. I fell in love with it the minute I saw it, but it's as if nothing else in the world matters. Every minute of every day, it seems, she's cleaning and polishing. I came back from up north and found there wasn't a scrap of food in the house. I just don't know what's been going on while I've been away.'

'Can you spend more time at home?'

'That's another problem. With this new job I've got twice the responsibility.'

'Maybe she should talk to someone about it.'

'Easier said than done. I did try. She point-blank refused.'

'And you, how is it affecting you?'

'Knocking the hell out of me, to tell the truth. I had

the worst nightmare of my life last night and found myself out in the road in front of the house in the pouring rain. I must have been sleepwalking and I don't want to go through that again.'

Alex turned his arm over. The weal was bright against the skin. 'It's very unusual to get an injury like that during somnambulance without waking up.'

'Spare me the big words, Doc,' Alan said in an attempt at levity. She caught it and threw it back.

'Sleepwalkers don't stay asleep when they fall and cut themselves.'

'This one must have done. For if he didn't, he wasn't dreaming, and that is something I'd rather not believe. Nightmares don't come true.'

'I'll give you a list of psychiatrists who will tell you otherwise.'

'They won't convince me. I dream weird dreams.'

'Tell me about them some time,' Alex said. She poured them each a small coffee which was cooling down in the pot. 'Speaking off the record, which of course we are, I'd try to get your wife to come down to see Dr Docherty. She's probably run down. I'm not going to advise tranquillizers, but I expect there's something that can help reduce the stress. And as for you, try not to worry. You're probably working too hard, and remember, the change of house has probably been as big a strain on you as on anybody. If you're really worried, I can arrange a health visitor to drop by. There's no problem there.'

'That might be a help. I don't know if she'd let anybody in the house though. It's becoming an obsession.'

'Hopefully it will diminish, but I can't say when. If I were you, I'd try to be at home as often as possible.'

Alan nodded. He drained his cup. The very act of telling somebody about the problem seemed to make it shrink to normal proportions in his mind.

'Want to join us down at the shore?'

'Sure I would,' she said. 'It's probably the only day in the year you can walk down there in your miserable climate.'

'Ah, we've evolved for it and we were born to it. Most of us try to get away from it, and some crazy folk actually choose to come here to live with it.'

'Some crazy folk don't go sleepwalking and cut themselves to ribbons,' she riposted as they closed the door behind them. The little bell tinkled mutedly again.

Along the shore, Beth and the girls were just wavery specks in the distance, caught in the glow of the shimmering light that struck up from the water in the glare of the morning sun in the east. Alan and Alex went down the pathway that was worn by the feet of thousands of fishermen and shorewalkers. They followed its snaking brown dirt ribbon between the trees and the bushes that had colonized the wide span between the high-tide line and the road.

The path fell away sharply after the first clump of trees and before the next thickly tangled patch of rough elm and birch. The slope was still slick from the night's rain. Alan got to the bottom first, in the little hollow that was only visible from the firth side. Alex came skittering down beside him, feet skidding on the smooth path, coming too fast. He tried to brace himself to catch her but she thudded fully into him, rocking him off balance. He teetered backwards and landed with a thump in the long grass. She heard the whoof of his breath being punched out with the impact as she landed right on top of him.

'Oh, I'm sorry, Alan,' she said, raising herself with her knees planted on either side of him. He lay with his eyes shut, face screwed up. She shook his shoulders and his breath came back in a big gasp.

She leaned forward, concern on her face, peering into his. 'Are you hurt?' she asked.

'That's some bedside manner you've got. I heard that doctors buried their mistakes,' he said with a big laugh that shook his whole body. She could feel it shake underneath hers.

'Oh, you . . . you,' she started, searching for the right word. She leaned forward and put both hands on his shoulders, about to shake them roughly when he twisted. She fell forward right on top of him, breaking her momentum with her hands just before their faces met. Both of them froze, suddenly aware.

Alan raised his head an inch and kissed her quite softly, quite chastely, on the lips. He let his head fall back to the ground again. Her clasp had fallen out, and her hair spilled down far enough on one side to brush against his cheek. He could smell its clean fragrance. He could feel her body against his, and for an instant he could feel nothing else. He raised himself up again and kissed her. She gave a small shiver and responded tentatively. He could taste her through his skin.

Alan brought a hand up slowly from the grass and held her head, feeling his fingers dig themselves into the thick dark waves. Gently he clutched her forward. Her lips opened, his opened and they kissed. Their tongues met tip for soft tip. He could feel the heat of her body, she the hardness of his chest. Without a thought they seemed to melt into each other.

It was Alex who broke it off with a little low moan that conveyed many things, including frustration, guilt and desire. She raised herself up, shaking her head, turning her face away.

'This is . . .' she started, faltered. 'We can't do this. It's wrong.' Her body was sending her a completely unfair and contradictory set of messages. They had fit like two halves. 'Oh *damn*,' she said softly. She turned to Alan, snaking a look with those dark-green, flashing eyes. 'We can't,' she said softly, simply.

'I'm sorry. It was my fault,' Alan began. His face showed everything she had felt.

'No. Don't say that. It wasn't anybody's fault. But we just can't. It's not right.'

348

'I know. I shouldn't have.'

'Neither should I.'

'It didn't happen. Nothing happened.'

'Right.' She nodded and looked away. Alan could see her trembling under the shirt. 'I'm sorry.'

'Come on. Let's get Beth and the girls,' Alan said and she nodded again, looking at the ground. He led the way, his mind a jumble of thoughts. Behind she raised her eyes and watched his back.

'Damn him for being married,' she said to herself. But she couldn't take her eyes off the way his shoulders moved as he negotiated the narrow, rutted track.

And on the way back with the girls' haul of shiny beach pebbles, she couldn't stop thinking about what had happened. When they came to the pit where the track was nipped in between the clumps of gorse that were powdered yellow with blossoms gleaming in the sun, their hands accidentally touched as they brushed close to each other. Both of them jumped at the contact. It was as if an electrical spark had leapt between them and drilled through them.

What was more, each knew what the other had felt, and it rocked them both. That night neither slept, but for different reasons.

There was only one car on the Creggan road when Tommy got up to the turn. Hector Lawrie whizzed round the corner in the red post van that he used every day whether there was a delivery or not. He tooted his horn, high and cheerfully toneless, and gave Tommy a big wave as he trundled past. Tommy smiled and waved back energetically. This was a nice place. Already he was getting to know folk and it gave him a great thrill for an adult to have recognized him enough to wave.

A hundred yards or so along the road he came to the cottage that was set back behind an old moss-covered dike. Seumas's old battered Morris Traveller was sitting

349

at the side of the house, like a trusty dog on its haunches, half out of the ramshackle lean-to garage. Docks and foxglove merged with lupins that had gone wild, great purple steeples that were stirred gently by a zephyr of wind. He got to the front door which was lying open, and knocked gently.

There was no reply, but through the house, from out at the back came the sound of an axe against wood, dull thuds muted by their passage through the rooms.

Instead of calling out, Tommy just walked into the dark little narrow hallway, following the steady beat of the axe. It was dark in there away from the sunlight. His eyes widened to compensate. There was a passage that went left or right, and Tommy took the former, where the sound was louder. Here at the back of the house was a living-room with a big black range set in a neuk on the far wall. The room was crowded with furniture, old and dark. The table was littered with pieces of machinery that were spread on sheets of old newspaper. There were a couple of fishing reels and an old penknife with a big blade stuck into a block of white driftwood.

Tommy's eyes swept across the clutter as his feet carried him towards the back door which obviously led out to the garden beyond.

Suddenly there was a sound in the stillness of the room and a shadow which blotted out the meagre light that came in through the small window on the shadowed side of the house. Something touched him scrabblingly, groping on his shoulder, and he jerked around with fright.

A face loomed up close to his. It was a grotesque wrinkled thing, the shrivelled face of a witch looming right into his from the shadow in the corner of the room.

Tommy gasped in terror as a hooked and horny hand that matched the one that gripped his shoulder came up and clamped on to his face.

He tried to scream. He could feel one, a great big one, start to lurch right up inside him. His ribs heaved and his lungs got ready, and nothing came out. A sudden feeling of faintness came over him, and the shadows seemed to spin.

I'm going to faint! The thought pelted right across the front of his mind, with a shocking impact. He was going to faint, in here with the witch. And that thought brought another surge of fright. If he fainted, there would be *no* escape from the thing.

The calloused hand scrabbled across his face, fingers like scuttling spider's legs, hard and horny, probing and scraping over his smooth skin. Inside him, Tommy's scudding heart was beating so hard he felt it would suddenly burst in a great big splash of blood. He tried to get a breath and failed. His whole body was rigid with the high power of pure fear that sang right through his every nerve. He was paralysed with binding dread.

The scuttling hand moved back from his face and suddenly his wide open eyes were faced with the thing that had grabbed him in the dark. From outside came a thump of the axe. Somewhere a wren burbled liquid song. They were miles away. He stared in shock, and his lungs seemed to swell up until they were ready to burst.

No eyes. It's got no eyes! his mind screeched at him, and instantly, in a supercharged, frightful rerun, he saw the face of the huge bird on the moor, the one that was the size of a big dog and had a huge black sword of a beak, and vast wasted craters where its eyes should have been.

The grotesque, raddled and wrinkled face that swam right into his vision had no eyes. He could see the puckered eyelids, hollow and sunken, dark pits that seemed to stare right through him. The mouth opened, another dark pit. A tongue poked out between sunken gums, and the thing laughed in a high-pitched chuckle. Tommy gasped in a hiccup. Inside him something

351

seemed to give. He let out a little fart that was awesome in its normality.

'Oh, Mother, put the wee fellow down before you scare the living daylights out of him,' said a voice on the far side of the room, a million miles away.

'Och, I'm just taking a look, where's the harm,' the thing with the dreadful witch face said in a high, cracking, old voice. 'It's the first visitor I've had in a wheen of earth days.'

Tommy's breath came back in a rush of air that bellowed into his heaving lungs. His chest seemed to be clutching air in huge waves. He felt both knees trembling, threatening to spill him to the floor.

'And put the light on, so the rest of us can see,' Seumas said, stepping into the room from the open door. He had a big axe in his hand. It looked too big for the small man's wiry frame.

Tommy was never so glad to see anybody in his life. Seumas switched on the light and the room jumped into sharp focus as the shadows scattered. Tommy jerked around when he felt the touch on his shoulder. His eyes widened. It wasn't a witch. It was just an old, tiny woman who wasn't much taller than himself. She looked incredibly ancient, and she was blind. Her eyes were just sunken pits in a wrinkled face. But the expression on that face was not that of a witch. What had seemed grotesque and terrifying in the sudden darkness of the room was now just old and curious, and strangely warm.

Instantly Tommy felt normality sweep back into the room.

'You'll not have met my mother, young Tommy.'

The boy shook his head, not yet trusting his voice to speak.

'I can see she gave you a right scare.' Tommy shook his head again, all the time knowing he wasn't fooling anyone. 'You'll be after having had a good look at him then, Mother?'

'Nothing any more than a wee glance, Seumas Rhu,' the wizened woman said almost crossly. 'We were only getting introduced when you came by.' The ancient woman's voice had that singsong quality of the Gaelic in it.

'Well, let me do the honours. Mother, this is a friend of mine. Young Tommy Crombie, who lives down at the big house. Tommy, this is my mother, who is the only person you're ever likely to see who's older than myself, and sometimes I can't believe it neither.'

The old woman let out a cackle that in the dark shadows would have sounded terrifying, but in the warm light of the room was just girlish laughter with a few decades added on.

'There's no need to be a-scared, Tommy boy. As you can see, my mother's only the height of a wee Scots terrier, though she's got a temper to match. She can walk under a bed with a lum hat on, if you catch my drift.'

'You're not that big yourself that I can't reach up and clatter you a dunt on the ear, Seumas Rhu,' the old woman said lisping toothlessly. Tommy smirked, feeling the fear fly off on wings of relief.

'See,' Seumas said with the air of someone who's been proved right. 'I told you she had the temper. Old *Sheela-na-brathadair*, all fire and fight.' He chuckled, throwing Tommy a sly wink. The boy smiled back tentatively.

'Come on away in,' the small man said, reaching a hand out. He pulled a chair and cleared off a pair of pliers and a hacksaw, dumping them on the table among the rest of the clutter. Tommy sat himself down.

'Mother can't see now,' he said. 'That's why the dark doesn't bother her. She takes a look with her hands to make up for it.'

'Thought we might have a burglar when I heard him tippy-toeing in, so I did,' the old woman said.

'Not Tommy,' Seumas said supportively. 'He's the fine straight fellow. But now take a proper look at him so you'll know him next time.'

The old woman raised herself up from the chair in the corner and crossed the room with the surety of the sighted and came right up to where the boy sat. She raised her hands and Tommy flinched back, but Seumas flashed him such a big, encouraging smile that he held still. She reached forward and cupped his face with both her hands. A little thrill of surprise ran through him. The hands weren't hard. They were soft and dry and warm. They didn't scuttle and scrabble. They slowly stroked his skin, gently feeling in at the sides of his button nose. Her thumbs came up and slid across the skin of his eyelids, the hands smoothed round his cheeks, softly probed each ear and then met each other in his thatch of tousled hair on the top of his head. There they stopped and the old woman took a deep breath. The wrinkles on her face seemed to shift into a different pattern, exactly as if she were closing her eyes to concentrate. Except for the fact that she didn't seem to have eyes, that was how it looked to Tommy who peered up between her outstretched hands. Beside him, Seumas Rhu watched quietly.

'Ah, you have a fine man here, Seumas, and with a touch of the old people in him too, for I can feel it. This is one of the real people, not an incomer. This is *Tomhais*, the riddle's key in the old tongue.'

Tommy could feel the warmth of the old woman's hands through his hair, it was making him feel drowsy. He didn't know what she was talking about, but now all threat had gone, all fear. He felt a slow wave of peace steal through him.

'And he's not the only one neither, is he, Seumas? You've got others, haven't you?'

Tommy swivelled his eyes to Seumas, who nodded. 'That's right, two wee sisters.'

'I know that, boy,' she said, and Tommy thought

she was talking to him until he realized she was address-
ing her remark to the old man. He felt a giggle begin
to bubble up at the thought of him being called *boy*.
'Two in one, they are, and faerie-kissed. They've no
need to speak, for they've got other gifts that tie their
tongues. Babes from Tir-nan-Og.'

She raised her hands from Tommy's head. A strange
expression flitted across her face as if she'd thought of
something else to say, then the wrinkles rearranged
themselves. Tommy felt the sudden warmth drain away
as the hands were removed.

'Well, I've got the measure of this one,' the old
woman said, and she laughed. 'But he hasn't got his
own measure yet, has he? So long as he has the faerie-
kissed to watch his sleep, he'll come to no harm.'

Tommy looked from the woman to Seumas. The
small man shot him another wink.

'Right, then, Mother, we can't be standing here
blethering all the day. I'll bet there's something your
dad wants me to do, eh?'

Tommy agreed, and the old man led him through
the house to the front door. The boy passed on the
message and Seumas told him he'd come down in the
afternoon. He patted the boy on the back and watched
as he went out through the old rickety gate and along
the verge at the side of the road, his fair hair gleaming
in the sunlight.

Seumas sighed and stood there at the door, thinking.

The last time he had been up on that roof, it had
been bad. He didn't want to go up there again, not on
the roof of Cromwath. There was enough of his mother
in him to feel the strange, alien foreboding when he
thought of it. He knew some of the history. But that
was then, and this was now.

And maybe what he'd been sent before was just an
echo from far back.

THIRTY-FOUR

It was after ten that Sunday night when John Lindsay came knocking on the front door of the Crombies' house. Seumas had located the burst in the pipe out beside the garage. He'd had to go down to the cellar to turn the cock back on again and he didn't spend too much time about it. Alan hadn't noticed that the old man seemed very uncomfortable and less chatty than he'd been before. Seumas had promised to come back during the week to replace the slack tiles.

Alan had let Tommy and the girls stay up a bit later than usual to watch Michael Douglas and Kathleen Turner romance their way through the South American jungle. As he said goodnight to Tommy, he paused. 'So you're quite enjoying it here?'

Tommy nodded. In the dim light Alan saw something quickly flicker on his son's face (*uncertainty? anxiety?*); then it was gone.

'Got some good friends, I see.'

'Yes, they're OK,' Tommy said fairly nonchalantly. Alan was not too far removed from the memories of his own childhood to be able to translate that into the values boys put on their friends when they tell their parents that they're OK.

'And how about this place, much better than down south?'

'I like the place. I mean the hills and the trees. You can go anywhere and play. We were catching crabs and Seumas is going to show me how to catch fish in the burn. That's a stream, you know.'

Alan laughed at Tommy's explanation. For most of

356

his own childhood, he'd only heard the word *stream* in books and poems. They were always burns to him.

'Me and Bobby and Jim are going to build a gang hut up in the trees. And maybe we can camp out during the holidays.'

'Sounds pretty good to me,' Alan said. 'And how about the house? Do you like living here?'

Tommy shrugged. Again Alan saw the shadow pass across his small clear face.

'It's all right, I suppose.'

'Just all right?' Alan probed.

'Well, sometimes it's kinda creepy. You know, like it's big and dark when you're on your own.'

'But you're never on your own,' Alan said.

'Except for the girls,' Tommy came back quickly. 'Mum's always doing something else. She's never there any more.'

'I think she's just busy,' Alan said quietly.

'Is she going to get better?' Tommy asked.

'Better than what?'

'I don't know,' the boy said with a hopeless little shrug. 'It's like she was before. It's scary.'

'She hasn't . . .' Alan cast around for the right phrase, the right question. 'She hasn't done anything to you, has she? I mean, if she gets angry?'

'Oh no, she hasn't spanked me since I was little. It's just that she never talks any more. She doesn't even seem to notice me and Laney and Katie. That's the scary bit. It's like we weren't even *there* some of the time.'

Alan didn't know what to say to that at all. Helen was different from how she'd been before. That had been straightforward, devastating but explicable. She'd had a complete nervous breakdown as a result of severe post-natal depression which all the experts told him was due to hormone changes, stress and exhaustion. This was different. She now seemed to be a different person. She was withdrawn all right, but not in the way she

357

had been. This time it looked deliberate, as if she didn't *want* to know.

Maybe Alex Graham was right, Alan thought; and as he did so, he felt a small thrill of guilt and a stronger thrill of desire well up inside him.

'I think she'll be all right.' He heard himself offer Tommy a platitude. Inside, he could offer himself none. 'She's had a lot of stress recently. I wouldn't worry about it.'

Tommy said he wouldn't, and it sounded unconvincing. Alan ruffled his hair again and told him he was a good boy and then he tucked him in again. He bent over his son's tousled head and kissed him on the brow.

Downstairs, he thought about what Tommy had said and again he felt the rancour rise up in him at how Helen's behaviour was affecting them all. He pottered about in his room which he'd finally got looking the way he wanted it, the books lined up on their shelves and the knick-knacks and pictures from his contracts all over the world planted on every horizontal surface. There were one or two pieces of paperwork he'd planned to have a look at, but he decided against it. Instead, he picked up Andrew Dalmuir's account of the building of Cromwath House and took it downstairs.

He'd stuck a till receipt in at the page where he'd left off. Dalmuir had started building his house and it was clear from what he said that there were problems right from the start. Latta hadn't been happy about moving the location further west to build the house over the depression between the five centre stones, especially since the land had dropped during the storm. He suggested that there was probably an underground stream or an old mine working there, but Dalmuir had been adamant and ordered bores drilled into the ground. The rock seemed solid.

There would be no standing stones there to tempt the tinkers or the folk of the four villages to hold their heathen ceremonies. He would be living right over the megaliths. For the first week, work went smoothly as the foundation lines were dug and the mortar rubble was compacted in hard wide strips to take the weight of the walls. Horse-drawn carts hauled the fine-grained red sandstone down from Callander's quarry to the site where the masons sawed and chipped it into shape. Barges floated the square blocks of a thousand bricks down to the pier where they were unloaded and hauled on steel-wheeled trolleys by the sweating labourers up the hill towards where Cromwath was taking shape.

It was on 10 January that the first man went missing. He was Sean Boyle, the joiner's mate. He and Patrick Byrne and Kevin Meagher had been sitting round their brazier sipping from their smoke-blackened tins of tea and shooting the gab in their thick Mayo accents. So far the weather had held out, still sharp and cold, and while few builders would start on a house in the depth of winter, the Irish crews were desperately glad of the work, even though they spent the chill nights in their smelly canvas tents and a sizable portion of their wages down at the Murrin Inn which was almost a hundred years later to be known as the Creel.

Sean Boyle was a big, weatherbeaten, grizzled fellow with the jug ears and long-faced look of many of the men who had been brought across from the wastelands of the west coast, most of them wrapped in their emaciated mothers' shawls, at the height of the famine in the forties.

Stuck in the ghettos of Glasgow and the Clydeside conurbation by a Presbyterian people suspicious of their Romish ways and fearful of the threat of masses of starving strangers, the immigrants huddled together in common poverty, picking up what labouring jobs there were in road, rail and house building which needed cheap muscle for the back-breaking donkey work.

It would be another generation before their accents smoothed out to the glottal abruptness of the lowland

Scots, and a century on they would still be separated by religion from their neighbours in their new homeland.

Sean Boyle thought little about this, and cared less as he rose from the warm circle of heat that expanded from the brazier where the branches from the trees that had been felled on the south side of the clearing crackled among the pine and oak chips from the woodwork. Kevin Meagher had taken his clay pipe out of the band of his crumpled felt hat and had begun filling it with the black plug tobacco that he cut and rasped with a small knife in the calloused palm of a huge, horny hand.

'Gi'e us a fill till the morrow,' Sean had asked, and Dalmuir had recorded the words in his bold script after hearing the verbatim report from James Latta. Meagher had demurred, claiming that Boyle had had two fills since the day before. Sean told him he'd left his pouch up on the joists that they had been laying over where the living-room was being built, and promised him a repayment when they got back to work. Kevin said he'd made the same promise yesterday, and huffily Sean stalked off to get his own makings. Paddy Byrne went with him to fetch something from his own box and was maybe twenty yards behind Boyle as the big chippy's mate climbed the ladder.

'He just went up and on to the wall,' he told Latta and the constable who was eventually summoned. 'Two o' the mortarmen were still laying stone on the far side, near up as high as the first window key. I got to the top o' the ladder and there was Sean walking on the joists. He was only half-way across when he took a tumble. I don't know how it happened, but he lets out a yell to wake the dead and goes down between the straights. I thought, Holy Mary, he's broken his neck for sure, and I slides meself back down the ladder and in through the doorspace, expecting to find him lying there on the rubble, or even across the floor joists down below. But sure, when I got there, he was nowhere to be seen.

'I called out to him, thinkin' maybe he'd been at the kiddin', you know, makin' play of me for a joke. The two mortarers, Paulie Ennis and Mick Cuddihy, they're up top and lookin' down. They heard Sean call out, though only Mick saw anything, and that just out the corner of his eye.

'I remember Sean callin' out too. It was like as if he was falling down a long way, much more than the fifteen feet it is from roof to floor in the place. But there was no sign of him there.

'I shouted over to Kevin and Paddy who were out by the fire havin' their dinner and they came for a look. But Sean wasn't there. I don't know where he was, but his tools were still there in their bale up on the boards, and his tobacco pouch an' all. It was like he just fell down there between the joists and disappeared, for I've no idea where he could have gone.'

Latta had had the site searched and on the next day when Sean Boyle still failed to report for work or to collect his belongings, including the jacket that he'd hung on a nail over the joists, they called the constable. He made a perfunctory search of the area with a certain reluctance, for after the work had been started in the centre of the Cromuath clearing the villagers had stayed away from the site, and the squad of Irishmen were treated with a mixture of wariness and disdain. There was no sign of Sean Boyle. Not then.

Seven days later, and still the weather holding out, the weak wintry sun burning off the early morning sea mist, Latta had a crisis on his hands when the Irish squad walked off the job. Dalmuir was called to the site, striding angrily down from the cottage that he had occupied alone since he'd sent his wife and sons back up to their townhouse in Glasgow.

He found the men huddled together round an open fire at the far end of the clearing where the big piles of stones were waiting to be cut. Latta explained they were refusing to work in the house and Dalmuir finally got it from him that one of the men had seen an apparition.

'It was Sean Boyle, the joiner's mate that ran off,' the builder explained.

It was Paddy Byrne who had sparked off the impromptu strike. 'I was layin' boards down this mornin',' he told Latta and Dalmuir, who had produced a hip flask from his long coat and allowed the distressed Irishman a large swallow, though he carefully wiped the neck of the silver bottle before recapping it. 'I hears this almighty cry from behind me, and there's somebody fallin' from the joists above. I look round, and there's Sean coming right down from up there. His hands are out to catch the spar but they miss and down he comes.'

Byrne's voice was as shaky as his hands when he recounted the tale to his boss and the owner at the corner of the site on the wintry morning.

'He was bound to come down and clatter off the floor-spars where I was laying boards, but that's not what happened. Holy Mother, he went right *through*. Not in between, but right through the joist, and that was solid oak an' all. He just slipped on down and I could hear him yelling like he'd taken a tumble down a well. But there was no stop, y'see. It went on goin'. I scrambled across the planks away from the boards I was nailin' down, expectin' to see him lyin' there in a heap. But, oh dear Mother, he was *still* fallin'. There was no floor where we laid the slabs down last week. It was like a black hole, and there was Sean fallin' arse over head, tumblin' this way and that, and the bawlin' came right up from that pot-hole until my ears was fit to burst.'

'You've been at the beer again, Byrne, haven't you,' Latta accused, but Paddy shook his head in vehement denial.

'No, sir. Not a drop. Sure after what you send to the missus there's hardly a ha'penny left beyond the

Monday. I swear I saw it, and I'm feared to go back in there again,' he said, jerking his head in the direction of where the walls of the house were taking rough shape, surrounded by wooden scaffolding.

'That's what the rest of the men are saying,' the builder told Dalmuir after he'd dismissed the labourer. 'They claim it was wrong to disturb these stones. They think there's some sort of magic or whatnot. I don't doubt they've been listening to too many tales down in the inn.'

'Well, that's on your own head, Latta. If a bunch of ignorant Irishmen are going to put a halt to this work, then I'll get rid of the lot of them, and you forbye if there's any more delays.' Dalmuir looked at the assembled squad who were sitting in a group on the pile of stones. 'You'd better get them back to work and I want no more of this nonsense. There's been enough blasphemy already and I want an end to it.'

It was a fortnight later that Dalmuir was summoned down to the site again. Somehow Latta had got the men back on the job, although Paddy Byrne was adamant that he wouldn't go within the house boundary and had spent a fortnight working on the outside cutting beams and planks to size.

'What is it this time?' Dalmuir demanded. Latta was in the little wooden hut that he used as a site office.

'I'm not rightly sure, but I think somebody's been up to some mischief. There's a whole wall's worth of stone gone a-missing, and nobody can account for it. I've been around the whole place, once I came back from Glasgow yesterday morning, and MacGregor who's the ganger on the masonry crew tells me they put up two of the inside walls on either side of the staircase over the weekend.' Latta paused, pondering what to say next.

'Go on, man, out with it.'

'Well, sir. I don't know whether there's been some mischief-making by the local folk or what. Either that or my foreman's been lying to me. You see, those walls aren't there no more, and nobody here can say why. Some of the Paddies say there's been people sneaking about at night, though none of them can swear as to who. But I can't see how ten tons of cut stone can disappear overnight, even if somebody made a mistake and just *imagined* they put up two walls.'

'I think your men have been on the drink again,' Dalmuir told him.

'I think maybe the villagers don't want this house built here.'

'If I waited for permission from a crowd of rustics any time I wanted to do something, I'd be a beggar today,' Dalmuir said. 'I'll tell you what. I've been thinking about it anyway. If you say ten tons of good stone have gone astray, I'm not going to pay a penny more for another cutting. There's some good stone there.'

Latta followed his indication towards the boundary of the site. Four of the standing stones were visible between the hut and the scaffolding of the house.

'That'll put an end to any nonsense. Once they're gone, then nobody will have any complaints. You'll see.'

Latta looked at his employer, then at the stones. The solid blue-black basalt pillars stood in a silent ring around them.

'Get your cutters on them. They'll do for the keys and borders, sills and lintels, plus the steps at the front. They'll last a million years.'

After he'd gone, Latta blew his whistle and summoned the mason with his gang and told him what was wanted. The masons were good, solid Scots stock, not superstitious Irishmen. That day they pulled the first megalith, like a great dark tooth, from the earth.

Nobody discovered what had happened to the two walls that were supposed to have been built.

Alan's reading was interrupted by the ringing of the

364

front doorbell. He waited a moment, as he normally would, to see if Helen would go to the door; then he realized she wouldn't and hauled himself out of the seat.

John Lindsay stood in the dimming evening light, a tall, thin silhouette. 'Mr Crombie?'

'That's me. And you'll be Mr Lindsay?'

The policeman nodded. 'My son's told me about you.' John Lindsay smiled. 'I thought you were English, the way your boy talks.'

'Oh, he'll get over it. I'm local, from Levenford. I never lost the accent.'

Alan stood by the door and invited the policeman into the house. John Lindsay took off his flat cap and twirled it in his hands as he stepped across the threshold. In the lounge, Alan pointed to a chair and watched as the lanky officer sat down and stretched out long legs.

'A drink?' Alan offered.

'Not supposed to on duty, but twist my arm.'

'I've got a good malt if that'll suit.'

'Ah, you're obviously a Scotsman, Mr Crombie.'

They raised their glasses and Alan sipped his drink. John Lindsay took a fair mouthful, held it, then let it go down. His face registered his appreciation.

Alan watched him quizzically. John caught the look and said, 'Not so much a social call, I'm afraid, though I should have been round a bit sooner after you moved in to say hello.' He paused and took another large drink of the golden whisky and set his glass down on the table. 'I was hoping I could speak to the lad. I know it's late, but it might be important.'

Alan felt himself stiffen, expecting a complaint. 'Is there any trouble? Has he been up to anything?'

'Och no, no trouble at all, and if they've been up to anything, it'll just be what boys do anyway. No. It's just that we seem to have lost one of the lads, and I'm hoping the wee fellow can maybe help me.'

'What's happened?'

'I'm not rightly sure. But one of my Bobby's pals,

Jimmy Rodger, hasn't been seen since before teatime tonight. He was out playing with your boy and mine this afternoon and he hasn't gone home. I'm trying to find out where he might be, hopefully before his mother starts to panic.'

'Well, the best thing is to get Tommy down. He might not even be asleep.'

'I'd appreciate that.'

Helen was in bed when Alan went upstairs to explain what was happening. At first she didn't seem to register his presence, then she opened her eyes and looked at him.

'Do you want me to come down?'

'No, it's all right. I'll get Tommy.'

She nodded, then closed her eyes again. Alan went into his son's room and stood silently in the dimness. The window was a lighter square against the larger dark. He could hear Tommy's muffled breathing and walked towards the bed.

'Huh, Dad?' Tommy said sleepily from his bed. He sat up, rubbing his eyes. 'I wasn't sleeping yet.'

'Good, because I want you to get up and come downstairs. I'll get your dressing gown.' Alan crossed to the closet and unhooked the little checked coat from the back of the door. 'Come on. Mr Lindsay wants a chat with the both of us. He thinks you can maybe help.'

Down in the lounge Tommy sat beside his dad, drinking a cup of hot chocolate that Alan had quickly warmed in the micro. Alan had poured John Lindsay another whisky but had made a coffee for himself.

'And what happened then?' the policeman asked encouragingly.

'It was the same man. The one who chased us down the valley. He was big and shouting at us. Jimmy let the rabbit out of the trap and it ran away and the man was angry. We ran away too.'

'And today, the same thing?'

'Yes, but we didn't *do* anything. We were playing up

in the trees and Jim came running out shouting about the man. He ran right past Bobby and me and then we saw the man coming along, waving his stick, just like before.'

'And what did you do?'

'We ran too. I was scared.'

'Where did you go?'

'We came along the edge of the trees. You know where the hedge goes along beside the wall?' The policeman nodded. 'Jim got through first and he went right across the road. I was next and Bobby came after me.' Tommy could remember the thrill of panic when he'd got caught in the hawthorn of the hedge as he scuttled through the narrow gap. Behind him he could hear Bobby's ragged breathing and could feel his pal's hands shoving at him, helping him through the space.

'We got on to the road and ran along. We could hear the man behind us. He wasn't shouting or anything, but we could hear him coming through the hedge. Jim went over the wall when we got along the road, up at the trees there.' He pointed out of the window at the coppice at the north end of the garden. 'We followed after him and came right down by the orchard. He wasn't there and we thought he'd kept on going right past the house. Bobby and I came in for a drink of milk and then Bobby went home. That's what happened.'

'And you think Jim went straight home?'

'It was getting to teatime anyway, and he was much faster than us.'

'But he didn't get home,' the policeman said softly. 'Would there be any other place he would go?'

'I don't know,' Tommy said. 'I don't think so.'

'And Jimmy was right in front of you? There was no way the man could catch up?'

'Oh no. He left him *miles* behind.'

John Lindsay looked over to Alan Crombie and shrugged his shoulders. 'Well, I expect he'll turn up,' he said. 'There's always a couple that don't find their way home at this time of the year. I expect they just want to start their summer holidays early.'

He thanked Alan for the drinks and the two men walked to the front door, leaving Tommy to finish his hot chocolate.

'He's told me the same thing as our Bobby. Now, if there's somebody chasing kids up in those glens, I'll have to take a look at it.'

'Do you think there's a nutcase about?'

'I surely hope to God there isn't. Probably just one of the tinkers getting all het up about the wee ones interfering with their snares. Maybe the boy just got a fright and he's scared to go home.'

'I hope so.'

'But I'd keep the lad out of the trees if I were you. For the time being anyway. I already told my boy that, and he was daft enough to forget it. He'll remember next time.'

'Well, if there are strange folk wandering about, that's a good idea.'

'Oh, it's not so much them as . . .' Lindsay paused, as if he'd started to say something and then changed his mind. 'There's been one or two odd things happening up at the farms. There's been some chickens killed, and some sheep have been worried. I don't know what's at the back of it. Probably a pack of dogs or some such, though a few people have got some funny notions. But if there's something that can kill farm animals, it could do a bit of damage to wee boys like yours and mine. I think for the next week or so it's a good idea to keep them close to the houses.'

'I will, Sergeant.'

'Och, I'm only sergeant when I'm arresting you,' the big man said with a grin.

'I'll try to avoid that.'

'Aye, and remember what I said about the trees and those glens. At least until I've got it sorted out.'

THIRTY-FIVE

They found Jim Rodger two days later.

John Lindsay had telephoned the police headquarters at Levenford. He spoke to a chief superintendent who asked if the local policeman wanted him to send a team up to help. Lindsay read between the lines. He could have a squad if he really wanted one, but the boy had only been missing for a few hours so far, and if he turned out to have been staying in a friend's house or fast asleep in a haystack on a summer night, then it might just be a waste of valuable man and dog power. Lindsay was a good, solid, country policeman who had a whole area to patrol, administering the law as he saw it. Levenford might be only fifteen miles away as the crow flies, but in the big diesel Land Rover, its white panels now spattered with mud from farm tracks, it would take a good hour and a half clocking up sixty-five miles to get from Creggan up the peninsula and down the winding road at the far side of the loch to near what anybody might consider civilization. He told the chief he'd muster some local men first before he called for any extra help.

Jim Rodger had last been seen running through the trees up at the north of the Dalmuir place. Little Jimmy had run through the trees and disappeared. Vanished.

There were a number of thoughts that followed on that. There was the possibility that he'd been so scared he'd kept on running and was now afraid to come home and face the leathering he'd no doubt get from Frank Rodger who ran the family joiner's business that fitted up most of the kitchen units in all of the four villages.

There was the possibility that he hadn't run through

the trees, but had somehow doubled back, and that was a worry, because somebody had chased the boys. Some stranger had come after them. And if there was some nutter about, then it kind of cut the realistic chances for wee Jimmy Rodger. The dark feeling that followed on the heels of that one was that his own boy had been one of the three that had been chased, breathless and panicking, down through the trees and across the road and into the coppice. John Lindsay had to fight down the red boil of anger that welled in the pit of his stomach. He was a policeman and had to carry out his job as calmly as possible.

But if they found the Rodger boy alive and well, he'd have time to go looking for the man who'd been after them. And then, John promised himself, he'd take off his blue serge tunic and he'd kick the living *shit* out of the man who'd scared the daylights out of his boy.

When there was no sign of Jimmy by noon the next day, John Lindsay called a meeting in the old village hall that now served as the meeting-place for the community council. He'd made a few calls to the farmers further up the peninsula, getting towards Mambeg where Tom Callander's quarry bit into the hill, and asked them for some help. They sent their lads down the winding roads in tractors and old battered vans and by two in the afternoon there were nearly a hundred men and older youths who'd downed tools and put off jobs to help in the search. The fact that it was a good, high summer's day helped, of course, but that was by the way. Most of them would have turned out in a snowstorm. There had always been a good tight community on the peninsula. Even some incomers like Alan Crombie had given up their time. Crombie had an interest, of course. John Lindsay knew that in the pit of *his* stomach bubbled the fear and anger over the *what-might-have-happened*.

The policeman organized them into teams to search the gardens along the seafront and the foreshore itself.

The rest of them he led up to the top of Creggan where the road separates into the front and back roads, and they hit out from there, beating their way through every stand, searching under deadfalls and in bramble thickets. Up in the Corrie Glen there were two old shepherds' crofts that were crumbling ruins, sway-backed where time had pressed on the rotted timbers and sagged the slates. Both were empty, though one had the mouldering carcass of a dog that had crawled in the space between the door frame and the sheet of corrugated iron and had died giving birth to its litter. Two of the small squashed and greasy bundles next to the maggotty remains testified to that. Further up there was a series of pot holes where the burn disappeared into old sumps in the sandstone. Two of the Reid boys from Scapesland Farm whose land was bounded by the fast-flowing stream lowered themselves down into the hole which every kid in the area knew as the Witch's Pot. They found nothing. Donny twisted his ankle and Hector, his younger brother, clipped his elbow a good one on a sharp outcrop of rock. Their language sur-prised everybody except their father, old Dixon Reid, who bellowed at them to shut the fuck up and get their arses out of there.

Twenty-four hours after Frank Rodger had reported his son missing, they had found nothing. Not a trace. No article of clothing, not a scrap.

John Lindsay did something he knew he should have done first thing in the morning. He went along to the tinkers' camp just outside Murrin. It was as well he did so, or he could have had a murder on his hands.

As it was, he drove past the first couple of shabby caravans into the clear space just as a range war was about to break out. There was a line of men standing way to the left of the big fire in the middle. Facing them and towering over most by a good head was Jake MacFie, a big dark shadow, limned with the flickering red of the flames.

It was like a scene from a western movie. The men from the town had come up to the travelling men's camp to do battle for whichever honour, practical or abstract, they'd been robbed of. There was a lot of muttering and a few shouts that could be heard from where John Lindsay had parked the jeep. Even at that distance, the policeman could hear the drink talking. All it needed was a Henry Fonda or a Burt Lancaster to step out into the light, although the accents were all wrong for that.

Pete Rodger, who was little Jimmy's uncle and the black sheep of the family – he collected rubbish on the peninsula while his two brothers ran their own businesses – was the main protagonist. He'd been down at the Creel with his drinking cronies and he'd let slip what John Lindsay had asked his brother not to talk about: the fact that the boys had been chased by a stranger.

Now, as everybody knew, the only strangers on the peninsula were the tinkers, Pete had declared, fired up on beer and whisky. And they had always been trouble, hadn't they? That got a general assent from the rest of the regulars, some of them men who'd been out beating the bushes and felt they deserved a quench. When the Creel closed its doors at half past eleven Pete Rodger had convinced himself and maybe a dozen others that wee Jimmy had been snatched by the tinkers for God knew what ends and they'd probably murdered him most foully, and *by Christ* they'd get what was coming to them.

John Lindsay arrived before they got what was coming to them. There were women standing at the doors of the caravans, silhouetted in the light, surrounded by the faces of small children who peered from behind their skirts. Behind Jake MacFie there was a bunch of hard-looking men, mostly fair-haired, broad-faced descendants of the highlanders who'd been displaced in the clearances. From the looks on their faces they were not going to take any lynch mob lying down.

'Good of you to think of it, Peter. I was coming myself to recruit more help for another search in the morn,' Lindsay called in a loud voice from the far side of the fire.

'I'm not here to get any fuckin' help,' Jim's uncle shouted back. 'This is between me and him.'

John strolled round the side of the fire, on the tinkers' side, and stood with his hands on his belt. 'And what would that be, now?'

'It's these tinks. They were after our Jimmy. We've been looking all over those fuckin' hills, and we should have been down here taking this place apart.'

Behind him somebody shouted that this was the very action they should have taken. Somebody else shouted, 'Aye.'

'And what good would that have done, now?'

'Get lost, Lindsay,' Pete came back, his voice rasping, only slightly slurred. 'They've been all over the hills. They took Jack Coggan's chickens and they killed Harry MacLeish's sheep. And now they've got Jimmy.'

'Is that right, Mr MacFie?' John asked the big man who stood solidly facing the crowd, his feet wide apart in big scuffed boots.

'No it's not. But don't worry about us. We don't need any help with this.'

'Oh, I'm not here to give any help. Just to keep the peace.'

'Are you going to arrest them?' Pete Rodger shouted. 'Or are you going to let them get away with murder?'

'Well, until anybody tells me that there's been a murder committed, I'm not letting anybody away with anything,' Lindsay replied softly, but there was an edge in his voice. 'Now why don't you all go back down the lane and home to your beds. It's getting late, and I'll be needing some help in the morning.'

'Fuck that,' Pete Rodger spat. Before anyone could

stop him he had walked the three yards right up to Jake MacFie and swung a roundhouse right at the big man's head. It was a mistake if ever there was one. MacFie outweighed Rodger by about six stone, and if he'd been drinking he didn't show it. A big hard hand came up and clamped on the smaller man's wrist. When the other hand came up, it was balled into a craggy fist. The air seemed to whistle as it came swinging round and there was a noise like an axe hitting a tree as it connected with Pete's face. The smaller man's head rocked back and his body followed suit. But Jake still had his right arm gripped tight, and while Pete let out a muffled yelp he had nowhere to go. One of the big scuffed boots came up in what seemed like a slow, lazy arc as MacFie swivelled his hips. It planted itself with a muffled thud right in Pete's groin. There was another yelp, maybe two octaves higher. Pete's breath came out with it and his body snapped double like a jackknife. Jake let go of the trapped arm and Pete continued the movement with a strange, fluid grace, slowly pitching forward until his face hit into the soft earth.

'Right, you bastard,' came a voice from the crowd of men. Archie Calvert, who was quickly pouring his late father's boat-hiring business into shot glasses of booze, came lurching out of the crowd on his skinny legs. He'd had even more to drink than Pete Rodger, though he hadn't been on the hill search that day, and it showed. He took about three steps forward, and in the same instant one of the tinkers matched him step for step. He moved in quickly and just seemed to nod at Archie. The thin man rocked back under the force of the head butt that caught him right on the bridge of his big, shapeless nose, crunching the bone with an audible squelchy pop. Blood splattered on either side of it, giving Archie a grotesque moustache that glistened wetly in the firelight.

'Oh, there's no need for that,' came another voice, raspy and with a slight quaver in it. Hector Lawrie came forward from the group who were now looking more than a little uncertain. The postman had come along with the rest more out of curiosity than anything else. He was sixty-two years old and not a violent man. John Lindsay stepped in quickly as one of the young tinkers, a squat fellow with broad hard shoulders, came forward to have a square go. John held up the truncheon that had suddenly appeared in his hand and barred the young man's progress by holding it right against his adam's apple. The youth gave a grunt and stopped dead.

'Right, I think there's been enough jollity for one night, eh boys?' He stood there with the nightstick against the young man's thick neck, but he was looking at the Murrin men who were shuffling their feet uncertainly. 'There's two down and a long night ahead, and the next one to make a move will be making it against *me*. Catch my drift?'

There was a mumble and a murmur. Somebody whispered, 'Bastards,' and at the back of the crowd two of the men turned and walked off trying to look casual.

'I hope you haven't brought your car with you tonight, Archie,' Lindsay said genially to the skinny man who had got himself to his feet and was now holding his face in both hands and moaning to himself. 'And you, Pete, it's yourself that won't be helping out tomorrow. You'll have a pair of balls bigger than a bull's in the morning. Seems you won't be up to much walking. Maybe from now on, you'll let me handle things.'

He drew the nightstick back and reached out to grab Jimmy's uncle by the collar. He heaved him to his feet. There was no way he could make him stand up straight. Pete's hands were clenched between his legs. There was a trickle of saliva dripping in slick string from his open mouth, and his moan was a fair imitation of Archie Calvert's. Both men lurched away towards the path. The rest of the men were out of sight.

When, an hour later, Lindsay left the camp it was well after midnight. By that time he had ascertained that indeed it had been one of the tinkers who had chased the boys into the trees. Alasdair McIver who had the most abysmal squint that John had ever seen in his life confirmed that one day he'd seen the boys take a rabbit from one of his snares, and the second day he'd chased them off because he thought they were up to the same thing. He also complained bitterly that he'd lost six rabbits on the last three nights.

'There's been somebody or something taking them and wrecking the traps, and if I catch them I'll put a boot so far up their backsides they'll be shitting leather for a week,' he declared.

'Well, if you do, I'll give you a wee holiday down in the station,' Lindsay warned him nicely. 'Anything like that, you come to me. And if I ever hear of you scaring wee boys again, especially *my* wee boy, then you'll have to answer to me, and I really don't think you want to do that now, do you?'

McIver shook his head. The policeman was tall and lanky, but he was no soft mark. The tinker had admitted chasing the boys. He said he'd stopped before they had got to the road, and then he'd come back over the hill and down to the camp. His wife, a broad-faced and quite spectacularly ugly woman with a surprising number of children – the surprise was that she had any, although John Lindsay thought she might look different to someone with such a devastating squint as McIver had – backed up his story. So did MacFie, and Lindsay was inclined to believe him. The tinkers were mistrusted and distrusted by most of the folk who lived in houses built on foundations. That didn't make them criminals. Maybe from time to time, when the opportunity arose, they weren't totally honest, but Lindsay didn't think they were into abduction.

On the way back to his station house, he thought about it some more. The memory of what he'd seen up at Henry MacLeish's farm kept coming back to the forefront of his mind. He recalled the carnage, and those humped scuttering shadows that had made a mess of the bull. If that could happen to an animal weighing close on a ton, what chance would a child have? The thought gave him a awful sinking feeling in his stomach.

Another thing worried him. Jake MacFie had asked where the boy had been seen last. Lindsay told him. And then MacFie had said a strange thing.

'If he's gone up there at the stones, then there's no use you nor me nor anybody looking for him. Not this close to the midsummer.'

Lindsay had asked him what he meant by that and MacFie had looked into the flickering flames in the fire. His black eyes reflected the red, and the lines on his weatherbeaten face looked like black slashes.

'The *thin* places. They get thinner,' he said.

'What are you talking about?'

'Don't take my word for it. You check. There's people gone a-missing up at those stones before and they've never been found again.'

'I've heard those old tales,' Lindsay replied.

'Think on them some more. We've been a-coming to this place four times in the year for ever, but none of our folk go up to those stones no more, not since the old man knocked them down more than a hunnert years back. There's badness up there.'

MacFie went back to looking at the fire. John Lindsay shook his head and got up and went to his Land Rover. Tinker talk, he thought. But there was something in the way that Jake MacFie had said it that kept coming back to him. Somebody else had used a phrase just like that. *The thin places get thinner, at the midsummer.* That was only a day or so away. And what could that have to do with wee Jimmy Rodger?

As he turned into the cut-off that led down to the station, John Lindsay shook his head again. There was no point in thinking about tinker talk. Even if it did keep forcing its way back into his head.

At two o'clock that morning Archie Calvert was wishing he'd stayed at home. Lindsay had been right on the nose when he'd asked if Archie had been driving his car, although noses were something the skinny, scarecrow-like man didn't want to think about. His own nose which had always been a conversation piece at the best of times now had a distinctly new geography, and it felt as if the earthquake that had rearranged its outlines was still going on. He'd gone back to the car and rather than face the mile-walk home, he'd swung up the creaky boot-lid and taken out the six cans of the lager they say is probably the best in the world and is known colloquially as leg-opener special, a tribute to its strength and its noted effect as an aid to romance.

Archie sat in the back seat of his battered old car and had a fair old go at anaesthetizing the pulses of pain that made his now strangely flattened nose feel like a neon sign flashing on and off. The rest of the men had gone home, and despite Lindsay's warning Archie was determined to drive to the far side of Murrin. He had four special brews while he sat and thought dark muddled thoughts about the big policeman and the man who had butted his nose into a pulp. As he reran the scene, his body jerked slightly every time he thought of the punches he would have thrown if he hadn't been caught off guard.

Just before two, he crawled into the front seat of the car, banging his knee on the gearstick, and with great effort managed to insert the key into the ignition slot. The starter moaned similarly to the way both he and Pete had done out at the tinkers' camp. It whined worriedly and then the solenoid clicked. He tried again, cursing out loud, and got the same response. The starter wouldn't even turn. He twisted the key angrily several times and all he got was an ever weaker series of gaspy whirs and a few more clicks. The car refused to start.

A few more curses followed, and then Archie hauled himself out of the front door, lurching as he tried to get his balance. He did a fair imitation of a drunken man, which indeed he was, as he wove his way along the road, swaying from side to side until he gathered enough momentum to keep on what couldn't be considered as a straight line but was as good as he was going to get.

He had got nearly a mile along the road, past the houses at the far side of the village and round the bend where there were steps leading down to the small wooden jetty that was stilted out into the cove.

It was just then that there was a sudden ruckus on the far side of the road, an almighty cacophony of sound that startled Archie round on his wobbly heels. The hawthorn hedge on the landward side seemed to whip about and then flatten. Something big and heavy lunged through, bellowing hoarsely. Another came clambering behind it, smashing the hawthorn branches with great weight. A third came blundering through the space before Archie realized what was happening. A herd of cows that had been quietly munching grass in the field on the other side of the hedge had suddenly stampeded. Twenty yards further along three more cows charged through the hedge, crunching the foliage to pieces. Two more came simply flying over the top of it like great clumsy steeplechasers and clattered on to the road. Their frantic lowing was incredibly loud in the night air. Archie stood for a second, mouth agape, trying to take it in when the herd came all at once charging across the road towards him. Behind them came a screeching sound that tore into the night, like a stone saw cutting granite.

With instant clarity despite the drink, Archie realized he was in the path of a herd of stampeding cows and was going to get trampled underneath them. He turned round to run in the opposite direction and went smack into the wooden post that held the notice board at the pier steps. Face first is perhaps wrong. He hit it nose first and for an instant a little galaxy of stars started spinning in front of his eyes. The pain was an enormous explosion that blistered across the front of his face and immediately twin gouts of blood splashed his cheeks again.

The stars faded and behind him he heard the frantic bellowing and the clattering of heavy hoofs on the tarmac.

'Oh shit,' he said, although through the blood and slaver it could have been anything. He jinked past the post and went lurching down the steps, holding his face in both hands, trying to bear the pain. At his back the stampede followed. He could hear the lurching of the animals as their flanks collided like carpets being beaten. There was a flight of maybe four steps and then a concrete ramp that led down to the pier proper. Archie half ran along it and the herd of cows thundered behind him, lowing deafeningly. Again there was the screech that made the hairs on Archie's neck stand on end. It was when his feet hit the heavy wooden sleepers that made up the pier's surface that he realized he was trapped. The cows weren't going to stop. Their feet pounded on the planks like a thundering drumroll.

'Oh fuck,' he said with feeling. The pier was thirty yards long and he was half-way down it. They were going to sweep him off the end.

The sudden realization made him swerve to the side, out of the path of the rampaging cattle as they loco-motived towards him. There was a wooden banister at each side of the pier. Archie grabbed it without stopping and literally threw himself over, turning his body just right in a way that he, no athlete, could probably never have done had he been sober and dived for the water. Behind him the beef express thundered.

Archie would have been fine. Cold and wet, but fine,

if the tide had been in. But it was just his luck. It wasn't. The pier went out to deep water, but there was a steep shelf just in from the head of the jetty and when the tide was out, there was only a short expanse of shingle and mussel beds and barnacle-covered rocks. Archie took a header into the darkness and fell twelve feet, landing nose first. It was not his lucky night. In fact it was third time unlucky as far as his nose was concerned, for it smashed straight into a big boulder that had been embedded in the shore for years. Again its geography was altered, this time out of all recognition. If there was anything lucky, it lay in the fact that he was spared the absolutely incredible pain that would have knocked the two other blows on his magnificent proboscis into a cocked hat on any night of the week. As it happened, the force of the fall broke his neck and killed him instantly before he felt a thing. He wasn't greatly missed, and later on the teenager who had been working his butt off for pennies down at the boathouse took over the business as there was no one left to claim it, and made it into a going concern. So some good came out of it anyway.

The cattle continued their flight along the pier. Only one of them crashed through the banister and on to the rocks. Two of its forelegs broke, cracking like kindling under the momentum, and one of its horns snapped off on a rock. It had to be put out of its misery by Sandy Tate the next day. The rest of them ploughed on, bellowing like crazy, to the end of the pier and went off the head in a great avalanche of meat that caused a huge wave to spread out for furlongs into the bay.

Behind them in the shadows, something big and fast screeched in fury as it scuttled along the planks. A light came on in the nearest house where Harry Shields the piermaster lived, and then a second shaft of light came from the lamp above his neighbour's front door. The thing that padded fearsomely, unseen by any human eye, on strange, blurring legs, screamed viciously at the glare of light and rocketed up the pier and across the road into the shadows.

John Lindsay, who was so tired he felt as if he could sleep for a week, came trundling along in his jeep about fifteen minutes later. By that time, two of the cattle had made it back to the shore. Another two swam right across the bay and came on to land at the hook that nipped the loch on each side. Three others were found three weeks later washed up, dead and bloated, on the far side of the firth near Greenock and the Gantocks. Everybody thought they must have been carried out by the tide although by that time, knowing what he did, John Lindsay thought they might have really tried to swim for it.

Of forty-five head of cattle, only nine were saved and lived to chew the cud another day. Five others were alive, including the one that had broken its legs on the ebb-tide shore. Two of them had terrible injuries on their backs. It looked as if somebody had taken a chain-saw to them and ripped them to shreds. One was missing an entire hind leg and how it could have run down to the pier was anybody's guess. The other one had no tail and no udders either. The whole mammary sac had been ripped right off, and the hide on its left flank had been peeled off down to the bone in a foot-wide strip from shoulder to the big hip-knuckle.

Sandy Tate had no explanation for that. Neither did John Lindsay, but he was up at the school the very next day and had Mrs Ross photocopy a letter for every parent warning that none of the children should be allowed out on their own. The big policeman went round all the classes from primary one up to seven, and gave all the kids the same message. There was an animal out there on the hills and it was dangerous and it would eat you. Everybody took his warning seriously, and everybody now thought that the same mysterious animal, a big dog or a pack of them, some said, a runaway panther or a cougar, said others, had taken wee Jimmy Rodger. There were a lot of nightmares later on, but John Lindsay preferred them to what could happen to a kid who didn't heed the warning.

As it turned out, Jimmy Rodger was found six miles away as the old crow flies, and twenty-seven if you go round the winding road of the loch and down the far side. He was found right at the top of Cardross Hill by a retired schoolteacher by the name of Campbell Ward who happened to be a friend of Beth Callander. He shared her interest in the local history and had gone up the hill to take pictures of the *cromlech* that stood on the peak. It was one of maybe a dozen or more old mega-liths that were found on the top of almost every hill in the west land and down the peninsula itself. It was ten feet high and built of three uncut stone pillars that supported a flat flagstone on the top; hence the name, which translated from the Gaelic means stone table. It was generally assumed that they marked the burial sites of kings or clan chiefs.

Campbell Ward had lined himself up and had set the aperture and shutter speed of his Minolta so he could catch the rays of the early morning sun coming in between the stones and through the light mist that swirled between the uprights on clear summer dawns.

This early, the sun was just heaving itself up behind the Longcrags on the far side of Levenford, ten miles to the west. The golden arc was sending spears of light into the morning sky. Campbell positioned himself behind the *cromlech* and waited for the right moment when the stones would be lit by the corona.

Then the world went dark, as if night had suddenly fallen. There was a low rumble that was almost below the human hearing range, and the heather under Campbell's feet seemed to shiver. Through the lens, the world seemed to wobble, as if seen through warped glass. The darkness faded to purple and dopplered up through red to orange back to daylight. All this hap-pened in an instant while the old schoolmaster was

383

preparing his shot. He looked up from the camera and there was a muted flash of light that came alongside a high-pitched rending noise as if a piece of fine fabric had been torn lengthways across the bias, and then a hissing noise as if something had been thrown through the air, whirring past his ear.

The day was suddenly silent and the sun moved its bright face over the longcrags and the first rays came lancing through the hill mist, limning the stones with magical morning light. Campbell shrugged and bent to his Minolta and clicked off a fast sequence of shots as the motordrive sped the film past the lens at a small aperture which gave him the best depth of field.

It was the thud, as if something had fallen on to soft earth, and the groan, almost an animal sound, that jerked his attention for the second time. He looked up, screwing his eyes against the direct rays of the new sun, and saw something moving between the stones.

He held an arm over his eyes and the shape resolved itself. A small boy was writhing on the dry earth underneath the flat flagstone. Campbell walked forward, more curious than surprised.

'What's wrong, boy?' he asked.

Jimmy Rodger's body heaved in a spasm and he rolled out from between the stones.

Campbell stepped closer. The boy rolled over again, hips bucking spasmodically, like a footballer who's been downed by a foul kick to the groin. As he did so, his body jerked again in a move that almost sat him upright. The old man took a step back, aghast.

'Nuh,' Jimmy mouthed, and a thick trickle of froth gushed from his mouth and on to the ground. His eyes were rolled so far back in his head that all that could be seen were whites. The left side of his face was puckered and blistered as if someone had taken a hot iron and held it against his cheek. A wide patch of red showed from his crown right down to his left ear where a hank of hair the size of a man's fist was gone.

'What's the matter, son? What happened to you?'

Campbell let his camera drop to swing on its strap against his chest, and bent down towards the small figure writhing on the ground, shivering uncontrollably in violent spasms that racked his entire body. He reached out and put his two hands on the boy's shoulders to hold him steady, and for a horrible moment he felt waves of dead cold come off the child. Underneath his fingers he felt the small body twitch and writhe. The front of the boy's shirt and the sleeve on the right arm were matted with blood.

As he pulled the child towards him, Jimmy's eyes rolled down from where they had been looking into the back of his head and stared at the teacher. Campbell felt as if he were looking into two fathomless pits. The pupils were opened so wide there was no colour but black. They looked vacantly blind, as if there was no life on the other side of them.

And then Jimmy let out a scream that tore right up from inside him and out into the morning. It was a high-pitched single-note screech that was so loud it rang right down the side of the hill and echoed from the steep side of the ridge. Campbell Ward jerked back from the sound as if he'd been struck, but the scream went on and on and on for an impossible length of time, tearing into the air. It continued for longer than any child could possibly squeeze air from his lungs. And then as if a switch had been thrown, it cut off instantly. The silence that followed was almost palpable. Campbell grabbed the boy's shoulders again and held the child to him. At first he feared he was dead, but even through the thick jacket he wore against the morning chill he could feel the boy's heart fluttering feverishly against his own chest, tripping alarmingly fast. Again the boy heaved against him, lungs gulping for breath. The old man held him tight, feeling the child's chill through the tweed.

At the age of sixty-seven, Campbell Ward should not

385

have been carrying Jimmy Rodger down the half-mile from the crown of the hill to the lane where he'd parked his car, but there was something dreadful about the boy's writhing and shivering that spurred him on. By the time he got to the car, his own heart was labouring painfully, but that slowed down once he was in, with Jimmy strapped in the back seat, soundlessly twisting and turning and dribbling from a slack mouth. Ten minutes later, at Kirkland General Hospital doctors and nurses were scrambling around the life-support machine and fighting to save his life.

THIRTY-SIX

John Lindsay called off the search as soon as he got word from the doctors at Kirkland General. No, he was told, there wasn't any point in him taking the long trip round the loch to question the boy. He was still on a life-support system. They couldn't say when he'd be able to speak.

Alan Crombie was at Tom Callander's house having a coffee in the old conservatory where the sun shone through the glass and made the air feel humid and warm, almost tropical. There was a fair crowd, though it was just after nine in the morning. Beth was running bacon sandwiches and mugs of tea and coffee through the house, aided by Alex Graham who had been more than a bit bashful when she met Alan at the front door.

The atmosphere in the Callander home, however, was much warmer than it had been in the Crombie household. Alan had called the office to say he was extending his weekend by another day or so. That wasn't a great problem, considering he'd worked solid on the northern contracts, and this had more than justified the partners' confidence in him. While he was on the phone, he'd spoken to Mike Toward and had put a couple of questions to the big American surveyor.

'What do you want it for?' Mike had asked in his blunt manner.

'I'll tell you once you work the sums out. Compare the amounts and see how they match my house. You've been all through it with the tape measure. There's something about the figures that just don't add up, but you're the quantity man. See what you think yourself.'

There was a silence at the other end of the line.

Obviously Mike was scanning the figures he'd noted down.

'I don't need any calculator to see that they're way out. I can tell you at a glance that either somebody's been ripped right off, or else you've got two houses here. There's enough brick and timber to put on two more wings and build a granny cottage into the deal. You sure you've got the figures right?'

'They're the only ones I've got, and they were written down a hundred years ago, near enough. I'll explain it when I see you. That should be the day after tomorrow. See what you can do.'

'Right. It'll make a change from working on thousand-ton quantities, that's for sure.'

Alan had hung up the phone and sat staring out of the living-room window. Outside, the sky was dark and threatening, almost purple with the promise of another storm. It didn't look as if it was going to be a day to be out. He was thinking about what he'd read the night before in Dalmuir's chronicle. The first owner had had further problems with the squads who were skilfully erecting the first big house down on the point. Three of the joiners and five of the labourers had walked off the site, swearing they'd never set foot on the peninsula again. Sean Boyle was never seen again after his workmate's hallucination. And the materials kept going missing. Latta, the builder, had already made up a great deal of the shortfall by using the standing stones for the keystones which had changed the appearance of the house for the better. The masons cut and shaped them for the corners, the steps up to the front door and the frames and sills for the windows. It gave the building a two-toned look, but the dark blue basalt stones contrasted so well with the fine-grained sandstone facing – and they were much stronger too – that it looked as if Cromwath had been designed that way.

What Latta couldn't figure out was how two walls which were supposed to have been built – and which his workers swore blind had been built – were nowhere to be seen. Between the main walls which were by this time up to roof level there was a blank space where the stairwell should have been. Right down to the foundations. And the bricks and cut stones, the lath and plaster for their construction were missing without a trace. But what caused the walk-off was the disappearance of plasterer Mick Mullen. It wasn't quite that he had disappeared. Only half of him did that.

As Dalmuir said in his book, and most of it was only hearsay anyway, Mullen had been floating the browning finish on the wall of the room which was to become the lounge. How he ended up in the top bedroom on the far side of the house, nobody knew, except for Mullen and he was dead by then. Two of the joiners who were nailing roofing planks to the joists could only say that they heard an almighty crash underneath them and that when they scrambled down the ladder to the room below, there was Mick Mullen screaming blue murder and writhing under a pile of stones which had collapsed on top of him. The only problem was, and nobody could explain it, that the pile of stones, obviously part of a wall, had no business being there at all. The two joiners, Gilbert Todd and Fergus Williams, didn't have much time to wonder about that until later. They scrambled over the rubble and started hauling off the big square blocks that were squeezing the trapped man down on to the floor. All the time he was screaming in agony. Two of the men who'd been working on the other side of the roof, laying shingles on the finished boards, came running into the room just in time to see the joiners haul the stricken man from the rubble. Half of him came tumbling out with a great ripping noise that everybody said sounded as if Mick Mullen was being torn in two. When this happened, the scream was cut off instantly and Mick Mullen came flying out from where he was trapped. There was only half of Mick Mullen, still wriggling on the floor. From navel to his feet, he was gone. He tried to raise himself up on his arms, looking like some dreadfully deformed creature. He made it high enough for his elbows almost to lock straight, then he opened his mouth, fell forward and hit the floor with a thump. Underneath him a huge pool of blood puddled out.

What nobody could understand, not Dalmuir or Latta or anybody on the site, or even a bemused and horrified Alan Crombie a hundred years later, was that the half of Mick Mullen's body was all that was ever found. Squads of men crowded into the room and carted off every one of the stones of the wall which should never have been there, expecting to find the grisly and thoroughly mashed remains of the joiner's other half. But they found nothing, not even blood. Somebody reported later that down in the lounge there was a mess on the plaster where Mullen had been floating the browning. It looked as if somebody had leaned against it, full face on. That raised an eyebrow then, but it wasn't the biggest problem facing the crews. Another plasterer finished the job and work went on.

On the following pages Alan read of more materials going missing, including an entire shipment of special slate from the quarry up at Ballachullish that had most certainly been nailed to the boards over the past week. They flew off in a big summer storm one night close to midsummer when bolts of lightning had streaked and fizzed all around the house. The men huddled in their sodden canvas tents heard them rip and whirr as they were torn off, but nobody dared look out from under the canvas shelter to watch. In the morning the whole roof was stripped to the bare boards.

Even stranger, there was no sign of the slates around the site. They had just been picked up and blown away. No one knew where.

This and the other set-backs hit Dalmuir's budget, and hard. But the more opposition to his building the house, whether human or accidental, the more determined he was to see it completed. Work went on.

Alan Crombie found it hard to close the chronicle. Helen was a vague silent shadow who worked about the house, never in the same room as him at any time, and there was a constant smell of polishing wax, domestic cleaners and air freshener throughout the place. They had had no contact since her rebuff at the bottom of the stairs. She went through the motions of being a housewife with such a distracted air that Alan determined to himself that he'd give it one more week, then he was going to take her to see the doctor – *and not Alex Graham* – if he had to drag her out of the house. Her skin had taken on a pale sheen that was partly due to tiredness, and also to the fact that she seemed determined never to cross the front-door threshold into the sunlight.

Tommy had been pale too that morning, but he assured his father that there was nothing wrong. Alan assumed that he was fretting over his friend who'd gone missing, but he let it slide. Alan strolled him to school before going up to Tom's where they'd agreed to meet.

'Do you think you'll find him?'

'We'll have a right good look, TC,' Alan replied. 'I'm sure he'll be found. Probably he's fallen and got stuck somewhere,' he continued, trying to sound hopeful and probably failing. In a rural place like this there were too many hills and glens where, if there was some nutcase around, a child could be taken and disposed of and never found again.

'Will *you* be all right today?' Tommy asked with sudden gravity.

'Course I will, why do you ask?'

Tommy shrugged. 'I don't know. It's just . . .'

'Just what?' Alan encouraged.

'The house. It's weird. Sometimes I get scared.'

'Why's that?'

'I get these dreams. Like I'm in the house, but some-where else. It's really scary.'

Alan felt a small chill creep up his back. 'When you say you're somewhere else, what sort of place is it?'

'I don't know. It's when I go through a door. Some-times there's an old man there. I dreamed that he had a gun and was shooting himself. It was all yucky. And then I go through a door and I'm somewhere else. It's like going outside, but *inside the house.*'

Tommy stopped and looked up at Alan to see if he was listening, and if so, if there was any understanding of what he was saying. Alan felt the chill creep up his spine again and did his best to keep his expression blank. *Outside, but inside the house! That was suddenly, creepingly familiar.*

'We all have dreams, son. Even I've had scary dreams. But the good thing is they can't harm you. You always wake up, and it's another day.'

'Sometimes I just don't like going to sleep.'

'All boys are like that. When you get to my age, you can't get enough of it.'

'No. I don't like going to sleep in the house,' Tommy came back quickly. 'And I feel better when I'm out again at school. But then I get worried again if you're not there.'

'Why is that, son?'

'I don't like leaving the girls, cos they're in the house.'

'But your mum's there with them.'

'I know,' Tommy said. But his tone told it all. Tommy was telling his father that he didn't think she was looking after the twins at all, and he knew he'd have to do something about that.

Man and boy walked the last twenty yards to school in almost complete silence, Alan thinking about what his son had said, and Tommy hoping his father had understood. What he had been trying to tell Alan was that when he looked at his mother he got the same feeling he got about the house. Tommy had a little bit of the gift that his twin sisters had in plenty, although only he and old Seumas Rhu MacPhee had any inkling of it.

When he looked at his mother these days, he thought of empty corridors that took you for ever to walk, and deep dark pits, and wild wet moorland littered with the bodies of slain men and overshadowed by great birds that had worm-eaten holes where their eyes should be.

Alan strolled back along the shore road, hands in the pockets of his light windcheater, thinking about what his son had said. The mention of Tommy's dreams had made him suddenly very uneasy; creepily uneasy. He decided he'd have to talk to somebody about it, and he didn't know who.

At Tom's it was Alex who opened the door and Alan felt the warm internal lurch that meant guilt was battling with attraction. She reddened slightly and turned her head away, almost schoolgirlish. Alan went in and as he did so, his arm brushed against hers. Both of them twitched as if some voltage had jumped between them.

'I'm sorry,' they both said simultaneously. Then Alan laughed a bit sheepishly and Alex smiled. Her face coloured again, but the smile remained. The last thing Alan wanted in his life was another complication, he told himself.

But as he looked at Alex Graham, neat and athletically limber in a pair of tight, faded jeans and a loose check shirt that looked comfortably worn, the slow rolling motion surged just under his ribcage.

'I need to talk to you some time,' he said very softly. There were voices from the living-room and the kitchen, but there was no one else in the hallway.

'Yes,' she said simply, and in that moment the voltage passed between them again, not a jolt this time but a current that was warm and strong.

Beth came out of the kitchen just then with a tray

which rattled with cups and saucers, and both of them turned towards the sound.

'Oh, it's you, Alan. Come away in.' She looked at Alex, who was still smiling. 'And don't keep a visitor at the door. Remember you're back in the old country.'

Alex's smile widened, showing her teeth against a clear tanned skin that looked darker under the shiny curls which framed her face. She didn't blush this time.

'Oh, and before I forget,' Beth said, turning to butt the door open with her rear. 'I've looked out some things for you. There's more history to your place than you'd believe. I'm surprised I've never found it before.'

'Well, I've got a surprise for you too,' Alan said. Beth had been fascinated with the copy of the Register of Sasines that he'd shown her and had borrowed it. She had wanted to elaborate on the bare bones, to flesh out the characters of the story. As a historian and an enthusiast, she told Alan, she had all the resources to find out about the people who'd lived in the house before the new owners.

Tom was sitting in the conservatory with half a dozen people. Alan had met them the day before when they'd all banded together to help in the search.

They were supposed to meet up with John Lindsay at half past nine and they were just preparing to go off when the policeman drove up the tarmac drive in his Land Rover. They clustered round the door as Tom Callander went to meet him and then listened as John told them the boy had been found. Everybody had questions. Where, when, how, who?

John held his hands up against the sudden flood. 'That's about all I can tell you. We don't know how he got up to Cardross Hill. He might have been taken there, or he might have walked. But he's in bad shape. Frank Rodger's been along at the hospital this morning already, and it's too early to say.'

'How was he found?' Alan asked.

'It was an old teacher fellow called Campbell Ward

from out Kirkland way. Seems he was photographing the old stones up on the hill. Found the wee fellow underneath them. The old boy nearly killed himself getting the lad down the hill, but if he hadn't done that, then the boy would have been a goner for sure.'

John Lindsay looked tired and drawn, as if he'd missed out on a lot of sleep. Tom brought him in for coffee and some breakfast, which the big policeman wolfed gratefully, although it was his second meal of the morning. It had been a long night.

In the relief of the boy's discovery, John told the now redundant search party about the cattle stampede the previous night and the death of Archie Calvert, who wasn't well known to any of them.

'I reckon there must be some sort of animals up on these glens,' he said. 'I'm thinking that seeing the boy's been found, I might get some volunteers to take a scout up the Corries and the Peatons. They've been after the animals, and I don't want them to start going after people. I don't know so much about them myself, whether they're likely to attack folk or not, but I don't want to take any chances.'

Alan said he was game, seeing they had an empty day ahead of them. Tom allowed that he'd not get a chance to use his shotgun for another two months till the grouse season opened, and he'd welcome a chance to warm up his over and under.

'All right,' John Lindsay said. 'I've just got to go down to the schoolhouse for half an hour. I'll meet anybody who wants to come along down at the station at the back of ten.'

As soon as he'd gone, Seumas spoke up. 'I don't reckon we'll find anything. Not during the day.'

'What do you mean?' Alan asked.

'I'm thinking we're not looking for any big cat, not a lion nor a puma. I think we're up against something else altogether. And it's coming from them standing stones.'

Everyone looked at everybody else. It was Alex who broke the sudden silence that descended. 'Is there something that we should know about?' she asked Seumas.

'I think there's something wrong going on.'

It was as if a small switch had been thrown linking circuit to circuit; a trickle of energy that leapt in a slow loop from one individual to the other.

It sizzled in the air around Tom Callander who had seen something up at those stones that had nearly given him a heart attack.

It riddled through Seumas Rhu who had nearly been swallowed by a stone whirlpool on a roof. It sleeted into Beth Callander, and it jolted into Alan Crombie who was closer to it than any of them. For some reason that she could not then, or ever, explain, it laced through Alex Graham. It joined them all together in a strange buzz of apprehension.

'Let's meet down here for lunch,' Tom suggested quietly.

'I think that would be a good idea,' Seumas Rhu said. They all nodded, and that was that. None of them knew why they decided it. None of them knew why they were each holding on to a piece of a strange jigsaw. It just seemed *right*.

THIRTY-SEVEN

The search went on until two in the afternoon. Fifty men had turned out, including a handful from the tinkers' camp, and split into five groups which scoured the Peatons and the Corries. Not a shot was fired. Nothing was found except two sheep carcasses that were pretty far gone and riddled with maggots, and nobody could say what killed them, if anything.

Alan knew that Tommy had a packed lunch with him at school, but he felt he'd been out long enough. He wanted to get back home to make sure the twins were being fed. After what Tommy had said that morning, and the way he had started to feel himself, he didn't like to leave them too long in the house. He knew he'd have to get some sort of childminder in, maybe a nanny if the budget would stretch to it. Then Helen could go on scrubbing the house until it was out of her system.

He told Tom he wouldn't make it for lunch but he'd be around later in the afternoon, and Tom agreed that that was a good idea. He hadn't realized they'd be out so long.

'I'll be stiff as a board in the morning, but it's good to stretch the legs for a change,' Tom said. 'I haven't been up this way in years, and it's a change from sitting at a desk all day, or in the cab of that bloody bulldozer.'

They agreed to meet back down at the Callanders' home at four, and they all headed back down the hill.

At home Alan opened the front door and as soon as he stepped past the lintel, he felt depression drape itself over his shoulders. Inside, the house was dark and silent.

'I'm home,' he called upstairs. There was no reply.

'Helen? Are you there?' His voice echoed up the stairwell and faded away.

At first the thought struck him that Helen had gone out, and his spirits rose a little. He went through to the kitchen and peered out of the window. There was no washing on the line. He went back and up the stairs and into their room. Then he stopped dead in his tracks.

Helen was standing naked with her arms outstretched and her legs spread. Her hands were pressed hard against the wall, fingers wide. Her breasts and belly and thighs were tight up against the smooth surface as if she was trying to force herself right into it.

Alan stood for a second, staring in surprise and bewilderment.

Helen's back was moving slowly and her buttocks flexed with each movement, doing a slow grind. He could hear her skin rubbing against the wall. She was moaning very softly under her breath. Alan couldn't take his eyes off the sight. Between his thighs, he felt a slow build-up of involuntary pressure as he watched the strange, sensuous motion his wife was making. She was oblivious to his presence. Then the sheer strangeness of it hit him like a blow and the turn-on turned itself off like a tap.

'What are you doing?' His voice found itself at last.

She didn't hear him. Her back kept on undulating as she rippled against the wall, the cheeks of her rounded backside swelled, then dimpled, as the muscles forced her against it again and again.

'Yes,' she whispered.

'Helen, what the hell's going on here?'

'Yes,' she said again, a little stronger, almost a moan.

Alan walked forward to touch her shoulder, and almost recoiled when he felt how cold and clammy her skin was. It was as if the contact with the wall had drained all her body heat away.

'Oh please,' Helen groaned, giving a little gasp between the words.

Alan gripped her shoulder and pulled her back from the wall. There was a sucking sound, as if he had ripped her off the surface, and Helen's body went totally rigid.

'What the *hell* are you doing?' he shouted, much too loudly.

Helen turned like a cat and her eyes blazed with something that was like fury and maybe like hatred. Saliva dripped from the corner of her mouth which was twisted in a grimace that showed almost every one of her teeth. She snarled something at him, and it wasn't words. It was just the snarl of an angry animal.

'Just what do you think . . .' Alan never finished the sentence. Suddenly Helen lunged at him, and hit his face with such force that he toppled on to the bed. He bounced back up again and she caught him on the rebound, raking her fingernails right down his cheek. Three stinging lines ploughed the skin from his ear to his chin. He raised a hand to fend her off and she lunged with her other hand. This time he blocked it, and despite the weirdness of it all, despite the sudden fright he'd got when she'd turned from the wall and he'd looked into eyes that were filled with poison, the voice at the back of his head was shouting at him.

The girls. Where are the girls?

That thought gave him the sudden strength to do what he'd never done before. Without thinking, he lashed out with a fist which, more by chance than any deliberate act of will, clipped Helen right on the point of her chin. Her head snapped back and her body seemed to draw itself up to its full height. Then her head came forward as if swinging on a hinge, and in that instant Alan saw that the vacuous hatred had disappeared from her eyes. For a moment that seemed to go on for ever, her gaze slowly swung across his, a tired, sick and frightened gaze, then her eyes rolled up and she just dropped to the floor.

'What in the name of God is going on here?' Alan muttered to himself, still shaken at the sudden violence of the scene. He slumped and sat down heavily on the bed, for a moment too bewildered for rational thought. Helen was lying at his feet in an ungainly attitude of sexual supplication that was strangely grotesque. He drew his eyes away from her vacant face and a cloud seemed to pass over the window, blotting out the light, throwing the room into gloom.

From downstairs there came a small noise, then the patter of small feet on a hard floor.

'Katie,' he called automatically, relief flooding through him. 'Laney.' He heaved himself up off the bed and stepped over his wife's pale, prone frame and crossed to the door.

He skittered down the stairs, taking them two and three at a time, and swinging his weight round on the smooth wooden ball that topped the corner of the banister on the landing.

'Girls?' he called out again when he got to the bottom. One of them laughed. The sound came from the lounge at the end of the hall. Alan strode down the passage and threw the door open. There was no one in the room.

The patter of feet came again. Alan stopped and cocked an ear. This had happened before, on the first day they'd moved in, when Tommy had got a fright when he couldn't find his sisters. Where the hell were they?

'Come on, girls!' he called out, flicking his eyes up and down the length of the hall. There was a bump and another titter of laughter. But it came from upstairs.

They couldn't have passed him.

He knew they couldn't have passed him. He'd almost jumped down the stairs. So, he told himself, in the echoing emptiness of the big house, he must have thought he'd heard them at the bottom of the house.

'Where are you, girls?' he called out again, this time showing more of the frustration he was feeling.

Up on the top landing there was silence. He passed

his bedroom door and Helen was still spreadeagled on the floor. There was a scuttering sound, small and slithery, up in the loft, the kind of noise starlings and jackdaws make when they've found a way into the roof space. For a moment his heart sank, thinking they'd found a way up there among the shadows and cobwebs under the slates. But then there was a click in their room and a small thud, as if something had fallen. He strode the five steps and swung the door open. Their cupboard door was open and a small plastic ball that was marbled with colour rolled slowly towards the door. Apart from that the room was empty. Alan swore softly and strode out of the room and into the hall again.

Just then, the door swung open and Katie and Laney stood there, smiling at him, holding hands. His heart did another quick flip, but this one felt good. He scrambled over to them and scooped them into his arms, feeling their tiny warmth settle into him.

Alex Graham was still with Tom and Beth, and she came immediately when he called. Up in the bedroom she briskly and efficiently examined the prostrate woman and got Alan to lift her on to the bed. From her chin to her ear, a blue-black bruise was beginning to blossom nicely.

Alan quickly explained what had happened and he didn't leave anything out, although he knew how this must look. He had three raked lines on his cheek, his wife was almost awake, though still stunned and dopy. It looked like another domestic set-to.

Alex looked at him straight in the eye and raised an eyebrow quizzically. 'What are you going to do now?' she asked.

'I haven't a clue. I just don't know what to do. I'll have to get somebody to watch the girls and Tommy.'

'No, I mean what are you going to do about your wife?'

'What do you recommend?'

'I thought you said I'm not your doctor.'

'Well, I need some advice. I don't know where the hell I am right at this moment.'

Right at that moment, Helen's eyes flipped open. Alan caught the movement and looked down at the bed. Alex caught his look and turned, just as Helen's hands shot up and grabbed her by the neck.

Alex gave a small, involuntary gulping sound as Helen's hands squeezed and Alan saw in horror that her eyes had immediately started to bulge. The young doctor's tongue poked out from between her teeth.

Almost with the same movement, Helen sat upright, hands still clamped around Alex's throat. The movement rocked both of them on the bed. Alan felt as if he were suddenly paralysed, unable to move. He watched Alex's hands come up to grab futilely at his wife's arms. Then, as if he'd managed to pull his feet out of a clogging mire, he stepped forward and grasped Helen's arms with his own hands.

Alex moaned and her legs jittered as she fought for breath. Her feet made a little drumroll on the floor. Alan heaved, suddenly aware of the power of Helen's grip. His wife was staring wide-eyed at Alex, and he could see the muscles stand out like stringy ropes on her thin forearms, showing the manic force of her grasp.

Right in front of him, Alex Graham was choking to death.

He braced his weight and, grunting with enormous effort, gripped two hands on her left and then using his leg muscles and his back, he jerked as hard as he could. It was like wrestling with a weight lifter. Sweat stood out on his forehead and he let out a huge yell. Suddenly Helen's hands shot apart, ripping right off Alex's neck. The girl was catapulted backwards on to the bed and tumbled off the far end. The unexpected give almost threw Alan off balance, but he didn't fall. Instead he thrust himself forward between Helen's scrabbling arms, and crashed on to her thrashing body. All the time she was mouthing and gurgling incomprehensibly. It was quite by accident that he drew his knee up and it smacked right off her pubic bone. If she had been a man, then the fight would have been over. Helen merely cried out in what sounded like fury. He heaved his weight up and then pressed himself down on her, forcing her shoulders on to the bed. Underneath him she jerked and bucked alarmingly. Up close, her breath smelt ripe and sweet, like purple plums from the bottom of the bag that have started to ferment. Her eyes were black and filmy, like empty caverns; craters.

Like the eyes of the crows on the dead moorland.

And then the fight went out of her. The film seemed to flicker up like a second eyelid and again the vague, despairing look flooded her face.

'What . . .' was all she said. Then she gave a great startling scream that seemed to tear through the whole house. Underneath him it felt as if a great electrical charge had surged through her body, bending her back-bone so hard she was arched off the bed. The shock-wave shivered through her rigid bow-taut body, and then it was gone. She collapsed under him on the bed, flaccid and spent. Through his clothes he could feel the cold. Her skin felt clammy and damp.

Alan held on to his wife's shoulders while he turned to Alex. 'Are you all right?'

She got up off the floor. Beside her, her bag was upturned, the contents strewn on the rug.

'I don't know,' she said in a husky voice that would have been enormously attractive but for the fact that it told of the enormous grip that had been clamped round her neck. She coughed, almost gagged, and then raised her head. 'I think I'll survive. How about you?'

'I'm all right. But I don't want this to happen again. Can you give her something?'

'I wouldn't know where to start.'

'Just something to make her sleep.'

'I don't know if that's wise,' Alex said.

'Who the hell knows what's wise and what isn't?'

'I'd rather you got Dr Docherty,' Alex said seriously. 'She's his patient.'

'Look, you saw what she was like. She tried to strangle you, for God's sake. What if she does it again? Maybe to one of the kids. Can we risk that?'

'All right. I can give her a sedative. But you'll have to get her down to the boss. I can't take responsibility. However, I'll judge this an emergency. She needs more than a tranquillizer.'

'Her and me both,' Alan replied wearily.

'Do you want me to prescribe something for you?' Alex said after she'd given Helen a small injection high on her shoulder. The prostrate woman didn't object. She didn't seem to know about what was happening.

'Maybe once I get to the bottom of this. It's either that, or I'm going to need to be locked up in a rubber room.'

Within a minute, Helen's breathing had subsided to a deep, regular rhythm. Alan pulled the coverlet up on the bed and tucked it under her chin. In repose, Helen looked wan and thin, drained and worn out. He felt a stab of guilt as he looked down at her. Beneath the guilt was the slowly rolling cloud of despair.

THIRTY-EIGHT

Katie and Laney played silently in the corner with their lego bricks while everybody sat themselves around in the room. Alex had called Beth and asked her to tell her father that Alan couldn't leave the house and had suggested they come over to Cromwath.

'Is that wise?' she'd asked Alan. She'd suggested that their arranged meeting might not seem as important as it had in the morning.

Alan shook his head. 'I don't know what's going on here, but there's something wrong. I don't know what it is. My wife might not be the only one going crazy, but today it felt *right* that we should all get together.'

'Maybe you're right. It did feel *important*. I don't know why.'

When the others arrived they sat around, fidgeting, unsure. They weren't so much an odd bunch as a group of individuals who maybe had something in common but weren't sure of exactly what it was. Alan sat in a chair in the corner and Tom sat opposite him beside Seumas. On the couch, Tom's daughter sat on the furthest side from Alex. Between them was a newcomer who had surprised them all. As Tom said to Alan later on: 'I haven't seen her in twenty years. I thought she'd died ages ago.'

Seumas had brought his mother, leading her slowly up the steps. The old woman had paused at the doorway, as if afraid to enter. She had made a small sign with her hand, just like a flick of the wrist, and then she'd drawn herself up to her diminutive height and crossed over the threshold. Somewhere in the clear air, thunder rumbled distantly, shivering the windowpanes.

Seumas had introduced his mother to them all and she had nodded to each one, turning her sightless face on them in turn. It was remarkable that she'd crossed the room without any assistance and stooped down beside the girls who turned and stared at her with their wide blue innocent eyes. They didn't laugh or smile; they just looked at her gravely. Alan watched as the old woman reached out her gnarled hands and placed them on each of the golden heads. She slid her hands across their upturned faces, memorizing them.

'*Cathair-Cailin*,' she said softly in her singsong voice when her fingers flitted over Kathryn's small face. 'Throne maiden, you are, close to the light.'

She turned to her sister, softly probing with wrinkled fingers. 'And *Aille-Ainne*, noon-day's glory, banisher of the night. Ah, there's old power in those names,' she said, just loudly enough for the rest of them to hear. Alan watched apprehensively.

She stood up again and retraced her steps, turning where Alan now stood and raising her face up to his.

'The faerie-kissed,' she said. 'Most precious of all.' She held him with her wrinkled, cavernous hollows and whispered: 'They know the *ways*. They have the gift of the *other*. Me, who has no eyes any more, I have some of the second sight. These babes have no voice, but they have the second *song*.'

Alan watched as the old woman turned and sat herself down on the couch, unerringly finding space between Beth and Alex.

'I don't know where to start,' Alan said when they had gathered round in position, drinking tea from the big mugs that he'd collected from filling stations around the country.

'Why not start at the beginning?' Tom suggested the obvious.

'He could if he knew it,' Mrs MacPhee said softly in a voice that carried. 'And there's few left who do.' Her tone didn't invite question.

'Look. I'll tell you what's happened to me first of all, because I don't know whether it's Christmas or Pancake Tuesday. Upstairs my wife is under sedation after having some kind of fit. There's been some things I can't explain, and from what I picked up down at Tom's place this morning, everybody has got something to say.' He paused.

Mrs MacPhee said: 'Go on, son.'

So he did. He told them everything. 'I've got to the stage where there's only two options. Either I'm cracking up, or there is something weird about this place. Both of them quite frankly scare the hell out of me,' he said when he finished his story.

'That's not surprising,' Tom said. 'It would do the same to me.'

'I know a lot of what I've said sounds really crazy. Even to me it sounds crazy. It's as if I've stepped into the set of the *Stone Tapes*. Maybe there is something in that after all. I'm beginning to wonder if there's a way the ground can act as some sort of recorder and play back scenes from the past.'

'You and me too,' Tom Callander said.

Mrs MacPhee came in quietly. 'And you, Thomas Callander, who's never been to visit these twenty years despite the fact that I was at your christening. What do you have to say for yourself?'

Tom looked sheepish at the mild rebuke and opened his mouth to reply, but Beth interjected, 'Just a minute, Dad. Can I say something?'

Tom looked relieved. Alan saw an expression flit across his face that told him Tom Callander didn't want to join in the Cromwath chronicle. He would, but it would cost him.

'Sure, go ahead,' Tom said.

'Well, I wanted to talk to Alan about the Register of Sasines. I've been doing some research on the history of the house.'

'That was before I found Dalmuir's history,' Alan put in. 'Now I think the less I know the better.'

'I was just trying to flesh out the previous owners for Alan. The register only gives their names and occupations and how much they paid for the property. That sort of thing. I did some checking through the old issues of the *Kirkland Post* and the *Finloch Times*. They're both defunct now, but they're all on microfiche in the library and we've still got lots of old parish records. They turned up some interesting things. I didn't see them as all *that* interesting until today. But now I'm not so sure.'

'Go on,' Alan encouraged Beth. Tom Callander looked at his daughter with fatherly concern.

'As I said, it didn't seem all that important. I was going to have it typed up, but I'm sure I remember it.' She stopped and stared into the middle distance, recalling. 'The last owner was Gerald McGrath. Everybody knows he took off just after the new year. There were some problems with his business. In fact there were a couple of pieces in the *Glasgow Herald*. Some sort of investigation. That seems about par for the course. He was one of those hail-fellow-well-met types and fancied himself a lot. But I think he left because he went bust, that's all. Nobody knew he'd gone anyway until the stories started about his firm collapsing, so it's probably fair to say that he just ran out of money and left.'

Tom Callander nodded. 'Never liked the feller. It was good to see some decent folk move into the place.'

'Before that it was Jessica and Philippa Kinross, who inherited the house in 1951. A couple of spinsters. Nice old souls. They both died in the winter of 1975. I remember I used to run errands for them. They were twins too. They always had an apple or an orange for any of the kids but they never went out much. They weren't in any of the local groups but they were nice old biddies. Always smiling, I remember, and they never forgot to send birthday presents. They kept the house just as it was before their father died.

'And that's the strange thing. Dr Kinross made a big splash in the papers at the time. There had been complaints from some of the local girls about how he was treating them. Sort of harassment kind of thing. There were rumours that he'd been performing abortions up at the house, and he had some sort of nervous breakdown. It was after this that they found him hanged from one of the trees up behind the house.'

'I remember that,' Tom said. 'It caused a real stink at the time. Your grandfather was living here, and we were round at the house on Mambeg. That would have been just after the war, eh?'

'Later than that. 1951 it was. In the summertime.' She went on: 'Dr Kinross had bought the place in 1930. The previous owner was a John Davidson who ran the partnership that Fergus Crawford inherited from his dad. He bought it in 1911 and had it for nineteen years.'

'And what happened to him?' Alan asked.

'It wasn't so much him as his wife and his family. According to the *Finloch Times*, he claimed they'd left him. But they were never found. There was a huge case about it. It was one of the big scandals of the time. It turned out he'd a mistress and fancied himself as a ladies' man. The wife came from money and it was felt that he'd done away with her and their three kids. Nobody ever got to the bottom of it. Davidson had some sort of breakdown half-way through the trial. The papers made a meal of it because he started raving on, and in the witness box too, about demons and doors into hell. Eventually he was committed to a sanitorium in Glasgow. I couldn't find out what happened to him.

'And before Davidson there was Alan Laing, who was the second owner. He only paid a thousand for the house because property prices seem to have slumped. He came here in 1895 and stayed for fourteen years.'

Beth paused and screwed her eyes up again in concentration. Light seemed to dawn again and she continued: 'Laing was a shipping agent involved in the Clyde trade. He had a lot to do with the paddle steamers and one of the first things he did was start up the ferry service to Gourock to save the long buggy trip round the loch. That's what started off the real building boom here at the turn of the century. He was quite big in local affairs. Chairman of the Burgh Council six years after he arrived. Those were the days when the four villages counted as one Burgh. He seemed to do quite well, and more than anybody made the peninsula the residential rural area that it is today.'

'What happened to him then?' Alan asked.

'He died of a heart attack in 1909. But things happened before that.'

'What were they?'

'Again you have to look in the *Finloch Times*. Laing considered himself a benefactor. There was a small poorhouse in Murrin then. There was still a lot of herring fishing going on and there were up to fifty boats putting out from the peninsula. The poorhouse was for the widows and their families of the men lost at sea. Laing used to organize trips for the orphans. He'd bring a paddle steamer down from Glasgow and take the families for jaunts in the summer. He also organized picnics up in the grounds of the house. In fact, the first photograph ever produced in the *Times* was a line-up of orphans in your orchard with Alan Laing in a top hat amongst them all.

'It was after one of those parties that two of the children went missing. Both girls, aged seven and eight. There was a huge search for them all over the place. At first nobody suspected Laing of anything, but then one of the others said they'd seen him talking to the kids inside the house. He denied it of course but the constable got a warrant to search the place. The first time they found nothing, but there was another search after a girl's shoe was found in the stables. This time they searched in the cellar and found a girl's dress. It was ripped and torn, although there was no blood. Laing was arrested and the constable threw him in the tollbooth that was down on the front. It was just a two-cell building.

'That night a crowd of villagers broke the door down and were set to hang him, but before that happened he had a heart attack. He just pegged out on the main street. Now that's not what the newspaper said. But there was a story about it in a history of the peninsula written in the thirties by an old chap called Hugh Mac-Feorlin. I knew I'd heard Laing's name somewhere before and checked it out. After that, they had another search of the house and lifted some flags in the cellar. There was some kind of pit, so the report went, where they found the bones of two children, and then there was more controversy, because the doctor who examined them said they'd been dead for years. What *was* very strange, and this was reported by everybody at the time, was that the bones looked as if they had been crushed. Nobody could tell whether they were the girls or not.' Beth halted and took a breath. She looked at everybody sitting in the room. They looked back expectantly.

'And then there was Alexander Dalmuir. Alan's told us about his book, and I'd really like to look at it some time. What we do know was that his wife took herself and her sons off to Glasgow not long after they moved in and Dalmuir stayed here alone. It seemed like his grand obsession. He lived here alone for a number of years and became some sort of recluse. In 1894 he simply disappeared into thin air. The house lay empty for a year and nobody could trace his wife and children. There was even an advert in the *Times* and in the *Glasgow Herald* offering them information "to their advantage", but they never showed. There was a nephew, but he didn't want the old place and put it on the market.'

'Looks like there's been a bit of bad luck about the place,' Tom said. 'Do you believe in that?'

'I don't know what to believe,' Alan said. 'But yes. There's something not right. That's for certain.'

'It didn't strike me until now that there's a pattern of sorts,' Beth said. Everybody looked at her. 'Look. Dalmuir built the house in eighty-nine. But he started it in the summer of the previous year. There's no pattern to his disappearance, but Laing lived here for thirteen years until 1909, which was twenty-one years after the work started, and that's when the girls disappeared. Then John Davidson. He was here, living quite peaceably until the summer of 1930, when his wife vanished and he went to the asylum. Next was Dr Kinross who moved in at the start of the thirties. He hanged himself in 1951. There's the pattern,' she said.

'I don't get it,' Alex said. 'What's the connection except a bunch of weirdos have been living here?'

'And thank you for that,' Alan said in an attempt at levity.

'Something has happened every twenty-one years,' Beth replied enthusiastically.

'Not quite,' Tom said. 'What about the Kinross sisters? They were here for near enough forty-five years. Nothing happened when they were here, except for the fact that their father was feeling up wee girls and hanged himself.'

'They were twins,' Mrs MacPhee said. 'Identical twins. It couldn't work through them.'

There was an immediate silence.

'What couldn't?' Alan asked, but the old woman held up a hand.

'Later, son. Let's hear it all, and then I'll have my say.'

'Well, except for them, there's been a pattern. After

them it was that McGrath man who was here until the turn of the year. And God knows what he was up to.'

'And now there's me,' Alan said drily. His throat was dry too.

'Does it really mean something? Can you get stone tapes? Or is this supposed to be like some Stephen King thing where the house stores up all its evil like a battery and lets it go every now and again.'

'No, not like that,' Mrs MacPhee said. But she didn't elaborate. 'Seumas Rhu, I know what happened to you, for there's no secret you can keep from me, and you've a wee bit of the knowledge of the MacPhees in you for all your daft ways. You tell them.'

Seumas looked out of place in the big lounge. He was wearing the boots that looked several sizes too big, and he twiddled his hat in his hands. It was hard to believe that somebody his age could be some mother's son, and that the mother was still in a position to treat him like a boy. Unlike the evidence of something wrong with the house, Alan had no difficulty in accepting what his eyes told him.

Seumas Rhu got through his story quickly, telling it in plain language, not elaborating. It sounded as though he'd had an hallucination. Alex thought that in normal circumstances she'd have considered it had been brought on by vertigo. Now she wasn't so sure.

'After that I got down off the ladder and went along the road to the Creel and had myself near enough a bottle of whisky before the place shut.'

'And I can vouch for that,' the old woman said. 'He came home like a smack in a gale and I had to put him to his bed. At his age, and all. And the cursing he did through that night never did any mother's heart good. And now you, Tam Callander,' Mrs MacPhee said, and Alan couldn't help smiling at the west coast diminutive. 'You've been holding back on us, it's my guess.'

Tom shook his head. 'No, I haven't. But what happened to me I've never made head nor tail of, and I don't know whether I imagined it or not. Anyway, it wasn't in the house. It was up at the trees.'

'Well, you might as well tell us.'

Alan stood up at this point and apologized. 'Can you hold everything for a minute, Tom? I have to check on Helen. And I want to make sure Tommy's gone down to the station with his friend. I'll have to go and pick him up at five.'

'I'll collect him if you want,' Beth said. 'You'd be better staying here.'

'That would be great,' Alan said, genuinely grateful. 'I don't want him coming home alone. He's made friends with the policeman's boy, and I can't think of a safer place for him to be than there.'

He went up to the bedroom where Helen was still fast asleep. It looked as if she hadn't moved. He stood and stared at her pale, drawn face and a wave of sadness flushed through him in a grey cloud. She would have to get some treatment, and he didn't know if he could go through that again. And after that? Was there any chance for them? He didn't even want to think about it. It filled him with dread because now he didn't even know if he wanted it any more.

He turned and left the room, closing the door softly behind him.

After the door catch snicked home, Helen lay still for a few seconds. Then her eyes flicked open. They were dead black. They stared straight at the ceiling.

Behind her the wall was vibrating very slowly and softly, like the ponderous, far-off beat of a heart. She heard it and acknowledged it without a flicker of movement. After a moment her eyes closed. She appeared to be asleep. But her body was resonating slowly with the distant beat.

Downstairs Alan sat back in his seat and looked at Tom.

'It happened only the other week,' the older man started.

'That was the night we met you down at the Harbour,' Beth interjected and Tom nodded, looking surprised.

'How did you know?'

'You came in looking sick, and finished nearly half a bottle of malt in one swallow. And if you *had* been sick, you would have told me.'

Tom nodded. 'Maybe I would.' Then he told them of the night he'd taken Gus for a walk up at the crossroads and had taken a short cut through the trees. 'It scared the living daylights out of me. I thought I was going to have a heart attack. And then I thought I was going mad. I've never seen the likes of these things before, and never want to again. There's no explanation in my mind for them. And it's not the first time I've seen something at those stones . . .'

He turned to Alan. 'You remember what I was telling you? I thought I saw my own son up there years back. That nearly killed me too, for he'd been dead and gone years past.'

Beth leaned on her father's shoulder, hugging him tightly.

'When did the accident happen?' Alan asked, keeping his voice low.

'It was midsummer of seventy-two. He was only fourteen.'

'That's the pattern,' Alex said into the silence. All eyes turned on her. 'That's another twenty-one years. When Beth explained it, I thought that something had to happen in seventy-two. Could that have been what happened?'

Everyone looked at the old woman who sat tiny but erect on the long couch, her small feet barely reaching the floor.

'It's something the old folks of these parts know of, though there's damn few left, and even fewer who know much. But I know a little of it, for that I got from my mother, and I was born in the year before

415

Andrew Dalmuir walked the dark path.' She stopped and looked around. She may have had only haunted hollows under her rutted brows but that's what she did.

'Some things you should know, even you, Seumas, who doesn't hold with the old things. You spell your name in the lowland way, but we are not of that clan that came down from the clearances. We were here a long time before that. We are the MacFiadh, the sons of the deer. And my uncle was the *Crom-druidh*, the keeper of the stones. He was Diarmad MacFie who stood against Dalmuir in the summer of 1888 and saw his sister's blood spilt on the *crom-leac*. That was how he cursed Dalmuir who had broken the midsummer. He put blood on the five stones of the dead days and took his people from here.' The old woman's voice had taken on the singsong quality of the Gaelic tongue as she warmed up.

'Since then the MacFie people have come back to this place in the great years. There is no undoing the *Fiadh* curse, at least none that I know of. My uncle told Dalmuir he was leaving the door open and that the man who broke the midwinter would remain to face the dark way.'

'What does that mean?' Alan asked.

'Listen and I'll tell you, as my mother told me. In the old calendar, the one by which we marked the seasons, there are *Great Years* when the heavens are in line. Every twenty-one years the sun and the great stars are in their appointed places and the moon turns in time to the months of the year. At those times the *thin* places, where all worlds meet, are joined. At the centre is the black keeper, the *Gleidhidh Gruamach* who guards the ways *between*. It has been so since the world was made and before the land parted and it will always be so.

'On midwinter of every year, the *Crom-Druidh* would make the sacrifice that would bind the *Gleidhidh* and open the door to give to this land the power. Ha, your teachers, and you yourself girl,' she said, nodding

416

uncannily towards Beth who was still sitting on the arm of the chair with her arm around Tom's shoulders, 'you write that these stones are calendars, while the old tales tell you different. No, they are not calendars. There were other ways of telling the seasons. These stones were the gateways to the middle kingdoms, and the Fiadh had the key to draw the strength from those places to here, the good and the bad. And the Druid folk used the stones to get through the dark ways and out through the *crom-leacs* while the keeper was bound with song.

'But what Dalmuir did was he fouled the ground at the year's end, in the dead days, and blood was spilt on the stone and the ceremony was never finished. The ceremony to close the gate, that was. And Dalmuir was cursed.'

'What did that mean?' Alex asked in a small voice.

'It meant that the black power from the dead kingdom came close in the great years and drew the owner of the house towards it, darkening his mind, bringing him down to the *Gleidhidh Gruamach*, the dark keeper of the ways. It meant that in those years, every one and twenty, the thin places, beyond where the dark one squats, are thinner still. Oh, he would like to come to this world, my mother told me, though I never believed her then for I was just a girl with summer in my heart. But that will never happen, not without the blood ritual.'

'Never heard of that,' Tom said. 'In fact, I've never heard of any of it. What's the blood ritual?'

'That's the way they open both sides of the gate, inside and out. To free *Gleidhidh* into this world. They must use virgin's blood and the blood of a bearing mother on the stones. And then they must use the blood of a first-born son. That would break open the doorway and make all the kingdoms meet, so my mother said, and she was blood sister to the Fiadh.' Mrs MacPhee stopped and swung her head around, eerily. She was tiny and wizened, but she was commanding the rest of them to listen. In the corner the twins played quietly with their building bricks, quite unaware of what was being said.

'So all this started a hundred years ago?' Alan asked.

'No. It started six thousand years ago.'

'And you really think there's some curse on this place?'

'I *know* it,' the old woman said. 'And if I had my eyes I would have known it sooner. I would have known the date. But I'm old. I get a telegram from the newcomer next year, don't you know?' she added with a small girlish giggle. 'For you, I can only say that you must leave this place for a while. After the midsummer the gateway narrows. The keeper will not draw you in as the gate closes, and he cannot come out because the ritual has never been done.'

'What about the dreams or whatever they were? When I walked into one room and found myself in another. And then when I got through the doors into places that don't exist?'

'Oh, but they *do* exist,' Mrs MacPhee said. 'Dalmuir, he broke up the stones, but they are still there. But not in the right order. There were thirteen gateways to the middle kingdoms and one gate to the dead lands where the dark keeper waits. And there are the wights, creatures of the dead lands. They are dark shadows, outriders of the night. They cannot exist in our light. But if the unbinding sacrifice was made, the *Gleidhidh Gruamach* would overcome the light. And if he came into this world, then this whole place would be in darkness.' The old woman stopped and hauled herself up off the couch. Seumas crossed the room to help her. 'That's my piece said. I don't know what you'll think of it, but I know it to be true, for my mother told me, and I've never told a living soul. Take heed, lad,' she said, turning to Alan who felt as if the woman was staring right into him.

'Take yourself and your family away from here a while. See what is happening to your wife. Get her out of here while there is time. There are powers of dark and powers of light. The dark powers use the weak and steal their hearts and minds. They move within and use the souls they conquer. Have no fear of those faerie-kissed,' she said, indicating the girls who still played silently in the corner. 'They sing another song. Nothing can harm them.'

'What do you mean, *another song*?' Alan asked bluntly.

'Can't you hear it?' the old woman asked. 'No, I suppose you don't, for you've not enough of the gift. The power of the two-in-one has been known since for ever. There's forces on the other side, and they are not all black. If the stones are a gateway, so are the souls of these faerie-kissed. The song of light comes from *there* through them. These babes have the power to protect against the dark, if they but knew it. Their song is clean and untouchable, and nothing from the dark side can harm them.'

She stopped and seemed to pin Alan with the shadowed sockets. 'There are many gateways, and your daughters are one of them. Your wife is another, don't you know. The dark has come in through her, and she has let it inside. She is at one with the darkness, the winter in summer. She must have some of the gift in herself, but it has withered and gone bad. Is she from around these parts?'

'No, but her grandmother came from around here.'

'Ah, the bloodline always shows,' the old woman nodded. She stood up slowly and swept them all with a blind gaze before turning away. The old woman walked out of the room unerringly, followed by Seumas. The small man turned at the door and looked back at the assembled group. He shrugged, but his face was solemn. His mother had spoken.

When they had gone, Alan went back into the living-room. The twins looked up and smiled, then went back to playing. He sat down again and said: 'Well, what do you think of that?'

'I don't know,' Tom said. 'I've lived in this peninsula all my life and I've never heard anything like it before. I'd heard bits and bobs about Dalmuir and Laing. Those kinds of stories hang around places like this for years.'

'It all seems to fit,' Alex said.

'Yes, it does,' Alan said. 'I don't know what to think. But to tell the truth, I'd rather believe a story like that than think I'm going crazy.'

'You're not going crazy,' Alex told him. 'Take my word for it.'

'I think you should leave for a while,' Tom Callander advised. 'You're welcome to stay down at my place if you like.' Beside him Beth, who was hanging on to her father's arm supportively and supportedly, nodded.

'Listen. Let me think about it. There's a million things I have to think about, and I don't know what to do about Helen.'

'I can send Dr Docherty along,' Alex volunteered. 'At the very least she needs some rest. He can get her into Kirkland for a couple of days.'

'That might be the best idea,' Alan said, nodding. Events were going too fast for him. He needed some time to think. He needed to sit down and consider everything that had been said that afternoon in the front lounge of his house. 'Can I give you a call later, once I've sat with it a while?'

'Sure you can,' Alex said. They all started to file out.

THIRTY-NINE

Midsummer

Alan went up to the bedroom where Helen was beginning to stir in her sleep. He shook her shoulder warily but gently, half expecting her to snap awake and launch herself at him. She slowly opened her eyes, looking a little dopy, and then, miraculously, she smiled at him.

'Hello, darling,' she said sleepily. 'Have I been dozing?'

Caught off guard, Alan didn't know what to say. There was a huge black bruise on Helen's cheek. You could almost make out the individual knuckle marks. He could have broken her jaw. 'Yes. The doctor gave you something to help you sleep.'

'Did he? What for?'

Alan sat down on the bed, feeling his knees go weak. 'You had some kind of seizure,' he said. That was close enough to the truth for him to tell it without stammering. He was never a successful liar.

Helen sighed. 'Oh, I feel so much better now,' she said. 'I feel as if I've been sick for ages, and now I feel well again. What day is it?'

Alan tried to think that one out. He'd lost track of time, he told her.

'Are you sure?'

'Of course I am. Why?'

'I can't remember anything. I've got to get your things ready for going back to work. You can't stay on holiday for ever, you know.' She made to haul herself off the bed, but didn't seem to have the strength.

'I've been back at work for weeks,' he said, looking at her oddly.

'Can't have,' she said dreamily. 'Silly. You've got a new office to go to. And a new job.'

'Can't you remember me going back?' he asked.

She opened her eyes and with obvious difficulty focused on him. She shook her head.

'You have been sick,' he said, feeling the relief and guilt surface within him.

'I don't remember,' she said. 'But now I feel good. As if I've just woken up. Where are the kids?'

'Downstairs having dinner.'

'What did you give them?'

'Noodles and chips,' he said, hardly believing he was having this conversation.

Helen smiled ruefully. 'I might have known. You men shouldn't be let loose in the kitchen. You just don't have a clue about what children should eat.'

'Don't worry about them. They're happy enough making a mess. I'll clean up after them.'

'And don't you worry about that. My kitchen's clean enough to be healthy and dirty enough to be happy. Tomorrow will be soon enough.'

Alan's mind was reeling with confusion. This was the woman who'd been copulating with a wall, for God's sake. She'd attacked him like an animal, and tried to strangle Alex Graham with her bare hands. She'd nearly starved the kids and she'd spent every waking minute cleaning and polishing the house to the total exclusion of all else.

He leaned over the bed, not knowing what to say. He had thought she was going mad, paranoid or schizoid. But obviously it had been some sort of withdrawal, probably brought on by stress. From the way she was talking, through the haze of sleepiness, she seemed so much like her old self. And with this thought all that had happened in the past few days seemed to fade into the background.

Alan put the kids to bed after taking them to see their mother. The twins were their normal selves, smiling delightedly when Helen hugged them, as if it had happened five times a day for months. Tommy was wary. Alan could see it in his stance, but even that faded when his mother put her arms around him and squeezed warmly. Later, when Alan was tucking him up in bed, he said, 'Is Mum all right now?'

'I believe she is, son,' Alan said, grinning down at the boy. 'She's been unwell, but the doctor gave her something and now she's better. I told you she would be, didn't I?'

Tommy nodded happily.

'Want me to keep the curtains open tonight?' Alan asked.

'Nah, it's OK, Dad,' Tommy said.

Dr Docherty came up to the house ten minutes later and gave Helen the once over. Downstairs at the front door, he told Alan that his wife seemed fine.

'I can arrange for a few days in Kirkland, if you want,' he said. Alan could tell that he was quite dubious about the whole thing. Docherty was a tall, elderly man with thin white hair and big horn-rimmed glasses. 'That's quite a bruise she has,' he said, making it sound both an accusation and a question at the same time.

'She had some sort of fit. I gave her the bruise.'

The doctor looked at him directly. Alan forestalled his next remark. 'I don't hit women. I don't hit my wife. Didn't Dr Graham tell you what happened this afternoon?'

'Yes, she did. Said your wife was very upset. Well, she looks a lot better now. Bed rest is what she needs, and she could do with some fattening up.' He gave Alan a prescription for some mild tranquillizers, 'just in case', and left.

By the time Alan went to bed, Helen was wide awake, and for the first time in what seemed like years, she was happy and animated. Alan had told her he'd take another day off work, and she tried to dissuade him.

'You've had enough time off already. You've got to get in there and earn that promotion. We need the money, remember?'

'We'll see in the morning,' he said, not yet convinced. Alan closed the curtains and pulled back the light duvet and slid into bed beside his wife. The turmoil in his mind had settled down to a slight swell. How could he have been so mistaken?

In the darkness of the room, his mind grabbed at justification. Alan Crombie was an ordered man. His whole career was based on the laws of physics and mathematics, chemistry and gravity. When he pressed the button on his expensive calculator, it always came up with the right answers because in the world in which he lived and worked there could only be one answer to any calculation. The strange conversation he'd had with Tom Callander and the rest down in the lounge tried to intrude on his mind, but he shooed it away. That was when he had been under impossible strain and his wife had been ill. This was now. He was back in the real world. Whatever he had thought must have been the result of the stress he'd been under. He'd been a fool not to have done anything about it, but now it was over.

In the dark of the room, Helen's hand stole slowly across his belly as he lay with his hands behind his head. Her fingers trickled through the hair and wormed into the cup of his navel. He felt warm goose bumps rise on his skin. Very slowly, very gently, she slid her hand further down, warm and soft. He felt himself react instantly.

'I've missed this,' she whispered. 'If only I wasn't so sleepy.' He could hear the laugh in her voice. She moved herself towards him, pressing her soft breast against his arm. For an instant he saw her against the wall, buttocks pumping slowly. He cast the thought away from him. That hadn't been Helen. That had been somebody sick.

Helen snuggled up to him and kissed him gently on the cheek. 'Maybe tomorrow,' she whispered. Within minutes she was asleep, nestling close to him.

Much later, before dawn lit the sky, Alan woke up with a strangled cry, springboarding out of the dream. His breath was hitching fast in his throat and his lungs were labouring like an old leaky steam engine. Down his back he could feel the sweat cold and clammy on his skin.

The image of the dream danced in front of his eyes in the darkness for several long minutes before it started to fade.

He'd been making love to Helen. She had been pressing herself down on him, undulating against him hard and fast, grinding her pubic bone against his. She had given a cry. *Yes. Oh Yes!* And a little grunt had followed it. She was pressing herself down on him, squashing him into the bed in the dark. Oh, she was going hard. With every thrust he could feel her weight, squeezing down, bending his ribs. His lungs had backed up and he'd tried to cry out, but the weight was too great. He had moved his hands across her back, trying to move her off so he could breathe, and he felt cold roughness. He opened his eyes, and inside his ribs his heart seemed to explode. He was in the room with four doors, lying on the floor, with his wife's hard, cold body ramming down on to him, threatening to push him down through the floorboards and into the cellar below and down into that great black pit that he knew was waiting for him. One of the doors was open, and Katie and Laney were walking hand in hand along an endless corridor. Aghast with horror, he tried to call out to them to come back, but the weight that was cracking his ribs had stopped his lungs. He swivelled and squirmed. He swung his head from under the shadow and saw Tommy outside the other wide door, writhing desperately on the moorland slope among the bones of dead men. Around him great black crows with craters for eyes were pecking at him. Their big black bodies were hopping on ungainly scaly claws, lunging with their huge shiny beaks. His son's face was covered in blood which streamed and gushed from gaping holes in his cheeks and in his golden hair, matting it with clotted red. Tommy was screaming for him, and his terror screech seemed to be whistling across the moor from a million miles away. Alan wriggled against the irresistible weight and tried to move from under. He was trapped. He was still inside her. He turned to look and the shock nearly stopped his heart. It was not his wife. It was a face made of stone, old and moss-covered, a grinning gargoyle that bore only a shadowy resemblance to the woman he'd been making love to. Moss covered the gaping eyes. Lichens moulded the stone teeth. Down between his thighs, he felt himself caught in a stone canal. It rasped hard, crushingly, against his tender skin. And then unbelievably, horrifying, powerful, it started to squeeze. The sides of the crevice began to close inexorably around him, trapping him inside the stone.

A huge and screeching chord of pain crashed through him as he felt his organ crushed flat. The agony was a supernova of white fire that burned through every nerve. He felt himself rise up on the bow-wave of pain that blanketed his whole being.

And inside that pain was the supreme agony of knowing that while he'd been playing, his children had been dying.

The shock was slowly fading. Alan was downstairs in the kitchen. He didn't reach for the brandy bottle. Instead, he made himself some hot chocolate and had a cigarette, the first for weeks. He hauled the smoke into his lungs and let it out again in a long, slow plume. The house was quiet. When he'd awoken with the images of pain and terror and horror dancing in front of his eyes, he'd been shaking with fright. Then he'd heard Helen's calm breathing beside him on the bed. After a couple of minutes, very tentatively and a lot fearfully, he had reached across to touch her. He had done so in the knowledge that if his hand touched anything rough and cold, he would scream and scream and not be able to stop. His fingers reached out in the dark and brushed up against Helen's side, just under her breast. It was warm and soft. It was feminine. It was human.

Down in the kitchen he realized again how wrong he'd been. This was proof positive. The strange room, the endless corridors, the huge grotesque sightless birds. They were all part of his imagination. Maybe Helen had been ill, but he hadn't been the picture of healthy rationality, had he? He'd built up a few coincidences and tried to make whole cloth out of shoddy. He'd stuck his nose into Andrew Dalmuir's century-old paranoia and had come up with the paranormal. He'd listened to a woman who was more than likely to be having delusions in senile dementia. They say that all old folk start to remember their childhood when the old cells start to falter and die off, don't they? And Tom, he'd seen his son, hadn't he? That was after a night down at the Harbour Inn. That kind of thing happened to bereaved parents. It was wish fulfilment.

And Alex Graham. Where did she fit in?

Alan sat down there in the quiet of the night kitchen, smoking his cigarette and drinking his hot chocolate. His dressing gown was slung over his shoulders and he was hunched across the pine table.

He didn't know where she fitted in. Either in any of this or with him. He remembered the kiss they'd had down at the foreshore when they'd fallen together. 'Let's be friends,' she'd said, and he'd agreed.

Now Helen was back and he didn't have a clue where he was in all that. His world had been on a roundabout that was out of control, but even then he couldn't deny the feelings he'd got when he thought of Alex. Had they been because of what had happened to Helen? Or despite it?

Alan believed it was probably the latter, but he didn't want to think about it just then. He didn't want to think about it primarily because when Helen had slid her hand across his belly and wormed it down through the hair sensuously towards his thighs, he hadn't seen Helen's face in the dark.

When he was reacting to that soft touch, it was Alex's face he had envisaged. He didn't know what to make of that, so he tried to avoid it.

He lit another cigarette.

FORTY

That morning had been the sunniest of the year so far. Helen had been up at the crack of it, and when Alan stumbled downstairs he was met not by the all too familiar odour of wax polish and bleach, but the tempting aroma of bacon crisping nicely under the grill. He went into the kitchen and Tommy and the girls smiled up at him.

'Morning, Dad,' Tommy said. The twins merely beamed wider.

'Hi, dear,' Helen welcomed him, straightening up from the oven where the plates were warming. She shot him a smile and followed through with a peck on the cheek. She swivelled her hips and bumped her thigh suggestively against his. 'Sleep well?'

'Like a log,' he said, unwilling to tell the whole truth. 'Now I need my vittles. What's on?'

'Working man's breakfast. I went down to the butcher's this morning. Awfully nice chap. They've got time to stop and chat around here.'

Would wonders ever cease? Alan wolfed the breakfast. The kids made inroads into theirs.

'I'm taking another day off,' Alan declared. 'I can make up the time later.'

'There's no need. I feel great. Honestly. I'd feel awful if you took more time off,' Helen protested.

'I think it's a bit soon. I'd just like to be sure.'

'Well, I *am* sure,' Helen said brightly but firmly. She leaned down and pecked him on the forehead. 'If I need a sleep in the afternoon, the girls and I can have a lie-down. But honestly, I'm feeling really great. Better than ever.'

'I could spend the day getting a few things sorted out. Just until you're back on your feet.'

'Don't you bother. I'll be fine. Honest. I've given you a hard enough time of late, and you'd better not push it with MacKenzie-Kelso. Not until you're a senior partner, and then you can stay home and play golf in the afternoons.'

'I was thinking of getting somebody in to help you with this place. I think we can run to it.'

'Oh, I shouldn't worry. This old place can take care of itself. And if I feel myself getting run down again, I'll let you know. But remember, you're not to let me get into the state I was in again, OK?'

Alan nodded. He wouldn't. Eventually he capitulated under her bright insistence. At the door, he again asked her if she was sure about this. She stood with her hands on her hips, head cocked to the side.

'If I wasn't, I'd certainly have another day in bed with you running around after me, wouldn't I?'

'Well, phone me if you need anything.'

'I will, but I won't have to,' she said. She leaned forward to give him another peck on the cheek, then pulled his head forward to kiss him on the mouth. Her tongue rippled over his. She pulled back after a while and looked at him, brown eyes bright.

'Work hard,' she said. Then she ran her forefinger down the front of his shirt. It bumped over the top of his trousers and continued lightly to his crotch. 'But not too hard, huh?'

At the office an hour later, Alan phoned Tom but got Beth on the line. He explained that Helen had had a sudden improvement, and asked her to contact Alex and let her know.

'What about yesterday?' Beth asked, and Alan decided not to tell her about the sea change that had come over him. He had driven away from Cromwath in the bright sunlight and had headed into the sun on the way east to Glasgow. The day had been fine. The night was past.

'I'll talk to Tom later. But I think things will be all right now,' he said, and hung up the phone.

In the morning he buried himself in the reports of the northern contracts with hardly a pause. He called home twice and Helen was fine. She scolded him gently for worrying too much. In the afternoon, Mike Toward arrived in his office and sat himself down on the edge of the desk.

'You were right about those quantities,' the big American said. 'They're way out.'

Alan looked up, bemused. He didn't know what his associate was talking about.

'Your house. The building materials, remember?'

'Oh yes.' Alan had forgotten all about them. In fact he didn't want to know now.

'I checked with the figures I'd taken down, and they're way out. Based on the area of the rooms and their height, the stone, bricks, timber and mortar are enough to make two houses. I've seen some contract scams in my time, but this one takes the prize. Your man Dalmuir, he was ripped off to a band playing. I thought you said he was a businessman?'

'Yes, he was,' Alan said distractedly. His mind was on the paperwork in front of him on the desk. The matter of Dalmuir's chronicle had receded from his mind, its seeming importance diminished.

'Well, he was no slicker. More of a sucker. Your builder – what was his name, Lappa? Zappa?'

'Latta,' Alan filled in.

'Yeah, him. He took old Dalmuir for the big one. He must have been some mover to get away with it. Shame all that good stuff went somewhere else, Alan. Otherwise you'd be living in a stately home, little buddy.'

'What makes you think I don't?' Alan asked him.

'Can't be stately, *compadre*. You ain't got no pool,' Mike said, and left, laughing at his own joke.

Alan looked down at the short set of figures Mike had worked out, probably on the Apple-Mac. He picked them up, scanned them quickly and shrugged. He opened his briefcase and slung the pages inside along with the rest of the documents. Then he went back to work.

At four, Alex Graham phoned to ask about Helen. Alan told her how she'd woken up and was back to normal.

'Beth told me. It's kind of hard to believe. I saw her yesterday and there's no way anybody can be just *fine* twenty-four hours after that.'

'I can't explain it either, but it's true.'

'I think you should keep an eye on her.'

'What do you mean?'

'Well, I know she's had problems before, and you told me what she's been like recently. That's not just something that evaporates overnight.'

Alan knew what she was trying to tell him, but his sense of relief over Helen's change was too great to withstand.

'Well, I will take your advice,' he said. 'I'll make sure she comes down to the surgery for check-ups.'

'And what about the thing we were talking about yesterday?'

'I don't know,' he said quickly.

'Neither do I, but you seemed so sure yesterday.'

'A lot of things have happened since then.'

'I see. I'm sorry to intrude.' She sounded a bit crestfallen and immediately Alan felt bad about it.

'No, Alex, you're not intruding, and I'm sorry if I gave that impression. It's just that she really does seem to be fine. Maybe what she needed was a good night's sleep. I know it's a bit confusing, but it's great to have some semblance of normality. And I promise I'll talk to you if there's any hint of anything going wrong. In fact I'll drop in at Tom's later tonight. I'll see you there and we can talk about it.'

'I'd like that,' she said.

It was a half-hour after that that Alan phoned home again. Helen answered on the third ring. She sounded bright.

'What sort of day are you having?' she asked blithely.

'Curate's egg,' he said. 'Some good, some just average.'

'I've had a great day. Sat on my backside and did nothing. It's been like a holiday.'

'Maybe that's what you need.'

'So I hope you're not rushing home. I'm giving the kids a fresh salad, but there's nothing big planned.'

'Oh, don't worry about me. I can grab a bite here.'

'Good idea. Why don't you take Mike for a pizza? He's missing his culture, and you two haven't had a boys' night in ages.'

He went through the routine of asking if she was sure, if she could cope, if she would be all right, then capitulated. She did seem on top of the world, and he hadn't had a night out with somebody normal in a month of Sundays. He promised he wouldn't be late, and meant it.

It was the pizza that did it. Alan and Mike worked until seven and then went to Sannino's where the big American was crazy for the Italian wine and they chewed the fat about the office and the big jobs they were working on as a team and everything else that came to mind. Mike was stuffing himself with a *calzone* and his huge frame seemed to soak up almost a litre of the dark red wine without effect, except that he became even more expansive and boisterous.

'Oh, listen. I never told you what happened Friday,' he said.

Alan raised his eyebrows.

'I sent Suzie to the photocopier with a whole bunch of stuff. You know her? Terry Kelman's secretary?

433

Sweet kid. I was up to my neck in reports and I was busting a gut to get them out. The kid takes her time and I'm bawling at her to get her ass in gear. Jesus, I could have kicked myself!'

'Why?'

'She never answered, so I went along the corridor, and there's the kid lying on the floor. I thought she was dead, you know? It turned out she was pregnant. Had a miscarriage right there. I couldn't believe I was giving her a bad time and all the while she's nearly dying. We got an ambulance right away and she's going to be all right. Pity about the baby though. Little Suzie only got married last year.'

Alan nodded absently. Something tugged at his memory. He chased for it and then the picture came zooming right back like a punch.

He saw Helen down in the basement, about two days after they'd moved into the house. He remembered he'd heard the cry. She'd been kneeling there, doubled over with cramp, and the blood had been dripping in a long, almost solid, thick stream on to the wall and the flagstones. It had been a sudden, unexpected flow, because she'd been pregnant at the time though he hadn't known it.

Pregnant. A bearing mother, he heard old blind Mrs MacPhee's voice in his mind.

Mike was saying something, but his voice was fuzzy, coming from far away. Alan saw the scene run through his head again. Then he heard the old woman, blind but somehow seeing.

'*The blood of a virgin and the blood of a bearing mother and the blood of a firstborn son.*' Even the singsong quality of the voice came back like an echo.

And in that memory, something else came back to him. Something else about blood on the stones. Inside him, his stomach did that familiar rolling loop as his muscles clenched. Dread simply washed through him.

'Hey, man, I didn't mean to put you off,' Mike said, and Alan's attention was grabbed to the present.

'No, it's not that,' Alan said, shaking his head in emphasis. 'It's just that . . .'

'Just what?'

'I don't know what. But I've got to go. I have to speak to somebody.'

'But you haven't finished,' Mike protested.

'Can't wait, Mike. I'll talk to you later,' Alan said distractedly. He got up from the table and dropped his napkin, leaving his half-eaten pizza and an almost full glass of wine. He walked quickly out of the door.

The big American watched him. 'OK, boss. I'll get the tab,' he said, and grabbed his fork.

Tom Callander picked up the phone and said, 'Hello.'

Alan didn't even introduce himself. 'Something happened up at the stones in the winter. What was it again?'

'Oh, it's yourself, Alan. I hear the wife's a bit better.'

'Yes she is, thanks. But listen, this is important. What happened up there in the winter at the start of the year?'

'It was the wee girl. Chrissie Watt. There was an accident up at the trees. She fell off an old pine log and it rolled on her. It was a right mess.'

'And she was crushed against the stone?'

'That's the way it was. Two of the youngsters found her. She was alive but pretty far gone. She died in the ambulance. Why do you ask?'

'It was something the old woman said yesterday. About the blood on the stones. You remember?'

'Sure I do. I'm not that old.'

'About the virgin thing. How old was the girl?'

'About nine or ten.'

'And Seumas's mother said something about a bearing mother too.'

'Yes, she did,' Tom said flatly.

'Well, that's happened too.'

'How do you mean?'

'My wife, man. She was pregnant when we came here. And she bled down in the basement.'

There was a silence at the end of the phone, then Tom said: 'Where are you phoning from?'

Alan told him.

'Maybe you should be a bit closer to home.'

'I'm on my way. But listen, could you take a look in? It's going to take me an hour and a bit even with good traffic.'

'Of course I will,' Tom said. 'I'll give Seumas Rhu a shout, and we'll both get over there.'

Alan was gunning the car three minutes later, heading down towards the Kingston Bridge which would take him along the motorway to loop round ten miles west to the Erskine Bridge that cut back over the Clyde and on to the road for home. He was doing ninety when he nosed the car up on to the first span. On the straight, he flicked a glance at his watch. It was nine fifteen, the night still bright. Then he looked again at the liquid crystal display. It gave the date, 21 June. Midsummer.

FORTY-ONE

Mrs MacPhee insisted on going with them. Tom had pulled in at Seumas's cottage, almost blocking the narrow road with his four by four. The sun was getting low over the Cowals on the far side of Loch Creggan. It was still light, but the shadows were getting longer.

'He sounded pretty agitated,' Tom explained. 'Something about his wife's blood on the stones, and he said she'd been pregnant.'

'Ah, that's the start of it,' the old woman interjected. 'Didn't I tell you? And that daft man never said a thing about it.'

'He phoned this morning to say his wife was all right. Beth took the call. She didn't know what to make of it, but you can't force yourself on somebody.' Tom stopped, then said: 'He asked me if I remembered what had happened up at the stones in the winter. I didn't know what he was talking about, but then it came back. That wee girl that was crushed under the tree.'

'Aye, that was a hellish thing to happen. Bella Watt's never been the same since her wee one died,' Seumas said. 'It was her blood on the stones. John Lindsay told me afterwards. He said he was nearly sick.'

'The boy,' Seumas's mother said in a voice that was more like an inward gasp. 'It needs the boy. Don't you see? Two parts of the ritual have already been fulfilled. If it gets the boy, his blood will be spilt too. All of it. And when it takes him, there will be nothing that can stop it, and all the wights of the dead lands, from coming through to this place.'

Tom stared at her.

'Look at me. These eyes have been closed for nigh

437

on twenty years. But I can still *see*,' she said. 'I can still see what was and what is and what is to come. You get that boy and those babies out of that house, for it is a black place. And unless that gateway is closed for ever you will let the *Gleidhidh Gruamach* through from the dead places to ravage this peninsula. There will be blood spilt the likes of which you cannot imagine.'

The old woman's voice had taken on that melodic quality, as if she was quoting from a far-off memory. The lines and creases of her face seemed deeper, like crevasses on brown earth.

'That's the truth of it. You get that boy and bring him out of there, and then you must destroy the stones and break the circle. Don't let anything stop you. If you do that this midsummer night, then it will *never* come through.' She stopped and turned to Seumas, who towered over her by a good span of inches and still only came up to Tom's chin. 'You take me down there,' she commanded.

'No,' he said flatly. 'You can't come, Mother. Let Tom and myself go down there and we'll bring those wee-uns up here to you.'

'And how are you going to get in there?'

'We'll just walk in,' Tom said. 'She can't stop us.'

'Ha. You say *she*.' She turned her face up to the sky. 'Feel the very *air* change. That poor woman no longer has any self, not if her blood was spilt on the stones in that place. It will not *let* you in.'

'We'll see about that,' Tom said. 'Come on, Seumas, let's get down there.'

With that, the quarryman and the old handyman left the cottage and got into Tom's rugged little jeep and drove the four hundred yards into a nightmare.

On the way Tom said: 'How are we going to do this? Maybe we should get John Lindsay?'

'Fat chance of him believing it,' Seumas said.

'What about Mrs Crombie? What do we tell her?'

'I reckon we'll have to worry about that tomorrow.

My mother's old as Methuselah, but there's nothing wrong with her head, except for the wee bit of lore she got from her mother. If she says a thing is true, then you'd better take it as gospel.'

We'd better be right, Tom Callander thought to himself. The two of them were preparing to go down to their neighbour's house, and if necessary abduct three small children. Under any circumstances what they intended was a crime of enormous magnitude. But the quarry owner was different from the man who'd taken his old dog for a walk up the Peaton Hill. That night he'd seen something that had kicked him in the soul. And after listening to the strange group as each told a strange tale, he had grasped the gaping truth of it. Tom Callander was a practical, pragmatic man. But he was no fool. If it looked like a duck and quacked, then there was no getting away from it. You just hoped it would fly close enough to train the twin barrels on it and slowly squeeze the trigger. For him, one and one made two, and if the equation added up to something so awful that it was sore to believe, then that was the way of it. You just took it and accepted it and decided what the hell you were going to do about it. His conversion had been total.

At the Crombies' house, Tom wheeled straight in between the stone pillars and powered up the driveway, sending stones scattering across the lawn in a hard spray.

The storm doors were closed. Every curtain was drawn over dark panes that seemed to swallow, rather than reflect, the fading light of the day.

Tom rapped on the big door. The noise seemed to echo down a hollow cavern. There was no reply.

'Try the back door,' he said to Seumas Rhu. The small man went off round the side of the house. It was more shadowed at the rear, in the pathway between the vegetable garden and the house. On one side was a tightly clipped box hedge that Seumas himself had shorn, running parallel to the stone wall. The back door, shaded under a small porch, was firmly closed. He tried the handle and it turned under his hand, but the latch never moved. It was locked. He moved away holding a hand up over his head like a sailor on lookout, and peered into the kitchen. It was dark in there. There was no light, not even the little red wink you would normally expect from a kettle plug or an immersion heater. The kitchen door was open, gaping black into the velvety darkness beyond. There was a slick of dust on the pane and Seumas pressed his face closer to see into the room, using the sleeve of his jacket to wipe a swathe clear. His reflection dimly stared back at him, a dim Seumas, vague and shot with shadow. Then the reflection rippled, and the small man pulled his head back in surprise. His image seemed to *flex*, and then it was suddenly clear, solid.

He looked at himself, startled, and then his own eyes widened as the reflection changed. Instead of looking into clear glass, it was like peering into a dark, warped mirror. The face grew broader, as if it were being inflated from within, and the lines that were already heavy creases on either side of the mouth became deep crevasses bracketing a coarse mouth. But there was something about the eyes that drew Seumas's gaze. They had retreated into dark hollows, throwing back none of the flimsy light. The skin around them puckered and shrivelled, burying the eyes in flaps of wrinkled skin. More creases appeared on his forehead and his ears seemed to twist and wrench, growing long and pendulous. From the thickened lips a drool of saliva dripped on to his chin. The lips curled inwards as the face crumpled, ageing dramatically, like an apple that has fallen and rolled to shrivel under a hot autumn sun.

Seumas, no youngster, saw himself decaying. In the space of two or three seconds he had a vision of what it would be like. The blindness, just like his mother's, the shrivelling and desiccating onslaught of senility. It horrified him so much and so suddenly that he jerked himself back from the window with a hacking gasp. In front of him, the reflection hauled itself away from the pane, into the dimness of the room. And then again he saw it change and grow and flow into something else. Something black and warped. He felt the force of pure evil reach out to him, pulling and tugging at him. He felt himself take a step forward and then a shudder ran through him and he twisted his neck, pulling his face away from the sight of it. The connection broke and he staggered back. Sweat was already running down the creases of his cheeks. Involuntarily, he shot a glance back to the window, expecting to see the black, looming shape come forward, crash through the thin glass, reach for him and drag him back into the house and those dismal shadows beyond the kitchen door.

But there was nothing there. There was not even a reflection of himself. The deep black in the house just sucked up all the light and swallowed it.

Tommy had known there was something wrong. The girls were in bed, put there by their mother who had washed them and looked out fresh nightgowns for them and made them cocoa. That day Tommy had seen the difference in her and had welcomed it with great relief, which was why his strange antennae, the knowing part of his mind which was aware of things that he didn't understand, had shut itself down. Like his father, he was so surprised at the change in Helen that he had wanted more than anything else to have things back to normal.

He was sitting on the couch, feet curled up underneath himself and reading a book, when suddenly the ambience in the room, until then still warm, went instantly brittle and cold. Inside his head, very faintly, he could hear the far-off sound of rasping, as if somewhere in the house wood was being crunched. His nostrils flared involuntarily as a brief stale whiff of damp rot and wet fungus spread from nowhere. It was the same smell that had hit him when he'd landed on the bleak moor among the mouldering bodies of the dead men. A little shudder worked its way up his spine, and on his neck the hairs started to stand to attention, tingling coldly on his skin. Apprehension surged through him before he had time to think. He whirled, dropping the book from his knee. It bounced on the couch and landed with a soft smack on the floor. The sound of rasping seemed to be all around, not coming from any one direction. It seemed to emanate from inside the walls. The air felt almost solid, thick and threatening, hard to suck into his lungs.

There was a sudden scraping sound from the kitchen. A chair being pushed back across the floor. Then his mother's voice: 'Bedtime, Tommy, come and get your coffee.'

Tommy didn't drink coffee. His dad never let him. In the wink of an eye, faster than the beat of his heart which was already beginning to power up high in his chest, he realized that his mother was not right again.

Against his wishes, his feet dragged themselves forward quietly on the carpet. He opened the door. His mother was at the end of the hallway, standing against the wall. 'It's time you were in bed,' she said.

'Yes, Mum,' he said quietly, trying not to look at her, knowing that if he did, she would be staring down at him with the emptiness in her eyes, and the blackness pulsing from behind them. He didn't want to see that. He wanted to go up to his bed and shut the door and pull the blankets over his head and pray for his father to come home. He turned to the right to walk past her, going towards the stairs. There was a soft snick and his eye caught the movement. Helen's hand was on the door that led down to the cellar. The knob twisted, the hasp clicked and she pulled it open. A line of darkness became a pillar of darkness and then a gaping black rectangle as it swung wide. He stared down there. The banister of the stair was only visible for three or four feet before it was swallowed by shadow.

'Tommy,' his mother said very softly. There was a strange echo behind her words, as if her voice was split in two and then joined together again, just out of phase. 'This way. I want to show you something.'

Tommy felt the blood drain from his face. A little nerve jumped and kicked behind his knee. He felt his head moving slowly from side to side in silent refusal.

'Do what you're told,' Helen said. She took her hand off the door handle and reached out towards him. Her other hand was behind her back. For the first time ever, Tommy disobeyed his mother. He jinked back instinctively, still shaking his head, now more vigorously. She had something in her other hand. What was it? A knife? Her free hand whipped past him, fingers curled into hooks.

'Come here, boy. *Do what your mother tells you!*' The undersound was stronger, almost a growl in her voice.

'I don't want to go down there,' Tommy said, his voice shaky and high. He backed off and almost fell on the first stair. She lunged at him again and he saw the glint in her other hand. It was a bread knife. His eyes, shocked and wide, flicked up to hers. It was like looking into black whirlpools.

'Come down here, or I'll make you sorry.'

I am sorry. Sorry. Sorry. Sorry. He wanted to shout it aloud. To make her stop. To change her. The words wouldn't come from his locked-up mouth. He whirled as she came at him, stretching to grab him. His muscles froze for an instant, then came back to life with a kick that sent him backwards a yard to land on his backside on the fourth stair. He whirled and scooted up there two at a time as fast as his legs could pump. Emergency bells were clanging up and down his spine and his skin puckered at the soft bit between his shoulderblades where, in his mind's eye, he saw the hooked fingers come down and grab right into him; or worse, where the point of the kitchen knife drove down and through into his spine. That thought hit him like a blow and the momentum carried him to the top of the stairs, feet pattering a tattoo on the treads. Behind him his mother's heavier footsteps pounded. He dodged right at the head of the stairs and skittered along the hallway. On either side of him, the walls bowed out elastically, bending towards him, shoving at him. It was as if the house was breathing.

The passage went suddenly dark, and a rasping, tearing sound filled the air. Above that came the sound of pursuit, a heavy drumbeat. Tommy slipped, stumbled and went crashing towards the far wall. He raised his hand to protect his head, and the whole wall opened like a mouth. He toppled towards it head first, and the split slammed shut on him, catching him across his waist. His legs kicked in the strangely pulsing corridor. Ahead of him, on the other side of the wall, there was blackness that went on for ever.

The rasping sound was loud in his ears. He kicked and struggled against the crushing bite of the wall that had opened and swallowed him.

And behind him came his mother with the mad blankness in her eyes, with the knife.

Seumas was panting when he got round to the front of the house again. Tom noticed, but didn't ask why.

'It looks empty,' he said. 'But I think they're in there. I'm sure I can hear something.' Tom put his ear to the door and listened. There was a deep pounding that sounded like a far-off, muffled pile-driver hammering down a shaft. And above that there was a rasping sound like an old double-handed spring saw ripping up an old log.

Behind them somebody spoke and both of them came close to breaking the all-time record for standing jumps. It was Beth and Alex who had come across the lawn instead of crunching up the driveway. Tom had

444

phoned his daughter at her friend's house to tell her where he was going. He had also told her to stay put and let him handle whatever was going on.

'What's happening?' she asked her father.

'Mrs MacPhee says we should get the kids out of here, and I think she's right.'

'What's happened to Mrs Crombie?' Alex asked. 'Didn't Alan say she was much better?'

'He did say that, but now he's not so sure. I think they're all in there, but there's not a light on in the place. I think we should get John Lindsay. Beth, you go. Tell him there's been an accident. I'll explain when he gets here.' He turned to Seumas, smiling a hard smile. 'If I can, that is.'

'If she's taken a turn for the worse, then I'd better have a look at her. Dr Docherty's down in Kirkland tonight.'

Alex walked up to the door and knocked on it. And in that moment the Virginia creeper which mixed with the honeysuckle that covered most of the wall at the front of the house seemed to flow off in a wave, whipping towards her. Thin, corded tendrils wrapped themselves around her, looping like snakes, almost in slow motion, but so swiftly she could not stop them. Two of the creepers lashed around her neck. Another, almost as thick as a finger, a length of fibrous, rooty rope, whipped around her body, pinioning an arm against her. Alex let out a small, strangled cry that sounded as if she was being choked. Another stringy sucker coiled itself around her legs, seeming to grow in a spiral from her thighs to her ankles in a mad spurt. Then it began to pull.

Alex felt hard cables dig into her. She lost her balance and started to fall, and her weight made the terrible grip on her throat monstrous. She tried to cry out, but the squeeze was too great. Blood surged into her face. She felt her eyes begin to pop under the pressure. There

445

was a buzzing in her ears. Her one free arm thrashed desperately.

She didn't even know that Beth Callander, faster than her father in this instant, had leapt right up to the door and launched herself at the writhing foliage. She was screaming with fright and panic and absolute fury. Her hands in front of her, she grasped the twisting stems and hauled at them, desperately trying to pull them from her friend's throat.

A tendril of honeysuckle draped itself over her shoulder and swung under her armpit. It rippled, then clenched, almost hauling her up into the air. The sweet smell of the high-summer blossoms filled the air, cloying and somehow sick. Beth's hands were still scrabbling at the loops around Alex's neck. She could see her friend's face go dark red and then purple. Her fingers wormed between the branch and the skin it was squeezing, and she pulled hard, letting out a high squeak of effort. Something gave. At first Beth thought it was her finger, but the tendril suddenly broke, flinging her arm back. Alex gasped, hacking hoarsely. Then the creeper on the left of the porch flung itself down off the wall and covered them both just as Tom Callander and Seumas rushed to help. There was a crunching and crackling and rippling as all four fought against the grip of the coiling, wriggling creepers.

Above them the sky darkened as a bank of cloud swirled in like a cloak to blot the fading rays of the sun.

FORTY-TWO

Tommy hung over the chasm of blackness while the wall twisted and vibrated, crushing him so hard he felt he was being bitten in half. His mouth opened in a silent scream because he couldn't draw breath.

Behind him he could sense the *thing* that was in his mother, that had invaded his mother, stalk him along the corridor. A voice in his brain shrieked: *'Help me. Oh please help!!!'*

The thought blurted out, directionless into the dark. And as it went, it was met by something that responded. A ringing sound cut through the ripping and rending on the inside of the walls and overpowered them. It was the sweet, clear notes he had heard inside his head, in the dream, when his sisters had rescued him from the endless corridors.

The sound swooped up on him in the blackness and instantly the wall convulsed in a violent peristalsis and just seemed to spit him out into the corridor. There was a snap as the hole in the wall closed, leaving a jagged line on the wallpaper, but Tommy didn't see it. He was tumbling backwards, head over heels, like a thrown doll. He rolled on the carpet runner and hurtled between his mother's legs as she stood in the corridor a scant two yards behind him. He twisted and sprang to his feet, moaning with fear, ran in the other direction and crashed against the door of the twins' room.

Despite the sudden freezing fear he was, somewhere in the high regions that floated above his swirling, horrified thoughts, aware that the change in his mother, the awesome metamorphosis, was not just a danger to him. That she meant to kill him was startlingly clear.

But just as clear was the fact that his little sisters would be next.

His fingers scrabbled for the handle and slipped. Behind him he could hear the pounding of his mother's feet, hard and ponderous, heavier than they could possibly be. Her shadow loomed on the wall opposite, where the hallway was swelling outwards. He grabbed for the handle again, fingers slippery with sudden sweat, and twisted hard. It turned, the door opened, and he tumbled headlong into the room. He kicked out with his foot and caught the edge of the door, sending it slamming closed. He got to his feet again and grabbed for the chair that was tucked under the little table against the wall. He hauled it out and jammed it under the handle of the door, the way he'd seen Tom Selleck do in *Magnum*. As soon as the top of the chair-back was fixed, there came an almighty crash against the door. It rattled from lintel to floor. Tommy staggered back and turned into the room.

The twins' beds were empty and his heart fell like a stone. There was another huge crash and the door buckled inwards with a screech of bending wood.

'*Come out of there you fucking little bastard!*' his mother screamed at him in that double voice that was underlaid by a roaring echo. It was not her voice at all. It was the voice of something else. It sounded riven by the cawing of the monstrous, unsighted crows that pecked and raved on the dead barren moor.

Tommy backed away on quaking legs. He crossed to the window and looked out into a jet-black night. The clouds were swirling like a whirlpool, deep and inky. There was a strange orange and purple tinge out there. It didn't look real. The door bulged in again behind him under a massive blow and a piece of the moulding splintered and whirred off past his ear. The old cupboard door set in the wall was open. Tommy scrambled over the beds towards it and leapt inside. It was the only haven. He pulled the door shut behind

448

him even though he knew he would be unable to lock it against the thing that was trying to batter down the other door. As he stepped into the closet he didn't even notice that no clothes were hanging there. The door snicked closed behind him, plunging him into total darkness. He took two steps forward and walked into the room with the four doors.

Out at the front door Tom and Seumas were struggling to free the women from the tendrils that were whipping in tight hard coils around them. Both men were festooned with the creepers which had snaked out of the green foliage like living ropes. Tom grabbed for Beth, ignoring the pain of one runner as it knotted itself around his bicep. Seumas had Alex by the waist and, incredibly, had lifted her off the ground.

Then across the lawn, patting the ground ahead with her gnarled stick, old Mrs MacPhee came quickly towards them, her voice harsh and loud, and the tendrils fell away from them. The old woman raised her stick and started laying into the green folds and loops of the creeper, almost singing in a high voice. She was chanting in Gaelic.

Where the *cromach* hit, the Virginia creeper just broke off and seemed to shrivel. Bits of it fell down on the stone steps and crumbled into brittle brown chaff. Alex felt the inexorable, unbearable pressure on her ribs suddenly give. Beth, who was screaming with pain at the grip of a tendril that had lassoed her chest and both arms, felt a huge relief as the pain cut off. The two men stumbled backwards as the grasp on them failed and their momentum threw them away from the mêlée. Tom almost knocked the old woman down as he spun out from the now crackling and dying creeper.

The four of them stood there, breathing heavily. Alex was standing with her head bent with exhaustion, hands on her knees. She felt the hot flush of nausea rise in her throat and swallowed it down.

'I told you I had to be here. Did you think it would let you in?' the old woman asked haughtily. 'No. This is where the kingdoms meet at the wrong time. This is the midsummer and this place is locked in the five dead days of winter. The chaos of hawthorn is rooted here, and only the rowan of summer can open the door.'

'What can we do?' Tom asked.

'The only thing is to save that boy. He is the key to the door that the *Gleidhidh Gruamach* needs. His blood is what will free him from the crossing of the ways. The boy must be found.'

'Listen, you two. Bring John Lindsay up here,' Tom said. He fumbled in his pocket, and threw the keys to Beth. 'Make sure he gets here quick as you can.'

Beth nodded and ran for the car with Alex on her heels. They almost clipped the pillar on the way as Beth steered round hard, all four wheels in drive, and on to the road beyond.

On the curve down at the foreshore, Alex said: 'What did she mean about the hawthorn and the rowan?'

'It's from the old Celtic tree calendar. Thirteen months and five dead days. The hawthorn is *Uath* in the old language. It stands for chaos and destruction and dreamlands. It's the thirteenth number. The rowan is *Luis*, which stands for the sacred fire, the clean force of light. It is the sixth month, and that means now. What the old woman meant was that something has happened to change all that. In the house, she says it's midwinter.'

'Can that be true?'

'Can what happened to us there be true? Either we've had a collective hallucination or I'm going to have to burn my history books. All the stuff I learned about our people, my ancestors and yours, I thought was all symbolism. The Celtic legends have always been alive for me, but now they really look as though they *are* alive.' Beth hauled on the wheel again and along the straight towards the little police station.

On the far side of the loch Alan was hammering along the road. His lights were on full beam and he took the bends like a rally driver, keeping the revs up high and bulleting into the corners at seventy. Twice on the winding road he'd come close to rolling the car when he'd booted the pedal to the floor only yards from the bright tail-lights of cars in front and he'd swung out to overtake on dark, blind bends. His luck was phenomenal. On one rare straight stretch he risked a flick of a glance across the water to the head of the peninsula. Over on the far side of the firth, the lights of Gourock winked orange and white. But on the peninsula itself, a huge black cloud rolled over the headland, a black, threatening mass that plunged Creggan into almost wintry darkness. When he saw that, his heart sank again. It just looked so wrong. The cloud swirled like a dark maelstrom, a black galaxy. It looked as if it was being churned up from the village itself and stirred by a huge mad hand.

In the house, in the strange, four-doored room, it was as if a huge tuning fork had been struck and then pressed right down into the house, sending an oscillating wave into its very fabric. Behind that was the rasping, crunching sound from within the walls. It sounded like saw's teeth biting or jaws crunching. Ahead lay darkness. Tommy peered in, casting his eyes left and right, looking for any sign of the twins, fearful of taking that step forward and between the door frames. Then behind him he could hear the screeching of what was chasing him and he turned, startled, and dived through the doorway and on to the stairs.

Except it wasn't the stairs.

He was on the roof over the stairwell, and yet it was flat beneath his feet. Above him the top banister on the stairhead was out of reach; the steps themselves going higher up the left wall and turning to reach away on the right were fading into the distance, narrowed by perspective. Far away, high up there, was the floor of the bottom hallway. The stairway was upside-down. The ceiling under his feet shifted and he slid down it, catapulted through the air to land on the now-righted steps in a dizzying whirl. His feet hit hard and his knees buckled, and then he went right through the tread as if he'd plunged into treacle. He could feel himself being pushed through a membrane, inside the skin of the stairs. It was a rubbing sensation on his skin and a cold, rasping feeling inside him as if the cells of his body and the molecules of the steps were suddenly merged in the passing. He sank very quickly, feeling the strange, inside-out feeling swamp up his hips and chest. His vision faded as the inside of the wood passed in front of his eyes. There was a soft tug on his hair, and then he was falling again, slowly, until his feet struck solid ground. He was in the room above the cellar again. The four doors were firmly shut.

At the back of his head the rasping noise still crackled and crunched. Tommy crossed to the window, fearful of going through the doors. He pulled back the curtain and looked out on a grey landscape. The moor was littered with dead bodies, some in armour and some in skins. A flight of crows were flapping in the distance, low and heavy against a sick sky. Tommy backed away from the window and a movement caught his eye. A mouldering, bony arm twitched. Close by, there was a glint from a shoulder-plate and a head turned, grinning, moss-covered, dripping with mould. He reached his hand out quickly and pulled the long drape closed, blotting out the sight. He didn't want to see any of that. The birds were nightmare enough.

On the home stretch down to Creggan, Alan pushed the big BMW onward, willing it to go faster. Ahead of him the black cloud was swirling fast like a sucking circular storm. And he felt the slow roll of fear squeeze his belly tight. Half a mile from the cut-off that led to the left down the shore road he almost rolled the car on the tight dog-leg and felt his rear bumper spang off the bole of a small tree. There was a screech of metal and the front wheels jerked as the back ones tried to slide across the road. Instinctively Alan eased the car into the skid and felt everything right itself, then he flipped the wheel over at the last second before he smashed straight into the bushes that hid the long drop into the loch. He could hear the blood singing in his ears. At last, forty seconds later, he stepped on the brakes, keeping the wheels turned a fraction to the right, and ground the car to a halt. It swung round, facing right at the entrance between the pillars, and he booted it hard up the driveway at such speed that he nearly mowed down the three figures standing on the wide gravel swathe.

'What's happened?' he asked breathlessly.

'We have to get those bairns out of the house,' Mrs MacPhee said, matter-of-factly. '*You* have to get them.'

Alan nodded, equally matter-of-factly, as if it was the most normal thing in the world. The fact that reality had taken a sideways shuffle and that overhead the sky was like a galaxy of devastating black holes and that nothing in or about this house was normal didn't seem to matter.

'It is not your wife. She is gone. It has her now,' Mrs MacPhee said. 'You have to go and face it.' She looked at Alan with those sunken hollows that seemed to serve as radar. 'Here. Take this. It's little enough as it is, but it's a piece of summer for the winter that waits in there.' With that, she handed him the gnarled rowan walking stick.

Alan took out his key and turned it in the lock. It moved slowly and he had to exert pressure. He was half-way through the clockwise turn when the key shot a knife of fire into his hand. Instinctively he jerked back and saw the round grip glow red and then flare white. It was like watching an arc-lamp sizzle. The surrounding lock took on a bright red glow, and the key abruptly started to melt. It twisted, crumpled and then dripped on to the stone with a short hiss.

Alan hit the door with his shoulder. There was a cracking sound from the lock and the door swung inwards, spilling him into the dim hallway. He sprawled forward, overbalancing, and caught himself before he fell to the floor. Inside, the air was icy cold. It was as if a big butcher's freezer had been left open and was sucking the heat from the place. Outside, Tom and Seumas took three steps forward to follow Alan into the house when the door abruptly swung shut. In the hallway, Alan spun round, startled by the noise. It was pitch black and numbingly cold.

'Tommy!' Alan called and his words echoed off the walls, ringing up the stairs, the final syllable of his son's name fading hollowly.

Outside Tom and Seumas stopped on the gravel, looking up at the house. All the windows were black.

'Do you hear something?' Tom asked, cocking his head. There was a far-off rumbling sound, like a distant, powerful explosion. Under their feet the ground trembled.

Then the house itself seemed to tense. There was a rattling noise from high up, and then a soft scraping sound. Something whirred down past Tom's ear, so close it tickled his eardrum, and hit into the pebbles with a thud. He looked down. It was a big slate that had slid down the slope of the roof and knifed into the ground like a blade six inches into the path. Tom stepped back in alarm and there was a series of soft rasping sounds in quick succession.

'Get back,' Tom shouted to Seumas and the old woman. Slates came whirling down in a line right across the front of the house like broad knife-blades.

One, two, five, ten, hitting the ground in a machine-like series of thuds. Seumas, instead of jerking backwards, dodged forwards to grab his mother's arm. One of the big slates *schocked* off the roof and skittered past the guttering, spinning as it fell. Tom never actually saw it until it had slammed into the old woman's head with the sound of an apple being hit by a hammer.

He saw Seumas, half turned, hand just reaching his mother's elbow. The tiny woman's head was slightly tilted upwards, just visible over her long brown coat, her dainty feet planted close together. Like a stone axe, the slate took her square on the top of the head and split it right down to her chin. For what seemed an eternity in the slow motion of shock, there was no movement. Not even a sound. The little woman and her son stood there like statues. The flat blade of stone protruded from the top of the old woman's head like an obscene cock's comb. The sickening thudding sound was ringing in a series of repeats in Tom's ears. On either side of the stone, blood gushed out from a red gap that was nine inches long, drenching the woman's collar. Then, if there could be more horror, the two halves of her head shifted slightly, widening the gap, and then hinged outwards, falling away from each other. The big stone slate teetered left and right, and then fell out with a small sucking sound and rattled on the stones. Old Mrs MacPhee took a step backwards and her body swivelled towards her son. There was a gurgling noise from her throat and Tom felt as if he'd been kicked in the stomach when he looked at the ghastly apparition. The old woman's eyes were still hollow caverns, but now separated by eight inches on either side of a bloody V-shaped mess of red and pink. The slate had cleanly sliced right down through her chin, cutting her nose slightly to the left, leaving only one flange of nostril on the right. Both sides of her mouth were opening and closing as if she were trying

455

to say something, but blood simply streamed from the flapping, ripped lips.

In slow motion, Seumas finished grasping his mother's arm, stepping forward. Tom heard words begin to come from his mouth as though from an old, wound-down phonograph, deep and ghostly. A great gout of blood splashed all over the small man's jacket and the old woman's head finally split completely into two halves which flopped down on to her shoulders. Tom heard a hoarse scream, realized it was his own, belting out of his lungs in a punch of sound. Behind him, he heard Seumas groan, and then there was a muffled double thud as the dead woman and her son fell on to the stones.

Tom straightened. From high on the roof there was another series of rasping sounds. Without thinking, he dived at the small man who was lying on his back with the mutilated, grotesque body of his mother sprawled on top of him. Tom grabbed Seumas's arm and hauled him backwards. A fresh series of slates socked themselves into the ground where Seumas had been. Two of them hit his mother and impaled themselves right through her coat. Tom dragged the small man off the path and on to the grass, away from where the slates were falling in serried lethal lines. Seumas's eyes were bugged right out of their sockets, his face a twisted picture of horror. He was clearly out of it. Tom shook him and got no reaction. He slapped the small man quickly on his cheek and Seumas gave a little start. His eyes flicked up to Tom, then across at the obscenity which was his mother, and he groaned again. Then he started to cry. Tom held on to him as the sobs racked him.

FORTY-THREE

A mile up the Corrie Glen there's a place where two streams meet and flow down to the firth between Creggan and Murrin. On the east side there's a dry-stane dike just beyond the trees, then a small hollow where the grass has been cut short by the grazing sheep. It has always been a favoured spot for generations of lovers partly because of its tranquillity but mostly because the hollow can't be overlooked. And on summer nights, the east slope catches the last rays of the setting sun, while the rest of the glen is thrown into shadow.

Danny Burgoyne was just seventeen and about to lose his virginity. Sheila Thomson was sixteen and a year and a half more experienced than Danny, and while he suspected it was not her first time, he wasn't entirely sure, and he cared less. The two of them had strolled arm in arm up the glen, stopping to kiss each other under the spread of lime trees that marked the boundary of Andy Noble's farm. Sheila was small and cuddly with a mass of brown curls that framed a face full of freckles and beginning to lose its puppy fat, refining itself down into what would surely become quite striking. As they kissed, she pressed herself up against him. He could feel the warm, pneumatic swell of her breasts low on his chest and her tongue wormed its way deliciously between his teeth, coiling with his own. Her hips were making slow, circular motions against him and already he could feel the urgency in his core. Further up the glen, the shadows were lengthening. They crossed the stream on the stepping stones, she leading, and climbed the old dike. In the hollow, Sheila sat down on the short grass and pulled Danny down beside her, reaching her hand out to cup the back of his head, drawing his face on to hers. He shifted his hips and pressed down on her and she let her body undulate against his. Inside she could feel the warm needy sensation. They had been kissing for five minutes or so when she slid her hand down and slowly brought his up to her breast. He squeezed on the outside of her shirt and massaged the swelling. She felt her nipple stiffen with the friction of the material against it, and her breath quickened a little, matching his. She squirmed again, showing him her appreciation, and contrived to move so that her shirt was pulled wider. Danny took the hint, still a little fearful in case she put a stop to all this, and fumbled with the two buttons. They finally opened and he slid his hand inside, feeling the wonderful warm swell of smooth skin. His fingers riffled one by one over the taut nipple and she gave a little gasp of pleasure. Encouraged, he tweaked it softly and she gasped again. Her hand moved slowly down his back and came slyly over his hips and slid down the outside of his thigh. She twisted her wrist and drew the flat of her palm up on the inside, slowly, teasingly. There was an agony of anticipation as Danny felt her fingers flutter on the outside of his jeans, closer and closer and closer, and suddenly the hand was rubbing softly against the hardness in the denim. He thought everything was going to explode down there in a huge gush, but instinctively she sensed it and let her hand slide away.

Danny drew his own hand from inside her shirt and let it trail almost nonchalantly down the side of her ribs, over her hip and down on to the girl's thigh. Her short skirt had ridden up and his fingers felt silky skin again. Learning quickly from her, he lightly brushed the skin, feeling the soft matte of fair hairs. He turned his hand, bringing it up agonizingly slowly on the inside straight. It was incredibly soft and warm. Up and up and up he drew the fingertips until, shockingly, they stopped against the yielding bulge. Danny's hand seemed to have taken an instant attack of palsy. It was shaking with the excitement of anticipation. Sheila swung her own hand down and quickly pulled away the soft material of her french knickers and suddenly his hand just seemed to slip into the wet warmth. It was utterly and absolutely astounding. It was the weirdest, most wonderful physical sensation his hand had ever encountered in his seventeen years. Danny gave a little groan and Sheila moaned very softly and shifted her hips again so that his fingers felt as if they were being sucked inside. She felt wet and swollen and silky and he thought the top of his head might just blow off with the internal pressure. She pressed against his touch and at the same time scrabbled with his zip. He heard the rasp as it dragged open. She fumbled for the brass button, gave a push and a pull, and his jeans opened completely. With deftness born of experience she slipped her hands over the top of his jockeys and quickly grabbed him. Her hand was cold and warm at the same time. Every nerve down there went into a frenzy of jittering and he felt himself pulse. It was happening. He was going to lose it. He was going to make a mess. And then she gripped him very firmly and squeezed hard. The urgent feeling slowly subsided. She drew her hand away and put it on his, between her thighs. She moaned, this time taking her mouth from his, sounding as if she was in pain, but he continued. After that everything happened very fast. Her right arm forced against his shoulder, pushing him over and on top of her, while she tried to slide her hips underneath him. Urgently, almost painfully, she pulled at him with her left hand, almost dragging that big swollen thing to where his hand was moving on her.

It was going to happen. It was finally going to happen. The realization was like a punch in the solar plexus. It almost knocked the wind right out of him.

She pulled him on top and spread her legs. He moved

459

his hand out for balance and she guided him. The sensitive part hit off the spongy warm place, rasping against the soft tangle of hair. His hips bucked and he felt himself press against bone. He couldn't find it. And then it felt as if his whole being had slipped into paradise. He drove right inside that silky wetness until he felt the bone at the base grind against her. There was a rasping sensation on the outside as their hair met and inside, oh inside, that was the sum total of every good feeling in the world multiplied by infinity. Afterwards, they lay in each other's arms as the shadows lengthened around them until, a while later, she fluttered her hand down on him. She smiled when she found he'd recovered. Danny grinned back proudly.

He had started again, rubbing softly, when Sheila stiffened against him.

'What was that?' she whispered in his ear. Danny stopped what he was doing and lifted his head away from hers.

'Huh?' he said with the stupidity of any teenager whose brain is completely focused on what's between a girl's legs.

'I thought I heard something,' Sheila said, craning over his shoulder.

'Probably a rabbit or a blackbird or something,' Danny said, not caring if every matron in Creggan were observing them from the belt of trees. There was a crackling sound in there between the trunks. Something skittered and scampered. Danny turned his head at a slight movement. Two rabbits came shooting out of the shade on blurring legs, and scooted past them. They heard the thump of paws on the hard ground. There was a flick of white tail and they were gone. The hollow was dark and quiet.

'Told you,' he said, grinning. 'There's nobody up here but rabbits, and they're just after the one thing.'

'A bit like you,' Sheila said with a twinkle in her eye. She lowered herself back on to the grass and pulled him on her. He went straight inside this time, plunging into that delicious warmth.

And then something bit him.

There was a huge explosion of intense pain on his backside. It was as if a part of him had been ripped off and the blue flame of a blowtorch had been held against the wound. Agony bucked his hips so hard that his whole back arched.

'*Aaagh*,' he yelled out across the hollow.

Sheila mistook his cry for an orgasm. 'Yes. Do it, Danny. Do it hard.'

But Danny had suddenly lost interest in the girl. Incredible pain rocketed through him and he turned instinctively.

'What's . . . ?' Sheila said and that was one of the last things she ever said.

Danny was lying on the grass beside her, twitching himself off the ground in a series of epileptic-like spasms. Sheila pushed herself up on one elbow and looked at him, then something moved out of the shadow right beside her and took a bite the size of a dinner plate out of her side. It happened before she even had time to feel it. There was a movement and a snap and a kind of wrenching sensation and then there was a great hole in her body, a bite-shaped red space between her hip and her ribs where there was absolutely nothing.

'Oh don't . . .' she said in a small voice, and that was the last thing she said. There was a small, popping sound from inside that red mess. A little hiss, and the air in her left lung bubbled through a dark liquid mass. Sheila gave a little hiccup and something lunged at her again, blurringly swift, with the speed of a striking snake. There was another snap and her whole body was wrenched to the left, hauling her three feet across the grass. Her legs crossed over themselves and the movement drenched her short skirt in a flood of blood. There was a ripping, crunching sensation that seemed to be very far away, and her whole arm came off at the shoulder with a wet, creaking sound. An involuntary scream tried to force itself out of her wide open mouth, but there was no sound except a soft hiss. Sheila's eyes were wide open, though everything was suddenly very dark. She got an impression of something grey and scaly with a wide mouth and a million needle-like teeth and terribly thin, many-jointed legs, and then a curtain of dark just enfolded her and she was dead.

Danny Burgoyne shoved himself back and away from Sheila. The wound on his backside rasped against the grass, but he hardly noticed it. The grey thing in the shadow of the hollow swivelled great black saucer-like eyes on him and seemed to leer. It was like a gargoyle with an emaciated, humped body and long legs. Too many of them. From one corner of its mouth a hand and part of a forearm beckoned at Danny as the jaws worked up and down in lizard fashion, gulping on the arm.

If Danny hadn't been led up to the hollow in Corrie Glen by Sheila Thomson, then he would have lived. If he hadn't just lost his virginity and been preparing for an action replay, he might still have lived, although he would have had a huge cratered hole on the right cheek of his backside to show for it. He might just have been able to sprint away and outrun the monstrosity that sat chomping in the hollow. But the fact that his jeans were down around his knees was the death of him. He hauled himself to his feet and started to run, his mind blank with horror. But his blood-soaked jeans slipped further down to his ankles, and because his maximum stride was five inches he got about ten steps. He started to topple, righted himself and glanced frantically at the horrible thing that was still chewing on Sheila's arm. It fixed him with those immense eyes, but didn't move. Danny turned and staggered, still caught in his jeans, toppling towards the bushes, in the opposite direction from where he wanted to go. Something shot out a long, eel-like neck, and wrapped itself around his bare thighs in a swift coil. Danny gasped and saw a small round body that sat on a handful of stubby legs, and a long sinuous neck with a tiny head. Instant fire burned into the flesh of his legs. He staggered and fell headlong, trying to scrabble away. The pain from down at his thighs was so immense he felt as if he'd been injected with concentrated acid. He yelled out an incomprehensible stream of words, staring at the thing that was wrapped around him, and then he felt everything fade when he saw what was happening. The flesh of his legs was simply melting off into the eel-like rubbery skin that had him in a stranglehold. There was no biting and ripping. No crunching and rending. The flesh just dissolved into the grotesque creature. It happened so quickly that Danny didn't have time to take it in. The skin and muscle seemed to be sucked away. In a few seconds there was none left on his thighs. White slick bone showed between the looping coils. As the flesh shrivelled and ran, absorbed by the monstrous slithery thing, the coils tightened, swiftly working their way up, looping round his hips.

Danny screamed a piercing wail of fright and agony. He tried to kick the thing off but his legs didn't work. There was no muscle left to make them move. He shoved with the palms of his hands, his body frantically writhing and twisting, and his hands just seemed to flow into the mucousy surface. Some far-off part of Danny's young mind was curiously aware of how amazingly long his finger bones were, long and slender. Then the pain bubbling out from them added to the monstrous seething, burning sensation from his hips and the coils squeezed up further and over his testicles. It was as if the blowtorch and the concentrated acid had been applied by mad torturers. The boy felt his mind expand outwards on the crest of a vast wave of agony that knocked the sensation of half an hour before into a cocked hat as far as unforgettable experiences went.

This was the most incredibly momentous monumental feeling his body had ever known. High up on that white-hot surge of pain he looked down at himself, awfully far away, in a detached sort of manner. There was nothing from his groin to his knees. Above that flesh was rapidly being absorbed into the jelly-like opaque skin. Below that his feet twitched in a blood-soaked pair of wrinkled Levis under the creature's coiling motion. Then the sight blurred and darkened in the already dim hollow and shock hammered into every nerve that was left in his body in a merciful blow that simply winked his conscious mind out of existence.

It was not till a week later that the remains of the bodies were found. One of Andy Noble's boys stumbled across them when he was bringing the sheep down from the east side of the Corrie Glen. At first he thought a tramp had left some old scraps of clothing. Then he recoiled in horror when he saw that in fact one of the huddled lumps was a perfectly articulated skeleton. It wasn't quite a skeleton. There was only bone from just under the nose right down to the calves. Otherwise everything was intact. The feet were still inside the baseball boots and there was some meat in the parts of the legs covered by the jeans. A scrap of shirt covered the ribcage, and the neck bones, chin and both upper and lower sets of teeth were visible, white in the sun. Above that, Charlie Noble, who was only sixteen, saw with a gasp of pure revulsion and horror the face of Danny Burgoyne, staring at him with eyes that were already crumpling. After Charlie had vomited quite spectacularly on to the grass he staggered away from the sight and almost fell over what was left of Sheila Thomson. Both legs, one arm, and the head were completely gone. One sagging white breast that was splattered with blood was hanging out of the shredded remains of a shirt. The stumps of the legs, one three inches below the crotch and the other a bit longer, were ragged tatters of flesh. Between them the pubic mound under the thick tangle of brown hair was strangely intact and blood-free. It buzzed with black flies. Young Charlie ran screaming all the way home, scared to look round in case whatever did that would lope out from behind the dike and come after him. But all of this was a week after what happened on the peninsula.

On the night that Seumus Rhu MacPhee's mother was unseamed from nave to shoulders, John Lindsay was coming down the Peaton Road on the short cut which saved him a mile of driving. His back was getting stiff from hauling at the wheel on the drive round from Kirkland where he'd been hoping to speak to the Rodger boy who was still in intensive care. There hadn't been any chance of that. Young Jim Rodger wasn't able to speak to anybody, and the chances were that he might never be able to. The doctor in charge of the emergency care unit that served half the district from Arden to the west as far as Arrochar had detailed the boy's injuries. Frank Rodger and his wife had sat there by the boy's bedside, watching blank-faced and shattered as the machines gurgled and hissed and bleeped, keeping the semblance of life in their son's wasted body.

Fitzgibbon, who was tall and red-haired just like the policeman but who wore thick glasses that magnified his pale eyes, had told him that half the boy's body, from shoulder to shin, had been exposed to severe heat. The skin was blistered and puckered and would need extensive grafting. There was a fracture on the elbow and two cracked ribs, one of which had punctured a lung. On the right side there was some skin wasting and raised, discoloured lumps like insect bites, only much larger, that had festered and gone septic. Both hands had been blackened by what the doctor could only diagnose as severe frostbite. Three fingers on the right hand were gone. The other two might have to be amputated. Below the knees the boy's shins and feet were slimy and coated by a fungal disease that had not responded to any treatment. The doctor had sent off some of the stuff for analysis and was waiting for an answer. He thought it looked like a tropical infection, but he couldn't be sure. Twice in the hour after the little boy had been brought into the hospital by a very distressed elderly teacher, his heart had stopped and been started only by the jump-pads. Later that day it had gone into fibrillation, fluttering madly like a frightened bird's, and he had been given a direct cardiac injection. Now his vital signs were more or less stable although he still needed a ventilator, and there was a tube which combated the alarming build-up of fluid in the lungs. He was also catatonic. Totally unresponsive. There was not even a reflex when a beam of light was shone into his eyes. No, the doctor didn't give much for his chances, he told John Lindsay out of earshot of the white-faced parents.

'What do you think happened?' John asked, although he didn't expect an answer.

'I can tell you what it looks like.'

'Carry on.'

The doctor looked at him squarely, eyes big and blue behind the bulging glasses, measuring up his credulity. 'I'd say he was kicked, bitten, burned, frozen, dropped on Mars and then slung into an Amazonian swamp.'

John Lindsay raised both eyebrows.

'Well, you did ask,' the white-coated doctor said. 'That's between you and me, of course, and it's impossible. But on the face of it, that's what it looks like. I'm none the wiser.'

On the way back, John Lindsay was none the wiser. Jim Rodger had been running through the trees at the top end of the old Dalmuir place with the policeman's own son and the Crombie youngster, and he'd disappeared. He'd turned up twenty-six miles away injured and sick and almost dead. What happened to him and how he got there was anybody's guess. John Lindsay's guess leaned towards the probability that the youngster had been abducted and dumped on the Carman Hill. But even then, if he had been abducted, what the hell had happened to him? How had he suffered such a catalogue of injuries, from burning to frostbite? And those strange insect bites and the fungus that seemed to be growing like slimy lichen on his skin. How the hell could you explain that?

John Lindsay couldn't. As he drove down the Peaton Road, the thought in the forefront of his mind was that it could have been his own son. No matter how he tried to shove it away, the thought kept coming back.

It was almost dark when he got to the house. There was a great mass of cloud tumbled right up over the peninsula and a wind was shrieking through the telephone wires that were strung from the poles on the edge of the road. Marion had a cup of tea ready and he swallowed a burning mouthful almost as soon as he walked through the front door.

'Beth Callander was looking for you,' his wife said. 'Her and that American girl. They asked if you could go up to see that fellow Crombie.'

'Did they say what it was about?' he asked after his second hot mouthful. It tasted great. The last thing he wanted was a call out before he'd had his supper.

'No. They just said to give you the message when you came in.'

'Doesn't sound that important,' he said, feeling relieved. 'I'll take a look along later once I've had a bite.'

'They looked worried, but they wouldn't say what was wrong.'

'Well, I'll make it a quick bite then, but if I don't get something to eat I'll cave in.'

As it happened, John Lindsay never got his supper. He took another mouthful and just then the phone rang. He picked up the receiver, gulped down what he had sipped, almost scalding the back of his throat, and tried to speak but failed in a paroxysm of coughing.

When the fit subsided, he could hear a tinny voice screeching from the top of the receiver. He put it to his ear. A loud voice bellowed at him: 'It's that fucking thing back again. It's in at the byre and it's tearing the fuck out of my cows.'

'Hold on a minute. Hold on,' John said. 'Who is this?'

'It's Jack Coggan. You'd better get up here. And bring a fuckin' gun. There's a horde of them in the byre.' Behind the man's yelling, John could make out a high-pitched caterwauling that could have been women screaming but was too shrill and fierce. And above that there was a banging and crashing and the lowing of frightened cattle.

'What the hell is that?' he asked.

'It's those things that slaughtered the chickens. They're in the byre and they're at my beasts. Oh for Christ's sake, John, they're *murdering* the animals.'

'Right. Just hold on. I'll be up there in a couple of minutes. And *don't* go out there. Make sure the wife and kids stay indoors as well.'

'Aye, I've sent them up to the attic. But hurry up, John. I don't want to go out there by myself.'

Coggan hung up the phone. John Lindsay shook his head resignedly. He quickly went to the cupboard in the small lobby and took out the over-and-under twelve bore that he used for putting dogs which had been run over out of their misery but more often for knocking a few mallard out of the air as they winged past the point at dawn. He told Marion he was going up to Coggan's farm and that he'd see her later. Then he went out and back into the Land Rover. The seat was still warm. John sighed. He could have done without this. But if there was a chance of getting whatever was killing off the livestock in the farms around Creggan, then he could maybe start to relax a bit. Mentally he tried to predict what he'd find. An escaped leopard? A family of puma? It didn't matter. If they were still around when he got there, he'd blast holes the size of dinner-plates in them. There was no arguing with hy-max goose-shot. None at all.

FORTY-FOUR

Inside the house Alan felt his way along the wall in the dark. As soon as he'd stepped inside, he felt the temperature plummet. It was winter where he walked. He could hear his breathing, quick and agitated. If there had been enough light, he knew he would have seen a plume of condensation as his breath froze in the strange cold.

His mind was focused ahead, into the dim recesses of the house that had been his home for only a handful of weeks, and was now, in a mere hitch of time, unfamiliar territory. Under his hand the wall felt slick and damp and icy, as if the cold had penetrated right through the fabric, leaked in through the stone.

On the way down from Glasgow, foot jammed to the floor, Alan had felt the knot of panic clench and unclench in his stomach. Now that he was inside, the panic hadn't lessened, but at least he was closer; he was doing something. In beside the panic and the strange fear was the feeling of anger at himself. He had spent weeks watching his wife deteriorate. He'd had those weird dreams where he'd found himself inside parts of the house that couldn't possibly exist, and he had dismissed them all. His world of logic, his measurements and calculations, his metal stresses and his concrete weight loadings, they'd had no room for this kind of nonsense.

Then people had met at Tom's house and something weird had happened. There had been a thread that linked them all together and when they had convened their little discussion group in the front room of Cromwath, he had believed. He hadn't wanted to, but the truth of it had seemed to leap up and smack him on the side of the head for emphasis.

And after that he had thrown it all out of the window because, more than anything in the world, he had wanted not to believe it, and Helen had given him an out. He had snatched at that straw and had submerged himself in his world of girders and compression factors, drowning in reality. And then Mike Toward had told him about what had happened to the girl in the office and Alan's concept of reality had flipped a dizzy somersault.

Anger at himself spurred him on. Outside, a blade of slate was whistling through the air towards the top of old Mrs MacPhee's head. Up at Corrie Glen young Danny Burgoyne was minutes away from losing his virginity and half an hour from losing everything else except the top of his face. Night was falling in Creggan and Murrin, Corbeth and Feorlin and the rest of the peninsula, under a whirling cloud that was beginning to shake the trees.

Alan walked down to the turn and took a right. The house was not silent. There was a slow, creaking noise far off from the kitchen, as if an old door was swinging. And around him was a rasping, crunching sound that was muted and distant, like millions of woodworm grubs in the walls.

'Tommy,' he called out, startled at the loudness of his own voice. It echoed away up the stairs and faded fast. 'Katie! Laney!' There was no reply. Alan turned to go up the stairs. It was night. The children should be in their beds. A little blue flame of hope flickered in his chest. He took a step, then another, feeling his way, hand clenched round the old woman's rustic walking stick. It felt warm in his hands, the only heat.

He reached the half landing and turned, eyes wide and growing accustomed to the darkness. He looked back and his heart did a somersault. The nine stairs he'd walked up weren't there. He was still on a stairway, on a half landing, but it was a different stairway. Instead of rising in an anti-clockwise angular spiral, it was reversed. In the darkness, the house had changed itself. From far away up there he heard a cry, high and quick, muffled behind walls.

'Tommy!' he shouted. Adrenalin punched into his blood and he bounded up the stairs.

Tommy was running. He had spun away from the window that looked out on to the moor where the dead warriors were stirring to ungainly life. He had wrenched open the door and skittered along the hallway, riven with fear. He passed the six doors on the right before he realized that there should only be two. Before his momentum carried him forward and into the wall at the end, there was a flicker and a wrench and he was tumbled into a long, stony corridor that sloped down steeply. Light flickered dreamily.

Then from far ahead, he heard someone call to him: 'Tommy.'

A high, musical voice calling his name. Instinctively he ran for it. The corridor went on and on. His feet were pounding on the smooth stone floor. He came to the end where it forked into two.

'Tommy!' The pure note of his name called again from the right and he swung himself towards it, feeling the need of it. The voice was leading him onwards and it was real. He didn't know why, but the calling was so imperative and so clear that he knew it was the only good thing. Behind him he was aware of the black shadow that was trailing after him. He couldn't see it but it was there, hugely dark and ponderous and hungry, like the thing he had seen when he dreamed of the pit down in the cellar.

Its menace was real and it was terrifying. It flowed behind him in a poisonous black wave that would engulf him and carry him off.

The corridor narrowed abruptly, then widened into

472

a circular room with an arched doorway leading off. The sound of his name rang again in his ears, sweet and warm. He halted his headlong flight, casting for direction. It came again, and he realized it wasn't his ears that were hearing, it was his *mind*. But the direction was clear. He dived into one of the low, arched entrances. There was a strong wind blowing up towards him. The cloying smell that had been in the long corridor was blown away by a gust of fresh clean air and there was light ahead. He ran towards it, blood pounding in his ears, legs pistoning hard, racing towards the sweet clear echo of his name. The light got brighter and the walls on either side blurred by . . .

And he found himself in the open. It was as if the walls had just disappeared. Bracken crackled under his feet. On either side, trees were pillars flickering by. A clump of ferns was in front and he hurdled it gracefully. Behind him he could feel the black cloud rolling. There was a deep roaring sound that he knew was also inside his head, but no less menacing for that. He could feel the cold dark reach out for him, trying to flow over him, and he knew it was the black evil thing in the pit. His legs pumped harder with fright. Two grey shapes blurred past on either side and then he was skittering across the short grass, feet sliding. The ground sloped down abruptly and then fell steeply to the stream. Tommy tumbled down the slope and skidded, spread-eagled to a halt.

The air was clean and warm in the space beyond the standing stones. There was a wind picking up, and overhead, to the right, above the house, a storm was building up. But outside the rolling clouds, the full moon silvered down at him, catching the water that gurgled and fell between the stones and dropped into a sparkling pool. The vast black threat that had rampaged after him through the house and into the catacomb-like tunnels under it instantly receded. In his head he could sense its rage, poisonous and hungry, beaming fury right into him.

He lay on the slope, panting so hard his lungs felt raw, one side of his shirt and his jeans slick with the earth where he'd scraped himself in his fall. It was as if he'd stumbled into a dell of placid calm while everything bad and hungry raged around. A strange peace stole over him. He could have sat there in the moonlight for ever.

But Tommy knew his baby sisters were still inside the house. And though the very thought of it terrified him to the very tips of his toes, he knew that he'd have to get them out.

He hauled himself to his feet which felt like lead as he walked towards the standing stones that lay inside the shadow of the gnarled old pines. Fear sizzled coldly inside him as he walked between the megaliths. There was a wrench, as he instinctively knew there would be, and he was inside the house again.

Cathy McIntyre was already yawning when she came into her bedroom on the upstairs floor of her cottage at the north end of Corbeth. She'd had a good day and a nice night. Paul Ferguson, who with his sister ran the Gossip Shop next door to her haberdashery business, had stayed for another glass of port after the meal of steak au poivre she'd cooked for them both. Their romance was coming along quite nicely, although she hadn't chosen to let him know that as yet. Cathy had been widowed for eleven years, she told the friends she'd made since coming to the peninsula. In fact, the man she'd married had been a waster and a drunkard whose incessant demands had led to her throwing him out and divorcing him when she'd realized she'd had enough. He hadn't been a gentleman, not like Paul, who may not have been particularly good-looking, but his manners were impeccable and his bridge hand was formidable enough to make them a force to be reckoned with every Thursday night. This night, they had sat listening to Pavarotti, sipping their port. She had let him edge closer, feeling his thigh pressing shyly against hers, noticing the slight tremor that ran through him as she accidentally leaned against him. Yes, she expected a proposal very soon, and they could both live very happily a life of gentility on the peninsula. She had let him peck her on the cheek as he had said goodnight, again accidentally allowing her substantial breast to press against his arm. Paul was obviously an inexperienced man. She knew how to lead him, and he would be led. There would be no demands from him, as there had been from the other one. This time, she would decide.

She smiled to herself as she towelled herself dry, standing in front of the full-length mirror. Things were going according to plan. Cathy was fifty-two and had let Paul (and everybody else) think she was six years younger. Her hair had been ash blonde and the highlights helped to keep it that way. She had a fine, handsome face and good teeth framed by dimples when she smiled. She looked at herself in the mirror. Age was beginning to show a little. Her breasts didn't so much sag as hang heavily, centred by large pink aureolae. Her hips were wide, but she considered that an advantage. She had, she felt, good legs, which looked even better in high heels; she had a certain presence, a certain style. A mature quality that appealed to a man like Paul. She wanted to mother him.

Cathy was drying her back, holding the long pink towel by each corner and rasping it rhythmically across her skin. Everything wobbled from side to side in a motherly sort of way.

The small noise at the window made her turn her head. She'd forgotten to close the curtains, but as her house was the last one at the end of the small cul-de-sac it didn't really matter. She couldn't be overlooked from anywhere. She was about to continue when the noise came again, like birds' feet on the roof. She crossed to the window and peered out into the gloom, trying to see through her reflection. There was nothing there. She pressed the button and killed the light from the standard lamp, leaving only the dim glow from the reading light on the headboard. She leaned forwards, hands on the sill, and something loomed out of the dark. It was a face and it was upside-down. With a start she jerked back, more in surprise than fright. Somebody was hanging from the guttering. Her first thought was that one of the young men who drank down in the Creel had decided to become a Peeping Tom, and her first reaction was of prudish annoyance. She leaned forward again, trying to make out the shadowed face. As she did so there was an almighty crash as the whole window pane caved in, showering her with glass. She stumbled backwards in alarm, and the figure flipped in a somersault into the room and landed in front of her.

Cathy McIntyre nearly died on the spot. In fact she died six feet across the room.

It wasn't any of the young boisterous men whom she occasionally caught trying to look up her skirt as she dressed the models in her front-window display. It was something out of one of the late-night horror shows that Cathy always turned off as soon as the cello began to play those jangling low chords.

It was small and monkey-like with a strange, warty face. Its skin looked greasy and its eyes were tiny red beads that looked blind. The most grotesque thing about it was that it had great wide nostrils, but below them there was nothing. There was no mouth.

The nostrils flared and snuffled as if searching the air.

The thing had happened so suddenly that Cathy had hardly a chance to catch her breath. It came in a little gasp. The grotesque creature seemed to fasten on the sound and sprang towards her, knuckling the floor with huge splayed hands on the end of long, ropy arms. The hands reached up with many-knuckled fingers and grabbed her arms, the weight toppling her backwards to the floor. She hit with a thump that drove her breath out in a grunt, and she tried to wriggle away. The grip on her upper arms tightened fiercely.

Her legs were abruptly grabbed by the thing's feet. She raised herself up and tried to scramble away. The thing weighed less than her and it smelled sickly sweet. Her eyes looked down and saw that both her knees were clenched in feet that were just like the hands. The grip squeezed hard and she felt her legs being prised open wide. Still struggling and now whimpering out loud, she tried to pull away, head and shoulders arched up off the floor. And then she saw something that froze her rigid.

It was as if her mind had been suddenly kicked out of her brain. Between the thing's legs something long and curved was sliding out like a blade. In an instant of dreadful perception, she knew what was happening. The horny thing slid out of a wrinkled sheath and the apparition bucked on her. She felt something sharp on the soft outside between her thighs and her belly. It withdrew and quickly prodded her again, jabbing into her buttock. She couldn't move. It had her pinioned top and bottom. Then, without warning, immense pain, incredible pain, seared right up through her as the curved hard spike thrust right inside. She felt ripping agony and a tearing sensation high up, felt the enormous invasive pressure, and she screamed desperately from jaws that were wide with shock.

The thing pumped in a berserk hammering series of jerks. Something burst in her chest. She felt things inside her give under the onslaught and her whole body went rigid. There was a sensation as if her heart had abruptly pounded once, twice, and then the pain drained away as the internal blood pressure simply failed. Her heart was ripped right out of the membrane that held it inside her chest, and burst asunder. Still conscious for a few seconds more, and strangely removed from it all, Cathy felt the draining sensation as the inside of her body was sucked out. Above her the thing snuffled mindlessly as it fed.

At Corrie Glen Farm, Henry MacLeish was closing the gate on the south pasture. Way down there over Creggan a storm was building up, and he was glad he'd put his flock of blackfaces into that field where they'd have some shelter from the rain when it came. He leaned on the top spar of the five bars and looked down at the threatening storm before turning to walk along the track towards the distant lights of his small farmhouse. He had gone only a hundred yards, walking between the two grey bastions of the dry-stane dike that separated the north and south pastures when a movement caught his eye. He looked round, but there was nothing. The top of the wall was knobbed and even, a line of good whin-stone that he'd bought from Andy Noble who'd joined two fields together the year before and hadn't needed the stones. Henry kept walking, only a yard from the wall. The diker had done a good job here although, Henry noticed for the first time, the wall next to him was a foot higher than the one facing. He hadn't spotted it before. He stopped, looking at the top row of stones. That was funny, he thought. There were two lines of crown stones instead of one. That was another thing he hadn't noticed before.

Before he could continue the thought any longer, the top line of stones slipped right off in a serpentine motion with a rough scraping sound. Henry stared dumbfounded as it wriggled on the narrow strip of tussocks and then flipped, rasping stonily towards him. He didn't have time to react at all, except to realize that this wasn't a line of stones at all. Something that was like a vast, segmented rock snake wrapped a huge weight of articulated coils round him, dragging him to the ground. Henry tried to wriggle free and something that felt like a boulder hit him on the side of the head.

Little white stars spangled six inches in front of his eyes, then there was an incredible pressure on the side of his head. He felt himself being dragged between stones. The pressure moved down over his shoulders in a series of huge squeezes. Something in his shoulder cracked and splintered. The pressure quickly passed in a series of mighty gulpings down his chest, and the ribs imploded noisily. It clenched down on his thighs, then his knees. Something snapped on his feet and then there was nothing. A sound like a gobbling swallow went low and strange along the shadow at the base of the wall. Something coiled and rippled next to the wall with a sound like stone scraping on stone, and disappeared into the night. Henry MacLeish's shepherd's crook lay on the path.

John Lindsay got to Jack Coggan's farm and parked the jeep with its lights blaring on to the wall of the byre. He was thinking about the time he'd seen the shadows that had attacked Henry's bull and slaughtered the sheep in the field. He reached over the back of the seat and hefted his Webley and Scott. The byre was a riot of sound. The screeching and lowing was bedlam in the night air. John fought down an impulse to investigate it, but he wanted two guns out there. He crossed to the house and rapped on Jack's door. Immediately a voice came from within.

'Who is it?'

'It's John Lindsay. Open up, man,' the policeman said.

The door opened a crack and an eye peered out. Coggan recognized the policeman and swung the door open. 'It's in the byre,' he said. His eye were wide and scared.

'I know it's in the fucking byre. D'you think I'm deaf?'

'And there's a lot of them.'

'We'll see. Have you got your gun?'

Coggan nodded.

'Loaded?' Lindsay asked.

'Damn sure. Alpha BB's.'

'Right. Let's get to it.' Lindsay flicked on his big black torch. The beam angled up into the sky. 'Now I'll go in first. You stay behind me, but make sure that's pointed away from my back. As soon as I see anything, I'm going to shoot. You might lose a couple of beasts, but from the sound of things you've lost a couple anyway. You shoot on the left, I'll take the right, and for Christ's sake don't shoot *me*.'

Coggan nodded gravely. The policeman could tell that the last place he wanted to go was into the byre and he mentally saluted the smaller man's courage.

The farmer did as he was told. The big green byre door was on sliding rollers. From inside the noise was earsplitting. It sounded as if a whole circus-load of animals had been let loose in there to fight it out among themselves. Coggan heaved the door and it slid open. Lindsay stood at the entrance and held his torch against the barrel of the gun, the beam lighting up an incredible scene of rapid liquid movement. It seemed as if the shadows had taken life and were streaming and rippling all over the place. The smell of blood was sickly cloying in the air. Something black and incredibly fast like a huge spider came scuttering up between the stalls straight towards them. John pulled left, squeezed the trigger and the shotgun bucked in his hands. There was a screech that sounded far louder than the gunshot in the enclosed space, and the shadow seemed to explode into black rags. There was a movement to the left and John fired again at something that moved so quickly it was hard to follow. The gun crashed again and he heard the third cartridge click into place. A dreadfully cold liquid splashed over him. Beside him he saw the flash of Coggan's gun and saw something shatter as it scuttled over the concrete barrier. The policeman couldn't make out shapes, only movement, blurred and

480

humped. Down at the far end, a Hereford cross screamed, and a screech that was filled with spitting venom overpowered the sound.

The policeman strode forward and a black thing flew at him. He had the impression of great liquid eyes and a row of teeth that sparkled like shards of glass. His gun roared and the thing tumbled backwards, as if jerked on strings. It landed on the straw and shit-laden floor with a hard bump and turned swiftly. John finally saw it in detail. The thing that was crawling towards him was small and thin, with terribly slender insectile legs, maybe six, maybe eight, although two of them had been blown off and were wriggling independently two yards away, and beginning to squirm and steam in the torchlight. The head was squat, somehow flattened, and it seemed to consist only of eyes and mouth. Drool dribbled from the trap-like jaws and sizzled poisonously on the floor. A small cloud of greenish fumes drifted up from where it had splattered. John swung the gun and led it have an ounce of hy-max goose shot right in its ugly face, and the nightmare thing disintegrated.

Two more shadows flickered confusingly down at the far end where the screaming cows were bucking and writhing. John walked down, flicking his eyes from side to side. There was something moving next to one of the feed troughs and Coggan blasted it instinctively, instantly killing the calf that was sheltered half underneath its mother's torn body. Twelve feet from the far wall, John shot another of the weird things as it leapt on to the partition and spat at him. Coggan got the other that was scuttling underneath the cow it had been chewing. The byre fell silent, except for the moaning of the dying cattle.

'I think we got them,' Lindsay said, letting his breath out. He felt as if he'd been holding it pent up since they'd walked into the byre, and he probably had.

'But what in God's name are they?' Coggan asked, panting.

'Nothing in God's name,' John said. 'They're demons from hell. I never believed MacFie. I thought he was talking out of the back of his head.'

'What do you mean?'

The policeman was about to answer when there was a riveting screech from behind them. Both men turned and the light from the torch cut a swathe through the gloom. Something blurred from up in the corner where the milking pipes were suspended over the stalls. John swung the gun up instantly and the thing moved, jinking left and right, clambering with many legs over the pipes, and came running down the wall with spidery swiftness. The barrel followed it but Jack Coggan's body blocked its movement. There was a scutter of hard claws and a grunt as the thing bulleted out from the stall and hit the farmer on the hip, sending him crashing into John Lindsay who was thrown off balance. The gun clattered to the ground. Coggan's gun roared, and shot rapped like metal hail off the corrugated roof. The farmer let out a yell and fell heavily. The thing was on top of him, back lurching and head driving down into his body. Coggan screamed something that could have been words, kicking out with his feet, trying to get out from under. Lindsay spun his body and the flashlight beam followed the movement. A profusion of thin bony joints were scrabbling all over the fallen man. Lindsay didn't wait. He took two long strides and swung his big policeman's boot as hard as he could into the centre of the thing. Something snapped like dead wood and the gargoyle screeched.

It rolled off on to its back, did a flip, landed on those crazy legs and came charging straight at the policeman. Instinctively he swung his foot again and caught it right in the face. There was another snap, but this time it was jaws closing on his boot. An immense pressure gripped his toes. Something sharp bit right in, and then there was a terrible, burning pain like molten metal shooting up his foot and into his leg. He yelled hoarsely and kicked out. The thing held on. He could feel its jaws chewing into the thick leather and the rubber sole. Beside him Jack Coggan was rolling about moaning. His hands were slammed against his leg and there was a pool of blood flowing on to the crap on the byre floor.

Lindsay didn't think any more. He just dragged himself across the muck with the thing that was at the same time both reptilian and insectile trying to chomp its way through his boot leather. He reached the gun and grabbed it with frantic fingers, then he twisted round and lifted his trapped foot up as high as it would go and squeezed the trigger. A huge jolt kicked his foot down. It was as if someone had just smacked him on the toe with a sixteen-pound sledgehammer and squashed it flat. The foot went instantly numb. The thing that had been there was splattered all over the byre, sizzling where its various parts dropped. Beside him, Jack Coggan was moaning unintelligibly. John crawled over to him, not daring to put his weight on what used to be his foot. Even then he saw himself having to take retirement as unfit for police duty and watched his future gurgling down the drain. He rolled the farmer over and looked down. The leg was covered with blood in the torchlight. John got to his knees and ripped the man's trouser leg down below the knee. The muscle of the thigh was a torn mess. Very quickly the policeman took his belt off, ignoring the pounding that was now shooting up from his foot, and whipped it round the leg above the damage, cinching it tight. He hauled the man to his feet, and together they staggered out of the barn into the wind that was whipping up.

In the farmhouse, he lowered Jack Coggan on to the old sofa. The farmer was still moaning, shifting his body this way and that, trying to get away from the pain. John forced him down and looked at the wound.

Blood was still oozing there, but not pouring out from the mangled flesh the way it had been. It would probably heal. The skin around the wound was torn and mangled, and for three inches on either side it was puckered and festered as if already badly infected. John called upstairs and there was a muffled reply from the farmer's wife. He shouted to her to phone for an ambulance and then turned to attend to himself. With great difficulty he managed to prise the boot off his swollen foot. The leather was tattered right up to the eyelets. His sock was soaked in his own blood. He gingerly peeled it off, expecting to see a mush where his toes had been, and was surprised and enormously relieved to see them still wriggling, bloody and abraded, at the end of his foot. There were two lines of thin holes, bite marks, and the skin was burned and puckered like that of the farmer. In between the bite marks were half a dozen dark spots. He wondered what they were for a second, then realized it was goose-shot embedded under the skin. The leather had saved his foot from the unearthly creature *and* his own shot. He knew the foot would be the size of a football the next day and he would have a lot more pain, but he was going to walk again. The relief of that after what he'd come through on that strange midsummer night was overwhelming.

Just as John Lindsay and Jack Coggan were stepping into the darkened byre, Philly Brown, who worked up at the quarry, was weaving his way home towards Feorlin and a not very understanding wife. He'd had a skinful down at the Creel with his mates from Murrin, and despite the fact that his wife outweighed him by three stone and had done so since not long after the birth of their fifth child when she'd opted for food as her main source of satisfaction, he was not worried. He could face anything tonight. He could face anything on any night he'd sunk eight pints of heavy beer, so long as it didn't move around too much. Philly was a man of limited ambition, and even more limited imagination. When he heard the whooping sound over him he assumed it was the wind in the trees and kept on walking. After eight pints, he was not a man to jump at shadows, and even sober it wouldn't have crossed his mind. He walked on with that wonderful rolling gait of the blissfully drunk. The air whooshed by him again, right next to his ear. He turned as quickly as his balance allowed, which was pretty slowly, and stared belligerently back along the road he'd walked, thinking someone had thrown something at him.

'Wha' the fu . . .' he started to mumble when something swooped out of the air and struck him a blow on the face. As blows went, it was enough to knock him to his backside, but not hard. It was a soft, powerful smack, like being hit with a feathery pillow. Philly came down with a bump that jarred him from the rear upwards. He bit his tongue and swore comprehensively but incomprehensibly. He stumbled to his feet, lurching forward, drunk enough to be bewildered but unworried, and a huge bird hit him in flight before he had taken his second step. Philly got the impression of an amazing long black beak. There was a squawk right in his ear and the whooshing buffeting of wings, and he staggered across the road, still amazingly on his feet. Another bird landed in front of him and hopped on ungainly thick legs towards him. It nodded its head and pecked at his knee. Pain flared on the bone.

'Fuckin' bastard,' Philly yelled in alarm. Behind him the huge crow pecked into his thigh. It was like being stabbed.

'Get!' Philly bawled. The big bird drew back and to Philly's great amazement, he saw that it had no eyes, just great black holes that looked as if the eyeballs had rotted right in the sockets.

There was a whirr of wings and another bird flew down past him. He heard its feet scrabble on the road. It cawed loudly, like a jackdaw using a megaphone.

The one nearest lunged its beak forward again and got him in the small of the back. It was then that Philly realized this was actually happening. There was a flock of great crows that had no eyes and were the size of bloody great labrador dogs and they were trying to *eat* him.

The befuddled realization had an amazingly sobering effect on Philly Brown. Despite the fact that he had had difficulty in putting one foot in front of the other less than thirty seconds before, he suddenly found his feet were working very well indeed. One of the monstrous birds took a peck at him and he felt the point of its beak drive through his pants into the side of his buttock. That was enough to send him sprinting right off the road and through the copse of saplings towards his house. Before he reached the trees there were several great thuds on his back that nearly spilled him to the ground but, miraculously, didn't. He felt as though knives had been stuck between his ribs.

On that night, where bad luck was spilling out in a semi-circle on the end of the peninsula, Philly Brown, who was probably the most accident-prone man in the four villages, found himself in a little pocket of good fortune. His feet were working fine and he scuttled for the trees, hearing the great pinions flail the air behind him, and when he reached the copse he could hear the wings beating and crashing past the twigs at the edge of the trees. But the dense foliage stopped the passage of the big black birds while he scurried frantically between the trunks. All around him was the coarse cawing of the carrion eaters. Philly moved like the wind.

He staggered up the path towards his dingy little cottage, wrenched the door open and stumbled head-long, crashing into the old bentwood coatstand which clattered to the floor.

'I might have known,' Meg Brown screeched at him.

'Pissed as a newt and acting like a half-wit. Well, there's no supper for you, Philly Brown.'

The skinny man got to his feet, his face white, eyes rolling. 'Big birds,' he spluttered. He pointed over his shoulder. 'Big black birds.'

'If you've been seeing any big black birds down at that pub I'll split you like a kipper, you randy wee bachle,' Meg said stoutly. Philly just looked at her and wondered what the hell she was talking about. He turned around and his wife's piggy little eyes saw the puncture holes in the back of his jacket. They were encircled with red blotches.

'You've been fighting,' she accused. 'Fighting over those birds, eh?' She took two steps forward on legs that were like tree trunks and fetched him a clout right on the side of his head. As he fell, Philly wondered whether he might have been better staying out there with the crows.

FORTY-FIVE

Outside the house Seumas had stopped crying. The deadly stone blades of the slates had ceased their bombardment. The old woman lay in a crumpled heap on the pathway. Tom stretched down a hand and helped the small man to his feet. The expression on the old fellow's face was bleak.

'We can't help your mother, and I'm sorry,' Tom said. 'We have to get inside.'

'No. That's not what we have to do. My mother was right, we have to destroy the circle.'

'And how do we do that?'

'We finish what Dalmuir should have done, I think. Mother said the stones up there are what started all this. We have to break them.'

'Easier said than done,' Tom Callander said.

'Aye, that's true enough. I always knew there was something bad about those stones, but I never knew how bad,' Seumas replied. He nodded over to where his mother lay. 'There's the proof of it.' The flood of tears seemed to have composed the small man. The catch had gone from his voice. He was speaking straight, and Tom Callander could hear anger more than grief. He stopped and tried to get his spinning thoughts together. Light dawned.

'Of course, man. We *can* do it!' he said. 'I've been sitting in that damned JCB for the past fortnight. That's the answer.'

Seumas looked at him uncomprehendingly.

'The *dozer*,' Tom said in a near shout. 'That thing can take ten tons of solid rock.'

'Where is it?'

'It's up at the quarry,' Tom replied.

'Aye. But we'll have to do more than break them. We'll have to take those devil's teeth out by the roots.'

'Aye, well there's something else as well,' Tom said. His well-spoken voice had automatically switched to the idiom he'd used as a youngster working on his father's quarryface. 'I've got something up there in the storeroom that will blow these buggers to hell and back.'

'Just to hell would be fine, I'm thinking,' Seumas said, catching his drift. 'But first I have to get my mother away from here.'

Tom forestalled him. 'No. Let me do it.'

Seumas looked straight at him, eyes filled with anger and grief and something else that made him look bigger than he was. Then he nodded. Tom walked over to where the crumpled heap lay. He tried not to look at the grotesque split head from which blood and brains were spilling out like congealed porridge. Up on the roof there was a series of scraping noises. Tom bent quickly and picked up the scrap that had been the old woman in his arms. One side of the head wobbled jawlike, but he ignored it. He spun and retreated just as several big slates crashed to the ground where he'd been standing. He kept the injured head away from Seumas's sight and walked on to the lawn.

He made to put the old woman down on the grass, but Seumas said: 'No. Outside of this place. She won't lie here.' Tom walked down with the weight in his arms and laid the old woman on the verge outside the gates. Seumas didn't come with him. The stocky man went back up and got into Alan Crombie's car. The keys weren't there. He remembered that they'd dropped in the porch and he simply sprinted to the door, all the time fearful that stone blades would come crashing down on him. He scooped the keys up and got the hell out of there. Tom started the engine, swung open the passenger door to let Seumas in, and revved up fast.

Then the big wide wheels spun on the stones, making the car fishtail. He went down the driveway at high speed and swerved out through the gates.

The quarry at Mambeg was deserted. Tom let himself and Seumas in at the big iron gate and swung both halves of it wide. He fumbled with the mechanism on the office safe and brought out the keys to the concrete store room, then went through the passage to where the big steel door was shut tight. It took two twists of the wrist to send the bolts back. He switched on the light and crossed to the shelves where the blocks of semtex were separated in metal cases. He and Seumas lugged out a dozen of the heavy boxes to the front office and Tom went back, bringing two cardboard rolls of fine plastic-covered yellow cable. They loaded them into the cabin of the immense earthmover, Tom passing them up to Seumas and telling him to store them out of the way. He was almost up in the cab and ready to move when he remembered he didn't have the fuses. He jumped down, ran back inside and came out again moments later with a small canvas bag.

'OK, Seumas old friend. Let's get this show on the road.' It was something he'd heard in a film, but it sounded all right. It sounded a whole lot better than he felt at the thought of going back up there and into the trees.

Inside the house Alan's fist gripped hard on the old walking stick, ready to lunge at anything. He didn't know where the hell he was. There was nothing in the house that he recognized. He had been into the kitchen, where the wall that he'd knocked down was still intact. There was an old blackened range that looked big enough to cook banquets on. Up in the corner there was a box which encased a series of little brass bells. They were tinkling madly, jangling on the taut wires that were being pulled by unseen hands in the rest of the house. He'd turned from there and walked out and straight into the girls' room, which was upstairs, not down. Their beds were unmade.

'Katie!' he called out into the gloom. 'Laney! Where are you?'

His words echoed into the distance. It sounded immense and cavernous. Around him, within the walls, the rasping, chewing noise was getting louder. Cold sweat was trickling down his back. Inside he was filled with a black panicky dread.

There was enough light to see by, just enough. Alan stumbled along the top hallway and found himself in the living-room where they'd had their meeting the day before. The walls seemed to be pulsing in and out, like labouring lungs. He shook his head, but when he opened his eyes again he saw them still moving as if a great force was pushing from within. Cracks were racing across the surfaces in a spider's-web tracery. He turned, and light shone down from above. There was a sudden cry, and he jerked his head up. A man screamed past him, flying down from rafters that were open to the sky. His body should have bounced and broken on the struts that were suddenly there in place of the flat floorboards, but he seemed to pass right through them. His scream continued as he fell down and down and down into blackness.

He was upstairs again. He got his balance, heart racing, and pulled the door open. In the corner of the room there was a man in a black jacket leaning over a small girl who was lying on a bed with her skirt rucked up around her waist. The man turned and stared at Alan, then he gave a grin that was cold as ice and totally lifeless. Alan turned away from the vision and found himself on the stairs. He fell forward, with both hands outstretched.

The one holding the rowan walking stick hit the step face hard enough to stave his wrist, and the other hand went right through the surface of the stair. Instant cold that felt like fire burned through his arm. He tried

491

pulling back and found himself trapped. His hand wouldn't move. It felt as if it was being frozen into fingers of ice, but it didn't numb. The pain was wild.

Then a shock hit him like an arcing bolt from the mains. He could *see* his hand, sticking out of the wall on the flight of stairs above.

The fingers were grey and flexing feebly. He could see it there and he could feel it here. It was impossible. It couldn't be happening. Yet he knew it was happening. It was just another facet of the nightmare that the house had become.

Panic surged up again. Without conscious thought, he raised his free hand and rapped the rowan stick down on the stair tread with a yell that might have been a curse but was really just a cry of outrage and fear and horror. There was an elastic-like snap, like a rubber band stretched to breaking-point, and his hand suddenly popped out. The motion threw him backwards and he rolled arse over elbow with a clatter down the stairs. The stick flew out of his hand and he tumbled into the room with four doors. All of them were gaping open.

'*Tommy!*' he bellowed hoarsely. There was no reply. He shouted his son's name again, and then called for Katie and Laney. And way in the distance, he heard his son's voice, small and high.

'Dad. *Daddeee!*'

'Tommy. Tommy, where are you?'

'I'm lost, Daddy. I can't find them. I don't know where they are.'

The boy's voice was coming from the door on the left. Alan wasn't exactly sure but that's where he felt it came from. Without a thought, he dived into the door space and found himself sprinting along a narrow tunnel that was filled with orange purple light that reflected off the slimy wet trickling sickly down the walls.

'*Tommy!*' he bawled again. From far ahead his son's voice echoed back.

492

'Oh Daddy. Daddy. *Come quick. Come quick. Come quick.*'

Alan raced to the end of the tunnel, sensing the hard stone walls flashing by in the gloom. A darkness welled ahead and he went into it, skidding to a halt as he passed the threshold. He found himself in the cellar.

It was like a vast arena. The floor stretched away into the distance, a plain of immense flat stones. Tommy was standing there on the flagstones, and right in front of him the five great stones seemed to be writhing like stone fingers, looping towards each other.

Between them, the ground was opening in a spiral, like the aperture of a camera. It was just like the unearthly reflection of the big circular storm that was winding itself up over Creggan.

The boy was standing rigid with fear or shock. Here the rasping sound in the walls was overpowered by a great roaring that came from that expanding pit.

Then there was another shift. Alan felt it under his feet like a tremor in the earth. He caught his balance as the shudder in the ground threatened to tumble him. Stone ground on stone. The floor under him buckled and cracked in violent upheaval, leaving him standing at the edge of a pool of black. He couldn't tell if the entire surface had fallen away, for the strange half-light that flickered around wasn't strong enough to penetrate the gloom. He sat down on the flagstone and dropped his feet into space. Tentatively he probed for solid surface and found none. There was another series of ear-splitting cracks as if the whole cavernous cellar was shifting and settling. A stone fell from the far wall and through the space a shaft of strange green light speared the dark. There was another wrench of breaking stone, and then another. They were tumbling in a succession from where they had been lodged in the walls. And from every cavity, light from somewhere else lanced through, criss-crossing the empty space.

In the dim light, Alan could make out a maze of

ridges that had been left behind as the floor had fallen away. There were flagstones linked as in a path, oddly twisted and angled, precariously balanced on rock, between him and the flat surface where Tommy stood.

Alan lowered himself down on to the first flagstone. It rocked under his weight and he felt a swoop of vertigo. He took a quick step, then another, on to the next stone. Around him the beams of light seemed solid, confusing his eyes.

He reached the middle of the depression, turning left and right, trying to find the path that would let him cross, when the vertigo struck again, sending his stomach into a low dive. In the complexity of light shafts, Alan couldn't tell whether his next step would be on stone, or on one of the broad planes of light that looked like narrow paths across the chasm.

And it was here that he found himself back in his own nightmare.

The beamwalk. His father had taken that path high up on the scaffolding gantry in the hull of the ship in the old Clyde yard. Deaf from years of pounding rivets into steel, he hadn't heard his workmates' warning call. He'd stepped on to a shaft of light that caught the motes of dust, making it look solid enough to bear his weight, and he'd fallen in a silent dive to crumple himself on a mound of spars. In the aftermath of that fatal fall, young Alan Crombie had dreamed the scene in recurring nightly horror. In the dreams he'd been there, down below, watching that step into space, screaming the warning, knowing with dread certainty that it would never be heard, watching the fall in the slow motion of nightmare.

Now he was on the beams and the light confused his eyes. Planes of weird light branched off and intersected, each offering a pathway. He took one step with his right foot, keeping his balance on his left and probed nervously. His toes sank through the insubstantial platform. Dizziness looped through him. Then he heard the sound inside his head that seemed to cut through the roaring and crashing all around. It was as if someone was beckoning him in a language that included no words. He could feel the pressure of the sound deep inside him, tugging at him, and he recognized it as part of himself without knowing how. The sound pulled him insistently, piloting his wary feet on the solid stone, steering him away from the treacherous beams. It hung in his mind, a cool sonar note that was the only right in all of this wrong. And deep in the spirals within spirals in his cells, he recognized the silent song of his daughters as they gently led him across the chasm.

On the last flagstone, which rocked sickeningly, Alan fell forward and caught the edge of the drop, hauling himself up and on to the flat. The strange, tickling sound lessened in intensity but remained with him.

He got to his feet and started across the expanse that the cellar floor had become on this side of the chasm.

Alan felt as if he was running through syrup. He knew he was shouting but he couldn't hear any words. He ran and ran, and it seemed as if he was running for ever; as if the whole physics of the place had been changed and that distance had been stretched in a way that was impossible for the eye to follow. But still he ran towards his son who was standing on the lip of the pit.

The huge bulldozer churned up the verge as it powered along the road with the two men jouncing and bouncing inside the cab. It roared like a dinosaur as Tom took the turn up the narrow north road until he got to the small dike that marked the Crombies' north boundary. Without a pause, he swung the great yellow machine and felt the jarring bump as the big metal plates on the caterpillar tracks crumped the dike and crushed the loose stones. Ahead of them were three small pines and a birch. Tom considered himself a conservationist. He liked hedgerows and wild animals and the like. He didn't stop.

The trees that had taken twenty years to grow shivered under the onslaught, then toppled like standing twigs in a series of crashes. Tom jerked on the controls, missed a big beech tree by a foot, shot through a space and ploughed up a ten-foot-wide swathe of brambles and bracken. The dozer roared through a patch of rhododendron, shoved another pine hard enough to cant it over on its roots. Then ahead, in the beams of the big spotlights that ringed the cabin, was the pair of stones.

'Right, Seumas. Hold on and let's see what these big fuckers are made of,' Tom said. He shot the gears back to first, rammed his foot down on the pedal and the great machine surged forward. It got to within five feet of the nearest stone when the ground underneath the tracks buckled upwards and Tom and Seumas felt the JCB cant over, still roaring forward. One track went up into the air, pawing like a mad conveyer belt. The machine spun and lurched and came down again heavily. There was a crash and the world tilted crazily. The JCB started to roll slowly over.

The engine roared to a crescendo and the two men were thrown around inside like small animals in a cage. There was one almighty crump and a vast rending noise, followed by the ponderous crash of something heavy falling.

'What happened?' Tom asked, dazed.

'I think I broke my back,' Seumas groaned.

Inside the house, down in the cellar, Alan was battling against the dimensions of the place that showed him his son not twenty yards away but so far off it was almost impossible to reach. The pit expanded like a black eye opening. It was a foot away from where Tommy stood.

There was a ringing in his ears. High and clear, like the resonance of pure glass.

'*Get back, son!*' he shrieked, legs still pumping away, cutting the vast distance down.

Then from nowhere the girls appeared, standing together, hand in hand, their fair hair strangely white despite the sick glow of the light.

They walked towards their brother, separated and drew him back from the chasm. It was as simple as that. Tommy, who had seemed petrified, turned to stone with fear and horror, just walked backwards without even seeming to notice their presence.

The circular hole continued to expand as the girls drew their brother backwards. The distance between Alan and the children narrowed. He was getting there, awfully, agonizingly, slowly, but the distance was reducing.

He was half-way there, when the writhing standing stones seemed to merge together, winding around each other, becoming liquid, melted black. There was a kind of twist in the air and suddenly the space between them coalesced into something that clambered up from the rim of the pit. It hunched at the edge of the hole in a horrid fluid motion like tar flowing uphill and squatted there, a foul, grotesquely twisted shape from which radiated a shock-wave of terrible want. It was an *abomination*.

Alan's mind rocked with the force of the ghastly hunger that blasted out from the thing. He was still running, battling against the warped perspective, frantically trying to reach his children.

It moved shapelessly, a Stygian immensity. A limb propelled itself out like a growing root from the black bulk, formed itself into something that was like an arm. Great fingers grew from the tip, splayed, and came down on the flagstone with a ponderous thump that shook the floor and sent great cracks radiating outwards. Bunched muscles rippled and tensed, and on the

497

other side something else formed itself, drawing out like treacle toffee from the main mass, hardening quickly in the air. It was like a many-jointed crab's leg that flexed, raised and pawed at the ground like a probe. There was a ripple and the black monstrosity pulled itself further out of the hole towards the children.

Gleidhidh Gruamach. The phrase jumped into Alan's stupefied mind. *The dark keeper of the ways.*

This was what Beth Callander and the old woman had been talking about. This was the thing that sat at the crossroads of all the ways. Already the blood had been spilled twice on the stones and it needed the life-blood of a first-born son to free itself from the ring. The certainty of that hit Alan like a hammer blow.

The cellar, now a vast space that stretched out for ever, was ringing with a nightmare cacophony of noise. From all around came the chitinous rasping sounds of stone and wood being torn and ripped. From above, throughout the house, there was a shifting, rending noise as if the whole building was suddenly sinking and settling. And from the pit there was the blasting rumbling roar that emanated from the thing, ripping the air and vibrating the stones, so loud in the head and in the mind that it was a physical pain.

Alan's mouth was working non-stop. He felt the words bolt out hoarsely past his throat. '*No! No! Get away from them!*'

But against the huge noise that was battering around in the colossal space that the cellar had become, even he couldn't hear the words.

As Seumas said: 'I think I broke my back,' the JCB was lying on its side, its engine still a juddering roar. The nearside track was spinning madly, plates clattering round the rolling wheels, clawing at empty air.

Tom heaved himself up from where he was squashed under the small man. There was a throbbing on his temple, and he could feel a small trickle of blood down his cheek.

'Can you move?' he asked.

'I think so, but it's damned sore.'

'So long as it's sore, you're all right,' Tom said, feeling a hysterical laugh trying to bubble up inside him.

'If that's true, then I'm having a hell of a good time,' Seumas said, and this time Tom did laugh. It just came out in a rippling belly laugh that completely belied the moment.

'Welcome to the picnic,' he managed to splutter, and then went off into a paroxysm of laughter that only stopped when he started to choke. Seumas, who was sprawled on top of him, eased himself up with a groan.

'I'm never going in a digger with you again,' he said, and then, despite everything that had happened to them that night, he too started to giggle. It set Tom off again, and the two of them lay crumpled and bruised in the bottom of the cab laughing manically until the hysteria finally drained away. It was an odd little moment, but the uncontrollable fit of laughter seemed to help them.

Eventually Tom clambered past Seumas, swung open the cabin door and clambered out, reaching to switch off the engine as he did so. The big ring of spotlights flashed stroboscopically on the whirring plates until they slowed and stopped. Tom popped his head out and saw the whole stand of trees lit up by the blaring white lights. In front of him was the big standing stone. Off to the right was another, broken in half a yard up from the ground.

Seumas followed him out and they got to the ground. The big machine smelt of oil and sweat and crushed stone. 'What now?' the small man asked.

Tom shot the bolt on the carrier compartment and hefted two spades from the bundle of navvy's tools. 'We dig,' he said. They dug.

They both worked furiously, instinctively aware of

the need for speed. Tom was at the intact pillar and Seumas was driving his spade into the earth at the base of the broken one, throwing earth up like a badger. They had worked for ten minutes when again there was a rippling tremor through the ground that almost knocked Tom off his feet.

There was a shriek in the air like canvas being ripped with a knife in the dark space between the stones. Seumas stopped digging and stared. The air itself seemed to waver and squirm, and then something appeared to drag itself out of a hole in the dark about three feet off the ground. Seumas never clearly saw what it was. It looked like an animal, but the shape was all wrong. He clambered out of the hole that was already three feet deep, took six quick strides and chopped down at the thing with the edge of the spade. There was a grunt and a sizzling hiss and something dropped into the tangle of ferns.

'What the hell was that?' Tom called across.

'I don't know,' Seumas replied, 'and by God I don't want to know.'

Tom was about to say something else when the dark space just seemed to bulge out towards them as if things were pushing themselves into a taut membrane. A grotesque head appeared at the level of Tom's shoulder. He had the impression of great black eyes. Another something shoved its way through and a limb like an arm groped towards him with long gnarled fingers tipped with curving claws. It hooked quickly and so close that Tom felt the wind of it passing. He hefted his spade against the horrendous face that followed through the rip in the air, hitting it such a blow that the vibration tingled in a jolt all the way up to his shoulder. He swivelled and sliced at the other thing, driving the edge of the spade down like an axe, and split its head with a pulpy thud, just as the slate had done to old Mrs MacPhee. In beside the sudden terror that surged within him he felt a strange elation.

Then the whole great space between the stones just billowed out with shapes. Hands reached for them and heads squirmed at them, snapping jaws and beak-like mouths. Tom swung frantically. Seumas battled by his side. Something leapt to the side, trying for Tom's flank, and landed right in the glare of one of the spotlights. Immediately it screeched with a sound like a stonesaw and squirmed away. Tom got a clear sight of it, a long thin slithery shape with a multitude of legs and a great many teeth. It wriggled in the light and its eyes just seemed to implode, giving off twin puffs of vapour. Realization kicked him in the ass.

'The lights!' he bawled at Seumas. 'They can't stand the light. I'll hold them off. You get up there and swing the spots on them.' He dived across to where Seumas was swinging his spade like a warrior's axe and battered a thing that was lunging at the small man.

'*Go!*' he yelled. Seumas danced back, giving him room. Tom swung and jabbed. Something snapped at his calf and pain danced up his leg. He stumbled and went down. Something else with a squat body and gripping hands grabbed him. There was a sharp stabbing on his stomach as the thing bucked on him, trying to impale him, and then it just seemed to melt. The spotlight was a brilliant glare of white light that blazed right over him and through the space between the stones. A small head with piggy eyes and no mouth at all seemed to shrivel and run, dripping on to his jacket. A gagging foul reek billowed up from where the drops fell and the material began to smoke. He threw the thing off and rolled back towards the JCB.

In front of him there was a chaotic tangle of movement, like a bagful of black cats fighting. Screeches and screams rent the air. Things dripped and dissolved. There was a smell of burning and the tight corrosive odour of acid. The light swung in a series of arcs back and forth across the space between the stones, catching a small, flailing, fading movement here and there, and then everything went quiet.

Tom hauled himself to his feet and Seumas clambered down to join him.

'Well, that settled their hash,' he said when he got his breath back. His heart was labouring hard. 'Whatever they were.'

'They were the *Neachd*, the *Urraidh*,' Seumas said. 'They're wights, my mother said. From the dark lands. The outrunners of the *Gleidhidh Gruamach*.'

'Damned devils.'

'That's for sure,' Seumas said. He hefted his spade, jumped in the hole, and started to dig. 'We'd better hurry. They'll be back.'

That thought spurred Tom Callander on.

Beth Callander and her friend failed in their mission to get John Lindsay. They left a message, and sped back to the big house. By the time Beth braked the jeep on the drive, there was no one there.

'They must be inside,' Alex said. Above them the storm was whipping up to a frenzy. Beth nodded. They got out of the jeep and ran to the front door. Alex pushed it and it swung open. They walked inside and in ten steps they were hopelessly lost in a maze of rooms and corridors where walls dripped cold. They wandered, hand in hand, and suddenly very frightened, trying to find a way back to the front door.

'Where are we?' Beth asked.

'I don't know,' Alex whispered back. Around them was a strange noise that came from nowhere and everywhere, whispering and rasping. They reached the bottom of the stairs. Alex kicked something which slid rattlingly on the floor. She bent down and picked it up.

'It's the old woman's walking stick. She must be here.'

'We've been here before,' Beth said. 'Twice.'

'I know. What's happening? Where are they all?'

Beth was about to reply when something loomed out of the shadows and grabbed her by the shoulders. She gave a gasp, almost fell backwards. A face came right up to hers. It was Alan Crombie's wife. Her eyes were staring out of their sockets.

'What are you doing in my house?' she hissed in a voice that did not sound human, let alone feminine.

'I'm looking for my father,' Beth blurted.

'He's dead,' Helen said in a low snarl. A little flick of froth spat from her mouth and landed on Beth's cheek. Behind her Alex stepped forward, just able to make out the two figures in the dark. At this point she had only heard the voices. She hadn't recognized Helen Crombie.

Suddenly, Beth let out a loud squeal. Helen's hands leapt up to her throat and her fingers tightened around the girl's neck, squeezing her windpipe in a strong grip. Beth tried to pull away, failed, and stumbled to one knee. The hands held their grip, and then, with amazing strength, hauled Beth to her feet. Alex came up behind her and saw what was happening.

'Let her go!' she cried. Helen flicked her a poisonous glare and went on squeezing. Alex pushed herself past Beth who was struggling frantically, and grabbed the woman's arm. It was like getting a grip on a cast-iron rod. She shook at it and succeeded only in making it sway an inch. Beside her, Beth started to choke. Alex could hear the gurgling in her throat.

Without a thought, she whipped up the walking stick and struck Helen squarely in the face with it. Helen Crombie let out a roar that was more animal than human, far too deep and vicious for a woman, and recoiled. She tried to grab at Alex, freeing Beth who spun away. The young doctor just hit her again. The stick swished in the air and clattered across Helen's cheek. In the darkness, a line of fire streaked across the woman's face, like a small bolt of electricity leaping between two contacts. Alex struck again and there was

503

another flash. There was a smell of burning and Helen fell backwards against the wall, screeching like a cat. Alex stood, gasping for breath, feet planted wide, ready for another strike, when Helen just seemed to merge into the wall, arms flailing. There was a gulping sound and she was gone.

'We've got to get out of here,' Alex said. 'This is too much.'

'Not without my father. He's in here somewhere.'

'We'll never find him in this fun house. I think I'm going crazy.'

'Me too, but we have to try,' Beth said, grabbing her friend's arm, dragging her along the corridor. There was a door to the left. Beth opened it and they stumbled and fell together down a flight of wooden steps and into the cellar. They sprawled on the flagstones and Beth let out a cry of horror. In front of them the three Crombie children were standing together, hand in hand, and from beyond a monstrous shape was reaching for them.

Behind them, amid the horrendous tearing and roaring noise, Alex heard Alan Crombie's frantic yelling. She turned and saw him running towards them, but so slowly, legs moving like someone running in glue.

Beth got to her feet and ran towards the children. She grabbed them and started herding them back from the pit and the abomination that was lurching outwards. She turned her back on it for an instant, and something coiled out from the pulsating bulk and smacked her across the back with a blow that lifted her from her feet and spun her in the air to crash against the nearest stone. There was a horrible pulping squash, and Beth fell in a heap. She didn't move. Blood pooled out from where she lay. Alex was screaming incoherently. The children stood as if transfixed, while the thing bore down on them. She could feel waves of blackness coming off it, heliographing waves of energy across the space between them right into her brain. She could feel it beating down into her and fought against it, shoving herself on legs of lead towards the children. Above them the thing crawled and humped forwards. She reached them and grabbed at Tommy who was holding his sisters' hands. He came back and they let him go. The boy stumbled away from the thing and Alex threw him behind her. With a monumental effort she forced herself towards the twins and reached for them. Her hands landed on their small shoulders and both turned at once. Very clearly, inside her head, she heard them speak one word. '*No!*'

Then they turned, separated and walked round on either side of the pit. The nightmare thing ignored them completely. Another arm grew out and slapped claws down hard enough to dig into the stone. Underneath a skin blacker than night, things jittered and squirmed. Alex could feel it sensing, searching. Its questing wave swung past her in a surge of pure frost that chilled her to the centre of her soul, and swung away again. It found Tommy who was standing on the stone floor, rigid with shock.

Around them the noise rose to an awful crescendo. Alan was roaring and his voice sounded as though its speed had been thrown into low gear. The noise that was coming from the black thing went straight into the brain in a vibration that was overwhelming.

And above it, very clear in the darkness, came a pure note of sound that rose higher and higher, combating the cacophony with its perfection. Alex stood and stared. Alan forced himself that last half-mile and reached her side. She jumped when he touched her and moved slowly past her. Something made her reach out and grab at him, dragging him to a slow-motion stop.

On either side of the pit the two girls were standing stock still, and between them the black thing was roaring madly. It shook itself from side to side as if, in some way, this thing that was the embodiment of pain was suddenly in agony. The crystal notes rang in the vastness of the cellar. It was the most beautiful sound Alex had ever heard.

Tom planted the charges quickly and efficiently five feet down in the ground beside the stones. Seumas helped him unravel the cable and cut it into lengths. The small man pared the ends while Tom jabbed fuses into the sides of the conical moulds and ran them off towards the digger.

'What now?' he asked.

'We blow these bastards right out of the ground.'

'Will it work?'

'Man, I've been a quarrier all my life. And this stuff could take the top off the Peatons. It's the stuff they use in bombs, don't you know. If it doesn't work, then I'll be looking for other work.'

'If it doesn't work, neither of us will get the chance,' Seumas said. He pointed to between the stones. The darkness was beginning to bulge again.

'They're coming back,' he said.

Tom clambered up into the cab and Seumas followed him, agile as a cat, even at his age. Tom flipped open the housing behind the seat and exposed the double row of terminals on the battery. He wound the bared ends of the wires together into a twist and then looked round at the stones one last time.

'Oh my God,' he said in a dismayed whisper. Seumas raised his head and saw the boy standing there in the dark space, frantically waving. In the beam of the spotlights he was wearing an orange slicker and a yellow lifejacket.

'It's David,' Tom cried. 'It's my boy!'

Seumas stared. Tom grabbed at the door and clambered out, yelling at the top of his voice. He was up and over the raised caterpillar track and had started sliding down to the ground before it struck him. Orange coat? Yellow preserver?

A voice inside him was shouting *no*. It was wrong.

It was the wrong way round! As soon as the thought struck him, he tried to stop, scrambling for purchase on the wheels between the tracks. It wasn't David. It was an illusion. A trap.

In front of him, the thing started to waver and change. Arms reached for him, stretching out spindly and long, long fingers spread into claws, grabbing his jacket. Tom raised a hand to fend it off, but great hands grabbed him and dragged him forward. Terror worse than the fear that had riveted him when they had fought the wights riddled up through him. The thing was not his son. The face rippled and ran, becoming squashed and squat, broad and bestial. Jaws opened, getting closer as the immense stretched arms contracted, pulling him in.

In that instant, Tom Callander knew he was going to die. He could do nothing against the relentless force that was pulling him towards the foul warped thing. Suddenly there was a ringing sound in his ears, a sweet crystal note of amazing clarity. The fear sped away from his mind, allowing it to think with sudden definition. It came to him in a flash. Nothing else mattered.

From up at the cab, Seumas watched, rigid with shock. He couldn't move.

'Blow it!' Tom bawled. 'Do it, man. *Blow the fucking things to hell!*'

The clear note came ringing through the trees and into Seumas's head. He snapped out of the frozen immobility and scrambled into the hatch. Without pausing to think, he touched the wires on to the terminals. There was a little bright blue spark and then the digger just took off into the air, tumbling as it went, forty tons of machine that went rolling and crashing through the trees with eight stone of small old man tumbling inside it. Seumas was thrown hard against the roof and then down on to the gears. The JCB somersaulted slowly and landed on the cab. Glass flew and the little man was hurled out of the window like a thrown doll. He smashed into a pine tree and there was a crack like a branch breaking. Seumas's thigh snapped so hard the bone came right through the muscle like a white knife. There was no pain then. He hauled himself up to a sitting position. The side of the digger was stove right in. Across to the left where the stones had been there were two huge craters, each twenty feet across.

Of the stones, there was no sign. Not even dust. The base of one of the trees was burning redly.

Tom Callander was gone.

FORTY-SIX

The clear sound pealed across the vastness that the cellar had become and the black shape shuddered as it recoiled from it. The tarry, somehow fluid skin seemed to writhe of its own accord. The great claw beat hard down on the stone, sending black cracks radiating out from where it hit. What might have been its head swung left and right, on either side, coming close to where the girls stood, stock still.

'It can sense them,' Alan exclaimed. 'It doesn't know they're there.' It came to him in sudden realization. He was able to think again. The thing could see Tommy. It wanted him. But it couldn't find the twins. Even in that moment, something the old woman had said to him came right back.

'The faerie-kissed. They speak to the faerie folk and sing their song. One soul and two hearts. No evil can reach them.' Old Mrs MacPhee had said that. The little ancient, blind woman had unerringly walked across the room and had put her hands on their heads and spoken their names in Gaelic. *Cathair-Cailin*, throne maiden, close to the light. *Aille-Ainne*, banisher of the night.

She had said these babies sing the second song. And she had told them all that the power of the *two-in-one* was joined to the white side on the other edge of the *between* places. The old woman, in her calm and matter-of-fact voice, had said the souls of the faerie-kissed were the gateway to the light.

Instinctively, deep in the centre of his own self, as if an ancient tribal memory had unfolded, Alan understood. For some reason that the old people of this place had known and accepted, certain people had the gifts that locked and unlocked gates to other places. His daughters had been born mute, but they had other gifts, hadn't they? They had moved around in the house, silent but for the pattering of feet, and they had disappeared in one place, only to materialize, almost magically, in another. On those occasions, Alan hadn't considered, hadn't conceived of the notion, that they might have been travelling pathways he had only seen in the flip side of his nightmares.

And the song they sang set up a sweet vibration, perfectly attuned to his own soul. That was *power*. He could feel it. They had no fear, no concept of fear, because all the time, in their innocence, they were armoured in the song of light. And behind that song, what force existed for good Alan could not comprehend.

'Can't you hear it?' the old woman had asked. 'No, I suppose you can't, for you've not enough of the gift. Their song is clean and untouchable, and nothing from the dark side can harm them.'

The thing roared and the notes overpowered the shrieking sound. The blackness wriggled and writhed as if caught in pain, trapped in the agony of the purity of the song. The appendages drew back and it started to slither and slide back into the pit. The wonderful sound continued, rising higher and higher, not heard by any ear, but in the centre of the mind. Deep in the soul.

The twins, tiny and beautiful in the dim light, moved towards each other. They joined hands and there was a sudden doubling of the resonant sound. Then they seemed to merge together, walking into each other, becoming one.

In Alex's hands the old gnarled walking stick abruptly warmed and started to glow. She almost dropped it in fright, but then grasped it tightly for some reason she couldn't ever explain. The whole length of it flashed into pure summer sunlight that radiated to

510

the edge of the pit where the girls stood, now seeming to dance in and out of one another, merging and melding and focusing down until all she and Alan and Tommy could see was one small girl.

The singing soared, an unearthly but wonderful sound. The light flashed in a pulse and the girls caught it in their hands and merged with it. At the edge of the pit a bright pulsating shape danced to the music. Inside the dark well, the black thing was squirming and slithering, trying to get away.

And that was when there was a terrific thump that rammed through the walls and the floor. One of the five megaliths that had been writhing like a live thing shattered with devastating violence, sending deadly shards of stone rocketing into the air. Yards away, the next one exploded into dust.

Beside Alan a great crack appeared in the wall. Something squirmed through and dropped to the floor. He didn't notice. His eyes were on the incredible scene in front of him.

The floor buckled in a seismic ripple that sent flagstones somersaulting into the air. And then the edge of the pit started to crumple. There was a small hitch in the song and the brightness that was the little girls seemed to slide downwards as the ground tilted below them.

Alan just hurtled forward towards the hole and dived headlong. His belly scraped on the flags in a searing skid that took him right over the lip of the pit, almost enough to pitch him into the depths. But he stopped, just on the balance. His arms shot downwards into a swirling miasma and found nothing. The girls were gone.

'Kathryn! Elaine!' he bawled as hope slithered away and despair swamped him.

Then, miraculously, he caught a hand. He could see nothing, but his fingers clamped around it desperately and he heaved backwards. One of the twins came swinging up out of the hole and Alan just let her drop. Heart pounding, head bursting, he scrambled back to the edge of the pit where a mist was now billowing upwards, clouding the dark far below. He could see nothing. There was no sign of his other daughter. He reached his hand downwards, panicking, despairing, and was on the point of launching himself forward when there was a noise behind him. Alex was bawling at him at the top of her voice.

'Stop, Alan. Come back!'

He half turned, and then his heart simply leapt so hard inside his chest that it could have burst with the pressure. For there, in front of him, lying sprawled on the flagstones, Kathryn and Elaine were gazing at him.

'But I only had a hold of *one* of them,' his mind told him.

'*One soul and two hearts*,' came the echo. Alan crawled to his daughters and scooped them up in his arms.

Around them the stones were crumbling. The light seemed to flicker and dance as the floor tumbled into the pit, shuddering under their feet. For an instant, Alan got a glimpse of the original cellar stair and moved towards it. Alex grabbed Tommy, almost dragging him by the collar, and they struggled up the steps which were hazy and insubstantial, but now solid under their feet, though shaking wildly.

They got to the hallway above and the floorboards were beginning to warp and writhe, pulling their nails out of the beams. There was a flicker, and the room with the four doors yawned in front of them. It disappeared in a wink and there was a crash as one supporting wall in the hall buckled outwards and collapsed. There was a rasping sound and a hole appeared on the wall.

Alan got a glimpse of rasping, insectile chellae, and a huge grub popped out of the panel, chewing as it went. The living-room door fell off its hinges with a loud creak. An insect that looked like a centipede scuttered on legs that were six inches long across the carpet.

At head height, another massive fat grub bored its way out of the wall. Then another plopped, wriggling, to the floor. All around them the house seemed to settle and shrivel, finding its own form.

And while it did, the other part of the house, the part that should never have been built and which had no place in the real world, gave itself up to the rot that had been there for a hundred years.

They reached the stairwell and Alan grabbed hold of it as the floor tilted. There was another ripping sound and the skirting board spanged off. Tommy jumped and it missed him by inches, clattering and twirling through the frozen air.

'Come on. We're nearly there,' Alan panted. In his arms, the twins hung tight, each with an arm looped around his neck.

He got to the front door, wrenched it open and literally threw himself and the girls out on to the path. Beside him Alex and Tommy landed heavily. The small group didn't stop. They just ran across the lawn and down to the gate, not halting until they were on the far side of the road.

Up at the house, under the cloud that was swirling faster and faster, there was an immense cracking sound, and abruptly the roof caved in, sagging into sway-backed ruin. The gable wall just seemed to crumble and the windows imploded as if a mighty vacuum had sucked everything inwards. There was a great rumble and the front wall collapsed.

Alan Crombie stood and watched his mortgage disappear. At that moment he was very, very glad. They stood out there on the roadway for more than half an hour in numbed awe as the house just shrivelled and died and sank into its foundations.

Before it finished, Alan turned his back on it and walked along the road with the twins in his arms. Tommy came just behind, and after a moment or two Alex followed.

FORTY-SEVEN

Eleven Months Later

In the small front room of a house a man put down the book he'd been reading. It was still light outside. A fine summer's evening.

Alan Crombie opened the door of his son's tiny bedroom and winked at the boy who was sitting up against the pillows reading a book without any pictures. The boy smiled up at him.

'Head-down time, TC,' Alan said. 'We're going fishing tomorrow.'

'Hope we catch something,' the boy said.

'Me too. See you in the morning.'

In the other room, this one a little larger, he walked between the twin beds where his daughters lay asleep. He stood for a moment, staring down fondly at them, then bent to kiss Kathryn on her forehead. The movement disturbed her sleep and she smiled dozily.

'G'night, Daddy,' she said.

'Night, Katie,' he said softly. From the other bed, Laney, also smiling with her eyes closed, murmured: 'G'night, Daddy. Love you.'

Alan Crombie looked down at them both. 'Me too,' he whispered.

He closed the door softly and went slowly down the hallway into the warmth of the living-room.